HARMONY BLACK

ALSO BY CRAIG SCHAEFER

The Daniel Faust Series

The Long Way Down

Redemption Song

The Living End

A Plain-Dealing Villain

The Killing Floor Blues

The Revanche Cycle

Winter's Reach

The Instruments of Control

HARMONY BLACK

CRAIG SCHAEFER

47NORTH

Published by 47North, Seattle

www.apub.com

ISBN-13: 9781503950429
ISBN-10: 1503950425

Cover design by Marc Cohen and David Drummond

Printed in the United States of America

HARMONY BLACK

FIVE YEARS EARLIER

"How long have you been a practicing witch, Special Agent Black?"

I'd been called into SAC Wendt's office to go over the paperwork from my last field operation. The special agent in charge was nowhere to be seen, though, replaced by a smug-looking stranger in a three-piece suit. He leaned back, cupping his hands behind his head and kicking his Italian loafers up on Wendt's desk like he owned the place. His shoes cost more than I made in a month.

"Excuse me?" I stammered.

"You're a witch," he said, as if he were making a comment about the weather.

"I . . . believe that's an inappropriate thing to discuss in the workplace, and quite possibly a violation of—"

"Relax," he said. "You're among friends. Call me Linder. You can sit down, if you like."

I didn't.

"Are you replacing SAC Wendt?"

"No, just commandeering his office. I do that sometimes." His gaze slid down to the silver bracelet poking out from under my jacket sleeve.

Tiny leaf-shaped bangles dangled from the hoop, catching the light and glimmering. "Nice jewelry. You made it yourself?"

"I do some crafts," I said. "In my free time."

Linder swung his shoes off the desk, sitting straight up. He dipped his fingers into his breast pocket, pulled out a slender vial of smoked glass, and set it down between us. My stomach churned, just looking at the thing, and my bracelet grew hot against my wrist like I was holding my arm over an invisible fire. There was something trapped inside that vial, something that squirmed and hungered and hated, and it wanted *out*.

"I'm willing to bet," he said lightly, "that if I uncorked this vial, you'd have a good chance of survival. Better than most."

"What is—" I started to say, then caught myself. Sometimes the *what* doesn't matter. "Why do you even *have* that?"

Linder flashed a pearly smile and took the vial away, slipping it back into his breast pocket.

"I'm a big believer in mutually assured destruction," he explained. "I've made a number of enemies over the course of my career, and I feel more confident knowing that if one of them finally gets lucky, I won't die alone. The point is, now we can skip the talk."

"The talk?"

He ticked off his points on his fingertips. "Magic is real. You're a witch. I carry a demon in my pocket. See? Now we're on the same page, and you don't have to lie to me. Saves *so* much time. I'm here to make you an offer."

I pulled back a chair and sat down. My sense of balance was long gone.

"I'm with a special task force," Linder said, "representing a joint effort among select elements of the FBI, local law enforcement, and affiliated civilian friendlies, sponsored by a small handful of concerned senators who will remain nameless. It's not . . . officially recognized by the Bureau."

"Not recognized," I echoed. "You're talking about a black-budget program."

He slid a closed beige folder halfway across the desk, leaving it between us. The faded white label bore unsteady block letters from a manual typewriter:

Operation VIGILANT LOCK. Top Secret//Eyes Only// Special Control and Access Required (SCAR) Use Only.

"We run silent. You can call us Vigilant, but you won't find that name on any government document that you're *officially* cleared to read. So whatever you do, don't open this folder and start reading right now. That'd be highly illegal."

He nudged the folder an inch closer to my side of the desk.

"Let me bottom-line it for you," he said. "The United States is facing an existential threat, one it is in no way prepared to overcome."

"And that threat is?" I asked.

"People like you and me," he said. "Just a lot less patriotic. There are *things* operating on American soil, Agent, things you wouldn't believe. I've seen the pictures. Then I've shredded the pictures."

"What do you want from me?" I asked him.

"We have a triple directive," Linder said, ticking them off on his manicured fingernails. "Investigate, exterminate, obfuscate. The occult underworld is real, Agent Black, and your average beat cops—or even veteran federal agents, like your colleagues here—are incapable of assessing a threat that doesn't even fit into their worldview. Not like you can."

"This sounds like a recruitment pitch."

"Good," Linder said. "Then I'm making myself clear. You'd still work for the FBI, in name at least, but I'll arrange for you to receive . . . special assignments. Ones that require your particular skills, and absolute discretion. Living a double life takes some adjustment, I won't lie, but your file shows a real aptitude for tradecraft. I think you'll take to it like a duck to water."

I shook my head. I didn't know what to make of this, any of it. Part of me thought I was the butt of some cruel and overelaborate joke, and that any minute now Linder would open the closet and show me the hidden cameras. Part of me hoped he would. I'd brushed against the orbits of men like Linder before, alphabet-agency insiders buried so deep inside the Washington machine they might as well be ghosts. Or gods.

One thing I knew: once you slipped down that rabbit hole, into the black-budget netherworld, you never came out again.

"Look, I don't know who you think I am, or what you think I can do, but—"

"The Ballard Ripper," he said.

I blinked. He looked at me, expectant.

"I'm familiar with the case," I said. "It's stalled out—"

"For lack of evidence, yes. Because the key evidence has been suppressed. You're playing solitaire with no aces in the deck, and you can't figure out why you never win."

He leaned forward, resting his forearms on the desk, locking eyes with me. His face was forgettable, almost aggressively bland; he was the kind of man who could disappear in any crowd—but his gaze froze me in my chair.

"The Ballard Ripper," he said, "has murdered nine women in the last six months. He'll strike again, within the week. And he'll get away, as he's gotten away each time before, because he's not *like* ordinary men. He's a sorcerer. Near as we can tell, he's using their hearts for—well, that doesn't even matter, does it?"

He pushed the folder another inch closer.

"Right this minute," Linder said, "he's marking his next victim. Stalking her. You can save her. Say yes, join Vigilant, and I'll give you all the evidence, all the tools and resources you need to get the job done. Or you can walk out that door, go back to your ordinary life, and let an innocent woman die. Your call."

I looked down at the folder and weighed my options. It wasn't a hard choice to make.

The Ballard Ripper never took another victim. Officially, the case is still unsolved. He just disappeared into the Seattle mist, never to be heard from again. In Vigilant Lock's secret archives, though, he has a one-line epitaph:

Hostile Entity no. 59: Terminated with extreme prejudice.

ONE

Joining Vigilant was a one-way door, an express elevator with only one button: down. As Linder reminded me more than once, I'd broken a laundry list of state and federal laws in the service of a task force that didn't officially exist. Vigilant could shield me from prosecution, but only so long as I was a good team player.

So I was a good team player.

Five years in the shadows left me with my share of scars—some on my skin, some deeper. At the end of my last case, I put in for two weeks' vacation. I'd earned a lot of vacation time; I just never *took* any. My mother still had her cottage on Long Island Sound, a cozy Victorian with cornflower curtains and white lattice trim, and spending some time with family felt like a good way to find my balance again.

A week on the coast wasn't enough to shake my restlessness. I stood out in the backyard, the wet, cool grass stroking my sandaled feet, and looked out across the water to a distant rocky shore. It was peaceful until I closed my eyes, and then I was right back in the field again, reliving memories I'd rather forget.

A crisp, chill wind brushed its fingertips against my cheek.

"Harmony?"

My mother had hair like silver tinsel and wore a long lavender housecoat, looking like a silent movie star in retirement. She stood on the back porch. Linder stood beside her. I knew my vacation was over before he said a word.

"We need you back," he told me. He had the decency to look apologetic, even though I knew it was an act.

"I was approved for two weeks."

"It won't wait." He turned to my mother. "Ms. Black?"

She nodded and stepped back. "I'll give you some privacy."

"I was approved for two weeks," I told him again, as if it would change anything. "I haven't taken a single vacation day in—"

"It won't wait," he said. "Walk with me."

I led him down to the yard's edge. His polished Italian loafers glistened with dewdrops. He looked out across the water and shook his head.

"You picked a good vacation spot. Scenic. Me? I'm a Palm Springs kind of guy. Great golfing down there."

"I'm not very good at relaxing," I told him.

"I noticed. You've filed four amendments to your report on that Las Vegas op since you went 'on vacation,'" he said, putting the words in air quotes. "Relax. The directorate is very pleased with your work."

"Pleased? That operation was a disaster from start to finish."

He shrugged. "I sent you into the field with a list of names. Everyone on that list is dead or on the run. Investigate, exterminate, obfuscate. As far as I'm concerned, you pitched a three-hitter."

"It was the *wrong way*. It was sloppy. And, sir, I want to reopen the investigation. I'm certain Daniel Faust was—"

"Killed," he said. Stopping me in my tracks with a single word. He arched an eyebrow at me. "You didn't hear? There was a riot at Eisenberg Correctional. Thirty-eight inmates died, him included. No great loss to society."

I couldn't answer for a second. I didn't have the words. I didn't mourn the man—he was a sorcerer, an unrepentant thief, and a killer—but I felt his sudden absence like a jigsaw puzzle piece carved out of my life. Faust was my nemesis. My great white whale. Now I felt like the sheriff in an old Western, gearing up for a showdown at high noon, only to find out the black-hat outlaw accidentally fell off his horse and died from a concussion on his way to the gunfight. No satisfaction, no closure. That part of my life was suddenly over, leaving nothing but a hollow aching in its wake.

"Job's done," Linder said. "Bottom line? You got results."

"Tainted results. When I took my badge, I took the oath that goes with it. I don't take oaths lightly."

"And when I recruited you for this task force," Linder said, "I thought I made it clear that we're operating on the extreme edges of what the law is *capable* of handling. That requires flexibility in the field. Hard judgment calls."

I didn't have anything to say to that.

"You haven't let me down yet." He shivered a little as a stiff wind ruffled his hair. "Getting nippy out here. Let's go inside. Need to show you something."

We went in through the kitchen door, to the little octagonal dining room in the back corner of the house. A hand-knit lace doily decorated the varnished pine table, and an ornately painted dish took a place of pride on the top shelf of a freshly dusted china cabinet. Linder paused by the credenza, his gaze drifting over a cluster of photographs. Me, Mom, Dad in his uniform blues. Pictures faded by time.

"You were a cute kid." He looked back over his shoulder at me. "You used to have long hair. When did you start doing the '90s Meg Ryan thing?"

I just crossed my arms and stared at him. He sighed, pulled up a chair, and gestured for me to do the same. He set his slender black briefcase on the table and opened it, taking out an unlabeled manila folder. He held it lightly in his hands, like it was a bomb rigged to blow.

"You were all eager to put me to work," I said. "Now you're stalling. What don't you want to tell me?"

He ran a fingertip along the folder's edge.

"There's been an incident. Two days ago, an infant was abducted from his home."

"Then let's *move.*" The last threads of my patience frayed and snapped. "You know the recovery rates on an average kidnapping. Every hour we wait, the odds drop by—"

He held up his hand. "I've already mobilized a team. You'll be joining them in the field. There was a nanny cam in the child's room, and . . . based on the recovered video, the boys in the lab believe we're dealing with Hostile Entity 17."

I shook my head. The number didn't mean a thing to me.

Linder took a deep breath, opened the folder, and turned it around, showing me the grainy photograph inside. A single blown-up still captured from the nanny cam feed.

"I told them not to call it the Bogeyman," Linder said. "I'm sorry, Agent. It's back."

I couldn't hear a word he said. Couldn't talk. Couldn't think. All I could see was the photograph as the world fell out from under my feet.

TWO

"Her name is Helen Gunderson," Linder said, nodding at the woman in the photo. Her face twisted in mad loathing as she clutched the bundled infant in her arms. The picture was grainy, but I could still make out the tears of blood weeping from her eyes.

"That's not Helen Gunderson," I whispered. I couldn't breathe, couldn't move, couldn't take my eyes from the photograph. I was drowning on dry land. Lungs burning, muscles clenched.

"You know that, and I know that, but the real Helen is sitting in a jail cell right now. She's being charged in the abduction of her own child. Considering the 'evidence' from the nanny cam, she *will* be prosecuted for it—along with a murder charge, if we can't recover the infant."

"Where did it happen?"

"Talbot Cove, Michigan," he said. "Less than a mile from—"

I locked eyes with him. "How many?"

"Just one victim. So far."

"There will be others."

He nodded. "I know. And soon. Clock's ticking. You're the only operative alive who's had personal contact with H. E. 17."

I took a deep breath. Unclenched my hands from the arms of my chair. Straightened my back.

"Call it what it is, Linder," I said, shutting the folder and sliding it toward him. "It's the fucking Bogeyman."

# # #

I was six years old.

It's funny. I can remember everything about that night, except why I'd gotten out of bed in the first place. I padded out of my room in my footie pajamas, the shag-carpeted hallway seeming to stretch for a thousand miles in the dark. A tiny night-light cast the striped wallpaper in a warm, soft glow.

There was another glow, too, seeping out from a crack in the doorway up ahead. My sister's bedroom.

I heard whispering as I crept closer. A sibilant, singsong lullaby, but I couldn't make out any of the words. The door creaked, just a little, as I pushed it open and peeked inside.

My mother stood over Angie's crib, head bowed, cradling my baby sister in her arms. The dangling mobile over the crib turned slowly, casting strange, long shadows across the nursery walls. As I walked closer, I heard heavy footsteps coming down the hall behind me. *Dad,* I thought. *Angie woke everybody up again.* She'd been sick for a few days, sick enough for at least one frantic late-night drive to the ER.

"Mom?" I said. "Can I hold her?"

The light caught my mother's face as she turned toward me. She'd been crying, I thought at first. Then, taking a step closer, I realized they weren't tears. Her eyes were leaking blood. Two little trickles of crimson, dripping down her sallow cheeks.

"You, too," she whispered, her voice a hoarse rasp as she held her hand out to me. "You come, too. Come to Mama."

"Harmony?" said the sleepy voice behind me. "Are you awa—"

The voice stopped dead. I slowly turned around. My mother stood in the bedroom doorway, her face a mask of frozen horror as she stared at the impostor clutching her infant daughter.

# # #

Linder said something. Jolted from my memories, I had to ask him to repeat himself.

"You won't be going in alone," he repeated, sliding a sheaf of papers from his briefcase. "Like I said, there's a team on the ground already. This is a kidnapping—a federal crime, which gives us the perfect excuse to involve FBI assets."

"Not me, though," I said. "I'm still attached to the Seattle field office. I was able to follow the Carmichael case to Vegas only because it started on my home turf."

Linder rapped his knuckles on the paperwork.

"Not anymore. As of one hour ago, you've been reassigned to CIRG. The Critical Incident Response Group gives tactical and intelligence support wherever and whenever it's needed, which means I can drop you right into the hot zone. Officially, you report to SAC Walburgh of the Crisis Management Unit."

"And this Walburgh is a friendly?" I asked.

"She doesn't exist. You can't get friendlier than that."

"I've always worked alone before," I said.

Linder shook his head. "I'm not taking any chances. This thing's been dormant for thirty years. We miss our shot, it could be another thirty before it comes back again. I'm putting our best team on it, cell designation Circus. You're there to provide personal insight and occult support. They . . . recently lost a key member, so you'll be filling a gap."

"Circus?" I arched an eyebrow at him.

He shrugged. "They get results. Pack up and roll out: a plane ticket's waiting for you at JFK. I'll send the itinerary to your phone."

He locked his briefcase and stood to go.

"Keep me in the loop," he said. Then he was gone, walking out the door and leaving me alone with the past.

My whole body felt numb, but I pushed myself out of the chair and trudged upstairs to the guest room. Vacation was over. I traded my sandals for polished black shoes; my T-shirt and jeans for a crisp white blouse, black suit jacket and slacks, and a black necktie.

My mother waited for me down in the parlor. She sat in the gloom beside a drawn window shade, staring at nothing at all. One hand idly stroked the fat, purring Maine coon in her lap, but her attention was a million miles away.

"You know," I said, standing at the edge of the room.

"Grizabella," she said, nodding at the cat. "She hears everything."

"I don't want you to get your hopes up. Even if I can stop this thing, it doesn't mean we'll get Angie back. There might not . . . be anything to *get* back."

"But you'll try."

"I'll try," I told her.

I went back upstairs and packed my rolling suitcase, the home I'd been living out of for longer than I cared to remember. I was still paying rent on a shoe-box apartment in Seattle, but at this point it was just a place to keep my extra stuff. The packing went quickly, almost mindlessly, the preflight checklists a drill hammered into me by repetition. Toothpaste, toothbrush, hairbrush, check.

"Take this with you," my mother said from the doorway. She held out a tiny worn-out teddy bear with tan fur and stitched eyes, just a little taller than a baseball. I frowned at it. It looked familiar.

"You don't remember," she said. "He used to be yours. He chased away bad dreams, you used to say. The day we brought your little sister home from the hospital, you decided she should have someone to watch over her while she slept. He was . . . in her crib that night."

I took the bear and slipped it into my suitcase.

She pulled me into a hug, her breath hot against my shoulder.

"Your father would be so proud of you right now," she whispered.

"I do my best," I said, "but I can always do better."

She smiled sadly as she pulled away, holding me at arm's length, looking me over.

"That's what he used to say, too. All right. Get out there, Special Agent Black. Give 'em hell."

One last hug and I was gone, bound for another plane and another nightmare.

# # #

Two hours in the air—half of it with a kid drum-kicking the back of my seat—and I touched down at Detroit Metropolitan Airport. From there it was just a half-hour taxi ride to 477 Michigan Avenue. I spent most of the trip with my phone in my face, memorizing the details Linder sent me.

The Patrick V. McNamara Federal Building rose up from the Detroit skyline like a clenched fist of concrete. I waited in line at the security checkpoint just inside the front doors. Eventually I made it to the front desk, flashed my badge and credentials, then took an elevator up to the FBI offices on 26, where I had to do it all over again.

I almost cracked a smile. If I squinted a little and didn't look out the window, I could imagine I was back at my old field office in Seattle. Same slate-gray cloth cubicles, same rows of identical government-issue computers and desk phones, same information security flyer taped up over the same water cooler.

Once they'd checked my bona fides, the receptionist printed off a visitor's badge and passed it through a hot laminator before handing it over to me.

"Here you go, and"—she paused, glancing down at a visitor's log—"Special Agent Temple and her consultants are already here. They're waiting in conference room two—just go right up this hall, take a left at the end, and it's the first door you'll see."

Consultants? I hadn't been expecting that, but the way my day had gone so far, I shouldn't have been surprised about anything. I snapped the visitor's badge to a lanyard and put it on, bracing myself as I walked up the hallway. I came to the conference-room door and gave what I hoped sounded like a confident knock.

It opened a few inches. The woman on the other side was wiry, with deep-brown skin and black hair pulled tight in a frizzy bun. What struck me, though, were her eyes: they were too blue to be real, almost turquoise.

"*You* aren't an extra-large pepperoni pizza," she said.

"Uh, no. No, I'm not."

"Then you must be the witch we ordered. C'mon in!"

She shut the door behind me, grabbed my hand, and gave it a pump. "Jessie Temple."

"Harmony Black."

"We know. Linder told us you were coming. You were running that Enclave Resort operation in Vegas, right? Heard they had to scoop Lauren Carmichael off the sidewalk with a spatula. Your work? Very flashy."

"Not entirely," I said, wincing. "It's a long story."

"And we don't have time for it," said an older woman in a wheelchair sitting at the far end of an oval conference table. Her aged hands rested regally on the varnished beech wood, flanked by a cup of coffee and a pad of paper filled with neat, prim handwriting.

"True," Jessie said. "Harmony, this is Dr. April Cassidy. Auntie April was one of the original BAU pioneers—"

"Behavioral Science Investigative Support Unit, at the time," April said, a faint Irish accent lilting on the edges of her words. "Let's be thankful for brevity, hmm?"

"She pretty much has an encyclopedic understanding of freaks, monsters, fiends, and politicians."

"Dr. Cassidy," I said, the name ringing a four-alarm bell. "I've read your work! I studied your PhD dissertation when I was at Quantico. It was brilliant, years ahead of its time."

"Thank you, dear, and please, call me April." She shot a steely look at Jessie. "*Not* Auntie April. I regrettably left the Bureau quite some time ago—taking an ax to the lower vertebrae tends to limit your prospects for career advancement. I've been in private practice ever since, but Jessie was kind enough to bring me on as a consultant."

"Last but not least," Jessie said, walking around the table, "meet Kevin Finn, which is not his original name."

The teenager on the other side of the table, a string bean in a World of Warcraft T-shirt, looked up from his laptop and raised his hand in greeting. "Hey."

"Not his original name?" I asked.

Jessie clamped her hand on Kevin's shoulder. "At the tender age of seventeen, Mr. Finn learned a valuable lesson: if you're going to hack into a stranger's bank account, make sure it doesn't belong to a high-ranking member of the Gambino family."

"I ended up in WitSec," Kevin said, looking sheepish. "Jessie pulled me out and made me an offer I couldn't refuse. I mean, it was either join her team or work in a doughnut shop in Albuquerque for the rest of my life."

"Now," Jessie said, "he uses his big brain to fight for the forces of good, seeking redemption for his tragically squandered criminal youth."

Kevin touched his hand to his chest and bowed his head. "I am but your humble slave, m'lady."

"Ha." Jessie slapped his shoulder and walked back toward me. "You *wish* you were."

I blinked. "You . . . pulled an informant *out* of Witness Protection?"

"I needed a hacker." She shrugged. "Turned out he was useful, so I kept him."

"What about your fourth? Linder said you lost a member recently?"

Jessie's smile deflated like a pinpricked balloon, and the room fell silent.

"The job Linder pulled us off for *this* one," Kevin muttered, staring at his laptop screen as he sank down in his chair.

"We'll get back to it," Jessie told him, her voice low. "Don't you worry about that. There will be some righteous fuckin' payback, just as soon as we take care of business here. Little babies going missing? That's gotta come first."

"I know," he said. "It's just . . ."

"I know." Jessie looked my way and gave a little shake of her head. Dangerous territory. I recognized the signs and resolved to mind my footing.

"We should get started," I said, eager for a change of subject.

"Quite right," April said, gesturing across the table. "Kevin, set up the projector, please. If one of you ladies would dim the lights, we can begin the briefing."

THREE

We sat around the table in the projector's silent glow, watching the images Kevin's laptop tossed up on the blank white wall. The first was a police station booking photo: the woman I'd seen in the still from the nanny cam, but instead of blood, those were real tears staining her cheeks.

"Helen Gunderson," April said. "Twenty-six years old, single mother, lifelong resident of Talbot Cove. Woke up to find her son, Elliot, missing from his crib. She immediately reported it to the authorities, leading to her arrest once they played back the video from the nanny cam in his room. Kevin?"

He tapped a few keys and a grainy video flooded the wall. Elliot slept in his crib. A shrill, slow creak groaned from somewhere off camera, and then a shadow shuffled into the frame. It was a woman, hunched at the shoulders, bare arms spindly and her hands curled into hooks. She whispered to herself—some kind of raspy, singsong drone—but I couldn't make out a single word.

Just like the first time I'd heard the thing speak, thirty years ago.

She reached into the crib, scooping out the sleeping infant inside, and cradled him in her arms. She turned back, finally facing the camera. It was hard to see unless you knew what to look for—unless you knew what you were looking at—but I couldn't miss the thin trails of blood leaking from her bottom eyelids. They rolled down her cheeks and her chin, dripping onto the sleeping baby's upturned face.

The creature masquerading as Helen Gunderson shuffled out of the room. Then that same shrill creak, and silence.

Kevin froze the video on an empty cradle.

"Ladies and gentleman," April said grimly, "meet target designation Hostile Entity 17: the Bogeyman. Unfortunately for Ms. Gunderson, she's been charged with faking the abduction of her son and hiding the child. Unless we can find her boy, he will be presumed dead, and his mother will be prosecuted for a murder she didn't commit."

"Not the first time that's happened," Kevin said, tapping away. Faded newspaper clippings sprouted up over the paused video. "Thirty years ago, over a two-week period, there were five infant and toddler abductions in Talbot Cove. At one incident, neighbors out for a midnight stroll saw the 'father' through a window, taking his child from the crib, though he told the police—truthfully, as it happens—he'd slept through the night. He was arrested, handed a life sentence, died in a prison-yard brawl. He went to his grave protesting his innocence. Four of the abductions remain officially unsolved, and the last, whence we take H. E. 17's lovely nickname, turned violent."

Local Sheriff Murdered by Home Invader screamed the headline as Kevin magnified it on the wall. The black-and-white picture of my father was a file photo, taken in happier times.

"Now, Sheriff Harry Black was home with his wife, Elise, and his daughters, Angie and Harmony, when . . ." Kevin's voice trailed off. He looked my way.

"Linder didn't tell you," I said, answering the question on his face.

Jessie slumped back in her chair. "Fuck. Another Linder surprise. It must be a Tuesday."

"I'm sorry," Kevin said. "When I complained about getting pulled onto this case earlier, I mean, this has gotta be personal for you—"

I crossed my arms. "It was a long time ago."

Jessie fixed her bright-blue eyes on me. I realized something strange, just then: in the last ten minutes, I hadn't seen her blink once.

"Well," she said, "seeing as the newspaper account is probably bullshit, how about you tell us what *really* went down that night?"

# # #

"Harmony," I remembered my mother whispering from the doorway, "get behind me. Now."

I couldn't stop staring at her bleeding doppelgänger, still holding an expectant hand out to me, cradling my baby sister in her other arm.

"You come, too," it rasped again. "Come to Mama."

I took an unsteady step to one side, backing toward the corner of the nursery, getting out of the line of fire. Something swirled in the room, a slow-building maelstrom of pressure that made my ears pop and my teeth ache.

"You," my mother said, locking eyes with her twin. *"Put her down."*

The creature clutched Angie tightly. *"Mine."*

The unseen winds churned faster, building like a cyclone I could only feel under my skin. My blood shivered. It was the first time I'd ever touched the currents of magic, and I'd never forget the sensation, just like I'd never forget the look of absolute rage on my mother's face.

"Put. Her. *Down!*" she roared, lunging out with both hands, pressing her open palms toward the creature. The air rippled and turned to spun glass. Translucent, scalloped spears of hardened air blossomed like ice crystals, spearing toward the creature, harpooning its stomach and shoulder.

Blood guttered from its wounds as it twisted and thrashed, breaking free, still clinging desperately to Angie with one arm. The baby was awake now and squalling, struggling. The creature raised its free hand and brought it down in a smashing fist; my mother's spell broke, the crystallized air shattering into a rain of broken glass on the shag carpet. Then it hissed and charged, coming for my mother like a freight train, lashing out with a brutal backhand and sending her sprawling to the floor.

I ran after it. I don't know what I thought I could do. I just knew I had to try.

My father heard the shouting. He was in the kitchen at the end of the hall, wearing his boxer shorts and clutching his service revolver. Coming to the rescue.

The creature barreled toward him. He saw its face and paused, just for a heartbeat, confused.

"Elise?" he said. "What's wrong with—"

It lashed out with fingernails suddenly turned long, hard, and black and slashed his throat open.

I think I screamed. I don't remember that part. I just remember being down on my knees on the cold linoleum, grabbing my father's chest like I could hug him back to life, listening to him drown in his own blood.

The choking, gurgling sounds stopped. There was something left in his eyes, one last spark of light, and he gave me the faintest smile as his big, strong fingers squeezed my arm. Then he was gone.

Cherry- and snow-colored lights strobed outside the kitchen window. My mother took hold of my shoulders, pulled me off my father's dead body, and turned me to look at her. She fought through her own tears, making sure I listened.

"You were in your room the whole time. You didn't hear or see anything. Harmony, these men . . . you can't tell them the truth. They won't believe you. Just say you were in your room. *Promise* me."

The house filled up with uniforms, big clunky shoes tromping everywhere, the air filled with crackles and radio static. Barry, one of my father's deputies, took me into my room. He was a kind-faced man, still carrying some baby fat in his twenties, and he put a blanket over my shivering shoulders and brought me a mug of hot chocolate.

My mother spun them the only story they could accept. In her version, the intruder was a strung-out junkie with a straight razor. Probably somebody Dad had busted, looking for revenge or just cash for a quick fix.

"Don't you worry," Barry told me, crouching down beside my chair to talk face-to-face. "We're gonna get this guy, and we're gonna get your little sister back. Every policeman in this city is going to be searching, night and day. I'm also leaving people to watch the house, to keep you and your mom safe."

Even then, I knew better. The word *safe* never meant anything to me after that night, ever again.

"Officer Barry?" I said, clutching the hot mug between my tiny hands as he stood to leave.

"Yeah, hon?"

I looked up at him. "It was the Bogeyman."

He just shook his head and gave me a sad smile.

"It was just a bad man, sweetie." He tapped the star on his chest. "This badge means it's my job to find bad people and make them go away so they can't hurt anybody else. And that's exactly what I'm going to do."

He never did, though. That was the last kidnapping in Talbot Cove. The case went cold, then it gathered dust, then it rotted away in the dark.

# # #

"And that was the end of it," I told them. "Mom's family had some money, and roots in Long Island, so we moved out of town about a year later. I've never been back."

"You've been waiting a long time for this," Jessie told me. It wasn't a question.

I thought about it. Nodded. "Suppose I have."

"Distressingly," April said, "this isn't the creature's *second* emergence. Kevin?"

The projector flickered. My father's face disappeared from the wall, replaced by an older, faded, and yellowed front page from the *Great Lakes Tribune*. The headline trumpeted the triumph of Allied powers against the Nazi war machine, but Kevin slid the focus to a column buried farther down the page.

Talbot Cove Infant Stolen from Crib;
Second Abduction in a Week Stokes
Local Fears

"I went back as far as I could," Kevin said, "but this is the last time I found anything concrete. This has been happening since at *least* the 1940s. It comes out, snatches a handful of kids, then goes dormant again. No telling what it does with them. I mean, I could think of some possibilities, but . . ."

He trailed off, looking my way. I rested my palms on the table.

"We need to get something straight right now," I said. "One, I'm not made of porcelain. Two, I finished mourning my sister's death a long, long time ago. If any of you feel like you can't say something in front of me, that means we won't be able to work together. And that'd be a damn shame, because right this minute, while you tiptoe around the truth, there's a missing kid out there who needs us. I'm here to help. *Let* me."

Nobody said anything for a moment.

Jessie nodded slowly, her lips curling into an amused smile. "All right. Respect. Kevin, what else have you got for us?"

"Something freaky," he said, typing away and pulling up a neatly organized spreadsheet. "While I was combing the newspaper archives, I mostly looked at police blotters, right? Well, I noticed that when the creature is active, the blotters got bigger. And, well, kinda samey."

"What are we looking at?" Jessie said. Beside her, April leaned in, her eyes widening.

"It's not *just* kidnapping kids," Kevin said.

FOUR

"This is a sampling of crime statistics from Talbot Cove before, during, and after the 1980s incident, and from last month through yesterday," Kevin said.

I had a degree in forensic accounting, but I didn't need it to read these numbers. They laid it all out, crystal clear.

"The crime rates *spike*," I said.

Kevin nodded. "I know, right? This is a sleepy little town in the middle of nowhere. Not exactly a hotbed of violence and vice. But in both cases, starting about a week before the first abduction, you see a distinct rise in criminal activity."

"*Specific* crimes," April mused. "Domestic violence, battery, child abuse. Crimes against family. Look: burglary and theft? Doesn't change one bit. Homicide rises a little bit, and I'd wager those are all cases of someone murdering a family member."

"Way ahead of you, Doc. I already checked, and that's a bingo. Near as I can tell, while our target is awake and hunting, anybody with a predisposition to take a swing at their spouse and kids finds it a lot harder to hold back. Case after case: it's repeat offenders, even some people who were in therapy for years. This thing is influencing people's minds across an entire city."

"Baltimore all over again," Jessie muttered. She looked my way and added, "Demon possessed a mall cop, right around Christmas shopping season. Shoppers started getting Ebenezer Scrooge levels of greedy, like, shanking one another over the last discount TV set."

April picked up her pen and flipped to the next page of her notebook, jotting down a few quick words.

"This is good information," April said, "but it doesn't bring us closer to finding the target. We know what it does. We need to know *why*."

"Are we agreed—" Kevin said, then paused. He shot a guilty look my way. I arched an eyebrow at him. "Are we agreed, um, that it's most likely using the kids for a, uh, food source? I mean, since we've never found any bodies."

I held his gaze. "That's my theory."

"Law of averages," Jessie said. "Considering how many critters we've seen that just *love* a good people snack, it's pretty likely this one does, too."

Kevin relaxed a little. "Okay, so, what if it's literally hibernating? Hedgehogs and bears sleep through the winter after fattening up. Heck, there's a recorded case of a bat in captivity hibernating for almost an entire year. This is just . . . a supersize version."

"One flaw," April said. "If food is the drive, why children and infants? We know it's capable of killing a full-grown adult with ease. Bigger prey means less work and more meat."

The table fell silent as we retreated into our own heads. I stared at the spreadsheet projected onto the wall, searching for some detail I'd missed, something to offer.

"It's not a ritual," April said. "Not a compulsion."

I looked her way. "How do you mean?"

"Nothing is repeated, except the abductions themselves. There's a bigger gap between the first hibernation than the second, by almost a decade. The first time, it took six children. In the '80s, it took five. The abductions occur over a period of two to three weeks, with seemingly random gaps between incidents. Harmony, when it spoke to you, did it seem . . . surprised? It couldn't have known you'd walk in on it."

I thought back, picturing it in my mind. That first approach, when I thought it was my mother, and how focused it was on Angie.

"Yes. It hesitated. That's when it held out its hand, and tried to get me to go with it."

"It changed its plans, spontaneously." April frowned. "It is sentient, it is an opportunist, and it is not bound by ritual or compulsion. That's not good."

"Doesn't make our job any easier," Jessie said, "but it's still our job. Talbot Cove's a three-hour drive from here. Let's pack up and roll out."

# # #

Down in the dimly lit garage under the building, Jessie twirled a set of keys on a plastic tag and checked license plates.

"All right, let's see what they gave us to drive. I'm feeling lucky this time. C'mon, Dodge Charger, it's gonna be a Dodge Charger—"

We came to a dead stop in front of a paste-white Crown Victoria, its bug-spattered license plate about ten years newer than the rest of the car. An entire quarter front panel was a slightly different color than the rest of the body, and the driver's-side door sported a long, jagged scar in the paint, like someone had raked their keys along it.

"Every time," Jessie said, deflated. "They do this to us *every time*."

Kevin patted her shoulder. "Sorry, boss."

April pushed her wheelchair past them, rolling around to the side of the car. Kevin helped her into the backseat, holding her wheels steady while she pulled herself into the car; then we collapsed the chair and stowed it in the trunk.

Jessie tossed me the keys. "You drive. My enthusiasm is suddenly diminished."

I'd been gone for thirty years, but once we put Detroit in the rearview mirror, Michigan looked exactly the way I'd left it. We drove through wild woods just feeling the first kiss of fall, the leaves turning crimson and gold, and past sleepy, hilly towns that hadn't changed since the '50s. Eventually we hit the coast of Lake Michigan, the highway turning to follow its curves, and the slowly setting sun gleamed like molten gold on the water.

Twenty minutes and I'd be home again.

The digital clock on the dashboard felt like the countdown timer on a bomb. I tried to distract myself from the inevitable, but all I had was static-choked talk radio and the incessant typing sounds from the backseat as Kevin hammered away on his laptop keyboard.

"So why are you called the Circus?" I asked, aiming the question at nobody in particular.

Sitting beside me, after spending the last hour in a light slumber, Jessie's eyes snapped open. "Hmm?"

"Linder, he said your cell designation was 'Circus.'"

"Because he's a jackass," Jessie said.

"Because we fight evil clowns," Kevin said. "Well, okay, it was just that one time, but once was enough. Eeh, *creepy*."

"Because," April said dryly, "our reputation for results far exceeds our reputation for following protocol. It makes for messy reports, which Mr. Linder must then explain to his superiors."

"They love us and they know it," Jessie said. She wriggled a little in her seat, put her head back, and closed her eyes again. "Considering the scuttlebutt about what went down in Vegas, you should fit in just fine."

I gripped the hard plastic steering wheel a little tighter.

"That's not how I normally operate. I do things by the book."

In the rearview mirror I saw April shake her head, a slight smile on her lips.

"Oh, dear," she said, "an idealist in our midst. I almost remember what that feels like. Suffice to say, Harmony, that works only when confronting a situation that's *in* the proverbial book. Outside the margins, improvisation is key. We operate under special circumstances. Can you think on your feet?"

I nodded slowly. "I do all right."

"Then we'll get along just fine."

The sun was nothing but an orange glow on the horizon when we hit the outskirts of town. A big forest-green sign at the side of the road read, **Welcome to Talbot Cove: the Town That Works! Population 2,032.**

"Yikes," Kevin said, glancing up from his laptop. "Kind of place where everybody knows your name, huh?"

I just shrugged and said, "Small-town America."

We cruised down Main Street, a row of mom-and-pop stores in sturdy Midwestern brick, most of them already closed up for the night. The modern world had to force its way into Talbot Cove through the cracks, one piece at a time: I smiled at the sight of a PC café rubbing shoulders with a thrift store and a TV-repair shop.

In the distance, out toward the water, the tall scaffolding and smokestacks from the old paper mill rose up over the town. The crimson glow from the setting sun turned them into silhouettes of skeletal fingers, grasping at the sky.

"Find us a base camp," Jessie said, and I obliged. The Talbot Motor Lodge was right where I remembered it, a sleepy one-floor motel nestled on the outskirts of town and flanked by clumps of towering oak trees. A cartoon owl loomed over us from a lit plastic sign, its claws perching on a placard that offered HBO and a heated swimming pool.

The Circus might play fast and loose with the regulations, but even Jessie Temple wasn't about to break the Bureau's rules on travel expenses. We doubled up, renting the two rooms on the far end of the motel.

"All right," Jessie said to April and Kevin, stretching like a cat as she clambered out of the car. "You two set up here while Harmony and I introduce ourselves to the local legal beagles."

"Does setting up include dinner?" Kevin asked, pulling April's wheelchair out of the trunk.

"Order some pizzas. And get receipts. I mean it."

The police station was a squat gray concrete shoe box with three late-model Fords parked out front. They shared a lot with the Talbot Cove Library on one side and the town hall on the other, a colonial building topped by a redbrick clock tower.

"Memories coming back?" Jessie asked me.

I looked up at the clock tower, cold and still in the gathering dark, and shook my head. "Vaguely? I mean, I was six when we left town. I . . . recognize these places, I know most of the streets, but they don't mean anything to me. They're just places."

Inside the police station, an elderly receptionist sat behind a rolling desk and paged through a back issue of *People* magazine. We held out our badges, letting her take her time looking them over.

"FBI, ma'am," I said. "Special Agents Temple and Black. May we speak to the sheriff, please?"

"He's in back," she said. "I'll go fetch him."

She left us alone in the lobby, standing under stark yellow fluorescent lights. Jessie wandered, checking out the notices on the community bulletin board. She let out a low whistle.

"Uh-oh. Looks like some kids have been playing mailbox baseball out on Route 7. We got here just in time."

"Are you *always* this flippant?" I asked her.

She looked back at me. Smile gone. Eyes frozen.

"It's a coping mechanism," she said, her voice flat, "for spending a career wading through the worst shit the human mind can come up with, and then some. What's yours?"

I took a step back and shrugged, looking down at the scuffed linoleum.

"I . . . I don't."

"You don't have a mechanism," she said, "or you don't cope?"

I was still trying to answer that when the door behind me swung open and a big voice boomed, "Harmony!"

I turned on my heel and couldn't help but smile. Barry looked just like I remembered him the night my father died, but he'd put on two things: another forty pounds, and my father's sheriff star.

FIVE

"It *is* you," Barry said, beaming. "Last time I talked to your mama, years ago, she said you were going into the academy. When Mabel said an Agent Black was here to see me . . . man, I was hopin', and my hopes were answered."

"Hey, Barry. You running this town now?"

He grinned and tapped his star. "That's Sheriff Hoyt to you, young lady, and . . . no. No, I most certainly do not. Damn council's cut my budget to a shoestring, and they're still sharpening their knives. Hey, can FBI agents give hugs?"

"We can only hug sheriffs," I said. "It's a firm rule."

He pulled me into a bear hug, slapping my back with his meaty hand.

"Look at you," he said, pulling back. "Just look at you. Your dad would be so damn proud."

"I do my best. Barry, this is—"

"Jessie Temple," she said, sweeping in and offering her outstretched hand. "I don't hug."

"Handshake's just as good," he said. "I'm glad you girls are here. Town's going goddamn crazy and I'm at wits' end trying to keep the regular troublemakers in line, let alone find this kid."

Jessie and I shared a glance. "Regular troublemakers?" I asked.

"And the irregular ones, too." He paused, glancing toward the back hallway and giving a wave. "Hey, Cody! C'mere, see who came to visit."

He walks like a cowboy, I thought. Cody had a little of that old-fashioned swagger, like an Old West hero on his way out of the saloon and headed for a high-noon showdown. *Don't worry,* his body language said to the world, *I've got this handled.*

He had high chiseled cheekbones and broad shoulders that filled out his beige uniform shirt, but that's where the comparison ended. Instead of a gunslinger's scowl, he wore a bright-eyed smile, and the smile only got bigger when he looked my way.

"I'll be damned," he said. "Harmony?"

I just tilted my head. He looked so familiar, but I just couldn't place his face, like the opening bars of an old hit song you can't quite remember.

"Cody," he said, "Cody Winters. You probably don't remember, but before—before your family moved away—I lived right next door. My mom said we were pretty much inseparable."

"Your first girlfriend," Barry quipped. "First and only time in your life you had good taste in women."

"Cody," I said, paging through faint memories distorted by time. I remembered a game of hide-and-seek on a long summer afternoon, and the smell of fresh-cut grass.

"I heard you joined the Bureau." Cody looked me up and down. "Gotta say, it suits you. No pun intended."

"Tell 'em about Oscar McKinney," Barry said.

Cody let out a long, low whistle. "You remember him? Runs McKinney Drugs over on Main Street? Check this out: he's been clean and sober for twenty years, okay? Last night he went out, downed a whole fifth of cheap whiskey, and beat his wife and kid straight into the hospital."

"She might lose one of her damn eyes," Barry added. "Now, how do you explain that? But that's not what you're here for. I'll tell you, this Gunderson woman? She's a real piece of work."

"How so?"

"Fakes a kidnapping, stashes her own kid God knows where, and you know what she says when we show her the nanny cam recording? 'That's not me.' That's it. That's her whole defense. I just can't figure what she's trying to get out of this whole thing. Attention?"

"That's what we're here to find out," Jessie said. "Can we talk to her?"

"Follow me," Cody said. "Want me to set her up in the interview room?"

Five minutes later, Jessie and I sat across a steel table from a very frightened woman. Her stringy hair fell over her face, and her eyes were a teary, bloodshot mess. She didn't sit so much as huddle, hunching forward, keeping her hands clenched in her lap and her arms squeezed tight at her sides.

The room was barely bigger than a walk-in closet, lit by a single hooded bulb over the table. Barry left us alone with her.

"Ms. Gunderson," Jessie said, "we're with the FBI. We'd like to talk to you about your son."

She made eye contact, fleeting, terrified to hope. "Have you found him? Have you found anything at all?"

"No, ma'am," I said, shaking my head. "We just got here."

"Then I don't know what you want from me. I told the sheriff, I *told* him, that isn't me on that recording. It's *not*. It's some . . . camera trick, or some kind of mask, like in those *Mission: Impossible* movies. I asked him, I asked him why would I kidnap my own son, and leave evidence like that? I *knew* the nanny cam was there. It's *mine*, I *put* it there. So why would I do that?"

Her voice cracked. She looked halfway between screaming and breaking down in tears, and she just wasn't sure which direction to lose her mind in first.

I wanted to tell her the truth. *We know you're innocent,* I wanted to tell her. *We know who took your son. You're not crazy.* I wanted to reassure her, to give her some tiny bit of hope she could cling to. But I couldn't.

Besides, I had to wonder, *is "your son's been stolen by a monster, and we're not sure where to even start looking" much of a comfort, compared to this?*

"You are the prime suspect," Jessie said, "but our job here is to investigate *all* possibilities. We're not here to build a case against you, Ms. Gunderson. We're here to find your child."

She swallowed hard and nodded weakly. "Thank you. That's . . . that's all I can ask."

"Is there anything you remember from the night of the incident?" I asked. "Anything at all? The smallest detail might be useful."

She shook her head. "I put Elliot to bed at five. He woke up at ten, and I cradled him for a few minutes until he fell back asleep. I went to bed at eleven. I thought it was so strange, when I woke up in the morning, that he'd finally slept through the night. But he was . . . he was gone. This woman who took him, she didn't come in or out through the front door, I know that much."

"Oh?" I said. "How do you know?"

"The lock is going bad. The doorknob thingie doesn't quite catch on the plate anymore. The only way to close the door is to give it a real hard slam—otherwise, the first good gust of wind will push it right open. My bedroom is across from Elliot's, just a stone's throw from the front door. There's no way I would have slept through a door slamming that loud, and it was still shut tight and locked in the morning, so they had to have gone out a window. I was . . . I was gonna have that lock replaced this weekend."

"Ms. Gunderson," I said, "we're going to do everything we can to help. May we have permission to search your home? We may find something the police overlooked."

Her jaw clenched. "Do whatever you have to, I'll cooperate, just please—please don't stop looking."

Jessie gave me an odd look as we left the interview room. "You know, the house is already a crime scene. You didn't have to ask permission."

"I know. But if we have to go back later and ask her about anything we find there, now it won't feel like a violation of her privacy. She'll feel empowered, like we're all on the same side. Never hurts to build suspect rapport."

"Huh, nice technique." She paused as I took a left, peeking into the tiny cell block at the back of the station. "Exit's this way."

"Yeah," I said, "just playing a hunch."

A stocky man sat alone in a tiny cell, the bars painted dried-mud brown. He wept into his hands, his shoulders quaking.

"Mr. McKinney," I said.

He pulled his face from his hands. I'd seen catastrophe survivors, third-world refugees who'd lost everything to a hurricane or an earthquake. He had that same haunted, devastated expression on his face.

I flashed my badge. "Agent Black, FBI. One question for you."

He didn't answer. Just stared vacantly at me.

"Why did you do it?" I asked.

"The . . . the first week I quit drinking," he said, his throat hoarse from crying, "that was the worst. I was so *thirsty*. Wanted it so bad, the bottle was all I could think about. But I fought it. And I won. Kept winning for twenty years. I got past it. Then last night . . . it came back."

"The thirst?"

He nodded. "People say they need a drink? Well, I really did. I *needed* it, needed it so bad I talked down every reason why not I could think of. Told myself I'd just have one. Forgot that I *can't* just have one. Then I come home and my wife's nagging and my kid's crying and I just got so . . . damn . . . *angry*. But that wasn't the worst part."

I leaned closer to the bars.

"What was the worst part?"

"This wasn't about shutting 'em up or making 'em do what I told them or any of that crap. I wanted . . . God help me, *I wanted to hurt them.* That was the only reason. That was it, the beginning and the end of it. I wanted to hurt them, so I did, and *I don't know why.*"

He wheezed out the last words as he collapsed to his knees on the concrete floor, breaking down, sobbing into his hands. We left him there.

"Like Baltimore?" I asked Jessie, remembering her story from the briefing about the demon they'd faced in a shopping mall.

"*Exactly* like it," she said. "Once we got rid of the thing, none of the victims could explain why they acted the way they had. Is that what you think this is? A demon?"

I shrugged. "Too many unknowns. Every little bit of intel we get is helpful."

We poked our heads into Barry's cramped office. Every spare shelf was choked with plastic binders, old and mismatched file folders, and trophies from the Talbot Cove bowling league. I glanced to my right and tried to swallow the sudden lump in my throat. A big framed picture of my father hung on the wall.

"Don't suppose she confessed?" Barry asked. He sat behind his desk, looking up from a carton of Chinese takeout and a pair of egg rolls on a greasy napkin.

"No such luck," I said. "Hey, you mind if we check out the crime scene?"

He fished around in one of his desk drawers, coming up with a ring of keys.

"Here, be my guest—547 Oak Terrace. Let me know what you find."

"Did you take anything out of the house?" Jessie asked. "Besides the nanny cam?"

"Nothing *to* take. Whole situation's pretty open-and-shut."

I had to feel sympathetic for his point of view. For someone who lives in a rational, logical world, where monsters and magic don't exist, he had a good point.

Problem was, I had left that world behind thirty years ago.

Out in the car, I fired up the engine, then paused.

"What?" Jessie buckled her seat belt, eyeing me.

"I'm sorry."

"For?"

"Back there," I said. "In the lobby. I had no business calling you out like that. You're right, everybody has their coping mechanisms. I'm just . . . coming back to this town, it's bringing back a lot of feelings I thought I'd locked away for good. So I'm tense, but me being tense isn't an excuse to talk to you like that."

Jessie shook her head and smiled. "Forget about it. But you know, you never did answer my question."

"Which one?"

"How do you cope, or *do* you? You can't be stoic *all* the time."

I shrugged and threw the car into reverse.

"First time I ever came under fire," I said, "was two days after my assignment to the Seattle office. High-risk warrant delivery on a suspected counterfeiter. He saw us coming; we'd barely gotten out of the van before he unloaded on us with a black-market Kalashnikov. Nobody seriously hurt, thankfully. After we took him down, I found one of my colleagues, this . . . two-hundred-pound bear of a man, sitting in the van and crying his eyes out. He was cool under fire, but once he had time to process, the adrenaline hit him."

"Sure," Jessie said. "Happens all the time. Laugh, cry, scream. Adrenaline after a gunfight's like a coked-up rock star in an expensive hotel room. It doesn't leave until it trashes the place."

"After we debriefed, ASAC Flannery called me into her office. We had a mentorship thing, nothing formal, but she took me under her wing and showed me the ropes."

"How the Bureau really works, as opposed to how they taught you it worked at Quantico?" Jessie asked.

"Bingo. And she said to me, 'What he did today? You can *never, ever* do that. A male agent in tears is a veteran operator experiencing completely understandable post-traumatic stress. A female agent in tears is *weak*. One slip like that—just *one*—and you'll have a rep that'll follow you for the rest of your career. So whatever you're feeling when you're on the job, for any reason, lock it down. Lock it down until you're home, alone, with a bottle of wine and nobody to judge you for it.'"

Jessie whistled. "That's grim."

"It's the reality of the situation. So I do what Flannery taught me: when I'm on the job, nothing matters but the mission. I just put one foot in front of the other until it's done." I glanced at the dashboard clock. "It's getting late. Want to check out the Gunderson house tonight, or wait until morning? I'm good to keep working, if you are."

"You mean," she said, "do I want to go and hunt the Bogeyman in the dark? Why, I'd be ever so delighted. Let's roll."

SIX

Oak Terrace wasn't in the prosperous part of town. It was a stretch of cheap tract houses down by the paper mill, and the Crown Vic's headlights strobed over dead, rusting cars and broken windows.

"Now this," Jessie muttered. "This really pisses me off."

"What does?"

She waved a hand toward the windshield.

"These people barely have a pot to piss in. They're just working hard, doing what they can to get by, and along comes some supernatural asshole to spread a little more misery around. I've been working for Linder for six years, come November. Know how many times I've hunted for monsters in Beverly Hills or the Hamptons?"

"None, I'm guessing."

"They always go after the little guy," she said. "Monsters always prey on the people who've already been beaten down. The ones who can't fight for themselves. Though that leads to the part of this job I really like."

"Protecting the innocent?" I asked.

In the dark, her bright-blue eyes seemed to glow faintly, like two radioactive sapphires.

"The dumb, surprised look on their faces," she said, "when they realize they're up against someone who can fight *back.* So on that note, what's your shtick?"

"My shtick?"

"You know." Jessie waggled her fingers at me. "The witch thing. What can you do?"

"Well, most of what my mom taught me is . . . defensive, I guess. Stuff to help protect people. Wards, barriers, bindings, and banishments. I can cast out a possessor demon, banish unclean spirits . . . basically, if something's in our world that shouldn't be, I've got all kinds of ways to ruin its day."

"Huh."

I glanced over at her. "Huh? You don't sound impressed."

"No, no, it's cool, it's just . . . your predecessor could set people on fire with her mind. I mean, banishing spirits, that's *useful,* but—"

I took my right hand off the wheel, curling my fingers into a cup. I concentrated, only half focusing on the road, the syllables of a spell twisting through my thoughts like a spiderweb. The car took on an amber glow, warmed by the tiny globe of flame that now nestled in my palm.

"When I need to," I told her, "I can do some damage, too."

I closed my fingers, snuffing out the fire.

"But I'm better with a gun," I added.

Jessie leaned back in her seat, nodding. "All right. That's more like it. So, uh . . . personal question?"

"Shoot."

"What's it feel like?"

I tilted my head. "What's what feel like?"

"Magic," she said. "When you do your thing. What does it feel like?"

"It's like . . ." I trailed off. Looking for words to describe the indescribable. "It's like the universe is this giant machine. Billions of gears and levers and rotors, a giant clockwork. And you're inside. You're right there, up to your elbows in it, making the machine dance to your tune. Just for a . . . a fleeting second, you *are* the machine."

We drove in silence for a minute after that.

"So that's why so many of you people are nuts," Jessie said. "That's gotta mess with a person's head. Not you, though. Linder vouched for you, said you were saner than . . . well, *me*, anyway. How's that happen?"

"How do I not go nuts?" I couldn't help chuckling. "I just remember what my mom taught me. Magic isn't *for* me. It's for the people I help. We call it 'the gift'—but I'm the one giving it, not unwrapping it. What about my, uh, predecessor? What was her secret to staying sane?"

"Oh, Mikki?" Jessie shrugged. "Didn't have one. She was a narcissistic sociopath."

I glanced over at her, not sure if she was joking. She stared back, dead serious.

"When we found her, she was playing muscle for a gang of neo-Nazi gunrunners. Man, she *hated* working for me."

"Because you're black?" I asked.

"Nah, because Linder had her on a chemical leash. Experimental thing the lab rats cooked up. She had a poison sac implanted next to her appendix; once every couple of days, I had to give her an antidote injection or she'd die. It was a rehabilitation experiment. Worked okay, while it lasted. She was still a raging bitch, though."

"I'm kinda surprised. I mean, the way everyone reacted at the briefing when her name came up—"

"That's principle," Jessie said sharply, staring out into the dark. "Nobody puts one of my people in the ground and walks. Nobody. All accounts must be paid in full. As for Kevin . . . well, I played interference as much as I could, but he carried a torch about a mile high for that psycho."

"Kevin. And the neo-Nazi sociopath. Had a thing. I mean, I just met him, but that doesn't sound like his type."

"The deal with sociopaths is, they're *really* good at being charming when they want to be. Teenage boy with raging hormones, leggy twentysomething redhead who went out of her way to string him along . . . yeah, he followed her around like a puppy dog, and she loved every minute of it. Never had any idea what she was *really* like when he wasn't in the room. I told her once she broke his heart, her next antidote injection was gonna be tap water instead."

Jessie sighed. She slumped against the armrest.

"And she went and got herself killed and broke his heart anyway," she added. "So we'll avenge her death. Not the real woman, but the imaginary one Kevin fell in love with. So he can shed a few last tears for the person he thought she was, and we can all move on. Anyway. Don't feel like talking about Mikki right now. We there yet?"

I squinted, trying to read house numbers on the unlit road. "Should be right up . . . wait a second."

I pulled over and killed the headlights. The Crown Vic's tires rumbled on the gravel shoulder.

"What?" Jessie said.

I pointed up ahead. Three houses down sat 547, a ramshackle two-bedroom that might have been pretty fifty years ago. Even in the dark I could see the drooping, corroded gutters and the weed-choked lawn.

That, and the tiny orb of light that bobbed behind one curtained window. A flashlight beam.

"Somebody's in there."

Jessie pulled her pistol from under her jacket and checked the load. It was her service piece, a slim black Glock 23.

"So there is," she said. "What do you think? Reporter? Souvenir hunter?"

My own pistol rode against my ribs, snug in its shoulder holster.

"Somebody," I said, "who is about to sorely regret tromping all over an active crime scene. Let's go introduce ourselves."

We got out in the dark, shutting the Vic's doors as softly as we could. Gravel crunched under my shoes as I padded toward the house, staying low, with Jessie right behind me. We cut across the lawn. Up ahead, I could see the front door hanging open a few inches, only shadows behind it.

I drew my Glock on the doorstep, moving to one side of the door. Jessie took the other. I gestured to myself, then her. She nodded. We'd never worked together, but we had the same training. On a silent three count, I swept into the house, soundlessly pushing through the open door and covering the darkened living room with the muzzle of my gun. Jessie sliced the pie in the other direction, right on my heels, watching every angle.

Clear. No movement in the gloom, but we definitely weren't alone. The living room looked like the aftermath of a riot. Chairs broken, a sofa slashed to ribbons and all the stuffing pulled out, a porcelain lamp smashed on the cigarette-burned carpet like a kid's piggy bank.

Two exits, both wide open. One archway looked in on the kitchen. From just around the corner, a rattling sound. Someone rummaging in the refrigerator. In the other direction, up a short hall, heavy footsteps and dresser drawers banging open and closed.

Jessie pointed to me, the kitchen, then to herself and the hallway. I nodded. We passed each other like ghosts in the night.

My shoulders tensed. These weren't mundane thrill seekers, and they sure as hell weren't reporters. This was a full-scale ransack, and they didn't care about being subtle. I stepped lightly into the kitchen, nearly slipping in a puddle of milk from a ruptured carton. A man hunched over, concealed behind the open refrigerator door. He grabbed a box of fruit juice, gave it a shake, then tossed it over his shoulder to splatter on the linoleum. From the mess on the floor, he'd been at this for a while.

I spoke softly. Soft but firm, with the authority of my badge and the steel in my hand backing me up.

"Federal agent. Stand up slowly. Show me your hands."

He raised his head, and my breath froze in my throat.

His eyes were like two broken, runny eggs, scrambles of white and yellow pus. Black veins covered his face like a road map of hell, bulging and pulsing. He grinned and showed me a mouthful of curving fangs.

Cambion. Half demon. I'd seen them before. In a heartbeat I did the math: cambion survive in human society by hiding their true nature at all costs. There's only one time they'll show a stranger their real face.

When they're about to kill you.

Two quick gunshots echoed from the hallway behind me. A single moment of surprise. The cambion moved, blindingly fast, and hurled a tin can at me just as I opened fire. The can hit me in the face, smacking my cheekbone like a brick, and my bullet caught the half demon in the shoulder. He didn't even flinch. He lunged, and before I could fix my aim, he threw himself onto me. We both went down, hard, into the mess of discarded groceries on the kitchen floor.

I landed on my back. He drove a knee into my stomach, winding me, and pinned my gun hand. I shot out my other hand, not to punch him, but to grab his face. I wheezed the first line of an incantation—the twisting, doggerel Latin rolling off my tongue. The spell was designed to banish a bodiless demon from its unwilling host.

For a living human with demon blood, it just *hurts*.

The cambion let out a shrill scream and rolled off me, his face burned black and smoking where my fingers had gripped him. He landed on all fours, crouching like a jackal, baring his fangs at me. Then he turned and ran.

I chased after him. On the other side of the living room, Jessie had a fight of her own. I saw her stagger back, her lip cut and bleeding, reeling from a cambion's punch. A third man grappled her from behind, trying to pin her arms behind her back.

The one from the kitchen loped out the door, still running on all fours. I let him go. My partner took priority. I lifted my gun and dropped a bead on the closest half-breed.

"Federal agent!" I roared. "Get on your knees and put your hands behind your head!"

The cambion behind Jessie shrieked. She'd gotten hold of his hand—and wrenched it so far backward that the backs of his fingers were pressed to his arm, snapping wrist bones like twigs.

Jessie laughed with giddy delight. Before, it looked like her eyes glowed in the dark. Now there was no doubt in my mind. They blazed like blue fire as she spun the cambion around, still holding him by his mangled wrist, and broke his arm with a sound like a gunshot.

The third man, the one who had punched her, had hold of her Glock. He raised it to fire, but she snapped out a lightning-fast kick and knocked it from his hand. I heard the bones of his fingers pop. Jessie shoved the crippled cambion away, hard enough to send him sprawling to the floor, and went after her new target.

"Suffer!" she hissed.

He held up his hands, frantic, backing up against the wall. I tore my attention to the crippled cambion on the floor, keeping my sights on him. He kept his good hand tucked under his body, close to his pockets.

"Show me your hand," I said, looming over him. "*Right now.* Show me your hand!"

His fingers came out gripping metal, but it wasn't a gun. I saw the curve of some kind of amulet, a rounded disk of hammered brass engraved with spidery runes. He ran his thumb over the sharp edge of the disk, slicing skin, bleeding on the glimmering metal as he spat a guttural incantation.

The disk erupted with the fury of a flash-bang grenade. White light seared my eyes, a crump of deafening force pushing me back and knocking me flat. In my double vision I watched the two cambion run for it, leaning on each other as they staggered out the front door.

I couldn't move. Couldn't think. The sound of my blood throbbed in my eardrums, cranked up to eleven and pumping like a bass beat.

The spell faded fast. I slowly pushed myself to my feet, legs wobbly, and rubbed my eyes until the white spots faded away. Jessie knelt on the floor, head bowed and eyes closed, palms upturned on her knees.

"Jessie, are you—"

"Shh," she whispered.

"Are you hurt?"

"Keep your distance," she said. "I'm not safe to be near right now. Need to center myself. *Shh*."

We were going to have to talk about this.

I left her alone and stumbled to the front door. It hung wide open, looking out on an empty lawn and an empty street. The cambion were long gone. I stood there for a moment, on the threshold, drinking in the cool night air and catching my breath. My cheek hurt. I pressed my fingers to it, and they came away dotted with tiny specks of blood.

When I turned around, Jessie stood behind me.

Her eyes were still impossibly turquoise, but they'd lost their glow. I nodded at her.

"Your lip is bleeding."

"Your cheek's scraped up," she said. "What'd he hit you with?"

"A can of peas, I think. You want to discuss this?"

She shook her head. "No. I want to kick the shit out of some cambion. Barring that, I want to figure out what they were tossing this place for."

I shut the front door. It slowly swung back open, just a crack. The latch didn't catch against the strike plate. I leaned on it, hard, and it still didn't catch. Finally I pulled the door back and slammed it shut, loud enough to boom through the house. Now it stayed closed.

"Helen's telling the truth," I said. "Nobody could sleep through that. The creature didn't get in this way."

While I prowled the wreckage, Jessie got on the phone to April. She stepped into the kitchen, but I could hear her end of the conversation.

"Hey, Auntie April. We're over at the vic's house, and we just got jacked by three half-breeds. No, we're okay, but they got away. Yeah, she held her own just fine. Homegirl knows how to brawl. I know, I know, I have to have *the talk* with her. *Later*, jeez."

I poked my head into Helen's bedroom. A bomb would have done less damage. They'd torn apart her bedding, ransacked her dresser drawers, coated the carpet in sliced fabric and empty boxes.

"Need you to pull any intel you've got on the local occult underground," Jessie said behind me. "Yeah, cast a wider net, like, to the nearest big city. We need a player who can tell us the score around here, help us find these assholes. They're working for somebody. Also, have Kevin put a flag on all hospitals and emergency clinics within fifty miles of Talbot Cove. Guy with a mangled arm is going to need some serious medical attention, and I think another one's got a GSW. Hey, hold on. Harmony!"

"Yeah?" I called back.

"Did you wing one?"

"Think I hit him in the shoulder," I said.

"You hear that, Auntie? Yeah, shoulder wound. Cool. We've got a lot of ground to cover here, so don't wait up."

The door to the nursery was open, just a crack. I pushed it wide, the grainy wood gliding soundlessly under my touch. The cambion hadn't gotten this far in their search: Elliot's crib stood by a window, under a dangling plastic mobile. Stuffed animals grinned mutely from a long white shelf, leering in the dark.

Jessie hung up and joined me. She put her hands on her hips.

"So," she said, "witch senses tingling?"

Something was, anyway. I'd had the oddest feeling since I walked into the room, a nagging suspicion that I couldn't see the clue dangling right in my face. Then it hit me.

I closed the bedroom door, then opened it again. Jessie gave me a curious look.

"What?" she said.

"The nanny cam video. Right before and after the creature came on-screen, there was a squeaking sound." I closed and opened the door again. "These hinges were oiled, not long ago. No squeak."

Jessie turned to look at the opposite side of the room. I followed her gaze, my heart sinking.

The closet door.

"Shit," I said.

"Well," Jessie told me, "you did name it the Bogeyman."

SEVEN

Jessie covered me. She took a few steps back, raised the muzzle of her gun to target the closet door, and gave me a nod. I held my breath as I moved close, my fingers curling around the old, tarnished doorknob and squeezing tight.

As I slowly pulled the door open, the hinges gave a shrill squeal. The exact same sound we heard on the recording.

Empty. It looked like Helen had been using it for storing linens. A comforter leaned against one side of the tiny closet, zippered up in plastic, and a few old towels sat neatly folded on a high shelf. Not a lot of room. Just enough for a grown man to hide inside, crouching in the dark, waiting for a family to fall asleep.

A string dangled down, leashed to a single bare lightbulb. I reached in and gave it a tug. Stark white light washed over walls painted sunflower yellow, faded with dirt and time.

I knocked on each wall. Solid. I figured it would be, but it's best to rule out the mundane before you go hunting for phantoms. I took a step back and reached into my inside jacket pocket, fishing out a pendant on a long silver chain.

"What's that?" Jessie asked, holstering her gun.

"Belonged to my great-great-grandmother." My thumb played over the face of the pendant. It was a coin, ancient and tarnished, ringed with an inscription in Greek. A tiny hole, drilled through the edge, accommodated the chain. "First witch in the family, or at least the first to start writing things down for the daughters who came after her. Allegedly this is the first coin ever paid to the first Pythia, the Oracle of Delphi."

Jessie arched an eyebrow. "Seriously?"

"Allegedly," I said, shrugging. I strung the chain between my outstretched fingers like a cat's cradle, letting the Pythian coin dangle freely. "I think my great-great-grandmother was a bit of a huckster. What I do know is that it gets sensitive in places where reality's gone thin. Just have to concentrate a little, and . . ."

I took a step toward the closet. Slowly, as if nudged by an unfelt breeze, the coin began to turn.

The closer I came to the closet, the faster it turned, revolving counterclockwise at the end of the chain. Then I stepped inside. The coin spun like a top, and the chain links twisted until they pinched my fingers like tiny mousetraps. The coin hung in the air, straining, trembling.

I stepped out of the closet. The coin went slack. It spun the other way, suddenly lifeless, as the twisted-up chain unwound itself and relaxed. I slipped it back into my jacket pocket.

"It teleports," I said. "Came in and out of the closet, but it came *from* somewhere else."

"Any way to track it?" Jessie asked.

I shook my head. "Not sure. Let me think about it. Maybe I'll come up with something."

We poked around the rest of the house, but it was a lost cause. Nothing to see, and the cambion had turned the place upside down. If they'd taken something with them when they ran, we'd never know what it was.

"I've got nothing," Jessie said. "Just an aching lip and an empty stomach."

I didn't realize how hungry I was until she said it. "Yeah, sounds good. Let's call it. Maybe we can come back in the morning, see the place with fresh eyes."

Out in the front yard, trudging across the scraggly, tangled grass, something by the edge of the sidewalk caught my eye. It was a wicker ornament, about the size of my fist, hammered into the grass at the end of a short iron spike. I knelt beside it and waved Jessie over.

"Have you got a penlight? There's something here."

She crouched next to me and shined a thin, steady beam on the ornament. It was like a Möbius strip times ten, one long wicker ribbon twisting around and around and looping inside itself. The light caught the faint, almost invisible traces of needle-thin glyphs inscribed on the wicker, in a language I'd never seen before.

"Think the cambion dropped that when they ran?" she asked.

I shook my head. "Don't think so. That little spike is holding it into the dirt. Somebody planted it here, deliberately. Should be an evidence kit in the trunk; let's bag it up and take it with us."

"Good call. April can check it out. First, though, food. I need red meat and beer, not necessarily in that order."

# # #

It wasn't easy, this late at night, finding a place with open doors, let alone an open kitchen. We ended up at the Spit and Whistle, a barbecue joint with tables carved from tree logs and lit by strung-up Christmas tree lights. We settled into a booth by the kitchen while Lynyrd Skynyrd rocked out on an old Wurlitzer jukebox.

"The waitresses are wearing brown-felt fox ears on headbands," I said to Jessie. "I'm a little lost on the theme here."

"Red meat and beer," she said, buried in the sauce-stained paper menu.

She repeated herself when a waitress came over, then added, "Specifically, the brisket burger, and all the toppings. Rare. Rare as pirate gold. Just wave a candle in its general direction. What's on tap?"

"All the classics, plus we brew our own ale on site. It's an IPA with a medium body, a little nutty—"

"Sold."

"I'll have the barbecue chicken salad," I said when she looked my way, "and a Diet Coke, please."

"Living dangerously," Jessie said. When the waitress left, she stretched her arms over her head and yawned. "How's your cheek?"

"Stings," I said. "How's your lip?"

"Hurts. My pride took a worse beating, though."

"Jessie, we need to talk about this."

"My pride?" she asked.

I leaned closer, taking a quick look around.

"I watched you fold a man's bones like a piece of dirty laundry. And your eyes were glowing when you did it."

"Eh," she said, offering the waitress a smile as she brought our drinks over. She tossed back her mug, closing her eyes and smiling. "Mmm. Okay, that's good stuff. Goes down smooth. You should really have one."

"Jessie."

"I know, I *know*," she said. "I just hate this part. Fuck. All right. Better you hear it from me than from Linder. Or God, from Kevin. I just need you to be cool. Can you be cool, Harmony?"

"Test me," I said.

"All right." She took another swig of ale, then folded her hands. "Temple is my mother's maiden name. I was born Jessie Sinclair."

It didn't mean anything to me. I gave her a helpless shrug. I peeled the paper on my straw, giving my hands something to do.

"My father was Russell Lee Sinclair."

I almost dropped the straw.

"Russell Lee Sinclair," I echoed. "As in, Russell Lee Sinclair, the Dixie Butcher?"

She stared into her mug. "Yeah. That one. He didn't escape capture for as long as he did just because we moved around so much. I mean, that helped, but no. Dad's official designation, in *Linder's* records, is Hostile Entity 2. He's one of the reasons Vigilant Lock was created in the first place."

"So what was he?" I said. "Some kind of sorcerer?"

"Some kind, yeah. He was in contact with . . . something outside this world. That's H. E. 3, for the record, but he called it the King of Wolves. The killings were sacrifices. Part of his payment to 'ascend to a higher state of being.'"

"Part of the payment?"

"There were other rituals," Jessie said, her voice fading. "He had to . . . do things. And on my eleventh birthday, he told me he had a very special present. It was time for me to learn the family trade. So I had to do things, too."

"Jesus," I breathed. "I'm sorry, I had no idea."

She shrugged. "No reason you would. I was fifteen the year the feds gunned my dad down. Linder covered up as much of the story as he could, and April took custody of me."

"'Aunt' April," I said. I thought back to what I knew about the Sinclair story—the sanitized-for-the-public version, anyway—and blinked as the last piece clicked into place. "From what I heard, an agent was seriously injured when they tried to arrest him."

"That's right."

I regrettably left the Bureau quite some time ago, April said when we were introduced. *Taking an ax to the lower vertebrae tends to limit your prospects for career advancement.*

"It was her. Dr. Cassidy."

Jessie sipped her ale and sighed. "It wasn't maternal instinct that made April take me in. She wanted to make sure I didn't turn out as fucked up as my dad was. Joke's on her. I'm just neurotic. Could have been worse. Linder wanted me taken out on general principle. She convinced him I'd make a better tool than a target."

"Taken out?" I blinked. "You were fifteen years old."

She didn't answer right away. The waitress swung by, bringing plates laden with food. The rich scent of homemade barbecue sauce, spicy and honey sweet, made my mouth water.

"Spent four years 'learning' from my dad," she said, looking down as she spread a paper napkin across her lap. "Hunting. Fishing. Tracking. The best ways to shut up a naked, screaming, bloody victim while you're smuggling her across state lines in your trunk. Just your basic backwoods Serial Killer 101 stuff."

She looked up at me. "They called it Stockholm syndrome. That, and being too young to know right from wrong, being dominated by a parental authority figure, et cetera. Fortunately, I can report that years of therapy have done wonders, and now I have a serious problem with *all* authority figures."

I felt like I'd airdropped into the middle of a minefield. Reading Jessie was like trying to catch a bead of mercury. She slid from withdrawn and taciturn to smiling and gregarious in the blink of an eye, and it felt like she was daring me to push her.

"Your eyes," I said, "were glowing in the dark."

"Funny thing? In all my baby pictures, they're brown. Like I said: there were other rituals, besides the killings. Dad wanted to make me just like him, a chip off the old block. Had these grandiose dreams of starting a wolf-king cult. Just a happy little pack of serial killers, roaming the country and biting out throats. He was going to fix me up with some nice young man, and I'd pump out lots of evil babies. Everybody wants grandkids, right?"

"So," I said, cautious, "what you did back there, your strength—"

"When I get heated, when the adrenaline starts to pour? I'm stronger than most people. Faster. All my senses get sharper. It's not something I have to think about, like you and your magic; it just *happens*. There's limits: I'm not gonna outrun a freight train or leap tall buildings in a single bound, but it's a handy equalizer when hunting the sorts of creatures that go bump in the night. Love that stupid look on their faces, when they think they've cornered a helpless victim and suddenly realize they had it all backward. They show me their claws . . . and I show 'em mine."

She took a long drink from her mug, guzzling the ale down. She wiped her mouth with the back of her hand and sighed.

"My dad, he had a beast behind his eyes. Or maybe it was always there, and he just woke it up. I've got one in me, too. A smaller, sleepier one, but it's the same beast. I've got to toss it some table scraps every now and then, to keep it happy and fed."

"What happens if you don't?" I asked.

She smiled ruefully at her plate.

"Then it demands a three-course meal," she said, "and that wouldn't be good for anybody, now would it?"

EIGHT

We drove back to the motel with full stomachs and heavy eyelids. No lights burned behind the curtains of April and Kevin's room, so we decided to turn in and catch up with them in the morning.

Our room hadn't been freshened up since sometime in the early '70s. From the garish tree-patterned comforters on the two queen beds to the cheap paper-wrapped soaps in the cramped bathroom, I felt like I'd been in this room a hundred times before. Spend enough time on the road, and they all start to look the same.

"So you're really okay, bunking with me?" Jessie asked.

I sat on the edge of my bed and shrugged off my jacket. "Why, do you snore?"

"I mean, after what I told you tonight."

I tugged at my tie, loosening the Windsor knot. "I asked you for the truth, you gave it to me. I haven't seen a reason not to trust you. If you really thought it'd be dangerous, I think you'd insist on a private room."

She gave me a curious look. "Yeah, that's right."

I carefully rolled my tie and slipped it back into my suitcase, next to the four others I'd packed.

"Besides," I told her, "we're hunting the Bogeyman. I can't deal with that *and* be afraid of the Big Bad Wolf."

Jessie tilted her head. She was quiet for so long I started to think I'd offended her, but then she broke into a toothy grin.

"The Big Bad Wolf. I *like* that. But on the subject . . ."

She walked across the room and pulled back the accordion-style closet door.

"This? Stays *open*."

I couldn't argue. Sleep came fast once the lights went out, but my dreams were a labyrinth of empty houses and closet doors. I ran in slow motion and silence, through room after lonely room, looking for something I could never find.

# # #

I woke to the alarm clock's shrill whine, dragging me out of nightmares and into hard reality. I wasn't sure which was worse. Scarlet numbers in the dark read six o'clock, and the first glow of dawn peeked around the edges of the window curtain.

Jessie moaned, swore, and pulled a pillow over her head. "You can have the shower first," she muttered.

"So you can sleep another fifteen minutes," I said, pushing the covers back and forcing myself to sit up.

"Curses. You've seen through my cunning plan."

I'm a morning person, always have been. There's something about the start of a new day that just feels ripe with promise, even when a case isn't going my way. It felt like a metallic-green necktie day.

I thought about last night while I showered, letting the pounding water and rising steam clear the fog in my brain. The cambion were searching the Gunderson house for something. It had to have been something small, since they'd torn open everything bigger than a pack of chewing gum. Something hidden. Something well hidden, since they'd even gutted the upholstery and torn out pillow stuffing to hunt for it.

Maybe we needed to take another run at Helen and see if she was keeping any secrets up her sleeve. For all we knew, this could have nothing to do with the Bogeyman. Still, the timing was too close for coincidences.

I finished showering, toweled off my hair, and unzipped my little vinyl travel bag. I always go light on the makeup—moisturizer, eye shadow, lip gloss, mascara, done. The scratch on my cheek had faded to an angry little welt. I wished I'd packed concealer, but I could live with it.

"Bathroom's yours," I said on my way out. Jessie growled at me.

Eventually we got ourselves together and migrated to the room next door. April and Kevin had made themselves at home: the phone by the television was nothing but an exposed bundle of cables and parts, wired up to Kevin's laptop like something out of Frankenstein's laboratory.

"You're going to fix that before we leave, right?" I said.

On his screen, a medieval knight in shining armor stood on the veranda of an Italian-style palazzo, a massive sword strapped to his back.

"Oh my God," Jessie groaned, throwing herself on the closest bed. "You colossal geek. Kill orcs on your own time."

"I'll have you know, I'm mining for information," he said, and gestured to the chat window in the bottom left corner of the screen. "Hackers, extremists, undergrounders and fringers—everybody knows the NSA's all over IRC and e-mail these days, and phone security is a joke. Online games, though? *Nobody's* monitoring private chat there. It's the final frontier for unrestricted communication."

I took a peek, leaning over his shoulder and reading the chat as it scrolled up the window.

> (Private) Tomoe Gozen: Yeah, I'll be your Google.
> I need the cash to get out of the 702 for a while.
> Everything's going crazy here.

(Private) Grignr: Thanks, TG.

(Private) Tomoe Gozen: Anything for a guild buddy. Well, anything but cybersex again. That was a little weird.

Kevin lunged for the keyboard, snapping the chat window shut. He grimaced and looked up at me.

"I'm cultivating a confidential informant. A little privacy?"

April, sitting over at the table near the window and poring over a stack of heavy books, glanced up at us. "He's *also* slaying orcs."

"Hobgoblins, Dr. Snitch. Hobgoblins are not orcs."

"I," April said, "have something a little more grounded in reality for you two. I talked to Vladimir last night."

"Vlad's an antiquities dealer in New York," Jessie told me. "Specializes in stolen artifacts, real grave-robber stuff. We flipped him a while back. Now he gets to run his seedy little operation as long as he feeds us intel and vouches for us when we need cover."

"As it turns out," April said, "there's a sorcerer he's done business with living twenty miles from Talbot Cove. A man named Douglas Bredford. He's a small fish in a tiny pond. Vladimir says that if anyone can identify the men who attacked you last night, it's him."

I smiled. Finally, a lead. It wasn't much, but at least we weren't spinning our wheels and waiting for another kid to get snatched. "Great. Where do we find him?"

April held out a yellow sticky note, bearing an address in prim, neat handwriting.

"Most likely, this bar, at any given time of day. Mr. Bredford is, in Vladimir's words, 'a bit of a walking disaster.'"

# # #

Out in the parking lot, I asked if Jessie wanted to drive. She took a long look at the Crown Victoria, put her hands on her hips, and said, "It looks even worse in the morning light, doesn't it?"

I took that as her answer and kept the keys.

"We have a standard routine when we're approaching occult-underground types," she said. We drove away from the shoreline, pointing the car's nose along a forest road that coasted up and down massive, rough hills. "We prefer going in undercover. The fewer people who know about Vigilant Lock, the better it is for everybody."

"And this Vladimir, he's your cover?"

"Bingo. Anybody calls his number, he'll tell them we've been customers for years and totally vouch for us. Every major player in the underground either knows Vlad or knows of him, so that builds our cred. Just follow my lead; you'll do fine."

Douglas Bredford lived in a town that barely qualified for a name, just a crossroads and a trailer park on the far edge of nowhere. April's address led us to the Brew House, a gray wooden shack with busted-out windows and a front porch made from a line of two-by-fours.

The gravel strip of parking out front was almost empty, save for a battered old pickup truck that sported more rust than original paint. Rolls of twine held the back bumper on, and one of the side mirrors was completely gone.

"This job takes us to the nicest places," Jessie said as I pulled in a few spots down from the truck.

Scratchy speakers over the bar played an old country tune as we walked in, a screen door swinging shut behind us. The bartender didn't look up from his magazine. We were the only customers in sight, except for the man with the salt-and-pepper beard and trucker cap sitting in a booth in the back.

Deep lines marred his face, and the hand that gripped his bottle of Budweiser trembled like a leaf in a stiff wind. His rheumy eyes couldn't seem to focus on much of anything.

"Mr. Bredford," Jessie said. "Sorry to bother you, but we're with the Church of Starry Wisdom in Rhode Island, just passing through. Our friend Vladimir says you're the person to know around here."

He took a long pull on his bottle, looking us over.

"My 'friend' Vlad is a double-dealing son of a bitch, and if you two aren't cops I'll eat my hat. No." He looked my way. "Feds. I was on the job for almost thirty years, lady. Clocked you the second you walked in the door. Well, sit down, say what you're gonna say."

We obliged him, sliding into the booth across from him. Cracked red vinyl padded the bench, patched over here and there with strips of duct tape.

"Cambion," Jessie said. "Three of them. Locals. We want them."

Douglas snorted and drank his beer. "Forget you, lady. I don't need that kind of trouble."

"The bad news is, we're putting somebody in handcuffs today. Them, or you. The good news is, you get to choose."

"I ain't done anything," Douglas said, squinting at her. "You've got no grounds to arrest me."

Jessie smiled thinly. "Given that we know what cambion are, you've probably sussed that we're not the regular kind of feds."

"Noticed that, yeah."

"We don't take people to the regular kind of prison, either," she said. "You go to the special one. Offshore. And you never come back."

"You can't—you can't *do* that," he said, pushing his shoulders back and sticking his chin up, "I've got *rights*."

She was losing him. The shock-and-awe approach works on some suspects, but more often than not, it just backs them into a corner and clams them up. I gently put my hand on the table. Not touching him, but close.

"Mr. Bredford, a child has been kidnapped."

He looked my way. "Not their usual style."

"They didn't do it, but we think they know who did. This is a serial offender. He's stolen other children, and they've never been found. With every hour that passes, the trail gets that much colder."

He looked down at his beer. "Those boys are gonna kill me."

"Right now," I said, "there's a mother staring at the door, staring at the phone, wondering if she'll ever see her baby alive again. Minutes, hours, days . . . can you imagine how much that hurts? *You* can help her. Right now, you're the *only* person who can. Please. Help us find these men."

Douglas slouched back, the brim of his cap slipping down over his eyes.

"All right," he grumbled. "Goddamn it, all right. Fine. You're looking for the Gresham brothers. They hole up in a trailer park in Berrien County, just off Route 12. I can give you the address."

"What are they into?" Jessie asked, leaning closer.

"Meth, mostly, but they'll rip off anything that ain't nailed down. You know the saying 'Don't get high on your own supply'? Well, they don't think much of that rule."

"They work only for themselves?"

Douglas grunted. "If you call that work. Yeah, mostly, but every once in a while somebody from the Flowers throws a dirty job their way."

"Flowers?" I said.

He looked at me like I'd grown a second head.

"Yeah. Court of Night-Blooming Flowers?"

I looked at Jessie. She shrugged.

"You gotta be kidding me," Douglas said. "Special feds, huh? You don't know *shit*. You ladies get comfortable while I grab another bottle of Bud. I'm about to ruin your lives."

NINE

"Been in this game a long time," Douglas said, back at the booth with a fresh bottle of beer. "I was a cop, out east. We were working a gang beat in Little Vietnam, trying to roust some scumbags who were preying on the immigrant traffic. Then one night, my partner gets sick. Coughing up blood, buckets of the stuff. Ran him to the ER. Turns out, he had ninety-eight fishhooks in his stomach, like he'd swallowed them one by one."

Douglas took a long pull on his bottle, squeezing his eyes shut for a moment.

"After the funeral, I had a lot of questions. Didn't care about why—I knew why: we'd stepped on the wrong toes. I wanted to know *how*. Because my partner didn't swallow any goddamn ninety-eight fish-hooks, but there they were."

"Find what you were looking for?" Jessie asked.

"And then some. And then I couldn't stop. That's the thing, this world, it just . . . sucks you in. You start looking for the answer to a question, it leads you to a hundred more questions. You start looking to answer those, and there you go. Straight down the rabbit hole, and that's a one-way trip."

"What was that you were saying earlier," I asked, "about flowers?"

"The Court," he said, making grand gestures and rolling his eyes, "of Night-Blooming Flowers. Lemme bottom-line this for you. A few centuries ago, Lucifer took a vacation and never came back. Hell fell into a civil war. What was left, when the dust settled, were the courts. Each one with a prince, each one laying claim to some patch of dirt here on Earth. They call it the Cold Peace. Some really old-school factions, like the Bargainers and the Chainmen, they get an exemption and can go wherever they want. For most of hell's rank and file, though, they keep to their own courts. Plotting and scheming against one another gives the bastards something to do, I guess."

"Slow down," Jessie said. "Are you telling us hell is *organized*? They have a functional government, and they're claiming actual territory in the United States?"

"I don't know how functional I'd call it, but yeah. And they've got operatives. Hounds, they're called. Not hijackers who have to possess a human body, but incarnate demons. You know what incarnates are?"

I nodded. "I met one, in Las Vegas. He called himself Sullivan. I was told he was the only one in the country."

Douglas snorted. "Then you were told wrong."

Or lied to, I thought. Sullivan and his cambion followers came after me in a casino parking garage. He looked like a genteel schoolteacher until the gloves came off and he turned into a feral, mutating terror that took a bullet to the face without flinching. He damn near outran me, too—and I was on a motorcycle at the time.

Everything I knew about incarnate demons came courtesy of a thief named Daniel Faust, and he was knee-deep in brimstone. He'd had every reason to lie. Then there was the woman. I'd identified almost every member of Faust's crew, every thief and killer and warlock he ran with . . . except for the pale Scottish redhead who kept showing up at his side.

Every background check came back empty, I thought. *Image-recognition searches, nothing. Not the ones I did. The ones that I sent to the Bureau. Almost like somebody on the inside wanted to keep her anonymous.*

I didn't want to know, but I had to ask. "Mr. Bredford, how much influence do these demons have in our . . . social structures?"

"That's not the question you wanna ask me," he said, leaning forward and pitching his grizzled voice low. "The question eating at you is, are they infesting the hallowed halls of Washington, DC? And the answer is yes. Them and their human toadies."

He sat back and sucked at the bottle.

"There are agents of hell *in* the government?" Jessie said.

"You girls, God, you're cute. You've got your little shadow-op conspiracy going, probably got a name like Operation Cold Spectrum or something, and you think you're the secret hand of the president. The men in black, here to save the day from the hordes of hell. News flash, ladies: you're not the only conspiracy in town. There are only two reasons you haven't been shut down and left dead in an alley—either you're too weak to care about, or you're already their pawns."

"You make it sound hopeless," I told him. He just laughed.

"Don't you *get* it?" he said. "It *is* hopeless. That's the joke. The great cosmic jest at the end of the line. There's a hell, but no heaven. The universe isn't just apathetic toward humanity, it *actively fucking hates us*. What are you doing, huh? What are you doing right this minute?"

"We're hunting a monster," I said, my shoulders clenching.

"Sure, sure, good for you!" He applauded against his bottle. "And while you do that, a hundred others are out there in the dark, and a hundred more are waking up every year. The war is *over*. We *lost*. Humanity is like a . . . a . . . a crocodile with a bullet in its brain, too dumb to know it's already dead. We just keep kicking, keep moving, all the way to the dinner table."

"I don't believe that," I said. "There's always hope. And there's always a reason to fight. If I can save one life, it's worth doing."

"Even if you pay with yours? The things I've seen, I couldn't even begin to tell you . . ." He rolled his head back against the broken vinyl and clutched his bottle. "Well, that's why I'm drunk at nine in the morning, ain't it? I figure I've got two, three more good years before the cirrhosis kills me. How much horror do you think you can take before you're right here with me? Maybe I should save you a seat, huh?"

I locked eyes with him.

"You would be *amazed* how much I can take," I told him.

Jessie slapped her palm on the table. "Change of subject. When we crossed paths with the Gresham brothers, we left them bleeding. One's got a bullet in his shoulder. Are they dumb enough to go to a hospital, or is there somebody they'd call for an off-the-books patch job?"

Douglas thought about it for a second. He held up a finger, nodding.

"One guy, one guy I know, does that kind of work. Emmanuel Hirsch. He's a big-name plastic surgeon in Detroit, but he offers back-room surgery for anybody who can keep their mouth shut and pay in cash. Pretty sure he's in tight with the Detroit Partnership, mobbed up to the eyeballs."

"Got a number for this doctor?" Jessie asked.

"Been a long time since I cared what a doctor thinks," Douglas said. "What's he gonna tell me? Quit drinking? Yeah, sure, maybe I'll take up jogging and healthy eating, too. You got a name, you got a phone, he ain't hard to find."

I nodded. "I think we're done, then. Thank you for your help."

"You just keep my name out of it," he said as we slid out of the booth. "And you watch your asses around the Gresham boys. Demon-blooded and high on crank is one hell of a bad combo."

We were almost to the door when he called after me.

"You just remember, Agent. There's always more monsters. There's *always* more monsters."

# # #

Jessie dropped into the passenger seat and slammed the door.

"*Fuck* that guy. He wants to die so badly, I should have capped his miserable ass myself."

I shrugged and fired up the engine. I was numb, shaken, tired. The sky was crystal blue, but I still felt like I was sitting under a storm cloud.

"He gave us a good lead," was all I could manage to say.

"Sure. But the rest of it sounded like weapons-grade bullshit."

I paused with my hand on the shift. "One thing, though. I think he was trying to tell us something. Something else. Get Kevin on the phone?"

"Why not?" Jessie said. "Gotta tell 'em we're headed back to Detroit anyway."

She held out her phone and put it on speaker so we could both talk.

"Got an update for home base," she said. "Looks like our cambion buddies are headed to a mob doctor in Detroit to get patched up. We're on the trail."

Kevin's voice crackled over the speaker. "Cool. April's studying that wicker-ball thing you guys found at the crime scene, seeing if she can tie it to any recorded symbolism. I'm looking through the old newspaper archives looking for anything else like it. So far, no hits."

"One other thing," I said. "Can you or your hacker buddies dig up anything on old black-budget programs?"

"Depends on how deep they're buried. Whatcha looking for?"

"It's called Operation Cold Spectrum," I said. "I don't know anything else about it."

"Needle in a haystack, but I'll throw out a line and see if anything bites. Drive safe."

Jessie hung up and gave me a look.

"What?" I said. "That Cold Spectrum thing rolled *really* easily off Bredford's tongue. Like it meant something to him, but he didn't want to talk about it."

"Much like the alcohol rolled off his tongue, and down his throat, in vast quantities."

"Indulge me, okay?" I shrugged and backed out of the parking space, loose gravel rumbling under the tires. My shoulders sagged. "I just . . . I don't know how much of what he said was true."

We rode in silence for a moment. Jessie looked over, studying me. "Can't believe he made us the second we walked in the door. That's just embarrassing. I blame you."

I arched an eyebrow. "Me?"

"Well," she said, gesturing at me, "you do have this stereotypical lesbian FBI agent look going on."

My foot slipped off the accelerator. "What? Jessie, I—I am *not* gay."

"Really? Are you sure? Because you totally present as queer."

"Yes," I said, glaring at her. "I am *sure* I'm attracted to men, thank you."

"Hey, I'm just saying, don't worry about me hitting on you or anything. I don't date coworkers, even if you are really cute."

"Not gay, Jessie."

"But," she said, "you experimented in college."

"Where are you *getting* this stuff?"

She tapped the side of her head. "Finely tuned gaydar. And that wasn't a denial, was it? Okay, so what's with the men's ties?"

I glanced down. "They're . . . colorful. I like them."

"They're colorful." She eyed me, dubious.

"They're *organized* color. Black suit, ivory blouse, one splash of color always in the same place. That's my style."

"*Now* I get it," she said, nodding. "Have you been formally diagnosed with OCD?"

"Are you going to spend the entire drive to Detroit tormenting me?"

She looked in the backseat. "Is Kevin here? No? Then probably, yes. Now let's talk about your experimental phase in college . . ."

I couldn't help but laugh. It was the first time I'd smiled since we left Douglas Bredford to marinate in his misery, and the feeling of gloom he'd left us sloughed off in the sunshine. Of course, that was exactly Jessie's intention. Coping mechanisms.

If we'd known the horror that was waiting for us in Detroit, it might not have worked.

TEN

We hit the Motor City right around noon, sitting in a snarl of traffic under a hazy autumn sun. Like Douglas said, Emmanuel Hirsch wasn't hard to find. He ran his own practice, a swank boutique clinic in the Bricktown Historic District.

"People love this guy," Jessie said, thumbing over reviews on her phone. "Tummy tucks, face-lifts, implants, he does it all."

"And that's just the legal stuff. So what's our approach?"

She set the phone in her lap. "Hmm. Well, we could masquerade as prospective patients in need of emergency surgery, but unless you literally want to take a bullet for the team . . ."

"Yeah," I said, "that one's out. Besides, a guy like this is going to be careful. He'll want referrals, a voucher from an existing client, something like that."

"We could go in after hours, search his clinic."

"You think we can get a warrant?" I asked. "All we've got is Douglas Bredford's say-so, and that's not a lot."

Jessie tilted her head and squinted at me.

"Warrant? Why the hell would we need that?"

"Because," I said slowly, "it's . . . the law?"

"When we run these cambion punks down, they're getting off-shored. They don't *have* legal rights."

I merged from a slow lane of traffic to a slower one, edging toward the off-ramp.

"I don't like that," I said, "and you shouldn't like it, either, considering it'd be just as easy for *us* to disappear that way. Demon blood or not, they're still American citizens."

"You think I like it? It sucks, but what's the alternative? Tell the whole world that magic is real, and there really *are* things that go bump in the night?"

I shrugged. "Maybe we should. Maybe it's time."

"Wow," Jessie said. "Wow. No. Wrong. So very wrong. Case in point: not just anybody can learn to do magic, right? But it's safe to say, there's a lot of *potential* magicians out in the world who just never figure out that they've got the spark. Like, on an order of magnitude."

"Sure," I said, "that's reasonable."

"Okay. Now, how many of the sorcerers you've met are dangerous, deviant, murderous *assholes*? Most of them, right? So picture every Tom, Dick, and Harry Potter studying hard, trying to become a real live wizard. If just one-tenth of them succeed, and one-tenth of *them* let the power go to their heads—and it'll be a lot more than one-tenth, you *know* this—we'll be mopping up corpses around the clock."

"That . . . is a frightening mental image," I said.

"Then there's the simple fact that the law can't *handle* this stuff. How do you prove that someone cast a death curse on their boss? What happens when someone says, 'Oh, I didn't stab my neighbor to death, I was possessed by a demon'? How do you prove they *weren't*?"

"*We* do that. Figuring that stuff out is part of our job."

"Sure," she said, "on a small scale. Again, orders of magnitude. And even for us, there's a lot of judgment calls and leeway. Stuff that doesn't fly in a courtroom. Oh, and another good reason not to expose the truth? You just met him, back in that bar. Imagine a nation of Douglas

Bredfords. Some people can handle the truth, some people can't. And the ones that can't, well, they don't end up too good."

She had a point. I wanted to argue, but I couldn't come up with anything. It felt like I was digging my heels in for the sake of digging them in, so I just lightly drummed the steering wheel and focused on the traffic.

"The system sucks," Jessie said, her voice softer, "but it's the best one we have. The way I see it, it's not *about* the monsters; we're here to protect the innocent. The only way to stop these freaks from hurting people is to remove them from the equation entirely. So no, I'm not all broken up about the Gresham brothers' constitutional rights. In a perfect world, yeah, they'd get their day in court like everybody else. This isn't a perfect world."

"I can see it your way," I told her, "but there's one thing you're missing."

"Yeah? What's that?"

"Emmanuel Hirsch. As far as we know, he's just a regular garden-variety crook. Guy might be mobbed up, but he's got no occult connections."

"Yeah? And?" Jessie blinked at me.

We turned down the off-ramp. I braked at a red stoplight and looked over at her.

"So," I said, "as long as we're here, don't you want to bust this guy? He *does* have legal rights, and if we break into his clinic without a warrant, we can kiss any evidence we find good-bye. Play this the right way and we can take him off the streets."

"I might," Jessie said after a moment's deliberation, "have had a bit of tunnel vision. Okay, I'm down. Let's bust the mob doc."

"First thing we need to do is establish if the Gresham brothers are even here. Hmm. We can't poke around Hirsch's clinic without permission. So let's *get* permission. From him."

# # #

The Hirsch Clinic was a box of glass and steel, an elegant cube of new-wave architecture that stood out like a sore thumb on the historic district's streets. We walked into a dazzlingly clean lobby, sunbeams streaming off a pink-granite floor, and up to a pale-gray desk whose surface curved like the scallops of an ocean wave.

Big, wall-mounted LCD screens played a looping, endless advertisement, showcasing everything the good doctor could offer. *Create a Brave New You*, the scrolling text trumpeted. Behind the desk, a young blonde nurse in a salmon-pink smock flashed a flawless smile.

"Welcome to the Hirsch Clinic," she said, eyes bright. "How can we improve you today?"

We'd worked out our plan in the car. Jessie and I looked at each other, playing at being nervous and giggly.

"I'm, ah, thinking about having some work done?" Jessie said, pitching her voice low on the last two words.

I held up a fluttery hand. "I'm her moral support."

"Is there someone I could talk to," Jessie asked, "you know, about my options?"

"Oh, absolutely," the nurse said, checking her computer screen. "Let's see. Dr. Hirsch has appointments all morning, but it looks like his partner, Dr. Carnes, is just finishing up with a consultation. If you'd like to have a seat, she'll be out shortly."

The chairs in the lobby were as sleek as the building, gray canvas stretched across curving frames of beech wood. We took a seat by the wall of glass.

"Well," Jessie murmured, "so much for getting a read on Hirsch."

I glanced around the room. The door leading into the clinic proper had a heavy-duty lock, and the eye of a video camera kept a bird's-eye watch over the lobby from one corner of the room.

"It's okay," I said. "Long as we can take a good look in back, we can still get something out of this."

A tall, lean woman in a tailored suit, with sallow cheekbones and eyes as dark as her braided hair, strode out to greet us.

"I'm Dr. Victoria Carnes," she said, eyeing us like she was trying to peek into our bank accounts. She shot a pointed glance at my shoes. "A pleasure. I understand you're interested in our services?"

"That's me," Jessie said, raising a sheepish hand. "My friend Harmony is just here to keep me from going *too* crazy."

Victoria gave a polite, humorless chuckle. "Well, if you'd both like to join me in our consultation room, I'd be happy to go over your options."

The door leading to the back gave a slight click as we approached it. *Buzzer behind the reception desk,* I thought. They hadn't spared any expense in back, either. The polished granite floor was clean enough to eat off, and doorways along the salmon-pink corridor looked in on plush offices and a cutting-edge surgical suite.

"Business must be good," I said, trailing in the doctor's footsteps.

"Our facility is state-of-the-art. Dr. Hirsch and I have worked very hard to provide our clients with a safe, discreet, and comfortable place to embrace their becoming."

"Their . . . becoming?" Jessie said.

She nodded back at her, eyes widening. "Oh, yes. What we sell isn't vanity or ego. It's all about the ideal *you.* The *inside* you."

As Victoria turned her back, Jessie rolled her eyes at me.

Victoria ushered us into a windowless office, the walls painted lavender and lined with glossy, blown-up photographs. Close-ups of eyes and hairlines, breasts and thighs, all shot in hazy soft focus. There was something creepy about the display, almost fetishistic, but I kept a smile on my face as the doctor motioned for us to sit. The room was appointed with a curving glass-topped desk and a thirty-inch screen hooked up to a computer and a webcam. As we took our seats, the screen displayed a menu of three-dimensionally rendered limbs and the wire-frame outline of a woman's body.

The office smelled like faint vanilla spice. The air was warm, like bathwater or bedsheets fresh from the dryer. Victoria sat down on the other side of the desk.

"Our philosophy is simple: everyone knows, in their heart, how their body *should* look. Sadly, nature rarely meets those expectations. This leaves a person fragmented, incomplete. My job, as your surgical guide, is to help select the perfect procedures to bring your flesh into solidarity with your heart."

"Wow," Jessie said, nodding very slowly. "That's . . . so true. That's so real."

Victoria smiled placidly. "You won't regret choosing us. So. If I might ask, are you two . . . partners?"

Jessie reached over and rubbed my shoulder. "We are! Our first anniversary is next Sunday. Isn't that right, sweetums?"

"That's . . . right," I said, forcing a smile. "It's like every day is a honeymoon."

Victoria clasped her hands together and looked my way. "Ah, I thought so. I only ask because we do offer a couple's discount. For instance, if you wanted to do something about your nose, or perhaps a breast augmentation?"

Jessie nodded vigorously, eyeing my chest. "Oh, yeah. We need to pump those babies up. Double Ds, at least. Do they make quadruple Ds?"

"My . . . nose?" I asked.

"To unearth the beautiful woman," Victoria said, "who lives inside your heart."

"Let's talk about *me* for a while," Jessie said. "I've always been insecure about my thighs. They're so . . . thigh-ish."

I held up a finger. "Um, sorry, I need to freshen up. Is there a washroom I could use?"

Victoria pointed behind me. "Of course. Just go back out into the hall, turn left, and it'll be on your right-hand side."

"Great, thank you." I stood up and patted Jessie's shoulder. "I'll be right back, sweetheart."

I had no doubt Jessie could stall for as long as she needed to. What I needed, at the moment, was a better look at the clinic. First, though, I followed Victoria's directions and ducked into the washroom.

"There is nothing," I told my reflection in the mirror, "wrong with my nose."

All the same, I tilted my head left and right, checking from different angles. No. My nose was fine.

I was pretty sure, anyway.

Back in the halls, I prowled past empty surgical suites and recovery rooms. Victoria wasn't kidding about discretion: there wasn't so much as a stray slip of paper to be found, every file stashed out of sight, and every drawer and cabinet firmly locked.

Would he take care of his off-books clients here? I wondered, ducking into an examination room and tugging on cabinet handles. *Unless the whole clinic's in on his scheme, it'd have to be after hours. But where would they recover, then? That cambion who Jessie mangled is going to need serious reconstructive surgery. That's not an outpatient kind of deal.*

There just wasn't enough room here to hide a recovering fugitive, let alone three of them. I was thinking it over when I found a closed door with *Dr. Hirsch* etched on a brass nameplate.

My hand was on the handle, about to give it a try, when I heard an anxious voice on the other side.

ELEVEN

"And I'm telling you," a man said, "I have other buyers. Does the name Damien Ecko mean anything to you?"

I leaned close, putting my ear by the door. I could hear soft, rhythmic taps. He was pacing the office floor, and from the lack of any response I could hear, talking on the phone.

"No. It has to be *tonight*. Do you understand the kind of risk I'm taking here? This isn't normal product. I have *three* of them. And two are still breathing."

Three of them. I had a bad suspicion, and what came next only made it worse.

"No," he said, "I'm keeping them sedated. You can do whatever you like with them. *Whatever* you like. But you have to take delivery tonight, and it has to be cash. Yes. Ten thousand each, twenty-five if you take all three."

"Miss?"

I jumped. A nurse stood behind me, looking as startled as I felt.

"Can I help you, miss?"

"Oh," I said, fluttering my hand. "I'm a little lost. Which way to the washroom?"

"Around the corner, there. On your right."

I thanked her and took a walk. Back in Victoria's office, the doctor was giving Jessie the hard sell, and the computer screen had sprouted an itemized list of services. I felt a lump in my throat when I saw the total price on the bottom line.

"I know it's a lot," Jessie said, all wide eyes and sincerity, "but it's the only way to achieve my lifelong dream of looking just like a life-size black Barbie doll."

"We can make this happen," Victoria said, nodding solemnly.

"For as long as I've known you," I told Jessie, "it's been your guiding ambition in life. Still, that is a lot of money, and we *did* just spend several thousand dollars on those professional pole-dancing lessons for you. Let's sleep on it?"

Victoria beamed at us and rose from her chair. "I'll print off a copy of the quote, and you can take it home and talk it over. I think we can really make wonderful things happen for you."

To her credit, Jessie kept a straight face until we left the building. The second we hit the sidewalk, she let out a sputtering gust of a laugh, like she'd been holding her breath the entire time. She crumpled the quote in her hand.

"Man, fuck their fascist beauty standards. Do you believe that shit?" She turned to me and arched an eyebrow. "And . . . pole-dancing lessons? I was wrong, you *can* serve it back."

"I'm full of surprises."

"Gonna surprise me with a fresh lead?"

We got into the car, but I left the engine cold.

"Unfortunately, yes. The Gresham brothers picked the wrong family doctor. I heard him talking on the phone: near as I can gather, one's dead and he's got the other two doped up. He's going to *sell* them to somebody. Tonight."

"What are we waiting for?" Jessie nodded toward the clinic. "Let's go kick some doors in."

"They're not here. Can't be. I saw almost every room in the place. It's just not that big."

Jessie slumped back in the car seat and squinted at the clinic doors.

"Fine," she said. "We'll stake it out, wait for the doc to poke his head out, then follow his ass."

We sat in silence while I looked up and down the street, trying to guess which car was Dr. Hirsch's. No luck.

"Hey, Jessie?" I said.

"Yeah?"

"Is there . . . anything wrong with my nose?"

She crossed her arms.

"Seriously?"

"I'm just asking," I said.

"I hope she's in on it, too," Jessie grumbled. "Somebody needs a righteous ass-kicking."

# # #

The average stakeout involves all the thrills and excitement of watching paint dry. Still, Jessie made it bearable. We moved the car a little farther down the block as soon as street parking opened up, giving us a better view. We had some time to kill, so I held my post while she ran over to a Subway at the end of the street, coming back with sandwiches and two small bottles of water. As a rookie, one of the first things I learned was to never drink soda on a stakeout: it's a diuretic, and your options for a bathroom break may be severely limited.

Cars came, cars went, and the sun set over Detroit. We watched nurses leave the clinic, one locking up behind her, but no sign of the doctors. I hadn't seen Hirsch in the flesh, but Jessie was confident she'd recognize him from the picture on his website.

"You're sure they aren't in there?" Jessie said, slouching against her armrest.

"Positive. Besides, if they are, the buyer has to show up here."

"*Then* we can kick in doors."

"Agreed," I said.

She sat up straight, ears perked.

"Showtime," she said.

Victoria Carnes strode out of the building alongside a man who must have been Emmanuel Hirsch. He was stringy and bony, with a snow-white comb-over and a mustache too big for his face. They jogged across the street together, talking animatedly, and their body language told me it wasn't a pleasant conversation.

"Trouble in paradise," Jessie murmured as the doctors got into a shiny black Lexus. I revved the engine, waiting patiently until they pulled out into traffic, then I mirrored their move.

This was the tricky part. To tail somebody properly you need at least two chase cars, preferably three or four, in constant radio contact. The idea is to periodically let one car fall back and another chase car take point: that way, your target won't notice a familiar-looking vehicle hanging in their rearview for too long. Plus, if one car has to drop the pursuit—like if you do slip up and make them suspicious—the others can step in and pick up the slack.

We didn't have any of that. The darkness was our one real advantage, shrouding our faces and turning the Crown Vic into an anonymous blur. Even so, I made sure to hang back, keeping one car between us at all times. They took a twisting, turning path through the city streets, and as the drive went on our odds got slimmer. We headed into no-man's-land, a maze of broken streetlights and empty sidewalks, and with every passing minute it had to be more obvious we weren't sharing the road by coincidence.

"Hang back," Jessie said. "Give him a little more room."

Beyond a maze of warehouses and shuttered plants, we crossed over into Delray. The neighborhood was a ghost town, nothing but broken asphalt, boarded-up houses, and dead traffic lights as far as I could see.

About three hundred feet ahead, the Lexus signaled a left turn. I slowed down, giving them as much room as I possibly could without losing sight of the car, and waited for them to make their move.

Then I killed the headlights.

We weren't driving entirely blind, but it was close enough. The gathering clouds and the distant downtown lights choked the stars from the sky, and no electric lamps burned on the streets of Delray. We rolled through a fog of shadows, tires bumping on torn-up pavement, keeping the Lexus's distant taillights in view like some urban will-o'-the-wisp.

The Lexus turned in to a parking lot, and the taillights went dark. I stepped off the accelerator, slowing our ride to a crawl.

I couldn't imagine the building up ahead—a tall slab of crumbling bricks and rusted steel—had ever been pretty, but the years hadn't done it any kindness. A faded billboard propped up on warped crossbeams showed a smiling cartoon pig serving up a tray of steaming steaks. "Lombardi Meats," it read. "Come Meet Our Meat!"

"Well, that's not creepy or anything," Jessie said.

I pulled the Crown Vic over to the side of the road, about a block from the shuttered meatpacking plant. A barbed-wire fence ringed the parking lot, the fencing torn and uprooted here and there, but the front gate hung wide open. We kept low as we jogged across a weed-infested empty lot, trying to get a closer look.

The Lexus sat parked and empty. A few spaces down, a pair of delivery trucks with the Lombardi Meats logo lined up near a loading-bay door.

I gestured for Jessie to hold up. We crouched low in the grass, watching. Up ahead, a single light shone behind a wire cage, set into the wall over a sheet-metal side door. A man in a leather jacket smoked a cigarette, occasionally pacing back and forth or nudging loose rocks with the toe of his shoe. As he turned, his jacket hung open, and I caught the glint of steel on his hip.

"How long you think this place has been closed?" Jessie whispered.

"Years, why?"

She pointed at the delivery trucks.

"Those trucks look new."

The side door swung open. Another man, features too shadowed to make out, gave a wave. The thug at the door tossed his cigarette down, snuffed it under his heel, and walked inside.

"Two guys plus the doctors," I whispered.

"At least, but I don't imagine Miss-Find-the-Inside-You is gonna put up much of a fight. How do you want to play it?"

"Let's go in quiet, until we know what we're up against," I said. "Given what I heard on the phone, we've got probable cause to believe that human trafficking is in progress."

"You still think Hirsch is just an ordinary crook?"

I shrugged. "Depends on whether or not he knows exactly what the Gresham brothers are. Sounded like he did. Either way, he's going down tonight."

We drew our Glocks as we jogged across the parking lot, staying close and tight. Jessie covered me as I took hold of the door handle. They hadn't locked up behind them. It opened onto a hallway lined with cinder blocks painted dirt brown, riddled with open doorways on both sides. Too many angles, too many places a bad guy could be lurking.

Jessie put her hand on my right shoulder. I nodded. Breach and clear.

We moved together, hustling silently down the hall, muzzles sweeping to cover every opening. At Quantico they taught us proper technique in "kill houses" with plywood walls and random floor plans. There, though, paintballs were the ammunition, and the only consequences of failure were bruised skin and a bruised ego. Tonight we played for keeps.

We ghosted through empty rooms stripped of anything but chunks of corroded steel or the remnants of old chain belts. Machines rusted in the gloom, forgotten and abandoned. Then, around one corner, we found the operating room.

Calling it that was a stretch. It was just another empty storage room, but circled with thick plastic sheeting that dangled from shower rings. At the heart of the room stood an operating table, beside a sturdy wooden tool bench.

I smelled the blood before I saw it. The odor clung to every surface, metallic and pungent, so strong it pushed fingers down my throat and challenged me not to choke. Dried blood splashed the plastic sheets like some mad impressionist's painting, and coated the operating table like a sacrificial altar.

The operating table had restraining straps.

TWELVE

I turned my attention to the workbench. Scalpels, bone saws, chisels, tools for cutting and breaking the human body. Most hadn't even been cleaned off from Dr. Hirsch's last "patient." What really caught my eye, though, were the only sterile things in the room: a stack of small white Styrofoam coolers, each wrapped in plastic and waiting to be put to use.

Each one had a biohazard sticker on the side. Like the kind they put on organ-transplant coolers.

I heard voices up ahead. We kept moving, getting closer. At the end of a short hallway, an archway opened onto the heart of the old meatpacking plant—an open floor zigzagged by a dead conveyor belt, rusty meat hooks still dangling from the overhead track.

The doctors' hired guns lounged at a plastic picnic table in the middle of the room, keeping a watchful eye on the rolling gurneys where two of the Gresham brothers slumbered on a chemical drip. Sound asleep, they wore their human faces. The third brother, I presumed, had ended up in the black vinyl body bag on the concrete floor. Construction lights on tripods, encased in bright-yellow plastic, provided illumination; cables ran to a small portable generator in the corner.

"This is absurd," Victoria said, throwing up her hands as she paced. Her voice echoed through the drafty factory. "We're throwing money away. Do you *know* the aftermarket value of cambion organs?"

"She just said the magic word," Jessie breathed.

Emmanuel Hirsch followed Victoria like a puppy dog on a leash, his hands fluttering.

"And do *you* know how long it would take to find buyers?" he said. "We can't do that kind of volume without the Flowers sniffing our way."

"So we make a deal."

"You don't—you don't *get* it. You can buy off the police, you can buy off the feds, *you can't buy off the hound.* These men were working for the Flowers. They protect their own, and when hell comes calling, the Detroit Partnership isn't going to save us."

"Heard enough?" Jessie whispered. I nodded. Time to shut this operation down.

We slipped through the doorway and split up, her going left, me going right, crouching and using the shadows for cover. On the far side of the picnic table, she looked my way and gave me a nod.

"Freeze!" I shouted, springing up and holding my pistol in a two-hand grip. "Federal agents, nobody move!"

"Hands!" Jessie roared at the same time, dropping a bead on the guards at the table. "Let me see your hands!"

Emmanuel shot his hands straight up, his jaw dropping. Victoria froze. Their hired guns both sprang to their feet, startled, one of them going for his piece. He got it clear of the holster, a squat machine pistol in black matte, just in time for Jessie to give her trigger two quick squeezes. The Glock barked twice and the thug dropped, his shirt billowing red. His partner wised up and reached for the sky.

"On your knees!" I said, moving in with slow, careful side steps. "All of you, right now. Lace your fingers behind your heads."

"This is a mistake," Emmanuel stammered as he sank to one knee. "This is all a terrible mistake."

Victoria didn't kneel. She just stared at me. And whispered.

I couldn't hear it at first, but the sibilant lisping verse slowly grew in strength and speed, twisting like a knot in the air around my head. No. *In* my head.

I swung the muzzle of my pistol, aiming for center mass. My arm felt heavy, like the gun had put on ten pounds of weight in the last five seconds.

"You want to stop doing that," I told her. "Right now."

Over by the table, Jessie moved in, reaching under the gunman's leather jacket to take his weapon. Whatever Victoria was pulling, it hit Jessie harder than it hit me. Just enough to slow her reactions by a second or two. Just enough for the gunman to grab her wrist, spin, and draw his revolver. He held her like a human shield and pressed the barrel to her head.

"Drop your gun," he snapped. Instead, I turned and took careful aim. Right between the eyes.

"No," I told him.

He blinked. "Are you deaf? Drop your fucking gun!"

I kept one eye closed, sighting down the barrel. It felt good, closing one eye. *Why not close both?* The chant swirling in my brain said. *It's bedtime. So nice, so warm. Sleep.*

"A federal agent," I said calmly, "never surrenders her weapon."

"I *will* shoot her!" he shouted, looking desperate. Desperate wasn't good. Desperate people do stupid things. Desperate people pull triggers.

"No, you won't. Because your body drops one second after hers does. Something you should know: I took top score in my marksmanship classes at Quantico. If you're thinking I'll miss? Don't. The best, smartest thing you can do for yourself is surrender."

Jessie sagged in his arms, out cold. I could hear my blood pounding in my veins, pumping to the tune of Victoria's chant. Down on his knees, Emmanuel laughed.

"Quite a dilemma, Agent. If you don't shoot my friend Victoria, you'll fall prey to her enchantment in short order. But if you *do* turn your gun to aim at her, well, my other friend will shoot your partner, then you. What to do, what to do?"

"Last chance," I said, even as my vision started to blur. It felt like the sights on my gun were swinging slowly, rocking like a cradle, swimming away from me. I had once chance: shoot the gunman, hope he didn't reflex pull his own trigger, then spin and take out Victoria.

In other words, no chance at all. Too much risk, too easy for Jessie to catch a bullet. I could save myself, sure, but not at that price. We'd both survive this, or neither of us would.

That was the last thought that passed through my mind as my pistol slipped from my numb, slack fingers and I crashed to the concrete floor.

# # #

I woke to pain. My arms burned, wrists ached, shoulders pulled taut. As my vision slowly swam back, images unblurring and becoming one, I understood why.

They'd hung us from the old conveyor belt. Scratchy, stiff rope coiled around my wrists, tossed up and over the curve of an old, rusty meat hook. I dangled, helpless, my toes draping about an inch over the stained concrete floor. Jessie faced me, about ten feet away and hanging from her own hook, her head shaking as she slowly came to.

They'd taken our jackets, our guns and holsters, everything in our pockets, piling it all on the plastic picnic table. Emmanuel looked over at us and smacked his lips.

"Ah, look who's awake. Well, Agents"—he glanced down at the Bureau ID cards in his hand—"Temple and Black, I'm going to have to ask your patience. We have a very important customer about to arrive, and dealing with you will have to wait. You'll get your turn, no worries. Fredo, get the door, please?"

Fredo—the surviving gunman—ambled out of sight. I took a deep breath, as deep as I could manage.

"Clever scam," I said. "You put the word out that you offer fix-up services for criminals, totally off the books. They show up here, desperate for help, only to discover your *real* business: selling bootleg organs. This is a chop shop for human beings."

Victoria smiled, beyond pleased with herself. "We're performing a community service. We take beautiful, healthy organs from human garbage and bequeath them to needy people. Deserving people. Wealthy people."

"And not all of our patients end up on the chopping block," Emmanuel added. "Our connection to the Detroit Partnership is quite real. Can't go carving up mafiosi, after all. They have powerful friends. I suppose you could say that made men get our white-glove treatment, while *un*-made men get . . . *un-made*."

"We've got powerful friends, too, fucker," Jessie grunted.

He shook his head, gloating. "I'm afraid the FBI is quite incapable of understanding us, let alone pursuing us. Do you even know why you fell asleep? I imagine you must think it was some sort of gas, or a toxin. But what if . . . what if, my dears, I told you it was a magical spell?"

I caught Jessie's look and snorted. "Magic? You're crazy. No such thing."

"Poor, poor dears." He sounded genuinely regretful. "I'm afraid you've stumbled into a world you know nothing about and cannot imagine. And once you've entered this world, well . . . escape is quite impossible."

The loading bay door on the far side of the plant rattled upward, chains squealing. Fredo came back with a new friend, a barrel-chested man in stonewashed jeans and a cowboy hat. Gold chains and black chest hair poked out from under his half-unbuttoned shirt, and he licked his fat lips as he took a look around the room. His gaze traveled from the corpse on the floor, to the unconscious cambion on the gurneys, to us.

"Now, what the ever-lovin' fuck," he said, "happened here? Did I miss a party or what?"

"A minor setback," Victoria said, striding over to offer her hand. "You must be Buck."

He took her hand and pressed it to his lips. She cringed, faintly, as it came away glistening wet.

"And you must be the lovely and talented Dr. Carnes. Where's my meat at, sweet thing? I wanna check out the goods before we talk price."

"Right here," Emmanuel said, gesturing to the gurneys. "They're on a morphine drip, and restrained. Quite harmless."

Buck shook his head and pointed at the body bag on the floor. "Told you on the phone, I ain't interested in the dead one. My establishment don't cater to necrophiliacs. Not often, anyway. That's a special-request kinda deal. Besides, don't got a freezer on my plane. He'd be all squishy and smelly by the time I got him back to LA."

"We'd really prefer to make this a package deal."

"Look," Buck said, "live cambion? That's always a winner. Some of these freaks really get off on cutting 'em up and guzzling some demon blood. As a consequence, there's, ah, turnover in my stock that always needs replacin'."

Victoria strolled up from behind and rested her hands on his shoulders. "And you're certain that none of these . . . freaks can come up with *any* uses for a dead one? Even at a discount?"

"Ha. Honey, my place has all kinds of special attractions. Hell, we got a real live succubus chained up in the basement, if you're crazy enough to take that ride. It ain't a lack of possibilities, it's just that humpin' dead bodies is a niche kinda thing, and I don't see myself recouping my investment. I'll give you twenty grand for the two live ones, and that's the deal."

"Listen," I said. They all looked my way. "We're federal agents. You do *not* want to be associated with these people. Set us free and we can work something out. Something that keeps you out of prison."

Emmanuel snapped his fingers. "I've got it. Twenty-two thousand for all three cambion, *and* we throw in those two."

Buck frowned, scratching under his hat. "What are they?"

"What are they? Er, human."

"Now, what sounds like a better business plan to you?" Buck asked him. "Option A: I hold two feds hostage, have to keep 'em tied up and under constant guard the rest of their lives, and my customers get lousy service. Or, option B: I go to a couple of professional whores and say, 'Hey, ladies. Wanna be my whores? *I will pay you,*' in which case I get a couple of happy employees and a whole lot of happy customers."

"I . . . see your point," Emmanuel said.

"Trust me, there are enough women willing to work on their backs, I don't need to force 'em. Now, you *are* gonna end these two, right? Considerin' they've seen my face and all?"

"With great pleasure," Victoria said.

"Good deal. So. Twenty grand for the two live ones. Take it or leave it."

Emmanuel's shoulders sagged. "We'll take it. Fredo, wheel them out to the truck while our new friend gets his money. He has a plane to catch."

As Fredo shoved one of the gurneys to the door, rolling it on a spinning, squeaky wheel, I wasn't sure what was worse: that I had no idea how we were going to escape, or that the single lead we had for catching the Bogeyman was about to fly right out of our grasp.

THIRTEEN

Buck came back with a briefcase full of twenties, held in tight bundles by greasy rubber bands. Emmanuel didn't bother to count it. They just shook hands and called it a deal.

Jessie hadn't said a word in ten minutes. She kept her eyes squeezed shut, head bowed, burrowing somewhere deep inside herself.

I needed free hands. I needed to ease my burning arms, my aching shoulders. It felt like my wrists were being sliced open every time I swayed on the rough, scratchy ropes. I needed focus, to conjure up a defense. They didn't know I was a witch; that meant I'd get one shot, just one, to blindside them with my own magic. I had to make it count.

Fredo wheeled in a cart, bringing it to a stop right beside me. I looked and wished I hadn't. Scalpels, saws, a gleaming stainless-steel rib cracker—everything a mortician needed for an autopsy.

Before I could kick out, Fredo grabbed my legs from behind. I squirmed as he lashed my ankles together with another coil of rope, then pulled the rope taut and tied it to a metal ring set into the floor. I hung there, suspended between the two ropes, breathing through my gritted teeth.

Victoria hung back, watching from a few feet away, as Emmanuel moved in for the kill.

"You're making a big mistake," I told him.

"No, my dear, quite the contrary. Not only will your organs benefit many needy people—and, if I may be vulgar, my offshore bank account—but it's a very effective means of disappearing a person. You and your friend will simply vanish off the face of the earth. No muss, no fuss."

Behind him, Jessie raised her head.

"Let me out," she growled in a voice that wasn't entirely hers.

Emmanuel reached out and fumbled with my tie, his fingers unraveling the knot. "Patience, please. I'll be with you in a moment."

I tried to head-butt him when he started to unbutton my blouse, but the ropes kept me from anything but useless squirming. He reached for a scalpel.

"I will not be caged," Jessie said through gritted teeth.

With one quick slice, Emmanuel cut through the ivory fabric of my bra, right between my breasts. "Please relax," he said, as he pulled the fabric aside. "I'm a surgeon, not some *pervert.* You don't have anything I haven't seen before."

He set down the scalpel and picked up a new tool with a long ivory handle topped by a round horizontal blade about the size of my palm, saw-toothed and gleaming sharp.

"Now, then," he said. "I must apologize. We are a very *thrifty* operation, and competition requires us to cut costs wherever we can. As such . . . I can't really offer you any anesthetic for this procedure. That said, I've done this many, *many* times before, and while the first few minutes will be unpleasant for you, the pain will quickly lead to unconsciousness and death."

He flicked his thumb against a switch on the handle, and the saw blade whined to life.

"Out," Jessie grunted, eyes still squeezed tightly shut. She heaved herself up by her wrists and dropped down hard. The old track jolted on its bolts. She did it again and again in a thumping rhythm. "Out. Out. *Out.*"

"Oh, for the love of—" Emmanuel sighed. "Fredo, secure her, please?"

Fredo grabbed another coil of rope and strolled toward her, shaking his head. He reached for her ankles just as her eyelids snapped open. Her glowing eyes burned with hunger and hate.

"Uh, boss?"

That was all he had time to say. Her legs whipped up, scissoring around his neck, as she drew herself up on the ropes one last time. He fell backward, trying to wriggle free. Their combined body weight, one last sharp tug, was all it took: the upper curve of the meat hook snapped, rusty metal groaning, and they tumbled together to the floor.

Fredo rolled onto his back, and his eyes went wide. Jessie, wrists still bound but gripping the broken meat hook in her hands like a samurai sword, crouched low and lunged for him. She swung and drove the sharp end of the hook between his legs.

I didn't think a scream that shrill could come from a human throat.

It only got worse as she pinned his shoulder with one foot and dragged the hook upward with all her strength, disemboweling him one brutal inch at a time. Emmanuel dropped the saw, shaking his head wildly. It spun in circles on the concrete near my feet and kicked up sparks as the blade dug grooves in the stone.

"No," Emmanuel said. "No, no, *no*! Victoria, slow her down!"

He ran for the picnic table. For our guns. Jessie left the meat hook buried in Fredo's stomach. He'd stopped screaming now, and all that came from his tortured throat was a wet, mindless gurgle.

Jessie turned her gaze on me.

"Jessie," I said, "it's me. It's *me*. Get me down!"

She prowled toward me like I was a piece of fresh meat, ripe for the taking. Then I heard the chant. Victoria's sibilant whisper, trying to snake its way into my ears. I pulled on my ropes, deliberately hurting my wrists, focusing on the pain. The pain kept me awake. Kept me fighting.

Jessie snatched up the saw. She peered at it, then at me. She wobbled on her feet, Victoria's spell starting to take hold, but that didn't diminish her hungry smile one bit.

"The ropes," I said. *"Please."*

Jessie lashed out her arm. The blade whined as it chewed through the rope, a quarter inch above my clenched hands. I fell to all fours, hard, on the concrete at Jessie's feet.

A gunshot snapped through the air. It went wide, the bullet chewing into a cinder block. Emmanuel clutched the stolen Glock between his shaking hands, his aim wavering like a drunk as he fought his terror and lost.

Jessie bared her teeth, crouched low, and charged at him.

I didn't have time to cut the ropes on my ankles, but at least I could stand. Victoria was distracted, splitting her focus between me and Jessie, but her sleep curse still wove tendrils of warm velvet around my brain.

I unfurled the ropes around my wrists and tossed the severed ends to the floor. Shook my hands out, working the circulation back. Then I called to my power.

Earth. Air. Water. Fire. Garb me in your raiment. Arm me with your weapons.

Water coated me, coalescing over my body like a suit of armor. Not literal water, but the *idea* of water, pure and elemental, water like blue singing steel. I held up my left palm, blossoming in my second sight with a blazing equal-armed yellow cross. It spun like the blades of a fan and became a disc, a shimmering shield of elemental air. Her spell broke against my defenses, scattering into motes of violet light.

Victoria could see it, too. She blinked, taking a step back. "Wait, how are you—"

In my right hand, a sword. A sword of flame. I pointed its tip toward her. The air crackled between us and ignited as if someone had suspended a gasoline trail in midair. A thin streak of fire lanced across the factory and blasted Victoria in the face.

She went down, shrieking, clutching her burned face. Then she clambered back to her feet and ran for the door, leaving her partners to die. I fired another gout of flame, slicing across her shoulder. She flailed, trying to pat out her burning dress with her bare hand, still screaming as she disappeared into the night.

I moved to chase her and tumbled to the floor. Damn ropes on my ankles. The elemental energies flickered and snuffed out, my concentration shattered. Now I felt the cost, the rush of power paid for with leaden muscles and sudden, sharp cramps in my stomach.

Fight through it, I told myself. *Fight through it.*

I grabbed the saw and cut myself free. Jessie had Emmanuel pinned to the floor, her fists raining down as she pounded him into hamburger meat. I stumbled up behind them.

"Jessie," I said. "*Jessie.* It's done. Stop."

She froze with one clenched fist suspended over the doctor's bloody, terrified face.

I thought back to her reaction when she first spotted me, how she'd hesitated and cut me down from the ropes. Something in my voice had given her pause, pulled her just an inch out of her killing fugue. "Jessie," I said again. "*Listen.* Focus on the sound of my voice."

She didn't move. Her fist trembled, frozen.

"Come back to me," I whispered. "Come back."

Her hand slowly opened. She shook her head and tiredly pushed herself to her feet. I stood beside her, looking down at Hirsch.

"Emmanuel Hirsch," I said, "you are so under arrest, you have no idea."

My bra was a lost cause. Under my blouse I wriggled my way out of the shoulder straps, then tossed it aside. Funny. With all that had happened, with the sheer chaos of the last ten minutes, all I could think was, *Well, that's forty bucks I'm not getting back.* I buttoned my blouse and grabbed my holster from the table, slipping it on.

"Please," Emmanuel moaned, "it's not my fault. It was all Victoria's idea. She made me do it."

Jessie rubbed her eyes, now pale and soft, and winced. "Sorry. Spaced out there."

"You okay?" I asked.

"Yeah." She put her palms flat against the table and pushed herself up. She glanced back toward the overhead track, the dangling hooks. "How'd you get loose?"

"You cut me down. You don't remember?"

"Like I said, I spaced." She tilted her head. "Wait. I came at you with a knife, and I just cut you loose? Didn't hurt you?"

"It was an electric saw, actually. And no."

She rubbed the back of her head. "Huh."

"Please," Emmanuel begged, still fetal. "It was all Victoria. I'm innocent."

"Did you read him his rights?" Jessie asked me.

"Nope."

"Good. Because he doesn't fucking have any." She picked up her phone from the clutter on the table and hit the speed dial. "Special Agent Temple. Authorization ninety-three slash ninety-three. Yeah. We need a cleaning crew. Got two . . . wait."

She paused, then glanced over at me. "Is Fredo dead?"

I craned my neck to look. He lay flat on his back, glassy-eyed, the broken meat hook jutting out from his ruptured chest.

"Yeah," I said. "He's pretty dead."

"*Three* spills, one toxic," she said into the phone. "Also one package for offshore delivery. Also need an H. E. designation for one Dr. Victoria Carnes, details to follow in our debriefing report."

"Offshore delivery," Emmanuel repeated. "What does she mean?"

Jessie finished giving the details, hung up, and unceremoniously kicked Emmanuel onto his stomach. He groaned as she pinned his arms back and clicked the cuffs tight around his wrists.

"Funny story," she told him. "We've got this place; it's called Detention Site Burgundy. It's sort of like Club Med except it's not fun, there's no beach, and you can never leave. You're gonna make all *kinds* of new friends there."

"You . . . you can't do that. I want a lawyer!"

She stood up and dusted off her hands. "What was it you told us? 'You've stumbled into a world you know nothing about, and cannot imagine. And once you've entered this world, well . . . escape is quite impossible.'"

"Poor dear," I added, my voice a flat monotone.

Jessie looked over at me. "You good to fight?"

"Yeah." The stomach cramps ebbed away slowly, just the occasional stabbing tug to punish me for conjuring up that much energy that fast. I've had worse.

"Good," she said, holstering her pistol. "We've got a plane to catch."

FOURTEEN

Headlights strobed as the Crown Vic slammed over a pothole, tearing through the ghost town.

"We need details on anyone filing an FAA flight plan for Los Angeles," Jessie told Kevin over the phone. "It'll be a private plane, leaving tonight, if we haven't missed it already."

"Hold on, hold on," I heard him say, fingers rattling against his keyboard. "I have a hit. Got a Buck Wheeler, filed a route from Willow Run Airport to Van Nuys in the San Fernando Valley. He's due to leave in about twenty minutes."

"Shit," she said. "That's him. How far?"

"Willow Run is in Ypsilanti. You want to get on I-75, then take exit 41 to I-94 West."

"How *far*, Kevin?"

"It's, uh . . . about thirty minutes away."

"Drive *fast*," Jessie told me. "Kevin, get on the phone to the tower at Willow Run. They need to stall him. I don't care what they tell him, but they are *not* to give him permission for takeoff. Give them my number if they have any questions."

She hung up. I focused on the road, white lines flashing past like daggers in the dark. The Crown Vic bottomed out as I hit the on-ramp, speedometer needle kissing seventy, and we launched onto the highway.

I slid through the sparse late-night traffic like I was threading a needle, weaving and drifting. Every passing minute, every click of the dashboard clock, was another pound of weight on my shoulders.

Jessie's phone buzzed. She put it on speaker.

"Special Agent Temple."

"Yes," a hesitant man's voice said, "um, this is Miles Stanton, in the tower at Willow Run? Your supervisor, Special Agent Finn, said we should call you."

Out of the corner of my eye, Jessie arched her eyebrow at the phone.

"Yes," she said. "What's the situation? Is Buck Wheeler's plane still on the ground?"

"Well, that's why I thought I should call. We told him we had to delay takeoff due to unexpected air traffic overhead. Well, that was fifteen minutes ago, and he's not answering his radio anymore. We've hailed him twice, and nothing. I'm about to send a security guard over to his hangar—"

"No," she said sharply. "Don't do that. This man is dangerous. We'll take care of it."

She hung up and looked my way. "He knows something's up."

"I know what I'd do in his shoes," I said.

"He's going to run for it. And if he thinks we're onto him, he won't land at Van Nuys. No second chance. We'll lose him for good."

And the Gresham brothers with him. The Crown Vic's engine roared as I laid the hammer down.

The lights of Willow Run came into sight. I pulled a hard right, veering down Airport Drive, just as the phone rang again.

"Uh, Stanton again—"

"What?" Jessie snapped.

"He's . . . leaving. He's ignoring the radio, and I can see his hangar from here. His plane just taxied out onto the tarmac."

"What's it look like? What kind of plane?"

"It's a Cessna model 206," he said, "white, with a blue tail."

Jessie hung up on him. "You thinking what I'm thinking?"

"If I am," I told her, "you're crazier than I thought."

"Good. We're on the same wavelength."

The Vic shot through the open gate, turning a second too slow, and I winced at the shriek of steel against steel as the edge of the fence gouged a furrow in the driver's-side door. Up ahead was a forest of blinking cherry-red runway lights and brightly lit hangars, jets sitting silently on the tarmac, and canary-yellow carts ferrying pilots and passengers back and forth from the front office. I hit the brakes to veer around a sleeping Learjet, hooked a hard right, and punched the gas.

Buck's Cessna was up ahead, making a slow, lumbering turn as it rolled out of its hangar and onto the runway. We blazed past him, running parallel, and I gave it another hundred feet before slamming on the brakes, hauling on the wheel, and spinning the car out in the middle of the tarmac.

We jumped out and crouched behind it, using the car for cover as we drew our weapons.

He didn't stop. The Cessna picked up speed as it rolled toward us, faster by the second, propeller slicing the air with a high-pitched whine.

Jessie and I opened fire at the same time. The night erupted with short, sharp reports as we unloaded on his engine block, the front of the plane blossoming with bullet holes. Another round smashed into the tinted glass canopy, rupturing the windshield. He kept coming. We were locked in a lethal game of chicken, irresistible force against the immovable object, and I could feel the air tremble as the Cessna's wounded engine strained for power.

"Down!" Jessie shouted, grabbing my shoulders and dragging me to the tarmac. The Cessna wobbled, groaned, and took to the air, its fixed landing gear slashing just inches above the hood of the car. We watched as it seemed to hesitate, the airframe shaking . . . and then it plummeted.

The plane slammed back down to the tarmac, bouncing off its nose and snapping the propeller. The engine ignited in a shower of white-hot sparks. Landing gear rattling, the plane veered to one side and headed straight for the nearest hangar. We were already on our feet and running, breathless, as it crashed head-on into the hangar wall.

The front end of the Cessna was a mangled mess, the hangar wall buckled around a nightmare of burning slag. Billowing black smoke washed over us as we ran around to the side of the plane, and the air was thick with the chemical stench of spilled fuel and hot metal. Buck's plane was equipped with cargo doors. Coughing into my sleeve, I grabbed one handle and Jessie took the other, struggling to pull them open.

The warped metal screamed as we wrenched one door wide, greeting us with a rush of superheated air and a choking, roiling cloud of smoke. My eyes stung as I climbed into the back of the cabin to hunt for survivors. The Gresham brothers sat slumped in their seats, belted in and still adrift in a chemical coma. Up front, all I could see of Buck was a single beefy arm. Just the arm, nearly severed, hanging from a mangled seat by a single strand of glistening muscle.

I grabbed the first Gresham, unbuckled him, and hauled him back with my hands under his armpits. Jessie helped as I clambered out of the cabin, and together we dragged him away from the plane. I heard an electric popping sound as the engine fire flared and spread to the hangar. The flames climbed higher and licked at the night sky, insatiable.

"Come on," Jessie said, grabbing my arm. "We've got one. Let's go!"

"The other one's still alive in there," I said, pulling my arm away and running back toward the wreckage.

Sirens shrilled in the distance, but they wouldn't get here in time. It was all on us. I climbed into the cabin then immediately stumbled back, sputtering and choking. The brutal heat broiled against my cheeks. I could just barely make out the faint silhouette of the second Gresham brother, motionless in his seat.

I tried to take a deep breath. Smoke burst from my lungs in a hacking, wet cough, leaving me with the taste of bile in my throat. Jessie grabbed me from behind, wrapping her arms around my waist and dragging me backward.

"No!" I shouted, flailing. "He's still *in* there! He's still—"

The fuel tank erupted with an eardrum-shattering *crump*, flooding the compartment with fire and blasting out every window in a blinding explosion. For a heartbeat, white light drowned out the entire universe.

I remember lying on the tarmac, thirty feet from the burning nightmare, arm scraped bloody and bits of glass in my hair. Sirens shrilling and voices, too many voices. Hands lifting me up onto a stretcher. Then everything faded away, like ghosts in a burning rain.

# # #

I woke up on a stiff, scratchy mattress. My hand stretched out and bumped a plastic railing. Hospital bed. My eyes flickered open.

"You ever pull a stunt like that again," Jessie said, standing at my bedside, "I *will* kick your ass."

Sunlight streamed in through a dull window, giving the tiny room a soft glow. A television, mounted on a ceiling bracket in the corner of the room, softly played a news broadcast about last night's incident at Willow Run.

". . . the pilot, presumed intoxicated, died in the crash along with a single passenger. No one else was hurt."

I looked to Jessie.

"I had to try and save him."

"That was reckless," she said.

"It's my *job*."

"Laudable," April said, rolling in through the open doorway, "but Jessie is right. A dead agent does us no good."

"Hey, Auntie," Jessie said, "how's the prisoner?"

"Well secured. Double handcuffed, in a private room on the third floor with a police officer stationed outside. We're fortunate that he was unconscious during the crash. If he'd woken up, panicked, and forgot to keep his human guise on . . . well, that could have been a messier cleanup than it already was. Speaking of cleanup, Linder's men reported in: Dr. Hirsch has been secured for offshoring and interrogation. Good work."

"And Dr. Carnes?" I asked.

"On the run. She cleaned out her bank accounts—those we know of, anyway—and abandoned her home. We'll need to debrief you both with anything you might remember, for the file. She's been designated Hostile Entity 138."

"Oh, we'll catch up to her *and* follow up on Buck's little operation in LA," Jessie said, then looked over at me. "All in good time. You feel ready to get back to work?"

"Job won't do itself," I said, wincing as I sat up in bed. "Hospital gown isn't going to cut it, though."

"Fresh clothes are waiting in the bathroom. Hope you don't mind, I took the liberty of rummaging around in your luggage. I, uh, realized I left something important back at the motel, though, so I stopped at Carson's on the way back."

Jessie held out a salmon-pink necktie.

"Is the color okay?" she said. "I, um, wasn't sure."

I took the tie, running my thumb over the smooth silk.

"Yeah," I said, smiling. "Yeah, it is. Thank you."

"Go on, then. Suit up. We've got a cambion to crack."

FIFTEEN

"Where's Kevin?" I asked as we walked through the halls of St. John Hospital. April rolled her chair just ahead of us.

"He stayed back in Talbot Cove," April said. "Easier for him to get his research done if he stays put, and he's listening in on the local police band for anything odd."

A potbellied cop in uniform blues sat in a chair at the end of a long hallway, playing a game on his phone. He saw us, sat up straight, and made the phone disappear.

"He's been moaning all morning," he told us with a jerk of his thumb toward the closed door. "Wants to know where his brother is."

I blinked. "Nobody told him?"

The cop shrugged.

"Well, joy to the world," Jessie said. She opened the door without slowing her pace and strode on through.

Earl Gresham lay handcuffed to his hospital bed, one cuff for each wrist and shackled to the sideboards. I recognized him now, and the splints on his fingers; back at the Gunderson house, he was the one who'd grabbed Jessie's gun. The one smart enough to run for it when the tide turned. In his human guise, without the cambion blood rearing its ugly head, he looked like a hundred other tweakers: rail thin, bug-eyed, and twitchy.

A sheen of sweat drenched his hospital gown and soaked the mattress pad under his back. As he squirmed, the prison-ink swastika tattoo on his left shoulder flexed. He looked at Jessie and shook his head wildly.

"No, no, no," he stammered. "Police! *Police!*"

"We are the police, dipshit." Jessie sighed. She pulled up a chair to his bedside, spun it around, and dropped into it. I held the door for April, closing it after she rolled in.

"I'm not even talkin' to you," he said, wide-eyed. He looked to me and April. "Where's my brother, man? Where's Tiny? Mick was a goner, I know that, he bled out on the way to Detroit, but Tiny—he just had a damn bullet in his shoulder, man! You don't die from that!"

"I'm sorry," I said. "He didn't make it. I tried to save him."

Earl threw his head back, pressing it against the pillow and arching his back. A cry rose from his throat, his pain pouring out in a strangled screech.

"Everyone said we could trust those fucking doctors! Everyone said, you ever need help, that's who you see. Oh God, oh God, Tiny, I'm so fuckin' sorry—"

"No honor among thieves," Jessie said.

"He was unconscious when he died," I told him. "He didn't suffer."

Tears streamed down Earl's face, tears and sweat and snot in a glistening mess as he wept. He shook his head from side to side, as if he could make it all go away by denying it hard enough.

"It was an empty house." He moaned. "We didn't deserve this, it was just an empty fuckin' house, we didn't hurt anybody, we didn't deserve to fuckin' *die*—"

We let him get it out of his system. As much as he could. When he'd spent his grief, left with nothing but little shuddering shakes, I walked to his bedside. I plucked two scratchy tissues from a cardboard box.

"Here," I said, mopping at his face. The tissues came away gluey and cold. I held another couple of tissues to his nose so he could blow it. I grabbed a few more to wipe off my sopping fingers.

The whole time, I saw April watching Jessie and me. Her gaze ping-ponging back and forth, quietly measuring, assessing.

Earl's gaze latched on to me, too. "Thanks," he said, sniffling. "Man, we . . . we didn't deserve it."

"No," I said, "you didn't. Your brothers didn't deserve to die."

Jessie snorted. She gave me a quick wink before he looked her way, letting me know what she was up to. Textbook bad cop, pushing him my way.

"My partner's a little soft," she told him. "You ask me? You boys assaulted two federal agents. You got off easy."

"We didn't know you were legit! We thought you were working for—" He froze. Shook his head and clammed up.

"Working for who?" I asked.

"Worth my life, if I told you that. Nuh-uh. My brothers are gone, but I'm still breathin'. I aim to keep it that way."

"We can protect you," I said.

He let out a strangled laugh. "Like hell you can. You got no idea the size of the mess you stepped in here. Look, you seem okay for a cop, so I'll do you a solid and give you some advice: Leave. Get outta here as fast as you can and never, ever go back to Talbot Cove."

"Oh? Why is that?"

"Like I told you, you got no idea what's going on here. It's bigger than you can imagine."

"We know what you are," I told him. "You're a cambion."

He blinked. "A combo-what?"

"You have demon blood."

He sagged into the mattress.

"Oh. That. Yeah, me and my brothers, we call—we called it our genetic condition? On account of it sounds a little more reasonable than way. Far as we can reckon, Dad was the one with the horns. We were triplets. Mom died pumpin' me out, and the doctors had to go and cut Tiny out of her belly. Little guy almost didn't make it."

"You grew up as wards of the state," I said. "You didn't choose this life. You never had a choice."

"Yeah," he said, grabbing the lifeline. "Yeah, that's right. We were, what do you call it, products of our upbringing."

"Bullshit," Jessie said, poking him in the shoulder. "Nobody *made* you a criminal meth-head bottom-feeder. Nobody *made* you an errand boy for the Court of Night-Blooming Flowers."

"Damn right they did," he told her, too off balance to stay quiet. "You don't know what it's like. When the hound knocks at your trailer door and tells you to do something, you *do* it."

"What is it like?" I asked him, all sympathy. "I really want to know."

Something between desperation and gratitude shone in Earl's wet eyes as he looked my way. I gave him a tiny smile. Something to cling to, in the heart of the whirlwind.

"It's like . . . well, like your partner said," he told me. "Far as real demons are concerned, bottom-feeders is all we are. Some of the Flowers . . . they hunt people like us for fun. I guess they've got all kinds of rules and laws they've gotta follow—imagine that, laws in hell—but they can do whatever they want to us. Some of 'em . . . they call it 'pest control.'"

"I can't even imagine." I shook my head. "But you survived all that. You were strong enough."

"That was all Tiny. See, he played it smart, realized we had to make friends. Guys we could name-drop, if anyone came around to mess with us. I wouldn't say we got in *good* with the hound, but we made ourselves useful enough that the others pretty much left us alone, for fear of pissing him off."

"And this hound, he told you to break into the Gunderson house?"

"He just made the introduction. That was Fontaine's call. Hound says, 'Hey, this guy's a buddy of mine from way back, help him out while he's in town.' And you know, they're demons, so when they say way back they mean, like, back when George Washington discovered America. Fontaine is a Chainman."

The word rang a bell. Douglas Bredford had mentioned it when he was telling us about the courts of hell. *The Bargainers and the Chainmen, they get an exemption.*

"Chainman. What is that, exactly?"

Earl shifted on the mattress as much as the cuffs would let him, turning toward me. His body language telling me I'd captured his trust.

"Like I said, hell has laws, right? Well, they don't have cops. They have Chainmen. Bounty hunters, basically. Fontaine came to Talbot Cove hunting heads, and he wanted us to be his eyes and ears. He's the one that sent us to the Gunderson house."

"Is he after Helen Gunderson?"

He shook his head. "Naw, nobody wants to hurt that poor lady. Well, not us or Fontaine or the hound, anyhow. *Somebody* does, and don't ask who because I don't know a name. I just know that's the way this whole thing works."

As bad as things were, I had a feeling deep down in my gut that they were about to get a whole lot worse.

Sometimes I hate being right.

"You're talking about the Bogeyman," I said.

His eyes widened. "You know about that?"

"That's why we're here. Is that who this Fontaine is hunting?"

"Not directly," Earl said. "I think he wants the guy who's sending it."

Jessie leaned in. "What do you mean, *sending*?"

Earl looked back and forth between us. "I thought you said you knew? Man, that thing don't choose who it goes after. You've gotta *tell* it which kid to snatch. Whoever you want gone, you know? Wanna put a serious hurt on somebody, you call the Bogeyman, send it after his kids. Why do you think it's been gone for so many years?"

My stomach coiled in a sick knot. It was one thing when I'd thought we were dealing with a monster. Some kind of beast, born of cruelty, driven to stalk and steal. If that was true, then it was just following its nature. We'd find it and we'd put it down, like euthanizing a rabid dog. But this changed everything.

The Bogeyman wasn't a rabid dog. It was a weapon. A weapon aimed by someone else's hands. Aimed at Helen Gunderson's family, by someone who wanted to destroy her entire world.

Aimed at my family, too.

Jessie gave me a look, her brow furrowed. I just shook my head. Had to keep pushing.

"How?" I asked him. "How is it summoned?"

"I don't know, some magic . . . trinket or something. Tiny was the one who understood all that crap. You have to make it, with this special ritual, then you stash it wherever you want the Bogeyman to show up. See, Fontaine wasn't sure if the Gunderson situation *was* the Bogeyman, since it's been like thirty years since anybody's called it up."

"So you and your brothers were supposed to toss her house and see if you could find the magic trinket," I said, feeling numb.

They were looking in the wrong place. That strange wicker ball, the one that looked like a Möbius strip on crack, spiked into the lawn out in front. *That* was the key.

"Fontaine's really hot to get his hands on this guy before the trail goes cold," Earl said. "See, he was last here thirty years ago, and he missed his shot. That's the thing about demons: not a whole lot of patience, but they've got all the time in the world."

I'd assumed it was a different person. That someone new had found the ritual to call up the Bogeyman, starting the nightmare up all over again. But what if it wasn't?

What if the person who attacked the Gunderson family was the same person who attacked mine?

I guess that's the difference between me and a demon, I thought. *I don't have patience or time. Just a wound, thirty years deep, that won't stop bleeding.*

It's time to put things right.

SIXTEEN

"Did Fontaine give you a way to contact him?" I asked.

Earl shook his head. "We were supposed to show up at Norma's All-Day Café over on Stag Head Road. He said he liked the smell of the pancakes there. I wouldn't bother looking for him, though."

"Why not?"

"He's a hijacker. Man changes bodies more often than I change my underwear. He can be anybody. He can be *in* anybody. Grab you, too, if you're not careful."

"One other thing," Jessie said. "Earlier. You said you didn't know we were real feds, that we might be working for somebody else. Who?"

"Fontaine ain't the only Chainman in town. This is a hot bounty. He's got a rival, this guy he calls Nyx. See, they got a rule: Chainmen can't jack one another over a claim, no fighting one another. That rule don't apply to people working *for* them, though."

"So you thought Nyx hired us," I said.

"Better safe than sorry, considering if he did hire you, you woulda been there to cap our sorry asses." His voice trailed off. When he spoke again, it was broken, distant. "In the end, guess it don't matter either way. Killed two of us anyhow. We were just . . . we were just searching an empty house, man. Nobody was supposed to get hurt. Didn't . . . didn't deserve that."

Jessie stood up and looked at April. "I think we've got what we need. Call it in. Offshore him."

"Agent Temple," I said. "A word?"

I took her out into the hall, a discreet distance from the cop at the door.

"Come on," I said.

"What? He's a cambion, with direct ties to a court of hell. He needs to go."

I crossed my arms. "He's a small-town meth head. His 'direct ties' treat him like dirt and use him as cannon fodder. Come on, Jessie. He just lost both of his brothers. He's right. He didn't deserve that. And it's not like he's going to be plotting the downfall of the government. Hell, he could be more useful if we leave him in play: I'd like to have a grateful informant or two, wouldn't you? We can handle this another way. One where everybody wins."

Jessie squinted at me. "What do you have in mind?"

I told her. And she liked it.

We walked back into the room together, taking up our stances on either side of the bed. Earl looked between us, confused.

"We've got a place for people like you," Jessie said. "It's very dark, very cold, and there are no trials, no judges, and no appeals. You just rot there. For the rest of your life."

"C'mon," he said, suddenly wide-eyed. He looked at me like I was his last hope in the world. "C'mon, you can't do that. You can't *let* her do that."

I held up one finger. "Or, you can choose what's behind curtain number two. In about ten minutes, the police are going to come into this room and charge you with the burglary of Helen Gunderson's home. You will make a plea bargain, which we'll facilitate for you. You'll get probation and community service, and you'll repay Ms. Gunderson for the damage to her furniture. Every penny of it. As part of that deal, you'll also enter a court-ordered drug treatment program, which you *will* successfully complete."

He leaned his head back against the pillow and squeezed his eyes shut.

"Man, that's impossible. I can't get clean—you know how many times I've tried? I just can't."

"Have you ever had help?"

He opened his eyes. Looked at me. Shook his head, very, very slowly.

"We'll be watching you," I told him. "This is your one final chance. Your golden opportunity. You can either straighten your life out and make something of yourself, or get a bag over your head and a one-way ticket to a very unhappy place."

"Or," Jessie said, "if you're really that weak, you can give up right now and save us the trouble. Makes no difference to me."

"No." He looked up at me. "I want the chance. Lemme try."

"You've got it, then. Good luck. We'll be watching you."

I wrapped my fingers around his. Closest I could get to a handshake, given the cuffs. He squeezed tight.

Out in the hallway, I glanced at April. "You were quiet in there."

"Since it's your first time out with our team, I wanted to observe the quality of your fieldwork."

"How did I do?"

"More than adequate," she said. "You worked perfectly with Jessie, built a rapport with the suspect, and drew a full confession. One question. You know Vigilant Lock protocol. You should have arranged to offshore that man. Why didn't you?"

"He's basically harmless, he got a raw deal, and he's worth more to us if we cut him loose. Before Linder recruited me, I groomed confidential informants all the time. They're an essential part of intelligence gathering. I don't see why it should be different just because he's a cambion."

"Because Vigilant protocols demand it. It's the rule."

"Rule or not, it was the wrong move. I have to do what's best, regardless of—"

I stopped talking and shot a glance at Jessie and April. April leaned back in her wheelchair and offered up a faintly smug smile.

"Look at that, Agent Black," she said. "Showing a grasp of special circumstances. You *are* starting to fit in with us."

"Welcome to the Circus," Jessie said, checking her phone as we walked. "Hold on, got a voice mail from Kevin while we were in there."

Jessie's face turned to stone as she held the phone to her ear. I couldn't make it out, but I could tell from the pitch and the speed that Kevin was frantic about something.

"What?" I asked. Jessie hung up. She walked faster, balling her hands into fists as she strode down the hallway.

"We have to get back to Talbot Cove right now. The Bogeyman struck again last night. Another child is missing."

# # #

I drove the coastal highway like we had demons on our heels. *Except,* I thought grimly, *we're running straight toward them.*

We called ahead. Barry gave us the address and said he'd meet us at the scene of the crime. That turned out to be a rustic little bungalow on the east side of town, at the end of a forested lane. Barry's squad car sat out front, next to a Plymouth minivan. The minivan had those little family decals in the back window, a row of smiling stick figures. Mom, Dad, toddler, cat.

Barry met us at the door. Rumples creased his uniform shirt, and he looked like he hadn't slept in days.

"I was wrong about Helen Gunderson. It's really happening again, isn't it?" he said softly. "Like it did back then. It won't stop with two, either. This guy won't stop till he gets his fill. Just tell me how he did it, the nanny cam footage. Is he some kinda Photoshop expert? Was it a mask?"

I felt for him. He was supposed to be the law, Talbot Cove's protector, and he was up against a force he couldn't understand, let alone fight back against.

That's why we had to do it for him. I gave his arm a squeeze.

"We have some leads. Barry, this is Dr. April Cassidy. She's helping with the investigation."

"Ma'am," he said.

"Could we speak to them?" April asked.

Barry walked us into the living room. An empty box of Kleenex sat on the coffee table next to a small pile of used, crumpled tissues. The woman on the couch clutched one between her thin, trembling hands like it was her only possession in the world. The man hunched next to her, wearing flannel and built like a linebacker, looked like he was trying to be stoic and strong for her sake. He wasn't doing a good job at it. Their red-rimmed eyes took us in.

"Bill, Shelly," Barry said, "these are those FBI agents I was telling you about. They're good people. Just tell 'em what you told me."

"There's nothing to tell." Shelly stared at the dead television screen. Above it hung a framed family portrait: smiling parents cradling a cherubic toddler. It looked like it hadn't been taken very long ago. Happier times.

"We put Mindy to bed, then we turned in just after *The Late Show*," Bill told us. "I woke up around three. Had to use the john. Poked my head in, just to watch her sleep for a while . . . and she wasn't there."

"We have a security system," Shelly said. "There's not a lot of crime around here, but after Mindy was born, it just seemed like the right thing to do. They got through it somehow."

Bill pointed toward the front door. "Swear to God, it was working perfectly. Green light, all the doors and windows secure. I only turned it off when Sheriff Hoyt showed up."

"Could we see Mindy's room?" I asked.

Bill led us to the foot of the stairs, then gave April's wheelchair an awkward look.

"That's fine," she said. "My colleagues can handle it."

He walked us up. Mindy's room was on the second floor, a tiny nook with powder puff–pink carpet and teddy bear wallpaper. And a closet. Jessie put a gentle hand on Bill's shoulder.

"Why don't you head back downstairs and sit with your wife? We'll be only a minute."

As soon as he left, I fished the Pythian coin from my breast pocket and held out my fingers, suspending it from its fine silver chain.

"I'll check the alarm hookup on the window just to cover our bases," Jessie said, "but I think we both know—oh, yeah. There it goes."

The coin twirled on its chain, lifting slightly, tugging me toward the closet.

Nothing inside but a stack of empty boxes. They were crushed on one side, buckled inward, as if someone had squeezed themselves against the cardboard while crouching in wait.

We went back downstairs. There wasn't anything else to see. April sat with the parents, while Barry loomed in the corner of the room and looked anxious.

"—don't want to give you false hope," April was telling them, "but we're putting our full effort into this investigation."

"Question," I said. "Do either of you know, or have you ever met, a woman named Helen Gunderson? She lives here in town."

Bill and Shelly looked at each other, shaking their heads in slow unison.

"I don't think so," Shelly said. "Not by name, anyway. Maybe she's in my Pilates class?"

Bill frowned. "What's this about? Is she a suspect?"

"No," I said, "but we're investigating a lead and it might be relevant."

"We need you to make a list," Jessie said. "Every place you've been in the last two weeks. Your Pilates class, your job, where you bought your groceries. Everywhere you went outside this house. No matter how minor."

"You—you think the person who took Mindy is someone we know?" Shelly asked.

April folded her hands in her lap. "Someone who knows *you*. Child abductions are rarely crimes of opportunity, especially not from their own home. You came into contact with this predator somewhere in your daily life, and they took an interest in Mindy."

"Which is *not* to say it's your fault, or that you've done anything wrong," I quickly added.

"Have either of you come into conflict with anyone recently?" Jessie asked. "Had harsh words with someone, or maybe somebody picked a fight with you?"

"Is there anyone who would want to hurt you or your family?" April added.

"No," Shelly said, "I can't imagine—"

"No." Bill shook his head.

I believed them. With their child's life at stake, they had no reason to lie.

"So, how does this work?" Bill asked. "You're going to put a tap on our phone, right? Do you need our cell phone numbers, too? What do we say when they call with a ransom demand?"

We walked them through it, step by useless step, a drill they'd never have to use. There would be no phone call. Still, we had to let them believe.

I hated giving them false hope, but it was better than the truth.

SEVENTEEN

Barry followed us out of the house, keeping his thoughts to himself. Another squad car rumbled up to the curb. Cody jumped out, jogging over to us.

"Hey," Cody said, "I just heard. What are we looking at?"

"It's a goddamn copycat," Barry told him. "Of all the places and all the crimes in the world, some psycho is running loose in *my* town, trying to re-create the Bogeyman case."

"That's our working theory," April said.

"I still don't understand how he faked that camera footage. So what do I do about Helen? Apologize and cut her loose?"

"Warn her first," I said. "Her house was burglarized, and they trashed the place. Some thieves heard she'd been arrested and figured it'd be easy pickings. We caught one of them. Detroit PD is going to get in touch with you and send over the details, but it's not a pretty scene."

He rubbed his face. "Jesus, that's a fine damn homecoming, huh? Talk about insult to injury. All right, I'll see if I can't put her up in a hotel for a few days, maybe get some volunteers to help clean her place. We owe her at least that much."

"We'll also need the same information from Helen," April said. "Have her trace her movements, step by step, for the last two weeks. Every little detail is important."

"We're looking for commonalities," I said.

I was looking for one of my own. I scanned the manicured front lawn, slowly searching it up and down until I found what I already knew would be there.

"Jessie," I said, gesturing to a spot close to the curb. Another fist-size wicker ball sat in the grass. An offering to the Bogeyman.

"I'll bag it up," she said. She headed for the Crown Vic, but she didn't get far. The guy coming up the sidewalk toward us had the look of a used-car salesman, or maybe a professional golf sportscaster. His helmet of hair was too shiny to be real, just like his teeth, and he brandished the tiny video camera in his hand like it was a magical talisman.

"Ladies, gentlemen." He announced the words more than spoke them. "Can you comment on the Mindy Morris abduction? Can you confirm that this is the same perpetrator who kidnapped Elliot Gunderson?"

Barry's face turned lobster red. "How in the hell did you even—"

"This is an active crime scene," Jessie said, cutting him off, "and private property. You can't be here."

"I'm standing on the sidewalk." He pointed down, demonstrating how he'd kept his toes one neat inch from the edge of the lawn. "A wave of kidnappings is big news. The public has a right to know."

"Who are you workin' for?" Barry said. "The *Great Lakes Tribune* always *calls* when they want something from my office. You know, the polite way of doing things."

"And is politeness going to bring those children back home to their grieving mothers?" He lowered the camera and gave us a self-satisfied smirk. "The name's Tucker Pearlman. Field journalist for the *New Perspective*."

Cody groaned. "You're not a journalist, Tucker. You're a tabloid hack who couldn't cut it covering pet shows for the *Tribune*. What, hasn't Bat Boy done anything newsworthy this week? Maybe there's some more 'shocking 9/11 evidence' you haven't gotten around to revealing yet? I've *told* you about harassing people—"

"I'll have you know, we've won awards for our celebrity tell-alls. We stand on the cutting edge of news reporting. New-wave journalism, ferreting into the dark corners of the world that the big names are too afraid to touch. We connect the forbidden dots. Like this one, case in point."

The camera swung up and pointed right in my face. I had the feeling he'd been waiting for this.

"FBI Agent Harmony Black," he said. "Until recently, on temporary assignment to a Las Vegas task force. An assignment that ended, coincidentally, around the same time a massive scandal tanked the Carmichael-Sterling Corporation. Agent Black, care to comment on the rumors that satanic symbols were found inside the penthouse of Carmichael-Sterling's flagship Vegas casino?"

"Yes," I said. "It's an urban legend. Not true. End of comment."

"In that case, maybe you'd like to comment on the resemblance between these new abductions and the Bogeyman kidnappings from thirty years ago? Especially since that name came from, according to the *Tribune*, the frightened words of one Harmony Black, aged six."

Jessie strode toward him, balling up her right hand into a fist. "Shut that fucking camera off. *Now.*"

Tucker wagged his finger at her. "Ah-ah-ah, Agent. The Supreme Court has upheld the right of private citizens to film law enforcement personnel in the course of their duties. You're violating my civil rights."

"I'll violate more than—"

"Agent!" April snapped. Jessie snarled, but she took a step back. April rolled closer to her.

The camera lens swung back toward me.

"One woman, her life forever changed by tragedy." Tucker sounded like a movie-trailer narrator. "Walking in her father's shadow, she's taken up the shield of the law and returned to where it all began. Returned to face the madman who took her sister's life. *This* time, it's *personal*."

"Tucker," Cody growled, "knock it off. I won't tell you twice."

I shook my head at Cody. "It's okay."

"Harmony, you don't have to take that from him—"

"It's part of the job."

I looked into the camera's eye, somber. "Two children are missing. This isn't about me. This is about executing our professional duties as protectors of the public good, and ensuring the victims are returned home safely."

"But, come on, you have to admit, it feels like a cage match. Hey, you gotta figure the Bogeyman's following his own press coverage. All these creeps do that, right? So he's *gonna* see this. What do you want to tell him, Agent Black? If he was here right now, what would you say to the man who killed your baby sister and slit your father's throat?"

April's hand clamped down like a vise on Jessie's wrist. I didn't answer Tucker at first. I had to genuinely think about it.

"Give them back," I said.

"That's it?" He looked over the camera at me, eyebrows raised. "Seriously? That's all you have to say?"

"It's what we're here for."

"Okay," he said. "The Bogeyman is back, and he's taken two victims already. Do you think he'll go for six, like last time?"

"Five. There were five victims last time, and no, we have no reason to believe this is the same perpetrator, or if there's any connection at all to the so-called Bogeyman kidnappings in the '80s. There is absolutely no evidence connecting the two cases."

"There were six," he replied.

Jessie took a step forward. April tugged her wrist, hard.

"What do you know?" Jessie said.

He turned the camera off.

"Small town," he told me. "Lot of history. Lot of dirty secrets, too. I might have something you can use, but I don't give anything away for free. You've gotta throw me some red meat. Off the record, off camera. Just give me something I can go on."

"Withholding evidence is a crime," Cody said.

Barry stuck his thumbs in his belt and puffed out his chest. "Damn right. How about I run you in right now, and let you cool your heels in a cell for a few hours while you decide whether or not you wanna cooperate?"

Tucker held up one finger. "Correction, legal beagles. Never said I had evidence, I said I *might* have *something* you can use. That something was provided to me by a legally protected, confidential source. So go ahead. Bust me if you feel like a lawsuit and months of bad press. Or you can play ball, and we can all be winners here."

"You will *never* be a winner," Jessie muttered.

"Off the record?" I said.

He showed me the camera from all sides, proving it was turned off, though he didn't let it out of his grip. That didn't mean anything: I'd have been amazed if he didn't have at least one backup tape recorder running in his hip pocket. His promise of confidentiality? That meant even less than nothing.

Still, maybe it didn't have to.

The Bogeyman wouldn't be logging on to the World Wide Web to check out his press clippings. Thanks to Earl Gresham, though, we knew something else: the Bogeyman had a human master. Somebody sadistic enough to conjure the Bogeyman wouldn't be satisfied with just doing the deed. They'd want to read all about it, to vicariously enjoy their victims' suffering.

There was a very good chance that whatever I told Tucker would go straight to our quarry's ears. Had to be a way we could make that work to our advantage.

Sometimes you want to use the media to make a criminal angry. Get them good and pissed in the hopes they'll make a stupid mistake the next time they strike and leave evidence behind. Ever see a "profiler" go on TV and announce that a suspect is probably impotent, wets the bed, and has mommy issues? Textbook play. Dangerous, though, and you have to know whom you're hunting, how they're likely to react. Did we? Not nearly well enough.

Another good bit of media spin is to suck it up and play Keystone Kop. Make yourself look clueless to keep your quarry cool and confident. The safer they feel, the more likely they'll get careless and trip up.

"One second," I told him. I walked over to April and leaned in. "You're the expert. How would you play this?"

"Whether or not he's the original summoner," she murmured, "he's working on a timetable. If we frighten him, he's liable to step it up."

"So we play it dumb. Still, I want whatever this guy has. If we don't tell him anything interesting, we can kiss that lead good-bye."

"Sometimes it's not a matter of pretending you don't know anything," April said, her gaze enigmatic. "Sometimes it's better to pretend you know the *wrong* thing."

She had a point, but then there was the risk that anything I made up might accidentally be true—again, spooking our target and possibly derailing the entire investigation. I thought back to the conversation we'd had with Bill and Shelly Morris.

I snapped my fingers. "Jessie. Helen Gunderson's house didn't have an alarm system, right?"

"You kidding me? The front door could barely stay shut."

I walked back over to Tucker and gave him a careful smile, glancing back over my shoulder. Partners in crime. I led him out of earshot, to the far side of the lawn.

"Okay," I said, "but this is hot. Red-hot. If you connect me to it, I'll deny everything."

He rubbed his greedy palm against his camera. "All right, that's more like it! Quid pro quo's the way to go. Whatcha got for me?"

"Both houses had a full alarm system. Top of the line, from Polymath Security. Doors, windows, the works."

Tucker whistled. "That's hard-core security. How'd the Bogeyman get in?"

"That's the million-dollar question, isn't it? The alarms were totally undisturbed. You know what that means, right?"

His eyes gleamed. "Inside man."

"Exactly. Either the kidnapper works for Polymath, or he's paid someone to give him the alarm codes. We're on our way to the local office right now, to interview all the employees. If we're lucky, we'll have a suspect in custody by nightfall. On that note, do me a favor: sit on this until tonight, all right? Don't want to spook this guy into running."

Tucker held up three fingers. "Scout's honor. Okay, you did me right, so I'll do you right. I was digging around in the archives, over at the town hall. Did you know there used to be a local paper, up until the early '90s? The *Talbot Eagle.* Dinky little rag, but it covered all the local gossip."

"Every major news source we've seen said that five children were taken. The *Eagle* said different?"

"Sure, sure it did," he said. "Until they ran a retraction, the very next day, saying the child was safe and sound and the abduction never happened. Now, where would they have gotten the story in the first place? Kinda curious, considering the kid was from the richest family in town."

He slipped me a scrap of paper. Volume and issue number, date and column. I recognized the date right away, with a lurching sickness in my stomach. It happened two days before the monster came to *my* house.

"Go look it up," he said. "See for yourself. Way I read it, there's only two possibilities: either somebody made up a bogus story for no reason at all . . . or the Bogeyman gave a kid *back*."

EIGHTEEN

Tucker hit the road. I watched him leave, then walked back to the group in the driveway.

"What'd he say?" Barry asked me, looking nervous.

Or maybe I just imagined he looked nervous. Still, a nasty suspicion crept into my brain and carved out a little place to live.

"Nothing, he was full of crap," I said. "Look, we've got some leads to follow up on. I'll call you at the station later and catch you up, okay?"

"Yeah, okay." He gave me a brief, tight hug. I didn't say another word until his cruiser was rumbling down the driveway, turning onto the main road. Cody stuck around, lingering at the edge of the driveway, looking like he had something to say.

"What's on your mind?" I asked him.

He moved a little closer. I could smell his cologne, a musk that made me think of open fields after a fresh rain.

"I'm sorry you had to deal with that," he said, nodding back over his shoulder. "Tucker thinks he's a local celebrity. Local asshole's more like it."

I looked into his eyes. Longer than I needed to, but I was having a little trouble pulling away.

"It's fine. Goes with the territory."

He smiled and shook his head, his eyes lighting up. "True enough. So where are you off to now?"

I almost told him about Tucker's clue. Almost. I thought I could trust him. I *wanted* to trust him. But keeping him at arm's length was safer for both of us.

"Not sure yet," I said. "We have a few leads. Nothing major yet."

"Okay," he said, nodding but not sounding so sure. "Hey, I was gonna ask. I mean, tonight, if you have some free time . . ."

He trailed off. I tilted my head. "What?"

He looked over at April and Jessie, then shook his head. "Nah, it was nothing. I'd better get back to work before Barry starts squawking at me. Give me a call if you need anything, okay? Anything at all."

His hand brushed against mine as he turned to go. Just a fleeting, warm touch. I smiled and waved as he jumped into his cruiser and pulled away from the curb. Then I took a deep breath and walked over to April and Jessie.

"We've got a problem," I said through clenched teeth, still waving. Cody waved back and gave us a thumbs-up from his open window. "And Barry's in the thick of it. Bag up that wicker ball and let's get out of here."

"Barry?" Jessie asked. "Why? What's up?"

I relayed Tucker's story. "Barry was my father's chief deputy, and he took over as sheriff after he died. He was on top of the Bogeyman investigation from day one. He would have known about that newspaper article. Maybe even investigated it himself."

"And yet," April mused, "he never mentioned it to you. It *is* entirely possible that the article was a genuine mistake."

"Lots of things are possible. Until we check it out for ourselves, though, we don't trust anyone *but* ourselves."

Jessie snorted and unlocked the car. "Hell, that's standard operating procedure. So what about Cody?"

What about Cody? I'd been thinking about that. No, not really. I'd been thinking about *him*. Just him in general. His confident smile, the curve of his shoulder. That split-second touch of his hand. This was strange territory, and I didn't have a map.

"He's trustworthy," I said, "but no telling what he might slip to Barry by mistake. Let's keep our distance until we sort this out."

"That's all?" Jessie asked.

"Hmm?"

"That's your *entire* assessment of the deputy?"

"Yes," I said, "that's my entire assessment."

Jessie wriggled back against her seat and got comfortable. "Mmm-hmm. Whatever you say."

In the car, April leaned forward in the backseat and tapped my shoulder.

"Out of curiosity, why did you spin that particular story for our intrepid 'journalist'? About the security system, I mean."

"I couldn't risk a claim that might be true. Like, what if I said, 'Both mothers had the same hairdresser,' and it turned out the perp *was* their hairdresser? Serious long shot, but we'd be sunk. Whatever I told Tucker had to be believable—to him *and* to the Bogeyman's summoner—but unquestionably false."

"Which is why you asked me about the security system at Helen's place," Jessie said.

"The summoner leaves his tokens outside the houses he's targeting. As far as we know, he's never been inside. He wouldn't *know* that Helen Gunderson didn't have a security system—so if he reads Tucker's 'big scoop,' he's going to assume we're going off in the wrong direction and feel safe."

"And criminals who feel safe quickly become overconfident," April said. "Nicely done. Drop me off at the motel, would you? I need to update Kevin and see how his research is coming. Where are you two headed next? Records archive?"

"Food first?" Jessie asked, looking my way. "Seriously, I'm famished."

I hadn't even thought about eating—I get that way when I'm working—but now that she mentioned it, my stomach started growling, too.

"Sure," I said, "and I know just the place."

Norma's All-Day Café squatted on the edge of Stag Head Road, a four-lane highway that buzzed with eighteen-wheelers and tanker trucks on the way to bigger towns than this one. Norma's didn't look like much—just a long tin-roofed shack with dirty white walls and a gravel parking lot—but the number of trucks parked out front said good things about the quality of the food.

"You think this Fontaine guy is gonna be here?" Jessie asked as we got out of the car.

I shrugged. "Not likely, but we know he was going to meet the Gresham brothers here, and the Gresham brothers haven't shown up. He's bound to want to know why."

Spotting him, that was the hard part. From what I understood, most demons in our world arrive as hijackers: they aren't capable of creating their own bodies from soul stuff, so they jump inside any brain they can overpower. I know how to handle creatures like that. I can drive out a possessing entity, bottle it up, or send it screaming back to hell . . . but *finding* one, especially when it doesn't want to be found and it's masquerading as a human, that's another thing entirely.

Earl Gresham had told us that Fontaine liked the smell of Norma's pancakes. As we walked through the front door and onto a long rubber welcome mat, bells jingling behind us, I understood what he meant. I could taste the flavor in the air, a medley of fresh-churned butter and warm maple syrup.

"Shoulda brought Cody," Jessie said. "You know that's what he wanted, right?"

I blinked. "Huh?"

"You're kidding me. You *really* didn't pick up on that."

"Pick up on what?"

"He was trying to *ask you out.*" Jessie punched my shoulder. "He just didn't want to get shot down in front of me and Aunt April. He's totally into you. I could smell it."

Had he been? I thought back, walking through my memory like I was reconstructing a crime scene. I hadn't had anything resembling a date in three years. I guess if you go long enough without picking up those social cues, you just stop noticing them altogether.

Okay, more important question: Did I *want* him to ask me out?

Ugh, I thought, *complicated. Change of subject.*

"I don't care if it's lunchtime," I told Jessie. "I'm having breakfast. And what do you mean, you could *smell* it?"

"Look at you, living dangerously. And I mean, I could smell it." She tapped the side of her nose. "Pheromones. Told you, I'm a little sharper than most people in the senses department. Speaking of senses, are yours tingling? Spot anything weird?"

As a waitress in a pink frilled apron walked us to our table, a four-seater in the middle of the crowded room, I focused and took a long look around. Nothing suspicious, just a bunch of locals and long-haul truckers stopping in for a solid bite to eat.

Except for one.

The man in the corner booth had a waxy complexion, that jaundiced yellow look that alcoholics with bad kidneys get, and stringy, short hair combed in a side part. He wasn't eating at all. He had a full stack of pancakes, a side of hash browns, a steaming mug of coffee . . . and he was just *staring* at it, with his palms placed flat on the table and motionless.

"Seven o'clock," I murmured to Jessie as we sat down. "Guy with the bad haircut. He look hinky to you?"

She pretended to stretch and yawn, craning her neck to look. "Oh, yeah. Don't know if he's our guy, but he's giving off some serious creeper vibes. How do you want to play it?"

Demonic hijackers are bad news to start with, but if this guy was as good as Earl Gresham said he was—jumping bodies on a whim—the last thing we wanted was a violent confrontation in a room full of innocent bystanders. We needed to get his attention, subtly. Make him curious.

Flexing a little muscle might do the trick, I thought, and picked up the saltshaker.

"Little thing my mother taught me," I told Jessie. "African cleansing rite. Makes a room distinctly unpleasant for unclean spirits."

I held the saltshaker loosely and tapped it against the tabletop. *Tap. Tap.*

Taptap. Taptap. Tap taptaptap tap. Slowly, a rhythm grew, blossoming from the simple sound.

"Yeah, all right," Jessie said, nodding slowly. "Can I get in on this?"

"Please do."

Jessie's fingertips drummed the edge of the table, filling in the gaps and adding a strident beat. Focused now, feeling my power welling up, I willed it to spiral in time with the rhythm.

In the beginning was the sound. Music has the power to bind and compel, to stir the soul. Don't believe me? Turn on the radio. The universe was birthed in the beat of countless burning stars, and stardust is in our bones. Yoruban words spilled from my lips now, a low, keening song, shifting tones weaving in with the drumming.

We caught funny looks from the nearby tables, but I couldn't care. I was watching the white mist spread across the room in my second sight, glowing and warm, banishing all evils with the sheer joy of—

"Would you kindly stop doing that?" the waitress said, suddenly looming over our table.

The saltshaker slipped from my hand. Jessie missed the beat and froze, confused. The spell shattered.

I looked the waitress in the eye. Something moved in there. A squirming shadow behind her left pupil.

"Are we disturbing the other patrons?" I asked.

"You're disturbing *me*," she said, "which I assume was the point."

I glanced back toward the corner booth. The guy we'd picked out before was sound asleep, slumped back against the wall.

"Why don't you get out of that nice lady's body," I said, "so we can have a conversation?"

"You've got my attention," she said. The waitress turned and strolled back to the corner booth. She leaned in and brushed her fingertips across the sleeping man's shoulder. He woke with a jolt, sitting up straight and eyes shooting open, and she took a confused half step back.

The waitress rubbed at her forehead, looking like she had a headache coming on, and went back on her rounds like nothing had happened. The man just beckoned us over with a slow wave of his hand.

"Well," Jessie said, pushing back her chair, "this should be good."

We slid into the booth across from him. He leaned over his untouched plate and inhaled deeply.

"Isn't that just *divine*?" he asked in a syrupy New Orleans accent. "I've been near and I've been far, and there's nothing anywhere like a fat, fluffy stack of pancakes."

"You must be Fontaine," I said.

"Now, today's been chock full of surprises. First the Gresham boys stand me up—and I thought we had such a good working relationship—and now two lovely ladies who know my name have come to call." He sniffed delicately and wrinkled his nose. "Two lovely ladies with freshly oiled handguns. Now, that's fine, bullets don't affront me, but I'd love to know just who you are."

"Temple and Black, FBI," Jessie said. "We're here to regulate."

"You've stolen that body you're wearing," I added. "That's kidnapping. Now, there's a few ways we can address this situation, but that's going to depend on how helpful you are."

Fontaine laughed. "What, this old set of rags? Ladies, if you're going to pretend I'm a criminal, there's really only one thing you can charge me with."

His fingers moved like a violinist as he unbuttoned his shirt, going about halfway down. He pulled back the fabric to show us the Y-shaped autopsy scar running down his torso.

"Grave robbing," he said, buttoning back up. "Commandeering a corpse is a deeply unpleasant sensation—trust me, you can't imagine anything quite like it—but it does make for easier cleanup and fewer questions when a job is done. When it's time for me to move on, I'll just dump him back in the morgue where I found him. Only problem? Corpses can't digest food. No, no delicious pancakes for poor Fontaine, not this time around. I can just . . . *smell* them. Exquisite torment. Now, what exactly are you two playing at?"

"Playing at?" I asked.

"You know what I am. You're a fair hand at magic yourself, I can tell. So why would you think, in a million years, you could flash a badge my way? I'm not subject to your laws."

"You're standing on American soil. So yeah," I said, "I'm pretty sure you are."

Fontaine chuckled. "Is that where you think you are? Oh, darlin', bless your heart. This land belongs to the Court of Night-Blooming Flowers, and you live under their authority. You think you have a president? No. You have a *prince*."

"We don't accept that," Jessie said.

"Now that's just a foolish degree of stubborn. Let me pose you a conundrum. A man takes to drink and goes on a rampage. Smashing windows, hassling people. The constabulary arrives and puts him under arrest. He rages at them, saying he's a sovereign citizen and doesn't recognize the authority of the United States government. What happens to him?"

"He goes to jail anyway," I said. "It doesn't matter whether he accepts it or not."

Fontaine leaned back and smiled. "Now you two know what *you* look like, from *my* perspective."

"Earl Gresham told us you're a . . . Chainman," I said to Fontaine. "A bounty hunter."

"Speaking of, where are those boys? They're apparently late *and* loose lipped, neither of which I'm inclined to stand for."

"Two are dead and one's behind bars," Jessie said. "And you aren't laying a hand on him."

Fontaine's borrowed corpse arched a waxy eyebrow. "What, you think I'd *hurt* them? Now why would I do that? I was just gonna give 'em a good talking-to and cancel their bonus pay. Why would you think so poorly of me?"

"Because you're a demon?" I said.

"I'm a professional. The Chainmen's Guild holds itself to the strictest standards of conduct. We are the upholders of order. It's expected."

"Order," Jessie said, "in hell."

"You ladies are just adorable, with your little guns, and your little spells, and your entirely unearned sense of authority. Allow Fontaine to convey a bit of education. I'm just gonna need you to do one thing for me first."

"Oh?" I asked. "What's that?"

"Order breakfast." He wore a lazy, reptilian smile as he leaned closer. "I want to watch you eat."

NINETEEN

The pancakes, topped with a melting dollop of sweet butter and drizzled with maple syrup, melted in my mouth. The hash browns were lightly salted, crunchy, cooked just right.

I could have done without the staring, though.

"Swear to God," Jessie said, cutting into a sausage link and scooping up a forkful. "If your hands go anywhere near your pants, this discussion is over."

Fontaine cast a rueful glance downward. "Alas, that's another part that doesn't work on a corpse. My sensual pleasures, for the moment, are entirely cerebral."

"You were talking about order," I said.

"Right, right." He picked up his fork. "We are a rather . . . rambunctious people, my kind, prone to *excess*. When Big Daddy went on his permanent vacation, we all went a little crazy down there. Those were the Years of Iron and Fire, and they were a bad time. A bad time, indeed. What came out of that, though, was order. The courts of hell. Divisions of power."

He held the fork straight, rested it on its tines, and slowly pulled his hand away. It stood there, perfectly and impossibly balanced.

"But the courts feud," he said, "and the schemers scheme, and everybody's hungry. Everybody's hungry, but there's only one fork."

He inhaled and gave a little puff of air. The fork toppled over, rattling on the table.

"It'd be just that easy for everything to fall apart all over again. So we have laws. Laws with punishments, terrible and cruel. They have to be, to keep everyone in line. To keep the fork standing on its tines."

"And you . . . pursue other demons, who have broken these laws," I said.

"It's a living. Sometimes I hunt my own kind, and sometimes yours, if you cross certain lines. Word of general advice: if you make a deal with hell, you'd best keep your word, lest dire consequences ensue."

"A deal," I said. "Like the power to summon the Bogeyman."

"Ah, now that's a morbid tale indeed. But thank you for revealing why you're poking around this humble little town. Tell you what, ladies: Go home. Go home and forget all about the Bogeyman. That's one problem that'll take care of itself, once my work is done."

"Not happening." Jessie waved a forkful of pancake at him. "You think we're going to trust one demon to get rid of another one?"

Fontaine arched one thin eyebrow. "Is *that* what you think it is? Blessed innocents. I'm almost glad we crossed paths. You would've gotten yourselves ripped limb from limb, trying your little chants and exorcisms on *that* monster. That, ladies, is no demon. No . . . Bogeymen aren't born. They're *made*."

I was about to take another bite, fork halfway to my mouth. I set it down on the plate instead.

"Made, how?"

He shook his head. "Same way they always have been, miss. Same way as ever. But that's not a tale I feel like telling today. Again, I must request that you vacate this fine municipality, for your own personal safety."

"You threatening us?" Jessie said.

"Me? Oh, not in the slightest. Long as you don't block my road, I've got no reason to run you down. But a little crow tells me my competition just arrived last night."

"Earl mentioned him," I said. "Another Chainman, named Nyx?"

"*Her.* And she is not as cultured as I am, or as patient. Nyx is a daughter of the choir of wrath. She was personally trained by the matriarch of the House of Dead Roses. Believe you me, that's one bed you never want to find yourself sharing, not unless your sexual proclivities extend to barbed wire and rusty razors. If she learns that there are humans on her trail, aware of hell's influence and interfering with the hunt, she won't sit down to pancakes and pleasant conversation. She'll skin you alive just for kicks and giggles."

"We can handle ourselves," I said.

"Really?" He chuckled and folded his hands. "Have you ever faced the wrath of an incarnate demon, darlin'? Stared down a predator with eight hundred years of experience hunting and killing and lovin' every second of it?"

I thought back to Las Vegas.

"Once," I said.

"Oh?" His eyebrows went up in surprise. "Did you win?"

I shrugged. "I broke even."

"This time, sad to say? You won't."

"I don't see why you won't share what you know," I told him. "We're after the same thing."

"You don't even know *what* you're after. You're not ready for what's waiting at the end of this road, ladies. I'm trying to be kind. But I'm not dissuading you at all, am I?"

"Nope," Jessie said.

"Let me ask you something," I told him. "Is this just a job to you, or do you actually care?"

"That is," he said, "quite possibly the rudest thing you could say to a Chainman. If you were one of my breed, it'd be grounds for claws and teeth. But seeing as you're human and, well, ignorant, I'll let it slide. Yes. I care very deeply about my people."

I rapped my fork against my plate. "So do we. You're basically a cop. So are we. And that's why you should know we aren't leaving. We've got a job to do, and people to protect. We *don't* quit."

"All right," Fontaine murmured to himself, nodding slowly. "All right, all right. You'll do."

"Do what?"

He spread his hands and grinned. "What you will! You'll do what you will. I'm going to extend you ladies my professional courtesy. Go ahead. Stay. Hunt. I won't help and I won't hinder. Let's see how far you get on your own."

I didn't like it. I'd seen *human* bounty hunters less friendly than Fontaine claimed to be, and never one that was happy about people getting in the way of their claim. Did he think we were that insignificant, that we *couldn't* get in his way? Or did he stand to gain something by sharing the field with us? He didn't have any kind words to say about his rival Nyx, and they were obviously racing each other for—

I sipped my ice water, the answer suddenly obvious.

"And while we're doing that," I said, setting down my glass, "you're hoping we draw Nyx's attention and slow her down, so you can catch this guy first."

"Why, heavens, the thought hadn't even occurred to me. Though she is unlikely to be as considerate as I am. But as you said, you can take care of yourselves, isn't that right?"

"Watch and see," Jessie told him.

"Out of curiosity," I said, "who pays you?"

His gaze flicked toward me. "Hmm?"

"This is a job, right? So who pays you?"

"Oh," he said, "whoever hires me for the hunt. Usually the prince of a court, or some aggrieved noble. And they are *always* aggrieved."

"The guy you're after now, the one summoning the Bogeyman and sending it after people. He busted a deal with a demon, didn't he? And that's who hired you to hunt him down."

Fontaine shook his head. "Now, I didn't say that. I said words that could be construed in that particular pattern, but I did not *say* that."

"You didn't have to. So your client, he hired you and he hired Nyx. Who else? How many demons will converge on Talbot Cove before this is all over?"

He smiled. "You're asking the wrong question."

"What's the right one?"

"My client . . . did *not* hire Nyx."

"Who did?" I asked.

"That," he said, "is the right question."

"What's the answer?"

Fontaine took the unused paper napkin from his lap and daintily pressed it to his lips. Then he folded it, set it next to his untouched plate, and slid out of the booth.

"Worth pursuing," he said. "The answer is worth pursuing. Happy hunting, ladies."

Fontaine drifted through the restaurant, strolling away.

"We really gonna let him go?" Jessie said.

I sighed. "I don't see any other option. If we corner him, he'll just jump into another body. You've got to have a plan to take down a hijacker. A snare, binding wards, something to pin him down while I do a full exorcism. It's not improv work."

I tried another bite of my pancake. Suddenly, I wasn't hungry anymore. I set my fork down and shoved the plate back.

"So what do we know," Jessie asked, "and what do we think we know?"

I ran down the points on my fingertips. "We know that the Bogeyman has to be deliberately summoned and sicced on your enemies. You enchant the token, set it on the target's lawn, and the Bogeyman hits that house. It's a weapon. It's also—if we can believe Fontaine, and for the sake of discussion, let's say we do—not a demon."

"He used the plural, too," Jessie said. "Made it sound like people have been creating these things for a long time. Not only might this not be the same summoner from thirty years ago, it might not even be the same Bogeyman."

I thought about my baby sister, clutched in that monster's arms. Then I pushed the image away. It didn't help me work any harder.

"Either way, they're both going down," I said. "Doesn't matter. Okay. We know Fontaine was hired by another demon. We *think* we know he's here to hunt the Bogeyman's summoner. He pulled a double cross, and now Fontaine's here to bring down hell's hammer on him."

"I don't know." Jessie tapped her fingertip against her chin, thinking. "Isn't that . . . weirdly reckless? I mean, okay, you screwed over a demon. You've got two bounty hunters from hell, literally, tracking you down. Is that a good time to hang out in a small town, sending your pet monster to screw with people you don't like? If I was this guy, I'd go so far underground I'd burrow a hole straight to China."

"If he feels that injured by these people, if he's that obsessed, maybe not." I shook my head. "But neither Helen Gunderson nor Bill and Shelly Morris have any obvious skeletons in their closet. And then there's the place. If there's no connection to the last two times the Bogeyman showed up, why *this town*? What's so special about Talbot Cove? That's why I don't buy it. There's no way the Bogeyman was summoned here in the '40s, the '80s, *and* now, all by random chance."

"Or even farther back," Jessie said. "Remember, Kevin just couldn't find *proof* of any abductions before the '40s. He sure as hell found hints and rumors. Considering there's a human hand behind the monster, it can't be the same person calling it. They'd be ancient now."

"So. More than one perp. The current one may or may not be the same person behind the '80s abductions. Probably not the one who did the summonings in the '40s, and definitely not any earlier than that. And this all has to be tied to Talbot Cove itself, somehow."

"The Nyx thing," Jessie said. "That was weird. Fontaine really wants us to know who hired her."

"Yeah, but not enough to just make it easy and *tell* us. He wants us to blunder into her path. If she kills us, one less thing for him to deal with. If we slow her down, same outcome. Letting us stumble around blind is a win-win situation for him. Me, I'm thinking about what Tucker said."

"The newspaper article?"

I sipped my water. The ice had melted down to little slivers, bobbing at the top of the glass.

"The Bogeyman's victims are never found. No bodies, no trail, not even a trace. They just vanish off the face of the earth. If Tucker is telling the truth, and if the article wasn't a mistake, then one time—just *one time*—the Bogeyman returned one of its victims. We need to know why."

"You thinking what I'm thinking?" Jessie asked.

"Yep. Let's go do a little light reading."

TWENTY

We asked for the check at the front counter, but the cashier just shook her head and smiled.

"That gentleman you were with? He already paid the bill and covered the tip. He asked me to give you this."

She handed me a slip of cream-colored cardboard. A business card with no phone number, no e-mail address, just a name—**FONTAINE**—in crisp black type. Written on the back, a line of neat cursive read, "Next time's on you. —F."

I kept the card.

Talbot Cove's town hall wouldn't have looked out of place in a movie about colonial times, with its redbrick facade and whitewashed window slats. A great brass bell hung inside the open arch of the hall's clock tower, and the clock above was set to run exactly five minutes slow.

The police station sat on the far side of the parking lot. I didn't feel like stopping in to pay Barry a visit. Not until we knew how clean his hands were. I wanted to give him the benefit of the doubt. I wanted a lot of things I didn't have.

The Talbot Cove town seal, a vinyl decal faded and scuffed by time and shoe leather, was laid into the lobby floor. It depicted a giant eagle in flight, one talon clutching a fresh-cut log of pine, the other a sheaf of papers. I knew enough Latin to understand the motto that encircled the picture: *Through the grace of the land, we prevail.*

One wall bore photographs of the town's mayors, going back to the early 1920s. The current one, Mitchum Kite, was a plump and apple-cheeked man with a big, gregarious smile and a checkered sport coat. I was more interested in the directory on the opposite wall, where there was a corrugated metal board with big, white magnetic letters.

"Archives and public records," I said. "Sounds about right."

On the other side of a frosted glass door, the smell of mothballs and brittle paper clung to the humid air. A slip of a man in a tweed vest, who was peering at a ledger through his bifocals, sat on the opposite side of a long wooden counter. Jazz music crackled on an old portable radio, its antenna jutting out like a fencing foil.

The old man looked up and smiled. "Help you, ladies?"

"Special Agents Temple and Black," I said. We flashed our identification. "We understand that you store the old town newspaper archives here?"

Something flashed in his eyes, just for a heartbeat. Fear. He tried to put his smile back on, but it didn't fit his face anymore.

"Er, well, more or less. I mean, we did take in the old archival copies once the *Eagle* went out of circulation, just for historical sake, but only the first decade was ever properly placed on microfiche. Is . . . is there a reason why you ask?"

I took out the slip of paper Tucker Pearlman gave me and rested it on the counter. "We need two issues. This one, and the one from the next day."

He leaned in to read it, then sagged back in his wooden swivel chair. His hands gripped the chair's arms, like it might launch into the air at any moment.

"I'm . . . I'm sure we don't have that one anymore," he said. "The archives aren't perfect—I mean, there are gaps, years of gaps, even. Sorry I can't help."

Jessie shot me a look. I nodded. She rested her palms against the counter and leaned in.

"We'd like to look for ourselves. Just to be thorough. You understand."

"D-do you have a warrant?" he stammered. "I mean, I just don't want to get in trouble for not following protocol—"

"These are the public town archives, yes?" she asked.

"Well, yes—"

"Then do two things for us. First, walk us back there and show us where to find the *Talbot Eagle* archive. Second, get a dictionary and look up the word *public*."

He led us back into the stacks—tight aisles overflowing with cardboard boxes and bundled-up folders, piles of loose paper and rows of magazine binders.

"How do you find anything back here?" Jessie asked.

He looked back over his shoulder and smiled nervously. "Oh, there's—there's a system, ma'am. A place for everything, and everything in its place. Ah, here we are."

The *Talbot Eagle* archive consisted of twelve tub-size boxes of folded newspapers, with nearly illegible dates scrawled on each box in thick black Sharpie.

"As I said, it's . . . not very organized, or complete. Still, you're welcome to take a look for yourselves."

"Thank you," I said.

He didn't move. He just stood there at the end of the aisle, watching us and wringing his hands.

"*Thank* you," I repeated. This time he got the hint and doddered back to the front desk.

"That wasn't suspicious or anything," Jessie murmured.

"Agreed, but remember, last person through here was Tucker. Jerk probably bragged about how he was uncovering some big local scandal. That, followed by a visit from the FBI? Can't be good for the nerves."

"I still don't like it," Jessie said. She put her hands on her hips and stared down the wall of boxes. "So. You take one, I take one?"

We each pulled down a box, set it on the hardwood floor, crouched down and started hunting. The filing system was even worse than I'd feared. The dates on the boxes, at least the ones we could read, were more vague suggestions than firm commandments. The folded, faded papers mixed together with no rhyme or reason, stacked this way and that. The ink on the oldest papers had already faded to faint hints of words on yellowed, brittle pages—years of history abandoned to careless neglect.

"Kinda sad," Jessie said. "You'd think they'd want to preserve this stuff. Small-town pride and all that."

I lingered over a headline.

Kite Paper Mill Closes Its Doors

Below, a smudged black-and-white image of the factory on the waterfront, skeletal and lonely.

"Not always. Places like this . . . sometimes there's a lot of pain buried just under the surface. Some people think it's better to cover it up than to talk about it."

"What do you think?"

I glanced up at her. She watched me from the other side of the aisle, her turquoise eyes bright and curious.

I shrugged. "Doesn't matter what I think. People hide the truth. We dig it up. That's our job."

Something annoyed me, like a fly buzzing near my ear. Not her question, and not the tedium of searching through faded byline after byline, something I just couldn't put my finger on. I was halfway through the second box before I figured it out.

"Somebody's messing with us," I said.

"What, is it a day ending in the letter *Y*?"

"I'm serious." I gestured toward her box. "Let me guess. The papers on top are all out of order and jumbled around, right?"

"So far, yeah."

"Dig deeper. Go about halfway down."

Jessie lifted out an armful of papers, stacking them on the floor, then resumed her search. She looked up a moment later, frowning.

"They're in perfect order."

I swept my arm out, gesturing to the stacked boxes.

"So have the last two I searched. I bet they *all* are," I said. "This isn't carelessness. Somebody pulled the boxes out and scrambled them on purpose, mixing fistfuls of back issues at random. It was a rush job, though. They mixed up only the top layers to make it look like they were hopelessly out of order."

"Since most people would get just about that far before giving up," Jessie said. "And since Tucker Pearlman didn't have any trouble at all finding what *he* needed . . ."

"It happened after his visit. Somebody found out what he'd dug up and went back to make it harder for anyone else to do the same."

Jessie's gaze turned slowly toward the front desk.

"Let's go have a word," she said, and cracked her knuckles.

The archivist swiveled in his chair as we walked up the stacks, forcing a big smile.

"So, uh, Agents, did you find what you were looking for?"

"No," Jessie said, looming over him. "We didn't, because some asshole went and sabotaged the filing system. Know anything about that?"

He held up his open hands, eyes going wide.

"Now, now, ladies, I told you the newspaper archives are very poorly maintained. I *did* warn you."

I flanked his chair and slapped Tucker's paper down on the desk under the palm of my hand, loud enough to make him jump.

"Do you remember yesterday?" I asked him.

"W-well, sure, of course, but what does—"

"So do we. Because we weren't *born* yesterday. A reporter for the *New Perspective* came in here. He asked to see the stacks. Probably said some things you didn't like. Such as, for example, bragging about a news piece he's doing: Talbot Cove's history and the Bogeyman abductions from the '80s. Tell me if I'm warm."

"He . . . he did, yes, that . . . that happened."

"Spooked you, huh? And maybe you got to thinking, he might not be the *only* big-city reporter who'll come breezing through town, looking for some dirt to toss on the Cove's good name."

"Reasonable," Jessie said. "Nobody could blame you for that. You were trying to do the right thing."

His head jerked between the two of us, neck swiveling, as if his attention was a ping-pong ball.

"Sure, sure," I said, "nobody likes those guys. Muckrakers. They don't understand small-town life. Me, I was *born* here. And I'm not writing any articles."

"You don't understand," he said, his voice cracking. "I had to protect myself. It would have been too obvious . . ."

He bit his cheek and clammed up. I sighed and looked over at Jessie.

"What do you think he'll get? Twenty years?"

"Oh," Jessie said, catching my angle, "at least. He's lucky Michigan abolished the death penalty."

The archivist's eyes bulged. "*W-what?* What are you *talking* about?"

"Obstruction of justice," I said, "carries a maximum penalty equal to the actual crime itself. The obstruction, in this case, is that you're willfully withholding critical evidence. The crime, in this case, is at least six counts of kidnapping. Six. Counts. Maybe more. You can go behind bars with a life sentence for just *one* count."

"I say we run him in," Jessie said. "We don't need this guy. There's nothing useful he can tell us."

He grabbed the lifeline, just like we knew he would.

"Hold on, hold on! I can! I can tell you where to find them. They're not here—the articles, I mean."

"We're listening," I told him.

He slumped back in his chair. Beads of sweat glistened on his wrinkled brow.

"When that . . . reporter left, I called the mayor immediately. He stormed in, frantic. I guess he didn't realize we *had* that year in our archive. He demanded to see those two issues. And he left with them. He told me . . . he told me that if I said a word about it to anyone, I'd be fired or worse."

"Or worse?" Jessie said.

He shrugged, helpless. "I don't know what he meant, but he . . . I've never seen him that frightened."

"And the scrambled papers?" I asked.

"That was me. The mayor made it sound like other people would be coming to look for the papers. I just thought, if I made it look like a hopeless search, they'd just give up and I wouldn't have to lie when they found the gap in the records. I didn't know it was *evidence*! Please, believe me, I was just trying to protect my job."

Jessie and I locked eyes. We nodded simultaneously. I put my hand on the archivist's shoulder.

"We believe you," I said. "Now tell me just one more thing: Which way to the mayor's office?"

TWENTY-ONE

Mayor Kite's office was up on the second floor, just past a pair of curving staircases with alabaster rails. As we climbed up toward him, he stepped out of his office lugging a hefty, stuffed valise under one arm of his ill-fitting jacket.

"Mayor Kite," I said as we approached, flashing my credentials. "Special Agents Temple and—"

That was as far as I got. He spun toward us, a look of horror plastered on his face, then he turned and ran.

He bolted down the hallway, faster than his heavy frame looked capable of, and grabbed a clerk on her way out of a side door. He shoved her to the ground, a living obstacle in our way, and kept running. She went down in a flurry of papers and open, spinning folders.

I took two seconds to make sure she was okay, and kept going. Jessie got ahead of me, her lips curling back in a frustrated snarl. Kite grabbed a rolling mail cart and shoved it backward as hard as he could, sending it rattling our way. It hit Jessie full-on, metal cracking against her kneecap, but she knocked it aside with a violent sweep of her arm and kept going.

Kite slammed against the fire exit door and barreled on through. A klaxon wailed, red emergency lights strobing in the stairwell. We followed him through, but he was already almost to the bottom, taking the steps two or three at a time, running like the devil was on his heels.

He should have been so lucky.

"Mayor Kite!" I shouted, rushing down the stairs just behind Jessie. "We just want to talk!"

He wasn't in a talking mood. He tore through the lobby and out into the sunlight, climbing into a late-model BMW with a sheen of dried tree sap and gunning the engine. Jessie grabbed his door handle, but he threw the car into reverse and stomped the gas, peeling out of the parking lot.

"Fuck," Jessie hissed, rubbing her fingers. "C'mon, let's *go*!"

We jumped into the Crown Vic, and I mashed the gas pedal, clinging tight to the steering wheel as we spun out of the lot and onto the main road. I watched the redline, pushing the engine as hard as I could while we crept up on the mayor's rear bumper.

He turned off the highway, leading us on a chase along a winding country road that slithered over a chain of forested hills.

"When we get close enough," I said, "I'm going to PIT him. You cool with that?"

"Cool as a cucumber," Jessie said, buckling her seat belt.

PIT stands for Precision Immobilization Technique, and it's a hell of a lot safer—for you, the suspect, and any civilians within three hundred yards—than trying to shoot the tires of a fleeing car. Easier, too. It's a controlled crash, where the chase car comes up and carefully bumps into the target from the back corner, then applies engine force. Do it right and the target's wheels lose traction, they spin out, and you can force them to a more-or-less graceful stop. Or at least one where everybody survives.

We crested a hill, and down below I saw the narrow road straighten itself out. Taking him on a curve was too risky, but there was our chance, just ahead. Then something in the corner of my eye, something black and burning, flitted across the tops of the pine trees.

It *slammed* down onto the roof of the Crown Vic, shaking the car and making the shock absorbers groan. A fist, or something I thought was a fist, punched the roof hard enough to put a dent in the metal just over our heads.

"What the hell?" Jessie said. "Shake it!"

I held the wheel tight and swerved, veering from side to side, but whatever it was held on fast and punched the roof again.

I knew what it was. If I hadn't guessed, the flood of foul magic washing over me like a skunk's stench would have given it away. It was an aura of rot and ruin, like the taste of putrid flesh, and my stomach churned as I fought to control the car.

Nyx.

Jessie yelped as a face appeared in the passenger-side window, peering down from above. The incarnate demon didn't bother pretending to be human, not on the hunt. She had a face like a desiccated corpse, but her flesh was rubbery black and her lips pulled back in a permanent, skeletal grin to show jutting, curling fangs. Pupil-less eyes of molten copper glared at us through the glass.

She burned. A thin sheen of flame, so blue it was almost black, rippled over her head and down the bony black chitin armoring her shoulders like a mane of burning hair. If it bothered her, she didn't show it. She just reached out, curled a taloned fist, and punched through the window.

The safety glass shattered, spraying us with rounded chunks, and Jessie ducked as two-inch steel talons raked the air where her face had just been. She whipped her Glock out of its holster and fired two booming shots at point-blank range into the demon's face.

My eardrums throbbed with pain, the aftermath of the shots echoing in a receding ocean wave, but I could still hear Nyx's shrill scream.

She pulled back out of sight, clinging to the roof, and I heard the scraping of her claws as she scrambled to my side of the car.

"Coming around!" Jessie shouted. I scrambled for a warding spell, a banishment, anything, but I couldn't pay attention to the road and my magic at the same time.

"Take the wheel," I said, and let go. Jessie lunged over, grabbing hold and keeping the car on the road, as I brought my hands up and locked my fingers in a ritual gesture.

Focus, I thought, and took a deep breath. I couldn't care about the road, or the trees, or anything but the task at hand. One task. One focus. I thought back to my teenage years. Endless hours in my mother's study, kneeling beside her at the family altar, learning our craft. Learning patience. Learning to be calm in the heart of a storm. Sometimes we would go down to the shore and meditate on the water. Watching it lap up against the sand for hours, graceful and smooth and silent.

"Water flows," my mother told me. "It does not burn; it does not break. It adapts. There's a river in your heart; in panic, in chaos, that's where you'll find serenity."

Nyx dropped into sight on the other side of my window. The bullets had gouged two deep furrows in her skull-like face, drooling with black ichor, but they were already beginning to heal. Her gaze locked with mine. In my years with the Bureau I'd crossed paths with extremists, Klansmen, and even aspiring terrorists . . . but I'd never experienced the kind of hatred I saw in those burning eyes. It felt like a fire hose being turned on me, an utter torrent of loathing and rage without cause and without end. I let it flow. It washed over me without touching me. In my serenity, I could see Nyx—really see her.

She was born with this rage, I thought, *this fury. She can't be anything else. She'll never know anything else.* The waves of hatred hammered at me, trying to dig their hooks in, to tempt me to lash out and respond in kind. I couldn't.

"I feel . . . so sorry for you," I whispered.

Nyx shrieked and pulled back her claws to strike. That's when I exhaled a sharp gust of wind, carrying the spell I'd summoned to my lips and my fingertips. A word of banishment, a word of peace. Just a word.

Nyx lost her grip. She rolled backward, bounced off the trunk of the car and onto the country road, flailing. A five-foot barbed tail slashed like a bullwhip, gouging scorched furrows in the asphalt.

"Unless you've got something more powerful up your sleeve," Jessie breathed, "do *not* stop driving."

She didn't need to tell me twice.

# # #

We'd lost Mayor Kite. Part of me wondered if that was the intention.

"Two possibilities," I said once we'd caught our breaths and put a few more miles of road behind us. "Either we got on Nyx's radar when we went poking around at town hall—"

"Or Kite's the one who hired her, and he called her for a little emergency backup," Jessie said, finishing my thought.

"Would she do that, though? Fontaine made it sound like these Chainmen are pretty big on the law—or what passes for it in hell, anyway. Is offering an on-call assassination service part of the employment package?"

Jessie slumped in her seat, exhausted. Cool, crisp air billowed in through what was left of her side window. She tried to roll it down, making little pieces plink and shudder loose.

"He also made it sound like Nyx was kind of murder happy," Jessie said. "And you know what? I'm inclined to agree with his assessment. Either way, Kite's involved in this. Neck-deep."

"Agreed. He found out what Tucker was researching, flipped out, and pulled the articles. He doesn't want anyone knowing that the Bogeyman gave a kid back. I mean, given his reaction, I think we can take 'It was all a mistake on the newspaper's part' off the list of possibilities."

"We should rush to Kite's house. Maybe we'll catch him packing a bag."

I drummed my fingers on the wheel, thinking.

"We'll swing by just to be safe," I said, "but I have a feeling he's already gone underground. I hate to say it, but I know there's one person in this town who can tell us what really happened. And he *will* tell us."

We found Cody out in front of the police station putting a fresh coat of wax on his squad car. He stopped what he was doing, lowered the sponge in his hand, and stared at us blankly as we rolled into the spot two spaces down. I didn't realize why until we got out of the car.

In addition to the shattered side window and a huge dent in the trunk, the roof of the Crown Vic looked like the aftermath of a war zone. Rips, gouges, and long black streaks where the white paint had bubbled, boiled, and charred.

"Minor accident," I told him.

"Minor," he said flatly, staring at the car.

"Just a fender bender," Jessie said. "We exchanged license and insurance information with the other driver. She was very gracious."

Cody looked from me to the car and back again.

"Are you okay?"

No, I thought. *I just found out your boss might be hiding evidence about the night my father died. I'm pretty far from okay.*

I didn't say that, though. I just gave Cody a tired thumbs-up and said, "Copacetic."

"We need to talk to the sheriff," Jessie told him.

"Sure." Cody gestured to the front doors with his dripping sponge. "He's inside. Go on back."

We found him in the records room. I stood before him, silent as the grave, staring him down.

"Sheriff Hoyt," Jessie said, "we need to have a word with you. In private, please."

He furrowed his brow, looking uncertain. "Hey, ladies, why so formal all of a sudden? What's up?"

"This is a discussion," I said, "in a formal capacity."

"What're . . . what're you saying, Harmony?"

I gestured toward the cell-block corridor.

"I'm saying that we can talk in your office, or we can talk in the interrogation room. Your call."

TWENTY-TWO

Barry chose his office. We didn't say a word until we stood behind closed doors. He dropped into the chair behind his desk, looking pale.

"You gotta help me here, Harmony. I don't understand what's going on, but I know I don't like it any."

"Thirty years ago," I said, "you and my father were heading up the investigation into the Bogeyman kidnappings."

He shrugged. "Sure, I mean, you know that. Heck, the whole department—such as it was—was working night and day on finding those kids. We brought in reservists, volunteers from three counties around, every warm body we could get."

"And how many children were abducted?"

"Y-you *know* that," he said. "Five."

"Funny," Jessie said. "We heard six."

Barry's mouth opened, his lips moving but no words coming out, then it shut again. He clasped his hands on the desk.

"Except history says five," I added, "because one came back."

"I don't . . . I don't know what you're asking me." His voice was soft as cotton, but shaky as the San Andreas Fault. It was a familiar tone of voice. I usually heard it from suspects who knew damn well they'd been cornered, but still had the faint, false hope they could still talk their way out of prison time.

"The *Talbot Eagle* wrote it all up," I said, "then retracted it the very next day. Right before my sister was taken and my father was murdered. You remember, don't you?"

Jessie jerked her thumb back over her shoulder, pointing in the general direction of town hall.

"Your mayor just made himself a federal fugitive," she said. "*That's* how desperate he was to stop us from finding out about this. So don't feed us any lines about the article being a mistake. After the day I've had, I've got a seriously low bullshit-tolerance threshold."

"You were there, Barry," I said. "It was your case. You know what happened. You and my father."

"Harmony, you've gotta—you've gotta understand, it was a different time. Everything was crazy, we were running through a hundred leads a day and ninety percent of 'em were just nutjobs trying to get attention. Sometimes we had to play things loose—"

"*How* loose?" I said. "Barry, you know something about this case. Something you've been hiding for thirty years. Don't say you don't. You were there for me the night it all happened. You were there for my mom in the aftermath, until we moved out of town. Barry . . ."

I looked him in the eye.

"Please tell me you aren't in on this, and please make me believe you. Tell me you aren't bent. Don't break my goddamn heart."

His shoulders sagged, and he looked away from me. Staring at the portrait of my father on his office wall.

"Not bent," he said, almost too soft to hear. "Just a coward."

"Start talking," I told him.

He took a deep breath. "You gotta understand something. The Kite family . . . they *are* Talbot Cove. Maybe not so much these days, with most everybody flying off to the big city and the big paychecks, but they've been running things since the first homesteaders broke ground here in the 1800s. That paper mill on the shore—that was the town's lifeblood for nearly a hundred years. Everybody owed the Kites for their livelihood, and everybody knew it."

He drummed his fingers on his desk, straining his words through a sifter.

"I got the call that morning. Young couple, wealthy, kissing cousins to the Kites. Their baby went missing in the night. I took the report, searched the house, it was just like the other abductions. Nothing. Nothing to see and nothing to find, like the kid had vanished into the air. Later that afternoon, I get a frantic call, telling me to come back. And boom, there's the kid in his crib, right where he should be."

"From out of nowhere," I said.

He nodded. "From out of nowhere. And there's Mayor Jeremiah Kite—Mitchum Kite, the current mayor? Jeremiah was his dad. Jeremiah tells me that it was all a big misunderstanding, that he'd taken the kid for a ride in the country and his mother had forgot they'd squared it ahead of time."

"Forgot," Jessie said. "Mothers don't *forget* things like that. And what, he walked into their house in the middle of the night and borrowed their kid without saying anything?"

"I know, it was flimsy. But we were putting in eighty-, ninety-, hundred-hour weeks on this thing. Following dead end after dead end. I studied the case files in my sleep, when I *could* sleep. Now, I saw him with my own two eyes: the kid was sleeping in his crib, safe and sound. Case *closed*. Yeah, it was weird, but I didn't have time to investigate weird, especially when the most powerful man in town was standing right there and telling me to let it drop."

"And that's your story?" I asked.

He looked like he was about to say yes. Then he stared down at his desk, eyes burning with shame.

"I wish it was," he whispered. "Goddamn me to hell, I wish it was."

"What did you do, Barry?"

He took a deep, shuddering breath.

"Very next morning, Jeremiah showed up here at the station. He wanted the police report, the original one about the abduction. Not a copy, he wanted to take the actual report and shred it. Said it was a misunderstanding, but 'yellow journalists and muckrakers' could take it and make the Kite family look bad. He wanted all traces of the original report *gone*. Now, your dad, he always did things by the book. He said the police report wasn't public information anyhow, and he wasn't about to mess with department records just to make the Kite family happy."

"It got into the papers, though," Jessie said.

He shook his head. "Just the *Eagle*, which didn't exactly have a big circulation. Even the locals preferred the *Tribune*. You gotta remember, this was before the Internet. Tuesday's newspaper was Wednesday's bird-cage liner and Thursday's compost."

"And down the memory hole it goes," I said, "except for the one archival copy that ended up at town hall. So what happened next?"

He looked up at me.

"You know what happened next," he said. "That was the night your daddy died."

A hand of ice squeezed my spine, so hard I thought my bones might snap.

"Barry. Are you telling me . . ."

"No. I mean, I don't know. I mean . . ." He squeezed his eyes shut, steadying himself. "The next morning, Jeremiah Kite came back. He took me aside and congratulated me on my 'imminent promotion.' Then he asked how my sister's son was. My sister's nine-month-old son, in Three Oaks."

"He threatened you?" I asked.

"Never in a way I could prove. It was just the questions he asked, and how he asked 'em. Like, wasn't I worried that the kidnapper might start snatchin' kids in a different town, like Three Oaks. And wasn't I worried, given what happened last night, that next time he might kill everybody in the house."

"Jesus," Jessie breathed.

"His words were murky," Barry said, "but the meaning behind 'em was clear as glass. And then he said, hey, as long as we were standing right by the filing-room door, why didn't I just pop my head in, grab that police report, and give it to him so he could get on with his day."

"So you gave it to him," I said.

"So I gave it to him," he replied. "Because I wasn't going to sacrifice my sister's life, and her family's lives, for your daddy's principles. Jeremiah Kite was mobbed up and everybody knew it. When the paper plant tried to unionize, he bussed in a pack of gun thugs from Detroit to bust it up the very next day. He could pick up the phone and send someone to my sister's house, and do . . . do whatever he damn well wanted. Because he had the money and the power in this town, and everybody knew it."

"Barry, you *knew*. You *knew* Kite was connected to the Bogeyman abductions!"

He jabbed his finger at me, stabbing the air. "It was *over*, Harmony! Week after this all happened, Jeremiah got sick. Ruptured appendix. They rushed him to the hospital, but he died on the operating table. And that's when the kidnappings ended. Case closed: Jeremiah Kite *was* the Bogeyman. Going public would have gotten me killed, or probably just sued into the gutter. In case you haven't noticed, the Kites still own this town. I didn't have enough hard evidence to expose him—didn't have *any* hard evidence, at all—and it wouldn't have brought those kids back anyhow. Besides, you can't lock a dead man in jail. What was I supposed to *do*?"

"So you closed the case. Covered it all up."

"No." He shook his head. "No. I *never* stopped looking for your sister and those other kids. Never for one day since have I stopped looking. But you see? That's why I was so sure Helen Gunderson took her own kid: I *knew* the Bogeyman was dead. Didn't occur to me that it might be a copycat."

We knew what he didn't. That the Bogeyman was a real, genuine monster, not just a scary nickname for a human predator. Jeremiah Kite must have been his summoner, back in the '80s. Maybe in the '40s, too, if he was old enough. Who did that make the Bogeyman's new master? His son Mitchum?

"So all these victims," I said, "all did something to cross the Kite family."

Barry rubbed the back of his neck, shaking his head slowly.

"Besides your dad? That's the damnedest thing. Unless it was some scheme I couldn't figure out, *none* of them had. I spent years trying to suss out a connection. Every one of those families either was friendly with the Kites, or never had much reason to cross their path. Whatever this was about, with the exception of your family, it wasn't revenge."

"What about now?" Jessie asked. "Helen Gunderson and the Morris family?"

"Nothin'. I asked, believe me. Why, you think one of Jeremiah's kids is the copycat?"

"You," I said, "are no longer a part of this investigation, Sheriff Hoyt. We'll take it from here."

"C'mon, Harmony—"

"You had information about my father's murder and my sister's abduction. You had a suspect. And you refused to investigate."

"I *couldn't* investigate, and the guy was six feet under! What should I have done, huh? What would you have done in my shoes?"

I took a deep breath, trying to fight down the anger. Beat it back with my fists, down into the pit of my stomach.

"Did it ever occur to you," I said, "that the reason those children were never found was because investigators were looking everywhere *but* Jeremiah Kite's house? For all you know, those kids—*my sister*—were in his goddamn basement."

"I couldn't get a warrant if I tried! The Kites owned every damn judge in three counties. Harmony, I didn't have any—"

His phone buzzed harshly. Barry gritted his teeth and hit the intercom button.

"Mabel, I'm a *little* busy right now."

"Sorry, Sheriff, but it's Mayor Kite on the line. He says it's absolutely urgent."

Jessie and I shared a look.

"Put it on speakerphone," I told him. "And if he asks, you're here alone."

TWENTY-THREE

Barry turned the phone on his desk, swiveling it closer to us, and turned up the volume on the speaker.

"Mayor Kite," he said, trying to sound casual but failing, "such a pleasure. What can I do you for?"

"Need your help, Barry, pronto. No time to explain. Get out to County Line Road, near the twelve-mile marker. There should be a busted-up car there with a couple of bodies inside. You've got to make it disappear."

Barry leaned forward in his chair. "How—excuse me, did you say *bodies*?"

"Yeah, and brace yourself, they're not gonna look pretty. They've got to go. Burn everything."

"Now, just hold on one second, Mr. Mayor," Barry snapped. "This isn't like letting your sister off on another DUI or pretending I don't know about your nephew's little pot farm out in the sticks. I don't clean up *bodies* for you. I'm a goddamn *sheriff*."

"You're a man with access to a tow truck, and the authority to get things done. Authority you keep only so long as I *allow* you to have it.

Don't fuck with me, Barry. Not now, not today. Besides, this is covering your ass, too."

"Really. How do you figure that?"

"Those bodies," Mitchum Kite said, "belong to a couple of feds who were sticking their noses where they didn't belong. You know what happens if they turn up dead? A lot more feds come to town. A *lot* more. Who knows who they'll end up arresting, or what evidence they might find?"

"Say it plain," Barry told him.

"I'm just thinking 'small-town sheriff runs empire of corruption' makes for a great headline. Somebody's leaving Talbot Cove in handcuffs, and it *won't* be *me*."

I grabbed a notepad and a ballpoint pen with a chewed-up cap from Barry's desk, scribbling a fast note:

Say you'll do it.

I held up the note, and Barry gave me a nervous thumbs-up. "All right, fine, twist my goddamn arm. I'll go take care of it."

I jotted down a second line and showed it to him:

But you want to meet.

"But, uh, we gotta talk," Barry said. "I mean, this doesn't sit right with me, none of it does. If I take care of this, I think you owe me an explanation."

Mitchum let out a heavy sigh. "Fine, fine, just take care of it. Tonight, six p.m. Come to the paper mill. Alone. I'll meet you there."

Barry squinted at the phone. "Couldn't you just come down to the station, or I could drive by the house?"

"No! It's . . . this is a very sensitive situation. I can't be seen with anyone right now. The paper mill. At six."

"All right." He nodded slowly. "That'll do, then. See you at six, Mr. Mayor."

Mitchum hung up. Barry blinked at the phone, then looked up at us.

"He's gonna kill me, isn't he?"

"No loose ends," Jessie said.

"Well, you two are pretty damn big ones!"

"He sent his"—I paused—"his hired guns, to murder us. Obviously, he doesn't know we got away."

Barry scratched his neck. "Well, won't they tell him? I mean, he's gotta be getting a phone call or something."

"We took care of it," Jessie said. "And we'll take care of this, too."

"Not without me," he said. "I'm not letting you girls walk into an ambush—"

"It's not an ambush if you know it's coming," I told him, "and we're not girls. We're federal agents."

I pushed my chair back. Jessie did the same. Barry just watched us leave, silent, until I was passing through his office door.

"Harmony."

I looked back at him.

"Swear to God," he said, "I did everything I could."

"I know. Now we're here to finish the job."

# # #

I got in the car, leaned back against the cold vinyl-wrapped headrest, and stared at the police station like it was a million miles away. If I closed my eyes, all I could see was my father's face.

Jessie's boots crinkled against bits of broken glass on the floor mat when she got in on the passenger side. "Hey."

"Hey," I said.

"You gonna be okay?"

I shrugged. "Have to be, right?"

"No obligation." She leaned back, too, mirroring my stare. "Sounds like Barry was stuck between a rock and a hard place. Still is."

"He's off the hook. Don't know if I can ever talk to him again, but he's off the hook." I shook my head. "You know what the worst part is?"

"What's that?"

"He's dead." I turned to look at her. "If I'm reading this right, Jeremiah Kite was behind the Bogeyman abductions in the '80s. He summoned it; he chose the targets. He sent it after *my family* because my father stood up to him. And then he dies of a fucking *burst appendix*? Where's the justice in that? He was never exposed, never punished, never spent a single day behind bars for what he did."

"It happens," Jessie told me. "This isn't the movies. Lot of times the bad guy gets away, or at least he doesn't get what he deserves. All we can do is try our best."

I slid the key into the ignition. The Crown Vic's engine fired up with a sickly rattle.

"I was hunting this perp in Vegas," I told her as I backed the car up. "Daniel Faust. Sorcerer, mobster, all-around nasty piece of work. Typical sociopath occultist. Dime a dozen, right?"

"I've put a few down myself," Jessie said.

I shifted the car into drive and steered out of the parking lot. Cold air billowed in through the broken window, stroking the side of my face with icy fingers.

"This was . . . different, though. Something about him just got under my skin. He was this force of raw chaos. Wherever he went, people died, things broke down, *systems* broke down. I realized, at the end, that's what he was to me. A symbol. My order against his chaos. Taking him down should have been proof that order is better. That our *way* is better. I built it up in my head as this epic showdown. Guns at high noon."

"And was it?"

I shook my head. "Not even close. In the end? He got handed to me on a silver platter, and I'm pretty damn sure it was a frame job. It was just . . . wrong."

"But you *did* take him down, right? One more psycho with magic powers off the street is a pretty good deal for everybody."

"That's what Linder says. I don't know. It just wasn't what I wanted."

Jessie smiled. "Since when does anybody in this life get what they want? You fight your hardest, you make sure you can look at yourself in the mirror every morning, and you take whatever scraps of happiness come your way. That's my philosophy, anyhow."

We drove for a while. I drummed my fingers on the steering wheel, trying to jam together two corner pieces of the same jigsaw puzzle and wondering why they wouldn't fit.

"It's not Mitchum Kite," I said.

"What isn't?"

"He's the most obvious suspect, right? Back in the '80s, his father was behind the Bogeyman case. He inherited Jeremiah's money, power, and even his political office—why not inherit his magic, too?"

"Sure," Jessie said, "it scans."

"But it doesn't. Fontaine's in town because of the new abductions. He made it sound like he's after whoever is controlling the Bogeyman. He also said Nyx is hunting the same target."

Jessie nodded slowly. "Mitchum is either controlling Nyx or controlling the Bogeyman. He can't be Nyx's boss *and* her target."

"Bingo. And I think we can agree, given the evidence, that he sent Nyx to kill us. So he's not our perp."

"I'm still kicking his ass," Jessie said.

"Well, that's a given. He's just not the end of our hit list. So at some point, the secret to conjuring the Bogeyman slipped away from the Kite family. You know what else is bugging me? Revenge. Or the lack thereof."

"Oh, what Barry said, about your dad being the only victim who crossed the Kites?"

"For starters," I said. "Jeremiah was a pretty bad guy, right? But Barry mentioned that he used mob ties to get things done, like sending thugs after those union organizers. Now, if you had control over an undetectable, unstoppable monster . . . wouldn't you use it *all the time*? Why risk going down with some loose-lipped mobster when you can cast a spell instead?"

"So payback isn't the motive. What does that leave us?"

We coasted down a long forest road, across a blanket of fallen autumn leaves.

"Nowhere," I said. "Leaves us nowhere. But I have a feeling Mitchum Kite will have some answers for us."

# # #

We had a few hours to kill, so we headed back to the Talbot Motor Lodge to bring April and Kevin up to speed.

"An incarnate," Kevin said. "An *actual freaking incarnate*, and you fought it. Badass."

Jessie sat cross-legged on one of the queen beds. "We didn't fight it so much as ran like hell, but I got a few shots in."

"Yeah," I said, pacing the room, "my eardrums have finally stopped ringing. Thanks for that. I think you pissed her off."

"I hope so. It's important to make a good first impression. And you'd better have some fine tricks up your sleeve, because Mitchum's not gonna be at the paper mill alone."

"I'm working on that."

I didn't want to say I wasn't up to the challenge . . . but as far as I knew, I just wasn't up to the challenge. I can hold my own in a duel against another magician, and I've cast out my fair share of demonic hijackers, but a monster from hell that can take two bullets to the face and keep on coming? I wasn't ashamed to feel outclassed. Who *wouldn't* feel outclassed against something like that?

Twice in my career, I'd faced an incarnate and lived to talk about it. That said, I'd survived by running away as fast as my wheels could take me.

This time, running wasn't an option.

The speakers of Kevin's laptop let out a faint ping. He swiveled in his chair, taking a look.

"Cool," he said. "One of my contacts is running a search on that Cold Spectrum thing Douglas Bredford mentioned. I'll let you know if he digs anything up."

"Complete waste of time," Jessie said. "Bredford's a sad, old drunk telling sad, old drunk stories. Stay focused on *this* case, okay?"

April sat at the table by the window. Both wicker balls were sitting side by side next to a stack of reference books and a paper cup of coffee. "I've been studying the summoning tokens. I am . . . uncomfortable with the implications."

"I hate it when you use that word," Jessie said. "Your feeling uncomfortable usually means we're about to be hip-deep in corpses."

"These glyphs carved into the wicker strips? They're Sumerian, circa the fourth millennium BCE. Mathematical symbols."

"Ancient math?" Jessie said. "You're about to make my head hurt, aren't you?"

Kevin grinned. "The Sumerians practically invented math. Well, them and the Egyptians. Instead of a base-ten system like ours, theirs was base *sixty*. They invented quadratic equations, too."

"Yep." Jessie grimaced and pinched the bridge of her nose. "I knew it. Pain. Incoming."

April ran one finger along the face of a ball, tracing the elaborately woven wicker strip. "The curves seem to correspond to the equation written upon them. It all feeds together. And the two balls do not match. They share commonalities, but the mathematics are starkly different, and the weave isn't the same, either."

"But they both tell the Bogeyman where to take his next victim," I said.

"Hence my uncomfortable theory. I've seen work like this before, generally connected to ancient necromancy. The idea of ferrying spirits to, and from, the lands of the dead."

"The Bogeyman's undead?" Jessie asked.

"No. No, it's not exactly the same. More to the point, this symbolism is tied to spells of *travel*. To the idea of forcibly sundering barriers between space and time. We've been going under the assumption that the Bogeyman makes its lair somewhere close to Talbot Cove, perhaps a cave or a clump of thick forest nearby."

I nodded. "That's right."

"We need to consider," April said, "that the Bogeyman's lair may not be on Earth at all."

Jessie whistled. "Because we needed more complications."

"It's geographical," I said, snapping my fingers. "The math is different because the places they were *put* is different. The balls aren't made to target the victims—they're made to target the *houses*. Like a landing beacon for an airplane."

"My thought exactly," April said. "It doesn't bring us any closer to finding their creator, but the knowledge could prove useful."

I checked my watch. "While we're out, can you two dig up anything you can find on Mitchum Kite's background? We need to get going."

"Got a few hours yet," Jessie said.

"We have to stop at the grocery store on the way, to pick up a few things. I've got an idea."

TWENTY-FOUR

They'd built the route to the paper mill wide, to accommodate logging trucks, but years of disuse had seen the forest slowly creep back to reclaim its own. We rumbled along the desolate road with nothing but the wind and distant birdsong to keep us company.

Then the birdsong stopped.

As we rounded a bend and hugged the shoreline, barely ten yards from a beach of dirty sand and jagged rock, the old mill rose up before us. The great waterwheel still stood on one side of the cavernous factory, chained fast against the currents and broken down under the powers of time and tide.

Given enough time, my mother once told me, as we sat cross-legged on the rocky shore behind her house, *a trickle of water can carve the Grand Canyon. Fire burns fast, and dies just as quickly. Given enough time, water always wins.*

The parking lot stood cracked and broken, the white lines faded to ghostly blotches of paint. I pulled the car up to the big double doors out front, stopping in front of a battered sign that read, **EMPL Y E OF TH MONTH**.

"Don't you want to hide the car?" Jessie asked.

"Nah. Let 'em know we're here."

"All right," she said, getting out and walking around to the trunk. She came back with a pair of bolt cutters. "Now we're having *fun*."

Thick chains wrapped around the door handles, right next to a bright-orange **Property Condemned by County Order** sticker, but the bolt cutters popped the padlock clamp like it was made of plastic. We unfurled the chains and let ourselves in.

Sunlight streamed down, stretching its fingers through broken skylights and spots here and there, where the ceiling had caved in. Pigeons roosted up in tangles of naked rebar, a good fifty feet above our heads, and their droppings spattered the waterlogged concrete floor. The dusty air smelled like dank mildew.

When the plant shut down, the Kites must have sold off everything for salvage and scrap. Empty bays with concrete frames lined the walls, with rusted pipes and disconnected fixtures jutting from the unpainted rock. A supervisor's office overlooked the factory floor from twenty feet up, but even the staircase to get there was gone; only a few bolt holes remained to show where it once stood.

"Well," Jessie said, "if we're ever in need of some creepy-ass waterfront property, I know where we can get a good deal."

At the far end of the building, a broad staircase next to a smooth loading ramp dipped down into darkness. Storage space, I figured. Someplace to keep the paper pallets dry and cool. All the same, I wasn't in a hurry to go down there. I walked back out to the car for the groceries I'd picked up. Nothing too extravagant, just a canister of sea salt and a few dried herbs from the cooking aisle, plus a plastic bag to mix it all together. That and four white pillar candles made from beeswax.

Jessie stood guard as I did my work. By the time I was done preparing for Mitchum's arrival, the sun was sinking fast and those fingers of light pushing though the tattered roof had turned crooked and gray. Night wasn't far away. We didn't have long to wait.

We heard Mitchum's BMW pull up outside. Then a long, long pause before the car door slammed. He was either deciding whether or not to risk coming inside, or calling for backup. Maybe both.

The double doors squealed as he pulled them open, striding into the factory twilight. Jessie and I stood side by side in the heart of the room, waiting for him in a ring of candles. They marked the cardinal points of a five-foot concentric circle, drawn with herbs and salt, anointed by my craft. We stood inside its bounds, the inner ring adorned with carefully laid glyphs drawn from memory.

"You shouldn't have come here," was all he had to say. He didn't look nervous.

"And you shouldn't have tried to kill us," Jessie said, pulling her Glock. "Wanna guess which decision was the worse one?"

"Oh," Mitchum said, "I'm thinking yours was."

He put his fingers to his lips and whistled. Nyx answered.

The demoness plunged through a hole in the roof, streaking down like a comet of blue fire. The factory floor shuddered when she slammed down, landing in a crouch, her cloven hooves driving half an inch into the concrete and scorching it black. She slowly rose to her full height—at least seven feet—and her tail whipped the air as she turned her molten-copper gaze upon us. Her chitin gleamed, covering her body like the armor of some hell-bound knight.

"There they are," Mitchum said, pointing at us. "Kill them! What are you waiting for?"

"Khlegota aham-ahaz t'nala," she hissed. The words sounded like they came from two tongues at once, squirming wetly against each other, and a wave of nausea washed over me.

"I don't understand," Mitchum said. "Speak English, damn it."

Nyx spun and grabbed the collar of Mitchum's shirt, hauling him close. When she spoke next, her words came out in sonorous, perfect English, dripping with ice and hatred.

"Watch your mouth."

She shoved him, sending him sprawling to the floor. While he sputtered and grabbed at his shirt—the fabric singed and torn by her claws—Nyx strode toward us.

Jessie shot a nervous glance at the circle of salt. "You're good at this, right? Because now is not the time to find out you flunked out of witch school. And if the plan was for me to wrestle that thing, I'd have appreciated a heads-up."

"Relax," I murmured. I stood at the circle's edge. Nyx walked around the outer ring, sniffing the air, probing, testing, then came face-to-face with me.

I stood my ground.

She lashed out her fist, fast as a rattlesnake's bite, straight for my face. The air rippled with a sound like thunder, and her claws bounced off the invisible barrier between us.

I didn't flinch. She let out what might have been a faint, raspy chuckle.

"Trapped yourself," she said. "Can't come in. You can't come out."

"Nope," I said. "He's the one who's trapped."

Behind Nyx, Mitchum pushed himself to his feet and straightened his shirt, trying to regain his lost dignity.

"How am *I* trapped?" he asked, wearing an ugly smirk.

Jessie leveled her pistol at him. "Because my partner here? She can banish Tall, Dark, and Spooky from *inside* this little circle."

"That's right," I said to Nyx. "You can leave the factory, or I can blast you straight back to hell. Your call, but you *are* leaving."

"Which leaves you alone with us," Jessie said, keeping Mitchum in her sights, "and unless you can outrun a bullet, you'll never reach the door before I take you down. Better start talking."

"You—you can't shoot me in the back," Mitchum said, "and I'm unarmed!"

"You can't imagine how little I care," Jessie said.

I shrugged. "She really doesn't. And I'm not inclined to stop her tonight."

"Do you know who this one is?" Nyx asked me. It took me a second to realize what she was asking. She seemed to have a weird aversion to the word *I*.

"Sure. We had a chat with Fontaine. I understand you're both after the same thing. So are we."

Nyx held up a single claw. She reached out and dragged it along the barrier between us, slow and sinuous, as if tracing the flesh of my cheek. Tiny sparks of errant magic erupted in her talon's wake and screeched like nails on a blackboard, turning amber and black as they drifted to the floor and faded.

"Why do you refuse your gift?" she asked.

"What gift?"

Nyx nodded toward Jessie. "She understands the blessing of wrath. Embraces it. She spread her legs for the King of Wolves and drank his filth."

In the corner of my eye, I saw Jessie's mouth twitch. The gun wavered in her hand.

"Go fuck yourself," she snapped. "You don't know anything about me."

Nyx laughed. It sounded like barbed wire rasping across a sheet of sandpaper.

"Was complimenting you, pup. You have been blessed by the power of this one's choir." She turned her copper eyes back toward me. "But you? This one can taste your pain. A trail of sorrow and regret at your back like an oil slick. Could be your greatest weapon, but you fear losing control."

"Seriously," Jessie said. "Enough with the fortune-cookie bullshit. Harmony, you wanna get this banishment under way already?"

"You could forge your pain into a sword," Nyx said, "and persecute your enemies. Triumph. Survive. But fear imprisons you. Fear of breaking *rules*. Fear of what people will *think* of you. Petty little fears."

Nyx inched closer to the circle's edge. The air blurred as she pressed her face to the magic barrier, inches from mine. When she spoke again, it was in a pitch-perfect parody of my own voice.

"This one feels . . . so sorry for you," she said.

I thought back to what Fontaine had told us. "I'm not the only one who believes in rules. That's the whole point of the Chainmen, right? You enforce hell's laws."

"It is so. We hold the line against chaos."

"Well," I said, "so do we. There are two missing children out there, somewhere, and we're going to bring them home to their families. That's *our* job. Nobody is going to stop us. Not Fontaine, not Mitchum, and not you."

"Why are you even *talking* to them?" Mitchum demanded. "*Do* something."

I glanced between Nyx and Mitchum. "Now, we intend to interrogate this man, because he has information we need. You can leave willingly, or I can cast you out. I think one choice is a lot less painful than the other, but I'll let you decide. Call it professional courtesy."

Mitchum fumed, pacing. "This is ridiculous. I don't know what we even hired you for. Just kill these two bitches, and let's *go* already."

Nyx held up one claw, giving me an oddly apologetic look. "Moment, please."

She turned, took two quick strides toward Mitchum, and ripped his throat out.

It all happened in a blur: just a whip-fast flash of her claws and then the mayor fell, clutching his throat, rivulets of blood flowing between his fingers like a river gushing through a broken dam. He looked as shocked as I felt. He twitched on the floor, flopping like a fish on dry land while he painted the concrete crimson.

Nyx turned without missing a beat, casually strolling back to the circle's edge. "You were saying?"

I wasn't saying anything. I just watched as the mayor gave one last wheezing rattle and died, his wide eyes fixed on the broken skylights.

"You didn't . . ." Jessie said haltingly. "You didn't have to *do* that."

Nyx shrugged. "You were right. It was a good trap. You could make this one leave, and he would have broken under questioning. Only solution: remove him. Also, he was insolent. Was already thinking about killing him anyway."

"You're that desperate to keep us from finding the Bogeyman's master?" I said.

"To keep you from getting there *first*. This one was trained well, in the House of Dead Roses: the prize for first place is a bounty. The prize for second place is suffering and shame. Besides, it is in your best interests to step aside."

"Yeah?" I said. "Why's that?"

"Because you cannot punish him like this one can."

"I can't argue that, but it isn't the point. This isn't about punishment. It's about justice, and saving those kids."

Nyx studied her bloody nails, like they were more interesting than anything I had to say.

"I'm sorry," I said. "Am I boring you?"

"Just thinking, almost want you to find him. Want to see the look on your face when you realize . . . hmm. Funny. Maybe you'd let the anger out, then. A chance for enlightenment. Ready to answer your question now."

"My question?"

Nyx turned her back on us, her tail snapping at my face.

"This one leaves under her own power," she said as she walked away. "No banishment necessary."

TWENTY-FIVE

"So," Jessie breathed, "that just happened."

Nyx was long gone. So was the sun, plunging the gloomy mill into darkness. We stood in the light of the four pillar candles, still protected by the circle of herbs and salt. In the shadows, Mitchum Kite's corpse was a mangled lump on the concrete floor, slowly cooling.

"She killed him," I said. "She actually killed the man who hired her just to keep us from talking to him. You'd think there'd be a rule against that."

Jessie holstered her pistol. She touched my sleeve.

"Wait a second. *Did* she? Remember what he said before she took him out: I don't know what *we* hired you for. Mitchum might have been in on the deal, but she made it pretty clear she didn't answer to him."

"Somebody else hired her," I said. "Somebody knows the answers we're looking for. Somebody connected to Mitchum Kite. And unless Nyx feels like volunteering the information, they *don't* know that Mitchum is dead."

"Unless we call it in," Jessie said, eyeing the corpse.

It wasn't even a debate. It should have been, but I ran the numbers in my head, and the math wasn't hard. Mitchum's next of kin, whoever they were, would wait to get the bad news. Keeping his murder under wraps could give us an edge, and we needed every edge we could get.

I hated this. All my training, all my experience, screamed that leaving a murder victim to rot in an abandoned factory was as far from good police work as I could get. *Still,* I thought, *it's not like anybody in this world can bring his killer to justice. Anybody besides us.*

"We're not calling it in," I said.

Special circumstances.

"So," Jessie said, "what now?"

"Now's the hard part." I looked down at the circle of salt. "How bad do you think Nyx wanted to kill us?"

"Not sure. Felt like she was laughing at us more than anything. Why?"

I pointed at the barrier.

"Because," I said, "to leave, we have to step outside the circle. Which means, if she doubled back and she's hiding somewhere in the dark . . ."

"Hmm. Yeah. May have been a tiny flaw in your brilliant plan."

"Well, I *thought* I was going to end up banishing her."

No point wasting time. Either she was lurking or she wasn't. I took a deep breath, pushed my shoulders back, and stepped over the line of salt.

Nothing. Nothing but a cool night breeze whistling through the broken skylights.

"I'm not going to say it," Jessie told me.

I stepped all the way outside the circle. Jessie joined me, hesitant.

"Say what?"

"I've seen enough horror movies to know how this goes down," she said. "If I say, 'I think she's gone,' that's gonna be her cue to jump out of nowhere and eat our faces. So don't say that."

"You . . . just did."

"Oh." Jessie shrugged. "I think she's gone, then."

I'll admit it, I flinched.

We didn't discover Nyx's parting gift until we stepped outside. She'd shredded all four of the Crown Vic's tires, nothing left but scraps of torn rubber clinging to bent rims. The mayor's BMW got the same treatment.

"Technically," Jessie said, "she did us a favor."

I couldn't argue that. We called April and Kevin, told them to rent a car and meet us at the mill. First they had to call a taxi, then they had to take the cab to the only rental place that was still open, at a small airport fifteen miles away.

We waited, in the middle of nowhere.

Jessie walked the lot, doing stretching exercises, kicking the occasional stray rock. Some people are good at sitting still and doing nothing. Jessie wasn't one of them.

"You all right?" I asked as she walked by me on her fifth lap of the lot.

"Huh? Yeah, sure, why?"

"What Nyx said back there, about your 'gift.'" I jerked my thumb toward the mill's front doors. "Sounded like she hit a sore spot."

Jessie's lip curled. "Nobody talks shit like demons. All that creepy woo-woo 'I glimpse the shadows of your soul and call to your darkness' garbage. Seriously, you ever read the lyrics to a Dio album? Exact same stuff, but at least Dio put some good guitar licks behind it."

She stopped a few feet away, her back turned to me. She picked up a rock, weighed it in her hand, and gave it a throw. It skipped across the parking lot and out of sight.

"What my dad did, that's got nothing to do with who I am inside." Her voice went a little lower, a little harder. "And I don't spread my legs for the king of anything. Best *believe* that."

Headlights flashed in the distance, glowing against a copse of trees.

"Either the mobile cavalry is here," Jessie said, suddenly flippant again, "or Nyx stole a car and she's coming back to eat our faces."

Fortunately, it was the first option. Kevin and April drove up in a chocolate-colored Hyundai SUV with an Avis bumper sticker. Kevin rolled down the driver's-side window.

"Need a lift?"

We climbed into the backseat. Jessie reached up and rubbed Kevin's shoulder.

"My hero. I could kiss you, if I was desperate and blind drunk."

"Love you, too, boss," he said. "Get anything out of the mayor?"

"Unfortunately," Jessie said, "he caught a terminal case of death. Nyx wanted to shut him up."

"What do we know about Mitchum Kite?" I asked. "Spouse? Kids? He wasn't the only person who hired Nyx. Her other backer, or backers, has to be somebody close to him."

"Practically a hermit," April said. "No children, never been married. Four brothers, two sisters, most of whom have moved away from Talbot Cove."

"No relationships and no real friends outside his coworkers," Kevin added. "And I get the impression even they don't—I mean, didn't—like the guy very much."

I buckled my seat belt as Kevin swung the SUV around in the parking lot.

"Good," Jessie said. "Then since nobody knows he's dead, nobody's going to be watching his house."

# # #

Special circumstances, I thought, standing in the driveway of Mitchum Kite's house. *These lines just keep getting easier to cross.*

"Tell me you're not going to ask for a warrant," Jessie said, standing beside me. We'd left Kevin and April back at the motel and taken the SUV.

"There is nothing in the world we could say to a judge to justify a search warrant," I said, "besides the truth, and that's the one thing we can't reveal."

"Now you're getting it."

"Doesn't mean I have to like it," I said.

Jessie handed me a pair of disposable latex gloves, then slipped on a pair of her own.

"Nope, sure doesn't," she said. "Now let's break into a dead guy's house."

The Kite family home was a two-story colonial with a gabled rooftop and a pristine, manicured lawn. It lorded over a cul-de-sac in the nice part of town, where the sidewalks were lit with modern "old-timey" street lamps and everybody was tucked in bed by ten.

"Yep, it's the original family home," Kevin said over the phone. I could hear his fingers rattling like a hailstorm against his keyboard. "I cracked into the municipality database, gonna see if they've got the original blueprints on file. Their password, for the record, was 'password.' I can't even feel proud of myself."

We circled the house, keeping low, our footsteps muffled by the drone of crickets.

"Okay," Kevin said, "want some weird? Here's some weird. We've got only partial blueprints, scanned in from the originals. I'm showing first-floor access to a pretty good-size cellar. The cellar itself? Not shown. Probably wanna check that out."

"The cellar," I said. "Great. Because nothing bad ever happens in the cellars of creepy old houses."

A brick patio with a barbecue grill stood in the backyard. Given how spotless the grill was, I figured it had never been used. Jessie crept up to a window and clicked on a penlight, casting a narrow, shimmering beam through the empty house. She carefully checked along the windowsill, then the back door a few feet away.

"Caught a break," she said. "No alarm system. Gotta love small towns."

"Doesn't get us inside."

"Oh, ye of little faith." She handed me the penlight. "Here, hold this steady and watch as I make my own kind of magic."

She crouched at the door and pulled a small black plastic case from her jacket pocket. The clamshell opened to reveal a row of stainless-steel picks.

"It beats using a battering ram," she said, picking out a thin, bent rake and a stout probe, going to work on the lock. "More importantly, we do this right, nobody will know we were ever here. Don't need to leave *more* unsolvable crimes to clutter up Sheriff Barry's case files."

At that moment, I didn't much care about Barry or his files, but she had a point. The more silently we operated, the less of a mess we'd leave for the civilians to clean up after we finally left town. As it was, the mayor's death would go down as a permanently unsolved mystery.

The tumblers clicked and rolled over for Jessie like a well-trained dog. We let ourselves in.

Jessie cupped her hands to her mouth and called out, "Hello? Sheriff's office. Identify yourself."

The house sat silent and still. Jessie looked back at me and shrugged. "Better safe than sorry."

We turned on a few lights, just enough to work by; it wasn't like anyone was going to come home and catch us. The late Mayor Kite had a flair for the spartan, furnishing his rooms with the bare minimum to get by and doing most of his shopping at antique stores: a Victorian end table here, an art deco lamp with a stained-glass hood there. Old, expensive-looking dinnerware stocked his kitchen cupboards, but the trash was heavy with fast-food takeout bags and paper plates and cups, like Mitchum had been afraid to use any of it.

I felt a lingering unease, growing as we poked around in the dead man's house. I wanted to chalk it up to the fact that we were committing a burglary, but that wasn't the reason. There was something unhealthy about the Kite home.

No, I thought, *that's just it. It's a house, but it isn't a home. It feels like a museum, a set piece, a stage for a play.*

We drifted through a living room with a spotless plush sofa and a single end table with a lamp, positioned to face an empty, blank wall.

"Nobody *lives* here," Jessie murmured, echoing my thoughts. "It's like a Charles Dickens orphanage collided with a furniture-store showroom."

Homes mold themselves around the rhythm of their owners' lives. Sloppiness and clutter happens, dust settles in hard-to-reach places. People leave things out on tables, intending to put them away later and never quite getting around to it. Not here. The Kite house could have passed a white-glove test from top to bottom, spotless and cold as a mortician's slab.

Un-lived in, I thought.

Unloved.

"Okay," Jessie said, standing in the threshold of Mitchum Kite's bedroom. "Now, *that* is creepy."

Stark white sheets and a single thin pillow lay upon the mayor's antique four-poster bed. On the opposite wall, centered perfectly, hung the first piece of artwork we'd seen in the entire house: an oil painting of a tall, balding man, staring down in furious condemnation.

Jeremiah Kite, read the brass nameplate at the bottom of the frame. **Our Patriarch.**

"This guy didn't just have issues," Jessie murmured. "He had multiple *subscriptions.*"

What drew my eye was the closet door. Well, not the door itself, but the little addition, bolted onto the frame with newer hardware than anything else in the house.

"Jessie," I said, "why is there a dead bolt on his closet door?"

TWENTY-SIX

Jessie squinted at the dead bolt keeping Mitchum Kite's closet securely shut.

"Clearly," he said, "he didn't want anything getting out. I can think of one good candidate. How about you?"

"Cover me," I said.

She pulled her piece and held it steady, standing a few steps back. I took hold of the dead bolt. A frosty chill clung to the brass, too cold to be natural. The bolt slid free with a low, slithering rasp. I took a deep breath and braced myself.

Ancient hinges groaned as the closet door swung open. No monsters lurked inside, just cedar walls and a dangling string attached to a single bare bulb.

I tugged the string. The little closet flooded with light.

Pictures covered the walls. Pictures in crayon, stick figures and stick houses, scribbled in a child's confused hand. A couple of broken crayons sat on the cold floor, next to a metal bucket. Scrawled words ran down the right-hand wall.

i'm sorry
i'm sorry

i'm sorry
i'm sorry

Jessie whipped out her phone, her eyes as hard as her voice the second Kevin picked up.

"Check your intel," she snapped. "You're *positive* Mitchum didn't have any kids? Yeah. Yeah, because there sure as hell *was* one here. Kevin, I—*listen*. I don't care, *triple*-check and call me back."

The psychic miasma that clung to the Kite house was almost overpowering here, bordering on a physical odor that twisted my stomach into knots. Hopelessness. Dread.

"This house," I said. "It's been passed down through the family, right?"

"That's what April says. Started with . . . Edwin, Edwin Kite, the paper mill's founder, back in the 1800s. Why?"

"So Mitchum inherited it when Jeremiah died. And he would have grown up in this house."

"That's right," Jessie said.

I looked to her, to the portrait on the wall, to the closet and back again.

"I think this might have been *Mitchum's* closet."

"Jesus," Jessie said. "Okay, let's . . . let's keep searching."

The last door we checked, on the first floor, offered another mystery. More extra hardware on the frame, but instead of a dead bolt, a pair of heavy-duty padlocks sealed it shut.

"And this must be the cellar door. Want me to get the bolt cutters from the SUV?" Jessie asked.

I stood in front of the door and held out my open hand, waving it slowly forward and back. The air, right in that spot, was at least ten degrees colder than the rest of the house.

"Hold off," I said, slowly backing away. "Let's check the rest of the house first. Whatever's on the other side, it isn't going anywhere."

A couple of rooms on the second floor might have been bedrooms once, but they'd been stripped of furniture. Nothing remained but bare floorboards and lace curtains. And closets.

Every closet in the house had a dead bolt.

We checked those, too, but they were just as barren as the bedrooms. Not even a speck of dust on the sanded cedar boards.

Mitchum had sent a demon to murder us—twice—but the more we saw, the more I wished we'd been able to take him alive. I couldn't get a grasp on this place, or the kind of man who would live here. Who was Mitchum Kite, really?

And what had been *done* to him?

He kept his private office at the end of the hall. It was the only room in the entire house that felt lived-in, and that wasn't saying much. He had a desk, a frayed olive oval rug, a stiff-backed wooden chair, and a cheap coffeemaker next to a stack of disposable Styrofoam cups. No pictures sat on his desk, no personal mementos, just the closed shell of a laptop computer.

"Now we're talking," Jessie said, sitting down in his chair and opening up the laptop. I stood at her shoulder, waiting as it chittered and hummed to life.

"Great," Jessie sighed. "Password protected. Okay, let's bring this back to the motel and see if Kevin can crack it."

I rubbed my thumb against my chin, thinking.

"Try 'Jeremiah.'"

Jessie rattled off the password. A red *X* popped up. *Username or password is incorrect.*

"How about 'father'?"

She tried again. Another red *X*.

Jessie turned in the chair, looking back over her shoulder at me. "Any other ideas?"

"Just one," I said. "'Closet.'"

Welcome, read the log-in screen.

We peered into the digital version of Mitchum Kite's house. No media, no games, hardly any utilities, his hard drive stripped down to its absolute bare essentials.

"E-mail," I said, leaning in over Jessie's shoulder and pointing to one of the only icons on the desktop. "Let's see who he's been talking to."

As it turned out, quite a few people. Mitchum did his mayoral business on this account, and his box was flooded with the day-to-day minutiae of running a small town. Meetings, bulletins and memos, interoffice requests, hundreds of bits and pieces, and none of it unusual.

One piece of mail stood out. Jessie spotted it at the same time and double-clicked to bring it up on the screen. It was part of a series of exchanges between Mitchum and someone calling himself CTide06. CTide's first message was an eye-opener.

> You've done enough. Your entire adult life, you've stood sentinel for the family, living in that damned house. Keeping that THING from escaping.
> I won't let you pay Nyx's price. It would be monstrous, after you've already lost so much.

Mitchum's response came fast on the first e-mail's heels:

> That's the point. I don't have a life. He took it from me. You have a family, people who love you. I'll pay so you don't have to.

"What does she charge for a hunt, anyway?" Jessie mused. "I mean, do demons need cash?"

"I'm focused a little more on the 'thing' part, in all caps." My thoughts drifted to that downstairs doorway. The one with the double padlocks.

> We're all in this together, Mitchum. We all agreed. The evil ends with us. We ALL have to pay our fair share, not just you. It's worth it, if it stops that bastard once and for all.

Mitchum's next e-mail was only six words long, and it chilled me to the bone.

> I am quite ready to die.

CTide06 hadn't responded to that yet. Mitchum had sent it just a few hours ago, before leaving to meet us at the paper mill.

"Got his wish," Jessie said. She looked back at me. "You know we've searched every part of this house except for one door, right?"

My shoulders slumped. "Let's get the bolt cutters."

Just as Jessie was about to close the laptop lid, though, the screen blinked. New incoming mail, from CTide06.

> It took her. Just found her crib empty. She's going to be the next Returned. THIS HAS TO STOP.

"We'll take this with us," Jessie said, powering down the laptop. "Kevin might be able to trace the e-mails, find out where they're sent from. Of course, if we get a call in an hour from Sheriff Barry, telling us about another abduction report, we'll know exactly who CTide is."

I shook my head. "We won't. 'The next Returned'? It's the '80s all over again. One child from the Kite family goes missing, and they don't want anyone knowing about it. They must know the Bogeyman's going to bring their kid right back."

"If that's so," Jessie said as she stood up, tucking the laptop under one arm, "why aren't they *happy* about it?"

We went out to the SUV and traded the laptop for the bolt cutters. It felt good, getting a few breaths of fresh air, leaving the oppressive gloom of the Kite house and standing under a canopy of stars.

The respite ended all too soon. We went back inside to face the final door.

Jessie braced one boot against the door frame, leveraging herself as she squeezed the cutters around the thick padlock arm. She grunted, straining, while the metal buckled and finally surrendered with a hollow *crack*. Thirty seconds later she'd gotten through the second one. She plucked the useless locks from their hinges, one after the other, and tossed them to the floor.

"Of course," she said. The door swung open, revealing a rickety wooden stairway descending into darkness. "Of *course* it's the basement."

Her penlight guided us down, catching motes of dust in the humid, dank air. Whatever horrors I was expecting, an empty cellar wasn't it. Mostly unfinished, the walls were crude stone coated in eggshell-white paint. Bare gray foundation concrete under our feet—no windows, no lights, no electrical outlets. We stood in a box. A cold and lonely box.

A smell hung in the air, mildew and something else. A faint, odd spice, a little like sandalwood incense, almost too subtle to notice.

Jessie swung her light in slow circles around the room. It settled on the one piece of furniture: an old wooden shelving unit, about six feet high and almost as wide, laden with a clutter of junk. Ancient, crusted paint cans, rusty tools, a stack of newspapers so old they were petrified, nothing worth hanging on to.

"How long do you think it's been since anyone's been down here?" Jessie asked me.

"Years," my voice answered back.

But I hadn't said a word.

I slowly looked to my left. Another me stood there, grinning, with empty eye sockets and obsidian teeth.

Earth, air, water, I thought, beckoning my power, then I froze. *What was next? Four elements. Wasn't there? Maybe it was just three.* The smell of incense welled up, rising over the mildew, overpowering me when I tried to breathe.

"You'll never get this right," I heard my mother say. Sunlight flooded the cellar.

No, not the cellar. Not anymore.

We were in her kitchen, in the old house in Talbot Cove, and I was six years old. I stood on a stepstool beside her, craning my neck to see over the counter as she chopped herbs for a magical poultice.

"Honey." She crouched down and held my shoulder. "It's not your fault. Sometimes the gift skips a generation, or it only goes to a single child. Your blood just isn't strong enough."

"But," I stammered, tongue slipping over a missing baby tooth, "I *am* a witch. It's what I do, it's . . . it's the only thing I'm good at. It's why people like me."

My mother smiled sadly and shook her head.

"Oh, sweetie, no. You're worthless. Why do you think we had a second child? Because we knew you weren't going to amount to anything."

"You're not even my kid," my father said, alive and smiling as he strolled into the kitchen. He opened the refrigerator, leaned in, and pulled out a bottle of beer. "You know that, right?"

My mother squeezed my shoulder in a parody of affection. Her adult fingers clamped down hard enough to make my eyes water.

"It's true. You were the product of, well, let's call it a one-night stand."

"I wasn't mad," my father said. "I just wanted a *real* daughter. Figured we should tell you the truth because, let's face it, kid: you're not exactly bright, are you? Not like you'd figure it out on your own."

My mother clucked her tongue and let go of me, reaching for the kitchen counter.

"Now, Harry, be nice. Oh, well. I suppose we should make the most of what we have. One real, healthy daughter." She picked up her butcher's knife, turning toward me with a hungry smile. "So I suppose we don't need this one anymore."

TWENTY-SEVEN

I ran. I ran as fast as my stubby legs could take me, out of the kitchen and down the hall. I heard my parents laughing behind my back.

The sunlight vanished. Night, now, and the hall went on for a thousand miles with darkness ahead of me and darkness behind. I ran past a hundred identical night-lights as the thick shag carpet grabbed at my bare feet and slowed me down.

The door to my sister's room was up on the left. It hung open a crack, just a crack. I peered inside.

Something squatted in Angie's crib. Something black and leathery and toadlike, something that rasped and wheezed as it strained to breathe.

"You hated me," came the creature's wet, sickly voice.

"No," I said, backing away. "That's not true."

"You *hated* me. You knew your parents didn't love you. You knew they wanted a better daughter, so they had me. To replace you."

"I was six years old!" I screamed.

"It should have been you. The Bogeyman should have taken you instead of me. And you know it. You've always known it."

My father bellowed, "It should have been *you*!"

I turned to see him coming, running in slow motion down the endless hallway. His throat torn open, just like the night he died. His eyes were pits of black rage.

In his muscular hands, he gripped a fire ax.

"It should have been you that died, not her. Not our *real* daughter!"

It should have been me, I thought.

Just like I had thought those words a thousand times before.

Tears stung my eyes as I turned and ran. All I could do was run, sprinting down the endless hall just ahead of my father's ax blade.

Why am I running? I thought. *I deserve this. I've had this coming for thirty years.*

A woman's distant scream jarred my thoughts. Not my mother, no, someone familiar. I struggled to remember, but my brain was as fogged as the hallway air, slowing time to the pace of a slow-dripping tap.

Someone needs help.

My senses perked. I was stronger, faster, *older*. Adrenaline kicked my nerves into motion. Someone out there was in pain and needed a rescue. That took priority over anything else.

Door up on the right. My old bedroom. Closed tight. I didn't hesitate, just threw my shoulder into it and stumbled through as it burst open.

A rippling curtain of water sheared my bedroom in half, with a vague, gauzy void on the other side. I heard my dead father's howls of rage, coming closer by the second. If I laid eyes on him, I'd be six again and helpless. I knew this in my heart. It was a brief, blinding flash—a moment of perfect clarity as I stood on the edge of my mind prison.

Images drifted by on the far side of the water curtain. Endless primeval forests. A bloodied hacksaw, bloodied limbs. A shabby bed in a trailer home, arms and legs tangled together and the bed rocking with brutal, loveless thrusts. None of it frightened me. This wasn't my hell, it was—

Jessie. This thing, whatever infested the Kites' basement, it latched onto our minds and twisted our nightmares. Feeding on us while we suffered. Eating our hearts.

"But there's nothing scary about somebody *else's* nightmare," I said out loud. "Jessie!"

I felt her. She heard me. Her mind turned my way.

I took a step back as my father's footsteps raced up the hall, only a few feet from the bedroom door.

"I'm coming in!" I shouted. "Reach for me!"

I ran for the edge of the nightmare, and jumped.

# # #

I floated, adrift.

Inky, fluid space surrounded me, a bubble displaced in time. A blank margin in the pages of the universe.

Jessie floated toward me. Our legs curled in zero gravity, hair flowing free. We reached for each other at the exact same moment. One chance to connect.

We grabbed each other's wrists. I pulled her close.

"If you'll fight my demons, I'll fight yours," I whispered. "Okay?"

"Okay," she whispered back. Her blue eyes flashed.

I pulled with all my might and then let go, sending us sailing in opposite directions, straight toward each other's dooms.

# # #

I landed in a crouch, wet peat under my fingers and toes. The scent of cedar pines filled the air, that and the song of night birds.

I rose up, standing in a forest clearing. I smelled the creature before I saw it. Its miasma washed over me, the stench of stale sweat and musty sheets and morning-after regret. Then came the other smells, the ones

I'd learned by heart from visiting a hundred crime scenes: rotting flesh and the coppery tang of human blood.

The shambling figure could have been an ancient Viking, with his shaggy mane and braided gray beard, naked save for the black furry pelt that he wore as a cloak. His skin was mottled, though, rotting, and the thorny nightmare dangling between his legs didn't belong to any *human* male.

He saw me and paused. He studied me with eyes that glowed turquoise, bright as bonfires.

"What?" I asked. "Not who you were expecting?"

His voice sounded like chicken bones in a garbage disposal, and a thick rivulet of drool ran from the corner of his mouth as he replied.

"I am the King of Wolves," he rasped. "You will feed me."

A fleeting memory rose up in the back of my mind. What Barry told me on the night my father died.

This badge means it's my job to find bad people, and make them go away so they can't hurt anybody else. And that's exactly what I'm going to do.

I reached into my breast pocket, took out my badge, and held it high. It caught the moonlight and gleamed like liquid mercury.

"You're nothing but a child's nightmare," I told him. "Just another monster. Do you know who I am?"

"Meat for my table," he grunted, shambling toward me. "Warm, screaming meat."

The night wind kissed my skin. The forest bed washed my bare feet in fertile loam, lending its strength. My badge grew hot in my hand. A purifying heat.

"Wrong," I said.

Earth, air, water, fire, be my weapons, be my strength.

"I'm the woman who makes the monsters go away."

The badge erupted with blinding light, turning midnight into high noon. As the monster staggered back, throwing up an arm to shield his eyes, I slowly twirled my other hand. I guided the flow of power, hastened it, stirring the light into white-hot streamers that floated in circles around the forest clearing. Treetops ignited in the streamers' wake, exploding with peals of thunder, and showered the world in orange-and-gold sparks.

The streamers of light circled all around us, faster and faster, leaving an inferno in their wake. Then I raised my hand and pointed at the King of Wolves. The lights blazed toward him like a school of piranhas on a bleeding calf.

They all converged on him at once, and the entire world erupted in flames.

I wasn't afraid. The fire was my friend.

TWENTY-EIGHT

Sudden, jarring darkness. My head rested on a pillow of cold stone. I jerked upright, eyes slowly adjusting to the cellar dark, then doubled over as my muscles clenched and the cramps set in. It felt like a snake made of fire, squirming in my guts.

"What . . . what just happened here?" Jessie murmured, coming to on the floor beside me. "Hey, are you okay?"

I bobbed my head, keeping my eyes squeezed shut and focusing on my breathing.

"We call it the family curse," I said, my voice tight and breathless. "I use my body as a conduit for the magic. More power I draw, the more I pay for it afterward. Just . . . just pulled a *lot* of power. It'll pass."

Her hand closed on my shoulder, rubbing in slow circles. Her eyes glowed faintly in the gloom, darting from side to side, checking every corner of the room. She'd pulled back her jacket, her free hand resting on the grip of her pistol.

"What the hell *was* that? And is there any chance it's coming back for another shot at us?"

"It's gone," I said. "I'd say it's dead, but it was never really alive in the first place, not in a way we'd understand. Psychic parasite, sort of a brain-eating guard dog. I've read about them. Never seen one in the flesh, though. The amount of power it takes to conjure one of those things up . . . we're not talking bush league here."

Jessie pushed herself up and clicked on her penlight.

"Well, now we know what Mitchum was keeping watch over."

I laughed. Just a little. It hurt.

"Joke's on him. These things stay where they're put. He could have left the basement door unlocked and wide open. It never would have tried to leave. Real question is, why was it here?"

Jessie turned in a slow circle, strobing the penlight off the stone walls. "You mean, why did someone set an occult guard dog to watch over a totally empty basement?"

"Exactly."

"I've got a theory on that," she said. "Stand back. I'm about to do some science."

She walked over to the shelving unit and began clearing the shelves. Carefully at first, picking up the old, rusted junk and setting it off to one side, but then impatience got the better of her and she just started sweeping the clutter to the floor. She leaned in, rapping her knuckles against the backs of the shelves. They sounded solid.

The cramps ebbed away, leaving me with a vague, dull ache in my abdomen. I got up and stumbled over to join her. Jessie ran the beam from her penlight up and down one side of the shelves, then the other, studying where they met the wall.

"Ha," she said. "Hinges. Give me a hand."

We took hold of the far end of the shelf and pulled. The old, heavy wood groaned as we dragged it back, scraping along the concrete. I stepped back and dusted my hands off, looking at what we'd uncovered: a door, set flush into the wall. Instead of a doorknob, it sported a flat brass disk with five shallow finger holes to grip and turn.

I reached for the disk, but Jessie held her arm out, blocking me. "Whoa. Hold up a second."

She crouched down, squinting as she shone her light into the holes, one at a time.

"There's a needle at the back of the pinkie hole," she said. "Probably smeared with something nasty. A little fatal poison, you know, just in case somebody got past the invisible nightmare monster."

"There's a dividing line between security conscious and full-blown paranoid. Whatever's hidden behind this door, the owner wanted to *keep* it hidden."

"Yeah, well," Jessie said, slipping her fingers into the holes—keeping her little finger clear—and giving it a turn, "let's just hope it's not *another* monster."

The door yawned inward. I tasted stagnant air, the odor of rot curdling in the back of my nose. Nobody had been down here in a long, long time. Jessie whistled as she drew the beam of light across the room, taking it all in.

I knew a sorcerer's workshop when I saw one. I knew evil when I saw it, too.

The stone altar, the centerpiece of the room, wore its history in rust-red stains. The aftermath of candle wax and blood. Jessie's light trailed down, hovering over the manacles set into the rock. A wrought-iron cage stood in the corner of the room, sized for humans, next to a wooden rack lined with knives, hammers, and chisels.

"So what do you think?" Jessie murmured. "Wizard, or serial killer?"

"I'm betting on both," I said.

The beam swept over a writing desk and a smaller set of shelves, stuffed to bulging with leather- and clothbound books. Some of the titles I recognized at first glance: a first-edition printing of Balfour's *Cultes des Goules*, and the banned *Profane Insights* of Dr. John Dee. Beside them were even older tomes, ones with no name at all, or their broken spines inscribed with alien glyphs that seemed to squirm and writhe in the light.

"You see anything less than a hundred years old on that shelf?" Jessie asked.

"No, and from what I recognize . . . this is the real stuff. The dangerous stuff. We're going to need a cleanup team in here."

"That, or a can of gas and a match," she said, checking out the desk.

A thin black folio, about the size of an album cover, sat out on the desktop. Jessie's fingers brushed against the cracked leather and gently swung it open. A small sheaf of parchment pages, brittle with age and embellished in flowing cursive script, lay within.

"'Be it hereby attested and known,'" Jessie read aloud, "'that this contract, signed and sealed under the witness of Asmodeus and Lucifu—'"

She stumbled on the name. I knew it by heart, and by the sinking feeling in my stomach.

"Lucifuge Rofocale," I said. "According to legend, hell's treasurer. This is an infernal contract."

"'. . . that the human named Edwin Kite doth hereby enter a covenant, of his own volition and free will, with the Marquis Adramelech.'" Jessie looked up at me. "Edwin. The Kite who founded Talbot Cove. This town's been rotten since day one."

Jessie passed me the penlight. While I read, she took out her phone. She paced the workshop, holding it up in the air until a single weak reception bar lit up on the screen.

"Auntie April? Need your big brain on research duty. Looks like Edwin Kite was doing business with hell's finest. Need everything you can find on a demon named Adramelech. One second, I'll spell it for you—"

While Jessie passed the details on to April, I kept reading. It didn't get any better from there.

> Edwin Kite shall receive power, wealth, and every
> good thing upon Earth, as well as the grant of a

> personal demesne in a place Not Here nor There, to enjoy for a span of thirty-three years, three months, three days, and three hours. At the end of this span, his life and soul shall be forfeit, and become the rightful property of the marquis.

Edwin even signed in blood, next to the date: October 17, 1882. His scrawl, dark and brown, sat beside a trio of swirling, ornate glyphs. Demonic seals.

"Sold his soul," I said when Jessie hung up the phone. I walked her through it, fast.

"So maybe he jumped the contract somehow," she said. "That'd be a good reason to sic demonic bounty hunters on his ass. Doesn't explain how he's still alive over a hundred and thirty years later, though. What's this personal demesne thing?"

I pursed my lips, thinking hard. It didn't ring any bells, but the wording caught my eye.

"Not here nor there," I said. "*Demesne* is another word for 'real estate.' Specifically, property attached to a mansion, if I remember right. So this demon was going to give him his own place."

"I hope it wasn't this one," Jessie said, flashing her light across the cobwebs in the corners of the room. "Totally not worth it."

"Neither here nor there, here nor—" I snapped my fingers. "Think about the capital letters, and who's signing the contract, where they're all from. 'Not Here nor There' means a place not on Earth, and not in hell."

"So Auntie's theory about the spell on the wicker balls, that the Bogeyman's lair might not be on Earth . . ."

We both said it at the same time.

"Edwin Kite is the Bogeyman."

"Okay," Jessie breathed, "so that makes him how old?"

Doing the math gave my brain something to do—something other than reeling at what we might be up against here.

"Couple of hundred years."

"So, judging from this room," Jessie said, "he was a pretty accomplished sorcerer *before* he made his pact with Adramelech."

"In my professional opinion?" I took another look at the altar. The Pythian coin vibrated in my jacket pocket, responding to the residual magic. Like the radiation from a nuke, clinging to the air and contaminating the soil long after the blast. "'Accomplished' might be an understatement. This is . . . this is a lifetime of occult study on display."

"And he's had two hundred years to get *better* at it," Jessie said.

I reached into my pocket and curled my fingers around the coin. It trembled against my palm. Edwin Kite had the powers of hell and two hundred years of experience under his belt. I had a trinket and a gun.

Jessie studied my face. "You nervous?"

I paused, then shook my head.

"Weirdly? No. Now we know exactly who and what we're up against. And he doesn't know we're coming for him. That's the best weapon we've got. *How* to take him down . . . we'll figure that part out as we go."

# # #

As we pulled into the Talbot Motor Lodge, April sat silhouetted in the doorway of her room. She waved us over.

"I'd say good news," she told us, ushering us into her and Kevin's room, "but only for a dubious definition of 'good.' I've identified Edwin Kite's patron."

"Check this out," Kevin said, pacing the room with one of April's books in hand. "This guy's so hard-core he got a personal shout-out in the Old Testament. Second Kings 17:31—'And the Sepharvites burned their children in the fire, as sacrifices to Adramelech and Anammelech, the gods of Sepharvaim.'"

"We don't know much about the city of Sepharvaim today," April said, "but it may have been Phoenician, which would link Adramelech's followers with the cult of Moloch. Both had an . . . affinity for proving their devotion through the sacrifices of innocent lives."

Jessie snorted. "Huh. Life must have been easy a few thousand years ago. Show up in some backwoods town, throw around a little hellfire, and declare yourself a god. Probably had the rubes falling all over themselves to worship him."

"And these days," April said, "earnest devotees are a bit harder to come by. The pattern is clear, though: in ancient times, Adramelech thrived through the ritual murder of children. Edwin Kite served him as well, which brings us to the Bogeyman abductions . . ."

Her voice went quiet. She looked my way. Everybody did.

"I know," I said. "My sister is dead."

Up until that moment, until it was torn out of me, I had no idea how much hope I'd been hiding in my heart.

Intellectual Harmony knew better. Intellectual Harmony had already come to terms with losing Angie years ago, and knew that it was better to assume the worst. Intellectual Harmony was too smart to let herself hope.

Now Emotional Harmony just came along and kicked me square in the teeth, to remind me that she was in my head, too.

Facts were facts. If Adramelech got his mojo by hurting kids—or just *liked* it—then his servants weren't keeping a stolen child alive. Not for thirty years, not for thirty days.

"I need—" I started to say, then paused. I wasn't sure what I needed.

"Sleep," Jessie said. "It's late, and we've had a hell of a long day. Everybody get some shut-eye, and we'll reconvene first thing in the morning."

I stood outside for a moment, between the two motel room doors, looking up at the canopy of stars. The lights inside the motor lodge's big cartoon owl sign flickered, on the edge of burnout.

"You coming in?" Jessie asked, her voice soft.

"Yeah," I told her. "In a second."

I listened for a while. I listened to the wind, and I listened to the stars, hoping they had something to tell me.

TWENTY-NINE

What I heard instead of the wind and stars, coming up behind me, was the slow crunch of wheels on gravel. Cody's squad car. He killed the ignition and got out.

"Hey," he said.

"Hey."

"Just . . . just thought I'd come over and check on you. I mean—I was in the neighborhood, anyway."

I spread my hand, taking in the night.

"It's Talbot Cove, Cody. It's all one neighborhood."

He chuckled and rubbed the back of his neck. "Guess you got me there. You okay?"

"Don't I look okay?"

"Depends. You want me to lie?" He sat on the hood of his cruiser, putting one boot up on the front fender. His palm lightly patted the steel. "C'mere. Sit down a second."

I swallowed. Glanced toward the curtained motel windows.

"I should probably get going—"

"You gonna tell me you've got somewhere better to go?" He had an easy smile. "It's after dark. This town is *closed*."

I shrugged and walked his way. The cruiser gently rocked as I climbed up on the hood and sat next to him.

"Talbot Cove has to have something going for it," I told him. "It kept you around, didn't it?"

He shook his head and looked up at the canopy of stars, taking a deep breath of night air.

"I almost made it," he said. "Escape velocity. Every small-town boy's dream: to get the hell out and never look back. I had a full-ride scholarship to MIT, studying aerospace engineering."

"So you're a rocket scientist," I said. I wasn't sure if he was joking or not. "You're *literally* a rocket scientist."

"That was the plan. Plans change."

"What happened?"

"Dad took off about a decade back, and Mom got sick." He bounced his heel against the fender. "Somebody had to come home and take care of her, and both my older brothers had careers and families of their own. So. That's what I did. Dropped everything, left midsemester, and came back to good old Talbot Cove."

I touched his arm. My fingertips brushed against the stiff polyester of his uniform shirt.

"I'm sorry. Is she—?"

"Lingered for eight long years. Passed last winter. And in the meantime, every opportunity I ever had outside the Cove dried up and blew away." He leaned back on his palms and gazed upward. "One nice thing, we're far enough from civilization that you can get a damn fine look at the stars. Can't *reach* 'em from here, but you can look all you want."

The night sky was so big. It made my stomach flutter, just for a heartbeat, thinking I might lose my grip on the earth and fall straight up. Tumbling into space.

"Imagine this is all hitting you pretty hard," Cody said. "Your sister and all. Swear to God, if Barry hadn't been around, I would have knocked that wannabe reporter Tucker flat on his ass."

"I can fight my own battles," I said, a little quicker and a little harder than I wanted to. "But . . . thanks. I'm all right."

Cody let out a little snorting sound and shook his head.

"I'm not sure what's worse. You thinking nobody can tell you're wound tighter than a steel spring, just by looking at you, or you trying to convince yourself everything's fine."

"Maybe I'm always like this."

"Sure," Cody said, "maybe you are. Life'll do that to you, if you let it. Hey. I want you to try something."

"What?"

He patted his shoulder. "Lean against me."

I arched an eyebrow. "You're joking."

"Not even a little. You're so tense *I'm* getting tense just looking at you. When's the last time you let your guard down, just for a minute?"

"I'm a federal agent, Cody. I let my guard down, people die."

He patted the chrome-barreled revolver on his hip.

"Well, then," he said, "good thing a duly deputized officer of the law is here to pick up the slack. C'mon. Please? For me?"

I grumbled, but I scooted a little closer on the car hood and leaned my shoulder into his.

It was all right.

"C'mon," Cody said, "you're holding yourself stiffer than an ironing board. Take a deep breath."

Then he put his arm around me.

That was all right, too.

We just sat like that for a while, sitting on his hood in the dark, listening to the crickets sing, looking at nothing in particular.

"It's okay, you know," he said. "You can let somebody else be strong sometimes. World won't end. I promise."

I felt my back and my neck unclench. I didn't know they'd been clenched in the first place. His hand was soft but firm on my shoulder, and his arm warm across my back. Stable.

"So why the badge?" I asked him.

I felt him shrug a little. "Wanted to be useful. If I couldn't have my dreams, at least I could help other people. This . . . this isn't my forever, though. Mom's gone, nothing's really keeping me tied down here. Nothing but not knowing where to go. I'm saving up a little nest egg. Figure I'll work through the winter and sort things out come springtime."

"How do you stay sane, in the meantime?"

Cody shook his head. "You'll laugh."

"No, I won't. I promise."

He squeezed my shoulder, gentle, and pulled his arm away. For just a second, I wished he hadn't. He fumbled in his pocket and pulled out his phone. He tilted the screen toward me as he tapped his way through a gallery of photographs.

A falcon soared, spread-winged and free, through a pale sky streaked with wispy clouds. A cardinal perched in a tree, a spot of vibrant scarlet in a sea of bristling green. Another picture captured the forest at dawn, dew-drenched and blanketed by a low sea of roiling mist.

"You're a photographer," I said.

"Don't know if I can rightly call myself a photographer," he replied with a chuckle. "But I do take pictures."

"You take *good* pictures," I murmured, lingering over a long shot of Talbot Cove's main street. Caught at dusk, lonely and empty and loveless and old. "These are beautiful."

"Can't paint, can't draw. I just try to shoot what I feel."

"I can tell," I said.

"Yeah? How?"

My finger slid over the phone's screen, changing a nighttime shot of the old paper mill—its girders bending like the bars of a rusted iron cage—to a bluebird taking flight under the summer sun.

"You want to fly," I told him.

He turned off his phone. He stared down at the blank screen, his bottom lip caught between his teeth, and nodded.

"Suppose that's right." He shrugged. "You don't always get what you want."

"Sometimes you do, though."

He met my gaze.

"Sometimes," he said, his voice sounding as uncertain as I felt.

He leaned in, just a little. I tilted my chin, just a little. My heart pounded, and I felt like a first-time parachutist, about to jump out of a plane at fifty thousand feet. All it would take was one little push, one little step forward—

Our lips brushed. I fell out of the plane. I yanked the parachute cord.

He jolted back at the same time I did, both of us wide-eyed and tripping over our apologies as we talked over each other. "I'm sorry," he said. "That was completely out of line—"

"No, it's me, I shouldn't have—"

"—I mean we barely know—"

"Cody," I said. I grabbed his hand.

He fell silent. Unsure.

"It's okay," I said. I squeezed his fingers. "It's okay."

He chuckled. "It . . . it was pretty okay."

"It was *very* okay." I shook my head, smiling. "Look, it's . . . it's late, and we've both got to be on the job tomorrow. I'm going to go get some sleep. But I'm glad we talked."

I let go of his hand and slid down from the car hood.

"Hey, Harmony?"

I turned.

"If you have time, I mean, after we catch this guy," he said, "would you maybe want to, um, get dinner with me? Or something?"

"Yeah," I said. "I'd like that a lot. Good night, Cody."

I let myself into the motel room. Jessie was already asleep, out like a light. I undressed in the dark and slipped into my own bed, head swimming, stomach fuzzy. I could handle mobsters, monsters, and demons from hell. Handling a cute guy who wanted to take me out to dinner? Outside my skill set. It felt dangerously normal. I didn't know how to deal with normal.

It felt nice, though.

THIRTY

“You’re still awake,” Jessie whispered in the dark.

To my left, numbers hovered on the digital clock on the nightstand between our beds—1:32 in deep crimson.

“How can you tell?”

“Can hear you breathing,” she said. “People breathe differently when they’re asleep. Different cadence. You smell worried, too.”

“You can’t smell worry.”

“My senses are a little sharper than most people’s,” she said.

“I just keep going over the case in my head. It doesn’t play.”

Jessie rolled over in bed and propped herself up on her arm, facing me.

“What doesn’t?”

“Fontaine and Nyx are in town because somebody broke hell’s rules.”

“Right,” Jessie said. “Edwin Kite. He had a deal with Adramelech, and he busted it somehow.”

“But that’s the part that doesn’t work. If the whole Bogeyman thing is about getting kids to sacrifice for Adramelech . . . why is he still doing it? His contract was up before the abductions in the 1940s, let alone the ’80s or today. He can’t be hiding from the guy *and* working for him.”

Jessie stretched, talking through a yawn. "Don't know. Do know that it's after one thirty in the morning, and if you keep yourself up all night you'll be useless come sunrise."

"Yeah," I said. "Sorry."

"Don't be sorry. Be sleepy."

The room fell silent.

"Jessie?"

She rolled over again. The silence turned expectant.

"About today," I said. "That parasite, the nightmares . . . are you all right?"

"Oh, is that what you want to talk about? I thought you'd want dating advice. Saw you and Cody from the window, sitting on his car hood like a couple of teenagers. You ought to get a piece of that before we leave town."

"Cody's a good guy, I think. I like him. But we're here on business. The job comes first."

"Oh, please," Jessie groaned. "Can I ask you an honest question?"

"Sure."

"Harmony, when's the last time you got laid?"

"Jessie."

"I'm serious," she said. "Now, I'm not saying you *should* pull Deputy Handsome into the nearest broom closet for some no-strings-attached boning, preferably with a level of energy and enthusiasm normally reserved for Olympic gymnasts, but I *am* saying it's an option."

"Stop changing the subject. I'm worried about you. Are you okay?"

She took a moment, thoughtful in the dark, before she spoke again. "You saw some things, huh?"

"A few," I replied.

"Well," she said, rolling onto her back and tugging the sheets tighter around her, "that parasite did a crap job of hurting me, if that's what it was going for. It wasn't smart enough to figure out what it was doing wrong."

"Yeah? What's that?"

Her eyes gleamed in the shadows, faintly luminous.

"That's what it *always* looks like inside my head."

I felt the hand of sleep wrap around my mind, dragging me down, tugging my eyelids shut. Before I slipped away, though, Jessie spoke again.

"Harmony?"

"Yeah?" I said.

"You know, I . . . I don't like letting on when I'm scared. Makes me feel weak, and I fucking *hate* feeling weak. But I honestly don't think I would have made it out of that basement if you hadn't been there. I'm glad you were. Thanks."

"You saved me, too," I told her. "Sometimes you just can't do everything alone. And that's okay."

She fell silent, and I fell asleep. Eventually.

# # #

I woke with the sunrise, my own words echoing back to me as I jumped out of bed and into the shower. I'd just given myself the clue I was looking for.

"The lead we haven't followed," I told the team once we'd all gotten back together, "is the one who came back. The Kite child."

"We haven't followed it because they'd be a pretty lousy eyewitness," Jessie said. "How much do *you* remember from when you were an infant?"

"Sure, maybe they don't remember the abduction, but listen." I opened up Mitchum's laptop, clicking over to the e-mail from CTide06 and reading it out loud. "'Just found her crib empty. She's going to be the next Returned. This has to stop.' You said it yourself last night: if they *know* the Bogeyman's going to bring their kid right back, why are they so upset?"

"What's your theory?" April asked.

"Let's look at the pattern. This whole mess is tied to Edwin Kite and the history of Talbot Cove. As near as we can tell, there's always one child who gets taken and then returned during every rash of abductions, and it's always a blood relative of the Kites. Thanks to the e-mail, we also know that at least some of the modern-day family members are aware of what's going on. Aware to the point that they hired a demonic bounty hunter to make it stop. And from the sound of Mitchum's last response? Nyx's services don't come cheap. They're acting out of desperation."

Kevin glanced up from his laptop. "But the kid *does* come back for good, right? There aren't any reports of *re*abductions."

"Right," I said, "so that's not what has them scared. What if it's not that cut-and-dried, though? What if the kid comes back . . . wrong?"

"Wrong?" Jessie said. She flopped back on one of the beds, lifting and stretching her legs one at a time.

I shrugged. "I don't know. There has to be a reason they're taking one child and bringing him back again. And a reason these parents *aren't* relieved to get their kid back. The only thing I can think of is, somehow, the kid's not the same."

"Changeling," April said.

"With George C. Scott," Jessie said. "Scary movie."

"I was referring to the folklore, but you're not far off. For centuries there have been tales, from Scotland to Nigeria, of infants being replaced by monstrous impostors in their cradles. Most often by fairy folk. I don't believe in fairies, but I do believe in evil, and you're quite right: there's a reason for these returned children. We just aren't seeing it yet. We need more data."

I picked one of the wicker balls off the table and held it up. The wood felt spongy against my fingers. Diseased.

"How's this for a reason," I said. "Like I said last night: because sometimes you can't do everything alone."

Jessie sat up straight.

"The balls. You think the kid who came back in the '80s is *summoning* the Bogeyman this time around?"

"It's a cycle," I said. "One kid comes back. Decades later, somebody creates these beacons and calls the Bogeyman, and more kids vanish. Except for one who comes back. And on and on it goes."

Kevin turned in his chair. "Makes sense. I mean, somebody's gotta be leaving those things all over town, right? And now we know it's not the Kite family, because they're trying to *stop* the Bogeyman. Who else have we got for a suspect?"

"Jack and Squat," Jessie said, "and Jack just left town. Okay, it's a valid lead. How do we follow it?"

"Barry," I told her. "He might have given away the old case report, but he didn't give away his memory. Let's go shake it up a little."

# # #

Mabel, Barry's elderly assistant, met us at the station door.

"Ah," she said, "you're back. I have to say, it's so exciting to see real, live FBI agents in Talbot Cove. We never get this kind of commotion around here. And lady agents, too! Are you the first ones?"

Jessie blinked at me. I forced a smile and said, "Er, n-no, ma'am, the first female special agents joined the Bureau in the 1970s."

"But you don't do all the same things that the men do."

"Yes, ma'am, we do," I said. "Same training program, same duties and standards."

Mabel looked dumbfounded. "Well, just imagine. And your husbands *let* you put yourselves in danger like that?"

Jessie gritted her teeth and swallowed. Hard.

"We really need to see Sheriff Hoyt," she said. "Now would be good."

Mabel waved her hand and smiled. "Oh, sure, sure! Just go on back. You know the way. I'll buzz his office and tell him you're comin' down."

As soon as we rounded the corner, Jessie leaned close and whispered, "I'm sorry. Did we just jump back in time to the '50s? That was some serious Mayberry shit."

I didn't know what to tell her. I flailed an empty hand.

"Small towns," I said. "They can be a little weird."

"Yeah, I'm starting to see how you ended up the way you did."

"We moved when I was *six*."

Jessie flashed a smile. "Whatever, Mayberry."

I rapped on the office door twice and let myself in. Barry didn't look happy to see us. He didn't look like he'd slept, either, given the bags under his eyes and the double-size, gas-station cup of coffee on his desk.

"What happened?" he said. "Did you find the mayor?"

Jessie spun one of his chairs around and dropped into it, leaning forward against the back of the seat. "He never showed up. We assume the meeting was just a ruse to distract you while he slipped out of town."

"He'll turn up eventually," I said, taking the chair next to her. "But let's talk about the Kites."

Barry wrung his hands. When he pulled them apart, I could see a little tremor in his left hand. Just a little one.

"Anything," he said. "I'm *trying* to cooperate. You can see that, right?"

"Sure," I told him. "But there's one detail we're missing. The child who was taken and brought back, during the abductions in the '80s. We need to talk to him."

"What for? He was just a baby, not like he remembers any of it."

"We believe our suspect may have contacted him, years later, or might be keeping him under surveillance. He may be in danger."

Barry slumped in his chair and rubbed his forehead.

"Great," he said. "More trouble. Yeah, he still lives in town. Any given Friday night, you could probably find him down the hall, in the drunk tank."

"He's got a drinking problem?" Jessie asked.

"He's got a *life* problem. Willie's . . . never really lived up to his potential, let's just say. His mom's a doctor, dad went to Harvard, they gave him every advantage, but his life pretty much revolves around cheap takeout and cheaper whiskey. He's not malicious, not what I'd call a hardened criminal, but I have to pick him up once or twice a week. He drinks, he picks fights—loses, every damn time, like he *wants* his ass kicked. I toss him in a cell to sleep it off and let him go in the morning."

"Have you ever tried to get him help?" I asked. "Counseling?"

"Sure. He doesn't want any part of it. I asked him once, I said, 'What are you doing with your life, son?' He tells me, 'Just marking time, boss. Just marking time.' Seems like some people are cursed from the day they're born, you know?"

Or the day they're taken, I thought.

"That's Willie Grandeen," Barry said, "not Kite, by the way. His mom was Jeremiah Kite's first cousin."

"Do you have an address for him?" Jessie asked.

Barry reached for his notepad and a chewed-up ballpoint pen.

"Sure," he said, jotting it down, "but this time of day, assuming he showed up for work, you'll find him at Sutton's on Main Street. Only grocery store in town, he's a bag boy or something—"

The bulky old phone on Barry's desk let out a faint click. Barry paused. A little amber light glowed on the bottom extension.

"Huh, intercom's on." He leaned in and smiled. "Mabel? You up there? You eavesdroppin' again? Aw, I'm just teasing, hon, but you left the comm on again. Hello?"

Jessie and I didn't need to say a word. We just shared a glance, and that was enough to send us charging out of Barry's office, up the hall and into the lobby. The empty lobby, with its empty front desk, and a freshly emptied space in the parking lot.

"Fontaine," Jessie snarled. "Skeevy body-jumping son of a bitch. That whole routine when we walked in—he was *playing* with us."

"Wait, what?" Barry said, bringing up the rear. "Who's Fontaine? Who's getting jumped?"

"We'll handle this," I told him. "Stay here."

"Well, now, hold on a second! Where's Mabel? If my secretary's in trouble, I need to be in on this. You can't shut me out like—"

"Barry." I held up my hand. "Stay. Here. Mabel will be fine."

I hoped I could back that up. As it was, we'd just handed our best lead's name and location to Fontaine, and he had a hell of a head start. What he planned to do with Willie, and with Mabel once he was done hijacking her body, I had no idea.

We'd just have to make sure he didn't get the chance.

THIRTY-ONE

Sutton's was the only grocery store in town, a slope-roofed supermarket in pastel pink and green that looked like a relic of the '50s. I swung the SUV around out front, leaving it in a standing lane by the double glass doors. Getting towed was the least of my worries.

We paused just inside the doors and took the lay of the land. Sutton's had three checkstands, each with a line of shoppers, and carts and strollers crammed the narrow aisles. I scanned the crowd, looking for Mabel, but came up empty.

"How do you want to play this?" Jessie said, eyeing the baggers at the checkout line. I followed her gaze. Two were women, and the third had white hair and sixty years' worth of wrinkles.

"Let's find a manager," I said. "See if he can call Willie to the stock-room or something. Fontaine could be anybody in this crowd. The sooner we get Willie alone, the safer he is."

We found a likely candidate on aisle six—a pimply faced kid running a price gun along a wall of canned peaches. His assistant manager name tag read, **Hi! I'm Dave!**

He saw us coming and flashed a can-do smile. "Good morning! Can I help you find something?"

I flashed my ID and said, "Yes. Willie Grandeen, please."

Dave's shoulders slumped. I guessed it wasn't the first time members of law enforcement had come looking for him at work.

"Oh God," he said. "What'd he do now?"

"Nothing, nothing at all, we just need to talk to him. Did he come to work today?"

"Yeah, he's got the truck today. We have a lot of elderly and housebound customers, so we offer a home-delivery service."

"We need to know his route," Jessie said. "Every stop he's supposed to make today. And do you have a phone number for him? It's important we get in touch right away."

Dave opened his hands, helpless. "Sure, for his landline at home, if it's still connected. Dude doesn't own a cell phone. Come on back to the office. I'll pull up his log sheet."

We followed him through a cluttered stockroom and into his office, a yellow-walled shoe box that might have been a washroom in a former life. He squeezed around the desk, sitting behind a bulky computer and an ancient dot-matrix printer, and gestured to a couple of mismatched plastic chairs.

"Just one second," he said. "I'll pull it right up for you."

He angled the monitor so we could see, and deactivated his PC's screen saver. Then he frantically scrambled to close the porn site that popped up on his web browser, flailing at random keys as he leaned across the desk in a failed attempt to block our view.

"Hot moms, huh?" Jessie said.

Dave grabbed his mouse and hammered the buttons until the window disappeared. He looked from us to the screen and back again while his cheeks turned beet red. We just sat down and tried not to laugh. I did better than Jessie did.

"One of the cashiers," he said, "uses the computer on breaks. I'm . . . I'm *so* gonna write that guy up. I mean, was that pornography? On a business computer? I find that, uh, highly unacceptable."

"He should probably be disciplined," said a voice from the open doorway. Smoky, with a thick Russian accent.

Dave's jaw dropped, and I could understand why. The woman in the doorway was a pale goddess with her golden-blonde hair woven into a single waist-length braid. From her motorcycle jacket to her boots, I didn't think a single thing on her body wasn't made of black leather—and from the dangerously low position of her jacket zipper, I wasn't sure she was wearing anything underneath.

She held out an ID fold. "Svetlana Tkachenko, with the Sunlight Bail Bond Agency. Looking for William Grandeen."

Her ID checked out, at least at a surface glance, so Jessie and I showed her ours.

"Special Agents Temple and Black," I said. "FBI. Whatever you want him for, it's going to have to wait."

Svetlana favored me with a faint condescending smile. "Sunlight invested a great deal of money in this man before he skipped out on his bail. They intend to have it back."

"I'll say this nice and clear," Jessie told her. "*Federal investigation.* Back off."

Svetlana stepped into the room. She rested one hand against the desk, her black-painted nails splayed on the wood, and she leaned in just far enough to give Dave a generous glimpse of cleavage.

"Even clearer," she said, "is Michigan Code of Criminal Procedure 765.26, which establishes the legal right of a bail enforcement agent to detain and arrest. In fact, said agent is *entitled* to the assistance of a peace officer."

"Ms. Tkachenko," I told her, "no disrespect intended, but you really don't want to be in the middle of this."

Svetlana reached across the desk and stroked her fingernails along Dave's cheek. From the enraptured look on the kid's face, I figured he'd start drooling any minute now. From the vague look of disgust on Jessie's, she had about as much respect for Svetlana's brand of tactics as I did.

"You can help, no?" Svetlana asked him.

"Of—of course," he said, fumbling with his keyboard.

"Of course you *can't*," Jessie corrected him. "Eyes over here, Dave. Look away from the Playboy bunny and toward the nice ladies with the badges and the guns."

"Okay," Dave said, wincing. "Okay, guys, help me out here. Who do I give this information to?"

"Us," all three of us said in unison.

My ears perked. Something had been bugging me about the way Svetlana spoke, but I chalked it up to her thick accent. Now I wondered.

"Ms. Tkachenko," I said.

She looked my way, head tilted, curious.

"We could arrest *you*," I said, stressing the word deliberately and hoping Jessie caught my meaning, "for interfering with a federal investigation. What do *you* think of that?"

Svetlana flashed a charming smile and strolled around to stand behind our chairs. She sank down into a crouch so she could whisper her answer into our ears.

"This one," she breathed, "thinks little girls should go home and play with dolls, and leave a hunter's work to a professional. This one also thinks . . . you're out of salt."

She thumped the side of her motorcycle boot against my chair.

It hadn't occurred to me that Nyx might have a form other than the flaming chitinous beast we'd faced twice already. It should have. The incarnate demon I'd faced in Vegas had turned from a perfectly ordinary man into a monster before my eyes. I should have guessed that Nyx could do the same trick. We'd just met her monster side *first*.

"Salt?" Dave said, distracted as he typed, "That's aisle four, with the baking goods."

"Don't suppose you're going to be reasonable about this," I murmured.

"This one is always *perfectly* reasonable."

"Here we go," Dave said. "Willie's supposed to visit twelve houses this morning. I'll run copies for you."

The dot-matrix printer screeched to life, whining as its printing head slammed back and forth across a roll of cheap paper.

"Hey, Nyx," Jessie said.

Nyx turned, her shoulders sinuous. "Yes, pup?"

"How fast are you?"

Jessie leaned forward in her chair, just a little, as the first copy of Willie's delivery schedule finished printing.

"Very fast," Nyx said. "But if the two of you were to snatch that page and run . . . well, this fine young man might prove to be quite *distracting*. Us together, all alone, *anything* might happen."

Jessie leaned back in her chair.

Dave tore the top page off. "Who gets this?"

Jessie and I nodded toward Nyx. "She does." I sighed.

"A head start," Nyx said, stepping forward and taking the sheet. "How generous of you."

Dave's eyes slid downward as he watched her go. And stayed there. Jessie leaned in and snapped her fingers in his face.

"We're really gonna need you to focus here, Dave," she said. Then she smiled at me. "She fell for it."

"Fell for what?"

"Head start, my ass—she has only half the information she needs. Dave, we're gonna want something else to go with these addresses: we want to know what all these people *bought*."

# # #

We kicked Dave out of his own office and commandeered his desk. Technically not an FBI privilege, but he didn't know any better. I spread out the lists of names, addresses, and the groceries in Willie's truck while Jessie got Kevin and April on speakerphone.

"Okay, campers," Jessie said, "two hostile entities are zeroing in on our target as we speak, and they've got all the powers of hell at their command. Know what we've got? *Brains.*"

I scooted my chair forward and leaned toward the phone. "According to the assistant manager, Willie drives a late-model Ford pickup and keeps groceries in a couple of insulated coolers in the back bed. Insulated, but not refrigerated. So we know—unless there's a quick stop on his way—he's going to deliver to any customers who have frozen foods on their list first, and save the ones with nonperishables for last."

"Hit me with his home address." Kevin's voice crackled. "I'll run a secretary-of-state search and get his plate number."

"Good thinking," Jessie said. "Auntie April, you got a street map of Talbot Cove?"

"Don't call me Auntie while we're working, and yes."

Jessie tugged over one of the pages, swiveling it on the desk so we could both read it.

"Harmony and I are going to number this list in order from the customers with the most frozen items to the least. Then we're gonna hit you with the addresses. I need you to pinpoint them on the street map and come up with the most logical route Willie would take. He's lived here his entire life, so he's gotta know these streets by heart."

"Understood. Ready for the addresses."

"He gets a lunch break, too," I said, "but he might eat on the go. Look for cheap places, fast-food joints, around the midpoint of his route."

"Dave says this is an average order, and he's usually back here around four o'clock," Jessie told me. "Does Willie sound like a diligent worker bee to you?"

I rapped my fingernails against the paper, thinking. "Not even a little. I guarantee he finishes his route by two and just knocks off somewhere for a few hours. By the time we get rolling, figure he's halfway done."

We ordered the list and April broke it down, working her street map with the precision of a calculus professor. Kevin jumped in to help after snagging Willie's plate number with a quick records search.

"Head for 282 Fairmont," April said. "Kevin and I will call each person on the list to find out if they've gotten their delivery, and if so, exactly what time Willie left. As new information comes in, I'll adjust your route to accommodate."

Jessie gave me a wolfish grin and shoved her chair back.

"C'mon, Mayberry. Let's go piss off a couple of demons."

THIRTY-TWO

I cornered the SUV hard, tires screeching around a corner as Jessie clutched her phone.

"Now a left on—wait," April said. "Kevin just contacted number seven, and Willie left that house fifteen minutes ago, but he hasn't been to address number six yet. I'm redrawing your route."

At least they don't have their claws on him yet, I thought. Sure, Fontaine could jump inside Willie's body and wear him like a cheap suit, but I doubted he'd finish his delivery route for him.

"Soon would be good," Jessie said, eyes riveted on the intersection up ahead.

"I've got it," April said quickly. "He's headed to address eleven. It's directly en route to the next house with frozen goods, so he can make a quick stop without going out of his way. Go straight through the next light, then take a left on Angleton."

I laid the pedal down and we blazed through the green light, swerving hard to dodge a mail truck. Autumn trees whipped by on both sides of the road, brown-and-red blurs, as our tires rumbled over a rough patch of road.

"We gotta slow down," I said as the road narrowed and the trees gave way to rows of parked cars and suburban bungalows. I eased off on the gas. "This is all residential. Could be kids out playing, bike riders—can't risk speeding without a siren and lights."

"Just keep it steady," Jessie said. "He's gotta slow down, too. We'll catch up."

"Update," April said. "He just left the house on Angleton less than five minutes ago. He's on his way to 1021 Elk Ridge."

Jessie craned her neck, looking out the window and scanning for house numbers.

"We literally just passed the Angleton address," Jessie said. "He's got to be up ahead."

I wanted to stomp my foot on the gas. Wanted to pour on the speed, close the gap, and save this guy before Fontaine or Nyx got to him. We'd flipped an hourglass the second Barry spoke Willie's name, and I imagined the last few grains of sand sliding toward the abyss. I squeezed the wheel hard enough to turn my knuckles white.

"Steady," Jessie told me. "We'll get him."

That's when I saw it, just around the next bend: a battered white F-150, trundling down the street about a block ahead of us. As we got closer, close enough to read the license plate, we knew we had our man.

"Come up on his left," Jessie said. "I'll yell for him to pull over."

I caught up and matched speeds, the two of us running side by side and dangerously close on the narrow suburban backstreet.

"Uh, got a problem here," Jessie said.

Mabel was driving.

Well, Fontaine in the old woman's body, anyway. She looked over at us, grinned, and hit the gas. My stomach clenched as the pickup rocketed ahead of us, swerving hard to dodge a parked car. As the pickup swayed, a figure in the back bed struggled to sit up: a stringy-haired man with wild, terrified eyes and a strip of duct tape over his mouth, his arms bound tight to his sides with a coil of rope. The pickup swerved around a hard right turn, and he fell back down again, thumping against the truck bed.

Jessie pulled her gun, then holstered it again, swearing under her breath. "I can't shoot at his tires. Too many houses, too damn close together. If I miss or the bullet skips—"

"Somebody could get hurt. And Fontaine knows it."

Another sharp turn, the pickup's tires squealing, and the street only got narrower. Parked cars on both sides of the road whistled past us, inches from our side mirrors. Fontaine sped up.

"Either he's going to run somebody over," I said, "or he's going to wreck that thing and kill Mabel and Willie. We've got to shut this down. *Now.*"

Jessie looked my way. "Any ideas?"

"Yeah. Buckle your seat belt."

The yellow sign up ahead read **School Zone**, and the road began to widen. We were a hundred feet and closing from the big yellow brick facade of Talbot Cove Elementary. The kids were all in class, and the bus lane lay wide open and empty. That was the extra space I needed.

I swerved left and sped up, closing in on the pickup's back bumper. Once we'd passed the bumper by about two feet, I gently eased the steering wheel right, hearing metal *clank* as our vehicles made contact.

Then I spun the wheel, hard, and plowed right into him.

The pickup skidded sideways, back tires losing traction, and spun out. We pushed him forward, our vehicles locked in a T-bone collision, tires screaming on the black asphalt. I fought the instinctive urge to stomp the gas pedal. *Smooth and steady,* I told myself, *just like they taught you. Smooth and steady.*

The pickup came to a juddering halt. Jessie was out of the SUV before I was, leaping from her seat with her pistol drawn.

"Check on Willie!" I shouted, tearing my seat belt away. "I'll take Fontaine!"

Mabel staggered out of the pickup, looking so shaken I thought Fontaine might have vacated the premises. Then she saw me coming, squared her shoulders like a boxer, and smirked.

"You wouldn't hurt a little old lady, would you?"

Fontaine had a point. We could do this the hard way, but it wasn't *his* body I'd be injuring. Then he drove the point home with a blur of a right cross. Mabel's wrinkled fist smashed into my eye and left me seeing stars. He came at me again, pressing the advantage, but this time I was ready. As another punch whistled toward my nose, I sidestepped, got inside Mabel's reach, and caught her wrist. I let her body's momentum carry her around, off balance, and swept her leg out from under her.

We went down to the asphalt together. I landed first, my kneecap slamming against the street and sending a jolt of pain up my leg, while I tried to cushion Mabel's fall as best I could. Still gripping her wrist, I yanked it behind her back and pinned her body flat.

"Twelve years of aikido classes," I snarled, clamping my other hand on the back of her neck. "I can take someone down *without* hurting them."

Mabel's skin flared with heat, and every muscle in my hands went rigid. Then my arms, then my shoulders, an electric wave coursing through my body. Thousands of nerve endings, one after the other, flickering and going numb. I felt a serpent under my skin, coiling around the base of my spine and slithering its way upward, straight toward my brain.

"Five hundred and seventy-four years of riding humans like ponies," Fontaine's syrupy voice drawled in my inner ear. *"So can I."*

Don't panic, I thought. *If you panic, you're dead. Stay in control.*

I'm already in control, sugar, I thought in response. But it wasn't me doing the thinking.

I felt like a passenger on a doomed submarine, racing from bulkhead to bulkhead, doors slamming shut as the cold ocean water flooded in from all directions.

Water. I seized the image and dived mind-first into the depths of my own heart. I tapped the elemental river, conjuring my spirit armor—not wearing it on my skin, but summoning it from the inside out. Pure water surged through my veins, cascaded over my bones, pushing Fontaine's corrupt spirit out of my body through the sheer force of the tide. I felt him falling, tumbling back. His disjointed essence streamed from under my fingernails, out through my eyes and nose, billowing out into the open air like a living heat mirage.

I watched the air ripple as it darted left and right, all but invisible, searching desperately for a new host. From what I understood about demonic hijackers, they could get a foothold in our world for only a short time without a body to live in: without that, they'd plummet back into hell where they belonged.

A chubby gray squirrel darted across the school lawn, not ten feet away. The heat mirage streaked toward it. Before I could do anything, the squirrel keeled over, kicked one frantic leg in the air, then went still.

I heard Jessie's footsteps running up behind me. She put her hand on my shoulder. "You okay? Where is he?"

I nodded toward the squirrel. It hopped to its feet, chittered at us, and waved one of its tiny hands before dropping to all fours and running.

Jessie brought her gun up. "Whoa!" I shouted, tugging her arm down and pointing. Tiny, wide-eyed faces crammed the school windows, jostling to watch the excitement, along with more than a few dour-looking teachers.

"Jessie? As far as these kids know, I just used the martial arts on an unarmed, elderly woman. Let's not compound that with gunning down a squirrel on their schoolhouse lawn."

"It's an *evil* squirrel," she said.

"We can't prove that."

Mabel opened her eyes, groaning. "Where . . . ?"

I helped her to sit up. "It's all right. You've been in a car accident, but you're going to be all right."

Jessie leaned in and murmured, "Willie's just shaken up, a few bumps and bruises. I'll go untie him and call an ambulance for Mabel."

Mabel rubbed her head, squinting. "I . . . I don't remember anything. I was at the station, and this salesman walked in and I was trying to send him away nicely, and . . . and that's *not* my car."

"You've had a light concussion," I told her. "Short-term memory loss is a common side effect. We're calling an ambulance to pick you up. Just relax, okay? Stress is the worst thing for you right now. Your memory will probably come back in a day or two, and everything will be just fine."

We don't have any exotic drugs or enchantments to blank a witness's mind, but we generally don't need any. When presented with the impossible—like losing a few hours of time, only to find out you've had an accident in a total stranger's car—people are generally happy to grab at whatever explanation just makes the upsetting stuff go away. Mabel sat there, nodding slowly, telling herself a story about her concussion.

Jessie led a shaken and confused-looking Willie over to the SUV, bundling him into the backseat. My tactical maneuver left us with a crumpled front bumper and deep paint gouges on the passenger side, but other than that, it was still perfectly drivable.

I was feeling good about that until I remembered the SUV was a rental. I hoped April paid for the extra insurance.

The ambulance showed up five minutes later. I flagged it down, flashed my ID at the paramedics, laid some fast bureaucracy babble on them, and left Mabel in their capable hands.

"We have to get him off the street," Jessie said as I jumped into the SUV's driver's seat.

"My thoughts exactly. If Nyx is working her way down the list one house at a time, she'll be coming this way any minute."

Sitting in the backseat, unshaven and dressed in a food-stained teal smock with a **Hi! I'm Willie!** name tag, our new suspect gave us a hangdog look. His breath stank like a sewer. A sewer filled with cheap beer, anyway.

"An old lady just tied me up and threw me in the back of my own truck like I weighed less than a sack of groceries," he said, his voice slurring. "Then you hit my truck, beat her up, and almost shot a squirrel. And the squirrel waved at you. I think I'd like to go home now, please."

Jessie pulled on her seat belt and muttered, "Welcome to *my* life."

THIRTY-THREE

"What do you think?" Jessie said as we pulled away. "Take him to the motel?"

I thought it over. Willie was our best lead—our *only* lead—and both Fontaine and Nyx had the exact same thought on the subject. Fontaine was out of the hunt for a little while, unless he planned to pelt us with acorns, but Nyx still had our scent. If we wanted to hang on to our new catch, we might have to hold out against a literal siege.

"We're taking him to the safest place in town," I said.

Barry kept himself busy by pacing a hole in the police station lobby floor. "Hey," he said as we walked in with Willie, "what the hell is going on out there? Mabel's being treated for bumps and bruises after a car accident that *you* caused. And she was driving *his* truck and says she can't remember anything."

"That last part's true," Jessie said, holding Willie by the arm as she escorted him past. "Mabel's in the clear. You should probably give her a few days off, though."

Cody came around the corner, making a beeline for us. Barry didn't look any less flustered. "And where are you going with him? What does he have to do with all this?"

"Take him on back," I told Jessie, then turned to face the two men. "I need you both to listen carefully, okay? Willie is a material witness to a crime, and there are some very bad guys in your town looking to do him harm. I need you to put this place on lockdown. Nobody, and I mean nobody but the four of us, finds out he's being held here, all right?"

Cody tilted his head, shooting a look at the plate-glass doors and the parking lot outside. "Very bad guys meaning what, exactly?"

"Very bad guys," I said, "who won't hesitate to burn half this town to the ground to get what they want, and they've got some locals on their payroll. So while we're questioning Willie, I want you two standing post out here making sure nobody—and I mean *nobody*, not your next-door neighbor or your family doctor—walks through those doors. Anybody could be involved."

Jessie sat Willie down in the interrogation room. We stood on the far side of the two-way mirror, watching him squirm.

"Not taking any chances here," Jessie told me. "This guy could be the key to this whole mess. Normally I'd say we just go in and have at him, but . . . we need some expert help."

The expert help, arriving ten minutes later, was April. She rolled her chair up to the window, moving in between us, and folded her arms.

"So what do you—" I started to ask.

"Shh," she said. Her purse rested on her lap. She fished out a pair of steel-gray bifocals and slipped them on, eyeing Willie through the glass like a raptor watching a plump mouse. I looked at Jessie. Jessie held up her hand, nodding silently.

"Blush and pupil dilation," April said, "indicate he's still slightly intoxicated. Good. Lowered inhibition can help us. Harmony. His body language. What's it telling you?"

I looked through the glass. Willie wrung his hands, glancing from side to side, rocking in his chair.

"He's nervous."

She arched an eyebrow but didn't take her gaze off him.

"I thought you said you studied my work at Quantico. Details *matter*, Agent. Flared nostrils, stiffness—there. Did you see that? He keeps trying to smile. It's a flicker, an affectation he instinctively knows he can't sell, but he keeps trying. That's not stress, that's guilt and shame. He's thinking about something he doesn't like. Something he doesn't want to confront."

"Shame," I echoed, trying to see what she saw.

April squinted. "It's the Salt Lake Sniper case all over again. I worked lead on that, back in the summer of '87. Two assailants, one dominant and controlling, the other submissive and placating. When we separated the submissive of the duo and put him alone in an interview room, he exhibited the exact same behaviors. What we're seeing is a man who knows he's done something gravely wrong, and his mind is desperately trying to reframe it in a way he can accept. To find an excuse that exonerates him from responsibility."

"How did you handle the sniper?" I asked.

She quirked a smile. "Gave him more authority and more responsibility than he was willing to accept. Jessie, roll me inside, if you'd be so kind."

Jessie blinked. "You *hate* when people push your chair for you."

"People associate that visual with weakness. I want him to utterly discount me as a threat. That'll help when I drop the hammer on him."

Willie looked up as we walked into the tiny room, brushing the stringy hair from his eyes.

"Hey," he said, "uh, thanks for the help back there. I don't know what happened. I was on my route, just coming back to my truck after dropping off some groceries, and this little old lady walks up and asks my name. Next thing I know—"

"We know about the wicker balls," April said.

He froze.

"You know," I said, "the ones you planted outside the Gunderson and Morris houses?"

Willie shook his head. It was more of a twitch. His neck muscles pulled taut.

"I—I don't—I don't know what you're—"

"We know it was you." Jessie rested her hands, palms flat, on the table. "And we know about the Bogeyman. We're not the regular police, Willie. And believe me when I say it's in your absolute best interest to tell us *everything*."

"N-no," he said, eyes going wide. His words spilled out in a terrified stammer, turning into a singsong chant. "I don't know, I don't *know* what you're, what you're talking about, I *don't* know. No. *No.*"

"Hey, Willie," I said softly, reaching for his hand. He yanked it away, curling his fingers against his chest. He made little jerking motions, almost punching himself.

"Don't ask me because I can't, I can't, I can't know anything—"

April held up a finger. "Just one question, Willie."

He looked up at her with moist, bloodshot eyes.

"What did they do to you?" she asked him. "I mean, I understand. You *hated* those families. You hated them so much—"

"N-no," Willie stammered, louder now. "No!"

April slammed the flat of her palm on the table. "Yes, you did! We know this was *your* idea, *your* decision, *your* design from start to finish. You hated those families so much you sent a monster to murder their children—"

"He made me do it!" Willie shrieked, throwing his head back and squeezing his eyes shut. "Edwin Kite made me do it!"

He collapsed against the table, clutching his face, feet kicking the floor as he sobbed into his hands.

April glanced sidelong at me. She mouthed the words, *Be the good cop*.

I pulled back a chair and slid it around the table so I could sit next to him. I rested my hand on his shoulder.

"Willie," I said, gentle now. "Where is Edwin Kite?"

"In his house," he mumbled into his hands. His shoulders twitched.

"We've been to the Kite house," Jessie said. "Nobody's there, Willie."

He raised his tear-drenched face and swallowed hard. "Not that house. The *other* house. The House of Closets."

"From his contract, I bet," I said to Jessie. "The demesne Adramelech gave him."

"Don't say that name," Willie said, eyes wide. "Mr. Kite *hates* that name. See, he can't ever leave his house or the monster will get him. But the monster can't come inside. He's safe as long as he stays inside."

"You were there once," I said, "weren't you? When you were a little boy. The Bogeyman took you there and brought you back the next day."

"I don't remember." He squeezed his eyes shut and stomped one foot on the floor. "I *don't remember*."

I held up a hand. "All right, all right. That's fine, Willie. You're doing just fine. Do you have any idea why they let you go? What made you different from the other children?"

"He said . . . he said I was the *lucky* one."

Willie ripped open his shirt, buttons popping, tearing the fabric aside to show us the horror beneath. His chest, from just above his left nipple to the curve of his shoulder, was a mass of faded burns, cuts, and scars. Mutilation after mutilation, one upon another.

And above it all, rising up from the surface of his ravaged skin, was an occult sigil about the size of a silver dollar. The intricate curves and whorls bloomed above the tortured flesh, thick and fish-belly pale.

"It always comes back," Willie whispered. "No matter how many times I slice it off. It *always comes back*."

Jessie motioned me away from the table. I got up and followed her to the corner of the room.

"Couple years back," she murmured, "we busted up this little cult in Jersey. Humans, carving up locals as sacrifices for a demon. They all had brands like that. Demon got away. Aunt April had a theory that the marks were some kind of psychic link. So when we busted the demon's little helpers, he got advance warning to leave town."

"Edwin Kite was human, though."

"We figure he busted his deal with Adramelech, right?" Jessie said softly, glancing over at Willie. "Maybe, before he split, he learned some of his old master's tricks. Hell, he's what, around two hundred years old and still kicking? That's not exactly normal, either."

"Willie," I said, walking back to the table, "if you don't remember what happened, when the Bogeyman took you, how do you know all this?"

"Mr. Kite comes to me sometimes. In my dreams. He can do it a-anytime he wants. He always reminds me. I can't hide. Anywhere I go, he can find me."

His fingers clawed at the sigil, like a nervous tic.

"And did he teach you how to make those wicker balls?"

"He t-told me what I had to do. He *told* me. It takes a lot of energy to go back and forth, and the Bogeyman can't stay in our world very long because Edwin is afraid the monster will catch it. So the Bogeyman needs to know—needs to know where to find the *good* houses right away. That's my job. Picking the good houses."

"Why the Morris family?" April asked. "Why the Gundersons? What does Edwin Kite have against them?"

He blinked at her, like the question had never occurred to him before.

"N-nothing," he stammered. "He doesn't even know who they are. He doesn't care."

I leaned closer. "Then why target them?"

His gaze dropped to the table.

"I had to make it fair," he said.

"Fair how?"

"He told me I should pick families I didn't like, to"—he paused, grimacing, spitting the words out—"to make it *fun*. I didn't want to do that. I didn't want to. So I made it as fair as I could."

He finally met my eyes.

"I used my delivery list."

"The groceries," Jessie said, her voice flat.

He pointed at her with a shaky hand. "Y-yes, see, you understand! Except for the third one, the one he told me I *had* to mark, it's fair that way. I didn't know if they were good people or bad people. I just knew which houses had children and which ones didn't. It was just . . . random. That's all. That's . . . that's fair, right?"

Jessie's hands clenched on the edge of the table.

"Willie," I said, "you don't want to hurt anyone, do you?"

The only answer was a mute, miserable shake of his head.

"Why target any houses at all, then? If the Bogeyman can't hunt without your help, then why are you doing it?"

He hung his head. Silent.

"Willie," I said. "Please. Tell us why."

"I already told you why."

"Then help us to understand—"

Fresh tears glistened in his eyes, droplets from an ocean of loathing. "Because I'm *afraid*," he spat.

"Of who? Who are you afraid of?"

"I told you: *he can always find me*. He shows me, in my dreams. He shows me his house. The . . . the things that happen there. The things that happen to the children. And he tells me . . . there's one person who doesn't need a beacon. There's one person the Bogeyman can always catch and bring to him. *Me*."

Willie slumped back in his chair. He sniffled and shook his head. "It's them or me."

THIRTY-FOUR

Jessie's voice was a graveyard whisper, her eyes blazing as she squeezed the table's edge.

"You son of a bitch."

"He told me," Willie said, "that he'll let me go if I give him six children. And he told me . . . it's proof."

"What is?" I said.

"That nobody is good in their heart, not really. He's been doing this for a long, long time. And he told me that not once—not once has the 'lucky one' ever refused. Not once. Because when it's you or them? No matter how good you think you are, no matter how brave you think you are . . . you'll *always* choose to save yourself."

"Bullshit," Jessie snapped. "You're just fucking *weak*."

"Agent," April said.

"No," she told her. "No! This son of a bitch is sacrificing innocent children to keep *his* neck off the chopping block—"

He mumbled something as his head fell. I couldn't make it out. His shoulders shook, and a tear fell to spatter his dirty jeans.

"What was that?" I asked, leaning closer.

"I was innocent, too," he whispered.

April nodded her head toward the interview-room door. We left, giving Willie time to think.

"Don't even," Jessie told us, turning on April and me. "I take a *dim fucking view* of people who hurt kids, and don't tell me you both don't feel the same way. I *know* you do."

"Yeah, I do," I said. "I also know a victim when I see one. Whatever Kite did to him, Willie is . . . he's crippled. Come on. The drinking, the fighting, that horror show of scars on his chest? The man can barely function. However much you hate him right now, I guarantee he hates himself about a hundred times worse."

"That doesn't excuse what he did."

"No," April said, "it doesn't. But it *explains* what he did. And he's opened up to us. We need that right now. He's the best lead we have, and I am asking you to *pretend* to be sympathetic."

Jessie pressed her palms flush against the two-way mirror, leaning in to watch Willie sobbing in the other room. She took a deep breath.

"All right. Fine. I'm cool. Where do you two wanna go with this?"

I held up my hand. "I had an idea. It'll be risky, but now that there won't be any more abductions, since we've got Willie in custody, do you think Edwin will follow through on his threat?"

April looked from me to Willie.

"You want to use him as bait," she said.

"He's ours now," I said, nodding to the window, "and we can set the terms of battle. If Edwin sends the Bogeyman to grab Willie, we can be standing right there when the closet door opens."

"And armed for bear," Jessie said. "Yeah, okay. Sounds like we've got a license for Bogeyman hunting season. Think Sheriff Barry's got any serious firepower lying around the station house?"

"It's rural Michigan. Guarantee we can get shotguns at least. Serious enough for you?"

"Mayberry," she told me, "I am an *artist* with a shotgun. Let's do this."

"Likewise," April said. "I approve."

We strode back into the interrogation room. Willie rubbed at his reddened face, then wiped his palms on his jeans.

"Good news," I told him. "We're going to save your life."

Willie shook his head slowly. "The only thing that can save me is giving him what he wants."

"That's not happening," Jessie said, "but we can do the next best thing. As of now, you're under our protection."

He laughed. It was a nervous, jittery, humorless thing, and his eyes widened.

"You don't get it. You *can't* protect me. As soon as Mr. Kite realizes I'm not setting out any more beacons, he'll send the Bogeyman for me. He'll take me. He'll take me to his *house*."

"Not on our watch," I said. "C'mon, we need to move you someplace safer. Don't worry. We'll be with you round the clock."

We got him on his feet, flanking him as we led him out of the interrogation room, with Willie protesting every step of the way. We weren't alone. Barry came hustling down the hall toward us, looking ten kinds of worried.

"Something weird's going on, and you girls have visitors. I don't know if they're, ya know, the people you warned me might be coming around or what—"

"Who's out there?" I asked, shooting a look past Barry's back, at the swinging door that led to the station lobby.

"Russian girl came by, real pretty but hard-lookin'; she flashed an ID and asked if you two were here. Says she's a bounty hunter and she's got a warrant for Willie."

"You can't protect me," Willie mumbled.

"Barry," I said, "tell me you didn't let her in."

He stuck his thumbs in his belt and puffed out his chest.

"Hell, no, I did not. Gimme a little credit, huh? We talked through the glass door. Told her we were having a possible contaminated-mail situation, and I couldn't open the door till the CDC got here. Also told her I hadn't seen you all day, but I don't think she bought it. So she leaves, and five minutes later, this shady-looking guy comes up, says he's selling magazines door to door. Well, he's no local, I know that on sight. While I'm giving him the brush-off, he keeps eyeing the lobby behind me, like he's trying to see who else is here."

"Are they gone?" Jessie asked.

"Well, that's the thing. I look out and the two of 'em are out in the parking lot, arguing up a storm. They knew each other, I can tell you that much. So the guy went and sat in his car. He's still out there. Just sitting. Watching the building."

"And the woman?" I asked.

Barry shrugged. "Couldn't tell you. I guess she left."

Cody came up the hall from the other direction, jerking a thumb over his shoulder, one hand on his holster.

"Something's weird," he said. "I'm hearing a rattling in the vents, like there's something crawling around in the—"

That's when we heard the rattling thump echoing from the station-house roof, right above our heads.

"It's here," Willie moaned. "It's here to take me. The Bogeyman is here."

"No, Willie," I said through gritted teeth. "Different monster entirely. Okay, Barry, we need the most secure room in this building, right now. We're all in serious danger."

Willie clutched the sides of his head. "I told you. I *told* you, you can't protect me."

"This way," Barry said, pushing past us. "Got a little armory in the back, for the gun cabinets. Ain't exactly Fort Knox, but it's built to keep people—"

In the heat of the moment, Barry made the same mistake we did: treating Willie like a witness in protective custody instead of a dangerous suspect. As he brushed past, getting too close, too careless for just a second, Willie lunged for his belt.

Suddenly Barry's big chrome .45 was in Willie's trembling hands.

Barry shouted as April grabbed the wheels of her chair and veered backward. Jessie and I pulled our Glocks at the same time, keeping Willie covered in our gun sights. Cody had the fastest draw, whipping out his steel like a cowboy at high noon. He edged toward me, trying to get between me and Willie's gun. Chivalrous, but bad police work.

"At your shoulder, Deputy," I said in a low voice, only as hard as I needed to be. "Watch my line of fire." Cody got the message and side-stepped the other way.

"Son," Barry warned Willie, "you don't wanna do that—"

"Put it *down*," Jessie said.

The revolver swayed drunkenly from side to side in Willie's grip as he took a couple of unsteady steps back, toward the lobby door.

"You can't protect me," he said.

"Willie," April said, "you're frightened. We understand that. But what you're doing is very, very dangerous, and you need to put the weapon down before someone gets hurt."

Another shuffling step back. As the barrel of the stolen revolver swung toward my face, his grip shaking like a junkie in detox, I struggled to keep my finger off my trigger. From somewhere behind us, metal scraped and groaned. Nyx, in the ventilation. Creeping closer.

"I *will* drop your ass," Jessie snapped. "Put. The fucking. Gun. Down."

Barry held out his open hands and took a step closer to Willie.

"Son," he said, "where are you gonna go? We're just trying to keep you safe, that's all. Now, you're frightened, and that's fine, but frightened people with guns make some bad, bad mistakes. The kind of mistakes you can't take back. Just put it down, and we can all pretend this never happened."

A single tear trickled down Willie's cheek.

"Don't you get it?" he whispered. "There's nowhere in the world I can run to. Nowhere is safe. He can always find me. Ever since I was little, when he started coming to me in my dreams . . . I never had a chance, not really. But it's okay. Now I understand. Now I know there's only one way to make it all stop."

"Willie," Cody said, *"don't—"*

"It's okay," he said, smiling as he blinked back the tears. "I understand now."

Then he put the gun to his head and pulled the trigger.

The shot boomed like a cannon in the narrow hallway, and spatters of blood and bone painted the drab beige wall as Willie's corpse tumbled to the floor.

Nobody said a word.

We just stood there inhaling the coppery, acrid tang of gun smoke and blood as we stared down at the dead man.

Even the rattling from the vents stopped cold. I felt a prickling sensation on the back of my neck.

"He's dead, Nyx!" I called out, holstering my gun. "Get lost."

A rumbling from the vent, and another noise. Something that sounded like a snort of disgust. The sound retreated into silence.

"Jesus," Barry breathed. "I didn't—I mean, I knew Willie had problems, but you didn't warn me he was nuts. I didn't *know*."

"Amateur hour," Jessie said, "is officially over."

She stepped around Willie's corpse and stalked out the door. April rolled after her, grim and silent.

"Barry," I said, touching his arm, "it's okay—"

He stared at Willie with a face of pale stone.

"A man just shot himself in my station house, with a gun he took off my belt. This is anything but okay."

I hated to ask, but I had to. I gestured toward the body. "Can you . . . take care of this?"

"Yeah." His chin bobbed. "Yeah, sure. Might need you to sign something later, I don't know. Don't even know the procedure for something like this. Took my goddamn gun off my belt . . . I didn't know he was crazy, Harmony. I didn't know."

Except he wasn't crazy, I thought. *Just hurting.*

And he wouldn't be the last one.

I thought back to what he'd said in the interrogation room. That he'd used his delivery list to pick victims, choosing them at random—except for the third one, the one Edwin Kite picked out personally. We knew about only two abductions, and that could mean only one thing.

The next Returned, Willie's replacement, had already been marked. If we didn't find a way to take Kite down, then in another thirty years or so, the cycle would start all over again. Cody followed me to the station-house door. "Harmony," he said. I stopped with my hand on the push plate.

"I might not *like* Talbot Cove," he said, "but as long as I've got this badge on, I'm responsible for keeping it safe. And the stuff I've seen and heard today . . ."

He trailed off. I waited for him to find the words he was looking for.

"What's happening to my town?" he asked me. "And please, don't tell me about Willie being a witness to . . . some criminal conspiracy. Barry might buy that line, but respect me enough not to lie to my face, okay?"

"I won't lie to you, Cody. But I can't tell you the truth, either. I need you to just bear with me, okay? When the time comes, I'll explain everything I can. Just trust me."

He put his hands on his hips and chewed that over.

"Okay," he said. "Okay. Just . . . let me help?"

"When I can," I promised, and went outside to find my partner.

THIRTY-FIVE

Jessie paced across the parking lot, head down, kicking at stones. April rolled alongside her, speaking in soft tones. No cars around but ours and a couple of police cruisers—looked like Fontaine had already cleared out, and Nyx had no reason to stick around, either.

"Hey," I said, walking up behind them.

"Our best chance at closing this case," Jessie said, "and he shoots himself. Well, I've got good news and bad news. Good news is, the Bogeyman abductions are over. Bad news is, thirty goddamn years from now we'll be right back where we started."

"Maybe not. We've got one last lead to chase. Let's head back to the motor lodge. We'll need Kevin's help."

Kevin was a step ahead of me. He sat huddled over the mayor's laptop in the motel room, muttering under his breath as his fingers flew over the keys.

"Trying to track down this CTide06 guy, but it's no good. He's using a free e-mail provider and routing everything through a proxy VPN. Makes it look like he's sending all his mail from Hong Kong. Which, I can confidently say, he isn't."

Jessie leaned over his shoulder to read his screen. "Can't you, I don't know, run a back trace on the proxy?"

"Did you just make that up? Words mean things. And no. I'm a hacker, not a wizard. I know, it's an easy mistake to make. No, this guy knows how to hide his tracks—which, to be fair, isn't all that hard. Our best bet, though I cringe to say it, is the legal route. Get a subpoena for his e-mail service provider so we can scope out their internal logs."

"Which will take weeks," I said. "I've got a better idea. We know that the child who comes back is always a blood descendant of Edwin Kite, right?"

April, sitting at the table by the window, glanced up from her notes. "Yes. Which, at this point, enumerates several *hundred* people in Talbot Cove alone. Over the course of two hundred years, any family tree tends to sprout vast, long, and leafy branches."

"But we can narrow it down. We're looking for a family with a young child—"

"Doesn't narrow it down as much as you might think," Kevin said. "I've already tried that. I've spent the last four hours searching through *years* of birth announcements and cross-referencing them with everyone who has a passing connection to—wait. Wait, wait, wait. I've been going at this wrong. There's an easier way."

"What is it?" I asked him.

"When people put numbers in an e-mail handle, it's always a historically significant date. Birthdays, weddings, graduation. CTide. Crimson Tide. That's the University of Alabama's football team."

His fingers flew across his keyboard. I watched his screen turn into a wash of white on scarlet, and words scrolled on a pop-up window.

University Bursar's Office
Employee Access

"If you only want employees to access your employee-only site," he muttered under his breath as he worked, "maybe update your firmware more than once every five years."

"So we're looking for an alumnus who graduated in 2006," April said, "with a relation to the Kite family. Hmm. Bigger needle, smaller haystack. I'll help with the search."

Kevin cracked his knuckles and glanced my way. "We've got this. Give us three or four hours, tops."

It took them only two. Which, coincidentally, was the number of Kites they found.

"Jacob and Ellen Garner," Kevin said, pulling up old photographs from a campus newspaper on his screen and lining them up side by side. "College sweethearts. Our buddy Jacob was a running back for the Crimson Tide and a short pick to go pro until he blew his knee out. Ellen, meanwhile, is a Kite cousin twice removed. It's a stretch, but she's got the family blood in her veins."

"They married the summer after graduation," April added. "Traveled a bit, and came home to Talbot Cove to start a family. Jacob is the branch manager at a local bank—"

Kevin produced a sheet of motel stationery with a flourish, handing it to me. "—and as of one year ago, Ellen became a stay-at-home mom. Can't say it's them for sure, but they fit every single one of the criteria."

He'd scribbled an address on the sheet along with turn-by-turn directions. If I remembered the spot, it was a nice little chunk of town just off Main Street. Affluent, quiet, nice place to raise a kid.

Or lose one.

###

Jessie and I sat in the SUV, parked curbside on a tranquil little side street. Big houses, white picket fences, and the last light of the setting sun filtering through orange and dying leaves. A beefy blue Subaru sat out in the Garners' driveway, and the shifting lights of a television screen glowed against their living room window.

"We need to agree on something," Jessie said, staring at the house, "before we go in."

"Name it."

"Unless we get something to go on here, a real lead, none of this goes in our final report. Not the Garners, not the third abduction, none of it. It ends with Willie."

"What? Why?"

Jessie pointed a finger at the front door.

"Edwin Kite is stuck in his . . . demesne, right? And the Bogeyman can't do squat without someone Earth-side to build and set out a beacon for him."

"Right."

"Well," she said, "with Willie out of the picture, that means the only link to Edwin Kite—and the only thing that can help him snatch more victims—is the infant in that house. Vigilant Lock doesn't leave loose ends."

"I assumed we'd, you know, keep the kid under surveillance. Maybe run some tests, when she got older, to try and suss out how the link works. It'd be good intel."

Jessie snorted and gave me a humorless smile.

"Our mandate is investigation and extermination. Emphasis on the latter. Vigilant isn't in the business of taking chances when it comes to occult threats. Remember, I was a kid when I landed on their radar, too—and Linder had to be talked out of sanctioning my ass because I *might* be dangerous."

"Jessie . . . are you saying Linder would give a kill order on an *infant*?"

"I'm saying he's a cold-blooded son of a bitch, and I'd rather not find out if he would or not. So I'm asking you: Are you down with lying to the boss?"

It sounded like an easy question at first. Sanction an infant? And the victim of a crime? Never.

But Willie had been an infant, and a victim once, too, and now two children were gone—maybe gone forever—because he helped Edwin Kite take them. In twenty, thirty years, if the Garner kid made the same choices Willie did, the cycle would start all over again. By covering it up, we'd be leaving a time bomb in the heart of Talbot Cove.

Take the kid out of the equation and Edwin Kite lost his meal ticket for good. A quick fix. A snip of the chain. It was attractive.

Quick fixes always are, I thought, *and they usually blow up in your face later on down the line. It's the wrong way.*

"One condition," I said.

Jessie turned in her seat and gave me an expectant look.

"If that's what it comes to," I said, "if the investigation just dead-ends here, the case stays open. Unofficially, I mean. I'm not waiting another thirty years for a crack at Edwin Kite. We come back as often as we can, we keep an eye on this kid, and most of all we make damn sure she doesn't turn into another Willie."

"Shit," Jessie grunted, shoving open her door, "that was *assumed*."

We stood on the Garners' doorstep. Their doorbell played the opening notes of "Ave Maria," ringing out on metal chimes.

"So," I said, "you lie to Linder often?"

"I like to think of our case files as a carefully constructed media narrative, where specific facts and incidents may be reedited or reframed in order to convey a deeper understanding and context. Sort of like reality television."

"I'll take that as a yes."

Jessie shrugged. "I've got two priorities: my team, and our mission. Everything else takes a backseat, and that includes Linder and all his shady backroom buddies in Washington. All I need from them is funding and intel so we can keep doing what we do. All *they* need is to stay the hell out of our way."

A dead bolt rattled, and the door swung wide. The man on the other side looked like an all-American gone to seed, broad-shouldered and square-jawed but hiding his potbelly under a cable-knit sweater.

"Jacob Garner?" We flashed our IDs. "FBI. Could we have a word with you, please?"

He got a deer-in-the-headlights look and stepped back, gesturing us inside with a shaky hand. "Uh, sure. Sure, c'mon in. What's this about?"

The Garners kept a clean house. More than clean, meticulous, from the plush white carpet to a molded wood entertainment system with a stereo and racks of vintage vinyl. A place for everything and everything in its place—except for the rolling suitcases stacked in a line by the front door.

"Going on a trip?" I asked, nodding to the luggage as Jacob shut the door behind us.

A woman swept in from the dining room, thin, long-necked, and shrouded in a gray tunic dress. She put on her earrings as she walked.

"Honey? I thought I heard the doorbell. Is it—oh, hello."

"Ellen Garner," I said. "Good. You're both here. Special Agents Temple and Black, FBI. We're here to investigate your daughter's kidnapping."

Bull's-eye. The color drained from Ellen's face like someone pulled a plug, and the look that shot between her and Jacob turned the room to ice.

"I . . . I don't know what you're talking about," she said. "Mallory? Mallory is just . . . just fine. We didn't call about any kidnapping."

"That's right," Jessie said. "You didn't call about it."

Jacob forced a nervous laugh. "You two are way, way off base. I mean, you must be looking for another house or something. There hasn't been a kidnapping! Mallory's fine."

"Then you won't mind letting us see her," I told him, "so we can verify that for ourselves."

"Do you have a warrant?" Ellen asked.

Jessie smiled. "Are you really going to make us get one? C'mon, if it's a mistake, no harm done. Just let us see her and we'll leave."

"It's okay," Jacob said. "It's fine. I'll show you."

Mallory's crib was in the master bedroom, next to a California king bed and a whole bunch of cardboard boxes with duct-taped lids. A dresser drawer hung open and empty. The Garners weren't going on vacation—they were just *going*, period.

The baby lay in her crib, dressed in a tiny pink-flannel onesie and sleeping with her little fists pressed to her scrunched-up face. Safe and sound.

"See?" Ellen said. "She's fine. Now . . . please leave."

I unbuttoned her onesie.

"Hey!" Jacob snapped, striding toward me. Jessie got between us. She was half Jacob's size, but she gave him a glare that stopped him dead in his tracks.

The pink flannel tugged aside, baring the sleeping baby's shoulder. Revealing the glyph burned into her skin.

THIRTY-SIX

"I'm going to save you two a lot of time and trouble," I said, buttoning the onesie back up and turning away from the crib. "We know about Edwin Kite and the Bogeyman. Jacob, we read your e-mails to Mitchum Kite. And we know you hired Nyx."

"Where . . ." Jacob said. "Where is Mitchum? We haven't been able to reach him since yesterday—"

"Dead. Nyx killed him."

"Oh God," Ellen moaned. She pressed her face against Jacob's shoulder. He curled his beefy arm around her, pulling her close.

"Who are you people?" Jacob said. "Who are you, really?"

"We're the folks you really, really want to cooperate with right now," Jessie said.

Ellen pulled away from her husband and dabbed at one eye with her sleeve.

"I'll talk to them. Just keep packing."

"Ellen—"

She squeezed his hand, then let go.

"I'll talk to them." She glanced our way. "Follow me."

The tiny room in the attic, up a flight of creaking steps and behind a locked door, might have been someone's office once. A quiet little retreat to get away from it all, with a porthole window overlooking the street outside. Most offices didn't have the faint residue of pale-blue chalk on the floorboards, though, marking the curves of half-erased pentacles, or a candle-laden altar draped in purple silk.

"Our family talks," Ellen told us, slowly pacing the room. "Not all the Kites, and not all of them believe, but we've all at least heard the stories. About Edwin Kite, and the Bogeyman."

Jessie's gaze slowly took in the room, from wall to wall. "I'm guessing you're one of the believers."

"When I moved back to Talbot Cove after college, I got in touch with Mitchum. We were kindred spirits. He knew all about monsters, growing up in his father's house. Jeremiah Kite saw Edwin as an . . . aspirational figure. He idolized him. When he wasn't busy torturing his own children, he was trying to re-create Edwin's work. Then the 'great sorcerer' died of a ruptured appendix, of all things, and left Mitchum with the family inheritance."

"And the monster in the basement," I said, thinking back to the psychic parasite we'd fought there.

"And that, too," Ellen said. "We spent years looking for a way to get past it, thinking it must have been guarding Edwin's old workshop. Best we could do is keep it contained. I'm afraid I'm not a very good witch."

She paused beside the window, the golden sunset light washing over her.

"This wasn't supposed to happen. The timing was wrong."

"What wasn't?" Jessie asked.

"We knew how it worked. Edwin is . . . feeding off the children somehow—they're keeping him alive, but he can't leave the House of Closets. So he has two tools: the Bogeyman and the returned child. They work together and send him what he needs. Then I made my mistake. The timing. I thought the timing would always be the same.

The last time he hunted, it was the '80s. Before that, the '40s. I thought we'd have another ten years before the Bogeyman came back."

Ellen clenched her hands into frustrated fists, her voice cracking.

"I thought," she said, forcing the words out, "it would be safe to have a baby."

"But once the abductions started," I said, "you knew."

"Oh, we knew. Our first plan didn't work. Find the last returned child and stop him. Just . . . I don't know. Stop him, any way we could. But that bastard Jeremiah shredded the original police report before he died. He covered up every mention of the abduction, and we couldn't figure out who it was."

"His name was Willie Grandeen," Jessie said.

Ellen tilted her head. "You said 'was.'"

"He killed himself today."

"He killed himself." Ellen sighed, leaning back against the attic wall. Her head thumped against the grainy wood. "He marked my baby girl. He gave her to that monster. *Then* he killed himself. *Bastard.*"

"So that was your first plan," I said. "What was the second?"

"*Nyx,*" she said with a bitter curl of her lip. "That was Mitchum's idea. He read about the Chainmen in one of his father's grimoires. You see, Edwin Kite is a fugitive in hell's eyes: he broke his deal with Adramelech, and even stole some of the demon's power. We thought if we could get the Chainmen's attention, they'd kill Edwin for us and end this nightmare for good. I found the summoning ritual. Didn't know what to expect, but Nyx answered the call. Once we found out her price, it was too late."

"What's her price?"

"When Nyx goes back to hell, she has to bring *two* souls with her: the one she's hunting, and the one who called her name." Ellen folded her arms. "Jacob volunteered. Said it's what any father would do for his little girl. *I* said there's no way she's growing up without her daddy."

The suitcases, the cardboard boxes—now it all made sense.

"You're running," I said.

"What else can we do?"

Jessie rubbed the back of her neck, thinking. "If Nyx doesn't get Kite, do you still have to pay up?"

"No, but Nyx doesn't fail," Ellen said. "Ever. At least, that's the story. I guess she'll be hunting us next. At least my baby will be all right."

I scuffed the toe of my shoe against a faint line of chalk residue. "You mentioned the House of Closets. What do you know about it?"

"Only what's been passed down through the family. Hints and whispers. They say it was the key to Edwin's betrayal. When he sold his soul to Adramelech, he crafted these elaborate designs for a mansion in . . . well, I don't know where it is or how it works, only that it isn't *here.* He tricked the demon into infusing his own power into the building."

"So why doesn't Adramelech just take it back?" Jessie asked her.

"Edwin designed the house as a trap. It's a siphon. Power flows only one way: inward, straight to him. He barred Adramelech from coming in after him, then took his precautions a step even farther. According to Jeremiah's journals, he merged with it. He became part of the house itself. He can't be removed. *Can't* be. The only way Edwin Kite can leave the House of Closets is under his own power and by his own free will."

"But you think Nyx has a way to get at him anyway," I said.

Ellen shrugged. "She thinks she does. You've met her, I assume. Do *you* doubt she can do it, if she says she can?"

"Excuse us a moment," I said and tugged Jessie's sleeve. We walked over to the far corner of the attic, conferring in low voices.

"What do you think?" I asked her.

"Nyx wouldn't take a job if she wasn't certain she could pull it off. You heard her at the paper mill: she's a little obsessed with coming in first place."

"And if she nails Kite," I said, jerking my head toward Ellen, "how much of a chance do you think these people have of getting away without paying her?"

"Somewhere south of zero and none. About the same as our chances of getting Kite first, considering we can't *reach* him."

"Maybe," I said. "Maybe not."

Finding a demon-crafted house that doesn't exist anywhere on Earth—let alone getting inside—is a little outside my wheelhouse. I'm good at what I do, but there's magic and then there's *magic*. Still, the inklings of an idea came to me as I looked over at Ellen's shrine.

I can't say it was a *good* idea, or even a sane one, but you work with what you have.

"Ellen." She looked away from the darkening window, toward me. "What do you know about the beacons?"

She shrugged. "The Returned uses them to tell the Bogeyman where to strike. That's all I know. They were a passion project of Jeremiah Kite's—there's reams of pages about them in his journals—but the symbolism and the math . . . it's like trying to unravel higher calculus when all you know is how to add and subtract."

"Those journals—may we have them, please?"

"If you think it'll help," she said. "Jeremiah thought he could reverse-engineer the spell. Turn it into a two-way gate so he could go meet Edwin and 'learn at the feet of the master.' As far as I can tell, he never pulled it off."

Jessie gave me a side-eyed glance. "Are you that good?"

"Not even close," I murmured, "but maybe I don't have to be. We just need to get a little creative."

Ellen dug out the books: four of them in all, thumb thick, with cracked black-leather covers. I opened one, the old binding glue splitting and flaking, and gazed upon a dense sea of cramped handwriting. My eyes glazed as I tried to follow Jeremiah's stream-of-consciousness ramblings. Maybe that was for the best. What little I did read made my skin crawl.

She bundled the books into my arms and asked, "Now what?"

"Now you stay put," I said.

"We *can't*," she said. "Are you crazy? Once Nyx gets Edwin Kite, she's coming back for Jacob. We can't be here when she does."

"Ellen," I said, "if Nyx can capture a two-hundred-year-old sorcerer who's hiding out in another dimension, how much of a chance do you think you and your husband have? Edwin has an otherworldly stronghold. You have a Subaru."

Her shoulders sank. I could feel her hope sinking with them.

"That doesn't mean we can just stay here and wait for her," she protested, but her voice had lost its strength.

"That's exactly what it means, and I'll tell you why. First, she's not coming back, because we're going to catch Edwin before she does. Second, if all of this has taught you anything, it should be that once you make a bargain with a demon, you *don't* screw with the terms. If you run, Nyx will know. It's not just your husband's life at stake: it's yours and your child's, too."

"Do you really think you can beat her?"

"Yeah," I said, "I really do."

Sometimes you have to try and sound more confident than you feel. What we really had was a chance. Just a chance, bordering on a long shot, but it was the only chance we—and the Garner family—had left.

THIRTY-SEVEN

On our way out, in the freshly fallen dark, Jessie flashed her penlight across the Garners' lawn. We found the third wicker ball down at the edge of the grass, sitting cold and still in the shadow of an oak tree.

"Bag it," I said. "Then we need to run by the motel and grab the other two beacons."

"You're thinking about something," Jessie told me. "I can hear the hamster wheel rattling."

"Jeremiah Kite had the right idea: to take the basic idea behind the beacons and turn them into a door that works in both directions. He just wasn't skilled enough to pull it off. Neither am I, but I think I'm a little more creative than he was. We're going to need help from a contact of mine. Chicago is . . . what, an hour, hour and ten from here?"

I tossed her the keys to the SUV.

"How fast can *you* get us there?"

Jessie snatched the keys from the air. "We'll be there and *back* in an hour."

She wasn't quite that fast, but we still made damn good time as we wound along the coast of Lake Michigan, carving down long and lonely stretches of highway.

"You're holding your cards close to the vest," Jessie said, leaning toward the steering wheel as she leaned on the gas. "How about a little hint?"

"Edwin learned to mark his servants, like a demon, right? But we don't know how tight the bond between him and Willie really was. Willie said Edwin always contacted him in dreams, never while he was awake."

"Okay, I'm with you so far."

"There's a good chance, at least until he tries to reach out to him again, that Edwin doesn't know Willie is dead. He'll figure it out pretty quick—maybe tonight, even—so we don't have much time."

"Sounds about right, but what can we do with that?"

"I'm thinking 'Willie' needs to summon the Bogeyman one last time," I said. "And when he shows up, he's going to have a nasty surprise waiting for him."

As the highway curved north and the Chicago skyline rose up in the distance, traffic became a slow-moving sea of scarlet brake lights. We cruised along, weaving from lane to lane, until we hit the off-ramp for Lake Shore Drive. We hugged the coast—black waters on our right, and canyons of granite and steel on our left.

The city at night became a carnival of harsh white light. Spotlights, skyscraper lights, antennae topped with pinpricks the color of ice or frost blue. The electric power blotted out the stars, turning the sky black, but the night had to struggle for a foothold here. Chicago was too busy to sleep.

The Field Museum stood stony and proud, like a temple to the Greek gods in the heart of the American Midwest. Eighty-foot banners dangled from the eaves atop towering ionic pillars. We were far too late for a tour—the museum closed at five—but I knew at least one employee would be working late. As we looked for a parking spot, I gave her a call.

"Not the front doors," she said. "Circle around the campus and you'll find a side door for the research wing. Just knock. I'll tell the guard to expect you."

We were knocking on the glass for a while, standing next to a row of manicured bushes that shivered in the wind. Eventually a guard in a pressed blue uniform wandered by. He gave us a wave before he scurried over to unlock the door.

I showed him my ID. "We're here to see Dr. Khoury. She's expecting us."

"Sure, sure," he said, pointing. "Just go up the hall that way. Soon as you come to a security grate, take a left. She's in the conservators' workshop. Can't miss it."

There's something magical about a museum at night. As we passed the steel grates barring us from the main hall and the shadowed exhibits beyond, I craned my neck to see everything I could.

"So where'd you meet this doctor?" Jessie asked. "She a friendly?"

"Not a registered friendly, per se," I said.

She gave me a look.

"So what you're saying is, you kept her out of your reports."

I shrugged. "It was a prerequisite for getting her help on a smuggling investigation. Halima Khoury is kind of a private person. Her intel was flawless, though. She's an expert in—"

"No, no," Jessie said, "back it up. What you're saying is, you lied in your field report. After you acted all shocked that *I* lie to Linder all the time."

"It was a very tiny lie of omission, three and a half years ago. And I've done it only once. Ever. And I felt bad about it."

Jessie punched my arm. "You're a *rebel*, Harmony Black."

"Stop it."

"Mmm-hmm. You are one badass rebel."

A rubber wedge propped open the door to the conservators' workshop. I slowed my step, hearing voices drift out from inside. Not happy voices.

"—why you'd think that I, of all the people in this city, would be harboring that *creature*," Halima snapped.

The man who answered her was slick, cultured, his words edged with a breezy British accent. "I don't think that. The fact remains, Doctor, that you've known Damien Ecko longer than anyone. You can understand why I'd want to speak with you."

Damien Ecko. I remembered hearing Emmanuel Hirsch drop that name when I'd eavesdropped on his phone call back in Detroit. Whoever this Ecko was, he got around.

"Interrogate me, you mean. I am not subject to your laws, Royce, nor do I go seeking conflict with your people. This is my tiny corner of the city. My little dominion. All I ask is to be left to my work in peace."

"Right, right, you have to be around when your girlfriend finally decides to wake up."

"How *dare* you!" Halima shouted, her voice punctuated by the crash of breaking glass.

I didn't have to say a word to Jessie. We moved as one, sweeping around the corner and into the workshop. It could have passed for a college science lab, the long room bathed in stark white light and lined with tables and cabinets. A clutter of projects in midcompletion filled every open surface, from tiny stone relics under glass to Tupperware beds of dirt and sand. Old hardcovers filled a rolling library cart, each one with a colored slip of paper sticking up from inside the front cover.

Halima looked exactly like I remembered her: almond skin and a long, narrow face, her body draped in a floor-length dress and a powder-blue headscarf. The man standing on the other side of a study table with his hands on his hips, I didn't know. He could have passed for a retired model pushing the edge of forty, with an aquiline nose and pale green eyes. He wore a tailored gray suit, and the tail of a tattoo—a black, thorny rose vine, it looked like—snaked up from under the collar of his crisp dress shirt to end just beneath his left ear.

The man—Royce, she'd called him—slowly turned to look at a shattered pile of glass on the floor just behind him.

"Really?" he said, giving her a cocky smile. "Now we're throwing things? Please, Doctor, everyone says you're the voice of *reason* in this city. Do grow up."

Halima's fingernails dug into her palms.

"The museum is closed," she told him. "You need to leave now."

"As you wish. Just remember: there are rewards for cooperation. Find Ecko's whereabouts for me, and I'll gladly make a generous donation to, er"—he waved a hand, taking in the room—"whatever it is you people do here. It's very cute, with the antiques and the placards and the learning about things. Not sure it beats television for sheer commercial appeal, but—"

"Leave!"

Royce gave her a wave and turned on his heel. As he strolled past us, his gaze slid right over me and looked Jessie up and down.

"Hello, ladies."

"Good-bye, douche," Jessie muttered in his wake, nudging out the plastic wedge and shutting the workshop door.

"I'm sorry," I told Halima. "Is this a bad time?"

She chuckled, sounding tired. "No, far from it. You probably saved me from murdering more innocent test tubes. We've had an . . . exciting few weeks here. Local politics, nothing you need be concerned over."

Jessie jerked her thumb back over her shoulder. "So who was he?"

Halima's eyes twinkled. "That's not what you came to see me about."

It wasn't the most graceful attempt at dodging a question, but I let her get away with it. I shook her hand. Her grip was firm, desert dry, with a texture almost like cheesecloth.

"Doctor, this is Jessie Temple, my new partner. Thank you for seeing us."

"Of course," she said, shaking Jessie's hand. "It sounded like you two had an interesting conundrum for me. I'm always up for a good puzzle."

Five minutes later, we stood behind her while she perched on a stool, studying one of the wicker balls under an oversize magnifying glass. The other two beacons sat to her left, next to Jeremiah Kite's journals. She turned the ball in her hand, slowly, occasionally reaching over to adjust the magnifying glass's boom arm.

"So far I can confirm your suspicions. Definitely Sumerian. Dimensional mathematics. Magics." She snapped her finger. "Mathemagics."

"Head," Jessie groaned, "already hurting."

I gestured to the other two balls. "Each of these beacons was keyed to a place. Willie, the person placing them, was no magician; he just did what he was told. So I figure they're pretty much fire and forget. Plant 'em in the ground and they guide the Bogeyman to the closest house."

"Where it arrives in a closet," Halima said, "and leaves from the same place, yes? Or at least tries to?"

I thought back to the nanny cam video of the Gunderson house, where the recording ended with the same creaking closet door. I nodded.

"Odds are, this creature isn't teleporting. It's opening a very short-term gateway between worlds. Closets are just a convenient place to manifest it."

"What difference does it make?" Jessie asked.

"Difference being, if it teleports, only *it*—and the victims in direct skin contact—make the trip. A gateway, though . . . well, theoretically *anyone* could jump through as long as it was still open."

I rapped my fingernails on the stack of journals. "Jeremiah was wrong. He didn't need to reverse-engineer the spell or come up with something *new*. He just needed to be there when the Bogeyman showed up."

"And cross over before the gate sealed up again," Halima said. "Correct."

I looked to Jessie, the implications loud and clear.

"I thought if we could make a new beacon, we could at least lure out the Bogeyman and take him down. If we can be there when the gate opens, though? We can go after his master, too. This is our shot at Edwin Kite."

"Hell, I'm game." She looked to Halima. "What do you think, Doc? Can you re-create a working beacon?"

Halima thought about it. Her eyes narrowed as she studied the wound wicker strip, and she reached up to stroke her chin.

"Can I?" she finally said. "Most likely, yes. *Will* I?"

She shook her head.

"I am sorry, but no."

THIRTY-EIGHT

"I'm sorry," I told Halima. "Did you just say that you could help us, but you won't?"

She swiveled on her stool, turning to face us.

"I'm afraid that's correct. You are very brave young women, but I won't be responsible for your deaths."

"We're brave young women with guns," Jessie said flatly.

Halima chuckled. "And that is why I know you aren't ready. Pitting gunpowder against the machinery of the universe. Tell me, what do you even know of this place, this House of Closets?"

"Just what I told you on the phone," I said. "Edwin Kite conned a demon into building it for him, and he turned it into some kind of energy siphon. He can't be forced out; he can only leave under his own power—and he won't do that because the second he sets foot back on Earth, Adramelech is waiting to turn him into a charcoal briquette."

"Which doesn't stop us from walking into his house and sanctioning his ass right there on his living room rug," Jessie said. "*We* don't need him alive. In fact, it works out best for everybody involved if we permanently revoke his breathing license."

"You assume he needs to breathe," Halima said. "You assume far too much."

"Then clarify it for us," I told her.

Her stool scraped against the tile floor as she pushed it back, standing up. She talked as she walked, clasping her hands behind her back and pacing the aisle between tables.

"I once entertained a brief fascination with these . . . otherspaces. Worlds abutting our own—some entire universes unto themselves, others no bigger than this room. Hell is the best-known example, regrettably enough. The small ones, the pocket worlds crafted by deliberate magic, rather than forming naturally—they are defined by their creators. You are imagining a literal house. A place of wood and concrete, glass and nails. A dangerous mistake."

Jessie put her hands on her hips. "So what is it, then?"

"An extension of Edwin Kite's mind and soul. If he's truly mastered his little kingdom, it will respond to his every thought and desire. Everything you take for granted in this world, even the very laws of physics, will be subject to his whimsy. How will you fight that, hmm? How will your little guns help when he turns your blood to gasoline, or the air in your lungs to concrete?"

"I know some magic, too," I said, trying to sound braver than I felt. Facing down monsters was one thing. Traveling to another dimension, though? That was outside my skill set.

"Not in his realm, you won't. You might as well try to tear down a skyscraper with your bare hands. From the inside."

"You'd be amazed," Jessie said, "how much damage I can do with my bare hands."

Halima spun in midstride, stopping still, fixing her gaze upon Jessie's turquoise eyes.

"No. I wouldn't. I can see right through you, Agent Temple, down to the *thing* slumbering in your heart. Do you think it'll help you there? Edwin Kite's house represents his own evil, animal hungers made manifest. When your beast awakens, smelling blood, do you think it will fight against him . . . or *for* him?"

Jessie didn't have an answer for that. Not a verbal one. She just locked eyes with Halima, glaring.

"Halima," I said, "two children have been kidnapped. A third's been marked with Edwin Kite's brand, and the last person who suffered *that* fate just blew his brains out right in front of us. If we don't do this, if we don't take this chance, Kite will get away with it. And he'll do it again and again, and he won't ever stop because men like him never do. He thinks he's untouchable. Help us to prove him wrong."

I approached her, standing almost toe to toe, searching in her deep hazel eyes.

"If you won't help us, we'll keep searching until we find someone who will. The one thing we *won't* do is let this go. And right now, with every hour that slips by, our chances of getting those two kids back alive gets smaller and smaller. We know the risks. It doesn't matter. This is our *job*."

She studied me, silent, for a moment. Then she let out a sigh and walked back to her stool.

"No promises," she said, "but let's see what I can do. Check that cupboard—should be a few bricks of modeling clay. I don't work in wicker."

# # #

We paced, and waited, and watched the clock while Halima crafted her beacon. She rolled a cylinder of stiff gray modeling clay, first recruiting Jessie to knead it until it was malleable, and flattened the ends. With Jeremiah Kite's journals opened at her side and all three wicker balls lined up in a neat row under her magnifying glass, Halima slowly worked at the clay cylinder with a stainless-steel dental pick.

"The spell," she said with thinly veiled distaste, "is overcomplicated. What we're building, at its core, is a transmitter. A simple device to send a simple message, bursting across the veil of worlds."

She gestured toward the wicker balls. "The shared sequences on each beacon, the formulas that don't change? That's where Edwin Kite is. The variant numbers pinpoint the beacon's location on this side. Where are you going to trigger it?"

Good question. One I should have considered earlier.

"Can't use any of the houses he's already hit," Jessie said. "Kite or the Bogeyman might figure out something's up."

"Has to be a house in Talbot Cove, and it has to be empty." I snapped my fingers. "I know who can find us one."

I called Ellen Garner.

"Thank God," she said. "Tell me you have good news. The dog's been barking his head off all night, and Jacob keeps thinking he sees . . . things outside, in the dark."

"We're working on it. I wouldn't worry: Nyx is a little too busy hunting Edwin to be stalking you right now. Just sit tight. Listen, I need a favor. Your husband works for the bank, right?"

"Yes, he's the manager, but what does—"

"So he has access to loan records?"

"Of course."

"I need a property listing," I told her. "A foreclosure, in Talbot Cove. Needs to be a freestanding house, no current occupants. And it needs at least one closet."

"Hold on," she said, and pulled the phone away from her mouth as she called out. "Honey? Are you on the computer?"

She put Jacob on the line, and I walked him through it. It didn't take long at all: he found a little single-family home, empty for almost a year, on the south edge of town. Perfect. Within minutes we not only had an address, but the house's exact latitude and longitude. Bent over her magnifying glass, scribing intricate glyphs into the clay cylinder,

Halima paused just long enough to give me a thumbs-up before getting back to work.

"So you really think you can stop this guy?" Jacob asked, sounding like he almost dared to hope.

"We have a chance," I said. "We're going to do everything we can, I promise."

He fell silent.

"The dog," he said, sounding quizzical.

"Dog?"

"He stopped barking."

I heard a window shatter, glass exploding, and Ellen's high-pitched scream. The phone rattled as Jacob threw it to the carpet. There were pounding footfalls and a vicious *crack* that sounded like breaking wood.

"Suitcases by the door?" I heard Nyx hiss. "Boxes of memories? This one thinks you were trying to escape without paying your due."

"We don't owe you *anything*!" Ellen shrieked at her. "Not until you—"

A short, sharp slap silenced her, followed by the sound of a body hitting the floor. I heard slow, heavy footfalls, and the sound of the phone lifting from the floor. Nyx's rasping breath flooded my eardrum.

"Is this the wolf pup," she asked, "or the frightened little witch?"

"This is Special Agent Harmony Black of the Federal Bureau of Investigation," I told her, "and if you've hurt either of those people—"

"Hurt them? Yes. Kill them? No. They are more valuable alive. To you, at least, no?"

I squeezed my free hand into a fist. Jessie came over, leaning close to listen in.

"What do you want, Nyx?"

"This one has been watching. Saw you meet the Garners, saw you leave town. Has been here, in the dark, listening close."

"Shouldn't you be hunting Edwin Kite?"

Nyx laughed.

"That is exactly what this one is doing. Cannot figure out how to remove Kite from his demesne. Believes *you* have, though."

"We have an idea, that's all. No guarantees."

"It is sufficient. You wish to protect the innocent, yes? Then you will capture Edwin Kite and make a gift of him. Once this one has her target in custody, this one will release the Garners, unharmed. A trade: two lives, for a single damned soul. This one is generous, no?"

"You want us to do your work for you?" I asked, incredulous. "You're *cheating*."

"Losers complain of cheating and unfairness. Winners win. And Nyx always wins."

I pulled the phone away from my ear and cupped my hand over the receiver, looking to Jessie.

"We don't have time to pull off a rescue. The longer we wait on the beacon, the more likely Edwin is to find out Willie's dead."

"Why a rescue anyway?" Jessie asked. "Nyx is gonna drag Edwin straight down to hell, which is exactly where *we* want to send him. So we grab him and we trade him for the Garners. Everybody wins."

"Remember what Ellen told us about Nyx's price? She takes her target *and* the human who called her. You really think she's gonna change her mind and play nice if we give her what she wants? We can't risk that."

Jessie pressed her fist to her forehead, eyes squeezed shut.

"Shit," she said. "Okay, just . . . stall her. We'll deal with this after we deal with Edwin, assuming we live that long."

I took my hand off the receiver.

"I assume you heard my conversation with Jacob," I said to Nyx.

"This one has exquisite hearing."

"That address he gave me. Be there, on the street outside, at dawn. And bring the Garners with you. If either one of them is injured or dead, all deals are off."

"This one will treat them like kittens . . . and not drown them in a sack, unless forced to. Attempt any betrayal and they will be the ones punished for it. This one knows ways of keeping a human alive, flayed and screaming, for *weeks*. And would be happy to demonstrate."

"Be there," I snapped, "at dawn, with the Garners."

I hung up on her. There wasn't anything else to say. My lip curled in disgust.

"Because the stakes weren't high enough already," Jessie said. "Okay, so how do we hand over Edwin and get the Garners away from her at the same time?"

"That's plan D."

"Plan D?"

"Yeah," I said, "we figure it out while we're driving. Dr. Khoury? I don't know how much of that conversation you caught, but—"

"Almost done," she said, focused on the cylinder like a laser beam. The steel pick turned in her hand, scooping back tiny rows of clay and leaving intricate Sumerian glyphs in its wake.

I hoped she was right. We were burning moonlight.

THIRTY-NINE

Halima finished her version of the beacon. She sealed it in an airtight plastic baggie and gave me a five-minute crash course in how to set it off.

"Consider it a miniature engine," she said. "All it needs is a bit of gasoline—or in this case, a tiny spark of magical energy—and it will fulfill its purpose. Simply feed it and let it work."

"Thank you, Doctor. This means a lot to us."

"Salaam alaikum." She bowed her head slightly. "Be swift and safe, and sure of purpose. I hope to hear of your safe return."

Then we were off. Even with Jessie behind the wheel, driving the SUV like all hell was chasing us down, it'd be almost an hour's drive back to the south side of Talbot Cove.

I called April and filled her in. She hadn't been sleeping. I got the impression she didn't sleep much at all. Kevin, on the other hand, was out like a light and refused to budge until she rolled over and yanked the sheets off his bed.

"*Now* he's moving," she said, sounding satisfied. "And I saw that gesture, young man!"

"Can you meet us at the house?" I asked her. "And bring my luggage from the motel? We've got no time to lose. Nyx will be there come sunrise, and if we don't have Edwin—"

"Say no more. I'll see if I can find a taxi service still operating this time of night. It may take some doing. Another problem: we'll need some equipment to prepare the staging ground. Basic hardware-store fare, nothing too elaborate, but nothing in Talbot Cove is open this late."

"I've got a better idea. Hold tight. I'll call you right back."

I got Cody's voice mail twice in a row. He picked up on my third call.

"Yeahwhuh?" he mumbled, breathy.

"Cody. It's Harmony. We've got a line on the perp. We're finishing this. Tonight. If that offer to help is still open, I sure could use it."

That woke him up. I could hear him jump out of bed, covers rustling.

"What's going on? You need backup?"

"Sort of. Go to the Talbot Motor Lodge and pick up our assistants; April, you met earlier. They're going to need some supplies. How tight are you with the owner of that hardware store on Main Street?"

"Hank?" he asked. "He's one of Barry's poker buddies. Why?"

"Get his ass out of bed and have him meet you there. He's opening up early today. Tell him we'll pay double the sticker price for anything my people need to buy, plus he'll have Uncle Sam's undying gratitude."

"I'm on it," he said. I heard him tugging on his pants. "Anything else you need?"

I almost said no, then I caught the side eye from Jessie.

"Shotguns," I said. "Bring *all* your shotguns."

# # #

The A-frame house had barely been lived in, and loved even less. Thick curtains of dust caked the windows, and three months' worth of crabgrass choked the front lawn to death.

We pulled up behind a pair of squad cars. April met us out on the sidewalk while behind her, Cody and Kevin lugged plastic bags and armloads of loose lumber into the house.

"We don't have half the equipment I'd like for an operation of this nature," April said, shooting a dubious glance at the house. "We should have the building wired for film and sound, heat sensors at every door—"

"Well, as usual," Jessie said, "we don't get to play with the cool toys. We'll make up for it with some creativity, a little elbow grease, and a buttload of two-by-fours. You did get the buttload of two-by-fours, right?"

"I believe you specified at least twenty. Is that equivalent to a buttload? I just want to be certain I'm following your precise scientific methodology."

"Yeah, close enough," Jessie said.

"I also brought the chalk you asked for," April told me. "Will five sticks be enough?"

I turned and surveyed the street. I'd come up with a plan to deal with Nyx, but it was more of a desperation play than a stroke of tactical genius.

"It'll have to be," I said.

Kevin strode back out of the house, hopping down the porch steps, with Barry right behind him. I stifled a groan; I'd hoped to keep him out of this entirely. Kevin pointed back toward the open front door.

"Okay, we've got two floors with a nice open layout. First floor has one closet just off the foyer, and a walk-in pantry in the kitchen. Do pantries count?"

"Better safe than sorry," I said. I held the plastic baggie with the beacon in both hands, gripping it by the seal like it was a bomb that could go off at any moment.

"Two, then. Second floor has a master bedroom and a guest room, one closet in each, and a linen closet in the hall."

"Question?" Barry said, holding up his hand. He looked a little lost.

Jessie cracked her knuckles. "Okay, time is *not* on our side here. What do you think, Mayberry? Board 'em all up except for one of the upstairs bedrooms?"

"Don't call me Mayberry," I said, "and yes. April and Kevin can cover the bottom of the stairs, in case it gets past us."

"Ooh, a desperate last stand," Kevin said. "I just love those."

Barry held his hand a little higher. "Uh, question? Why are we boarding up closets?"

"*We* aren't," I told him. "Go home. We've got this."

"This is *my town*, Harmony. Whatever's going on here, it's my job to be involved. I mean, you called my *deputy* but you didn't call *me*? If Cody hadn't needed my help with the hardware store—"

I sighed. "Barry, you aren't equipped for what's going on here. Please, trust me on that. Just go home and wait. I'll call you when it's over, and I'll tell you whatever I can."

He turned away. Took a few steps toward his squad car. Then stood still.

"This is about Willie, isn't it? The police report I gave to Jeremiah Kite. You still don't trust me."

"No, Barry, it—"

He turned around to face me, red-faced, eyes glistening.

"And you're probably right not to. I fucked up, I know that. It was thirty damn years ago, and I've woken up knowing it every single day since, wondering what might've been different if I'd stood up to the Kites. Afraid of what could have happened, and regretting what did."

"He threatened your family." I took a step toward him. "I don't blame you for that."

He took a long look into my eyes.

"But I was wrong, wasn't I? Jeremiah Kite wasn't the Bogeyman. That's what you're doing here tonight. You're not after a copycat at all. It's the same man."

I gritted my teeth. He still thought we were hunting a human kidnapper, and I couldn't tell him the truth. Not the whole truth, at least. Some of it, I guess he'd earned.

"That's right. Jeremiah was involved in the kidnappings. He helped with the cover-up, but he wasn't the man who took my sister. The real Bogeyman is still on the loose. But, Barry, you don't understand—"

He thumped his chest. "I'll tell you what I understand, Harmony. Your father was my best friend in the whole world, and that son of a bitch cut his throat open with a razor blade. If this guy is still alive, I need to settle accounts. I *need* to. Please. Don't shut me out now."

I looked to Jessie. No help there. April tilted her head ever so slightly.

"It's your call," April told me. "We'll back you either way."

I thought back to the night my father died. Blanket around my shoulders, mug of hot chocolate clutched in my small, trembling hands, and Barry. Barry, showing me his badge, telling me what it meant.

"You do what we tell you," I said to Barry, "when we tell you. No questions. No hesitation. Agreed?"

He nodded slowly. Taking that in.

I put my hands on my hips and looked toward the house. "All right, let's get to work. I want every single closet in that house, except for one of the upstairs bedrooms, boarded over tight."

"Why are we—" Barry started to ask.

I held up a finger. "No questions."

"Your luggage is in the trunk," April said.

I walked around the back of the squad car and lifted the lid. They'd bought me a shoulder bag from the hardware store, just a simple beige canvas satchel, and I loaded it with some odds and ends from my suitcase: a canister of sea salt, some colored ribbons, bits and pieces of art I could weave into a spell with a little time to prepare.

I didn't think time to prepare was a luxury I'd be granted on the other side of the closet door, but we needed every edge we could get.

I picked up one last thing, scooping it up from where it nestled in the bottom of the suitcase. My sister's teddy bear. It sat in the palm of my hand, its tiny paws open wide for a hug. I added it to the bag.

I popped the collar of my blouse, slipped my tie off, and rolled it neatly. I replaced it with a new one, made of stiff polyester and glossy black.

"Wardrobe change?" Jessie asked me as she walked by, raising an eyebrow.

I turned my collar back down and tugged the tie's knot tightly at my throat.

"It was my father's," I told her.

The night came alive with the sounds of banging hammers and clanking wood. Cody, Kevin, Barry, and I all got busy, each picking a closet door and nailing up slabs of lumber to keep them sealed shut. I hammered fast, throwing up two-by-fours at irregular intervals as I worked my way down the door, building my emergency barricade. I'd almost gotten to the bottom of the door, arms aching as I knelt down for the last plank, when I heard April's voice from the doorway.

"Agent Black? There's . . . someone here to see you."

Fontaine, back in his borrowed corpse, leaned in the doorway with his ankles crossed. He looked like a dead man imitating Gene Kelly.

I stood, holding the claw hammer loosely in my hand. Feeling its weight. Fontaine's gaze drifted down to the business end.

"Oh, my," he drawled, "I *do* hope that's not for me."

"That depends entirely on you."

He uncrossed his ankles and strode into the room, his fingertips trailing along the back of April's wheelchair. She glowered and rolled back.

"Now, now," he said, "such hostility. *You* called *me*, after all."

That I had.

I'd done it on the drive back to Talbot Cove, fishing the business card he'd given us at the diner—the one that simply read **FONTAINE** in crisp black type—out of my wallet. I knew I'd held on to it for a reason. Stroking the raised type with my fingertips, I conjured up a spark of magic. Just a single musical note, the chiming of a crystal bell. The note rang out as it sank into the card, then soared off to find its owner.

"Nyx has taken hostages," I said. "A couple and their baby. If we don't hand over Edwin Kite at sunrise, she'll kill all three of them. If we *do* hand him over, she'll kill one of them and take his soul to hell along with Edwin's."

"Sounds like you're in a pickle of a perplexing predicament, Agent. But I don't see what any of that has to do with little ol' me."

"What if I told you I had a plan that would let *both* of us get what we want? You can't pull it off without me, and I can't pull it off without you."

"I would say . . . you have my undivided attention." He threw his arms wide, smiling like a showman. "But are you sure about making a deal with a demon? Are you *allowed*? Should I wait while you call and ask for permission? I declare, I certainly wouldn't want to get a sweet young lady such as yourself into any trouble."

"Special circumstances," I said.

FORTY

I laid out the plan, and Fontaine liked it. He liked everything except for the part about helping us board up the closets.

"Manual labor? Mmm, I'll sit that part out, darlin'. Just let me know when it's showtime. I'll go put on my dancing shoes."

We got the job done without him. By the time the last board went up, my phone read 3:38 a.m. Just a few hours to sunrise, and something told me Nyx wouldn't wait patiently if we were late. I stifled a yawn as I trudged downstairs. *No time for that,* I told myself. *Can't afford being tired.*

We gathered the team in the empty living room, the stained carpet still bearing the imprints of repossessed furniture. Cody, at Jessie's request, passed out the fruits of the Talbot Cove police armory: Remington 870 pump-action shotguns, with long, sleek barrels and sanded walnut stocks.

"Oh, yeah." Jessie whistled and checked her sights. "That's what I'm talking about."

Cody almost held one out to April, then paused. "Are . . . you trained to use a firearm, ma'am?"

She just gave him a thin-lipped smile. Kevin leaned in and whispered in Cody's ear. His eyes went wide. He handed her the shotgun.

"All right," I said. "Jessie and I are going upstairs. I want you three down here near the foot of the staircase. If anything comes down that *isn't* us, you know what to do."

"Not sure I do," Barry said.

April loaded her shotgun and racked the pump.

"That's quite all right, Sheriff," she said, "just follow my lead."

"What about that guy?" Cody asked, gesturing toward the living room window. Out in the dark, in a rented sedan, I could just barely make out the form of Fontaine sitting silent and motionless behind the wheel.

"He'll be ready when we need him," I said. "Okay. This is it. Just one last thing to do."

I took the clay cylinder and a handful of fat white chalk sticks out to the lawn, alone.

First, the chalk. Working under the glow of a distant corner streetlight, I crouched down and scratched out the rough curves of a circle on the asphalt. A circle at least twenty feet across, covering the street and rising up on to the sidewalk at its outermost curve, and ringed with swirling runes drawn from memory.

As I'd shown back at the paper mill, an arcane circle could keep a demon like Nyx out.

Done properly, it could keep her *in*, too.

I left the last few strokes of the circle unfinished. An open circuit, waiting to be sealed. Then I slid the beacon out of its plastic baggie. The engraved glyphs felt rough under my fingers, like damp stone, and thrummed with faint power.

This is it, I thought. *No turning back.*

I took a deep breath, drew a trickle of energy into my hands, and let it flow as I slammed the cylinder against the overgrown grass. A pulse rippled out into the night, silent and swift, as a sudden gust of wind ruffled my hair and rattled windows in its wake.

Then it was gone. Message delivered.

I stood up, slid my canvas satchel higher up on my shoulder, and held my shotgun in both hands as I marched back toward the house.

Time for war.

# # #

Jessie and I climbed the stairs in silence, taking our positions. She stood in the shadows of the empty master bedroom, the only one with an unsealed closet, and put her back to the corner. I covered the room from the open doorway so I could watch the hall at the same time.

It came to the hall first.

I felt it before I heard it, a creeping dread that set my teeth on edge. Then the linen closet doorknob slowly turned. From the inside.

The door rattled, thumping against the nailed-up boards. It thumped, hard, an aggressive shove. Then silence.

Come back, I thought. *Come back and try again. Test your luck.*

It obliged me. Downstairs, this time, trying to come in through the closet in the foyer.

"What the—" I heard Barry say.

"Shh," snapped April.

The rattling stopped.

I glanced over at Jessie. She brought her shotgun up, training it on the bedroom closet door. Eyes hard and gleaming like stained glass in the shadows.

The closet doorknob turned.

The door swung wide with a creaking groan, and I heard the Bogeyman's voice call out. A rasping, rattling singsong.

"*Little one, liiiiiiittle one* . . . come to Mama."

It was my voice.

With no parent to copy, the Bogeyman's protective coloration mimicked the closest body in sight. Mine. I stood in the closet, hunched forward, nails like iron razors at the end of limp, dangling arms. Two trickles of blood ran down from my cold, coal-black eyes.

It looked over, saw me, and screamed.

The shriek split the air like nails on a chalkboard, drawing a knife across my eardrums as Jessie opened fire. Her shotgun roared, a booming thunderclap of death that caught the Bogeyman square in the gut and blasted the closet door into splintered scrap. The creature doubled over, clutching its stomach, convulsing as its form rippled and changed.

When it rose up again, flinging out gangly arms and sickle blades for fingers, it showed us what it really looked like.

The Bogeyman was a rag doll, a malformed puppet, with too-long arms and too-spindly legs, draped in rags and burlap tatters. Its hair fell down in long, filthy dreadlocks around a featureless porcelain mask. Jagged cracks ran along the creature's mask, up to slits where mad, anguished eyes peered out at us.

Not at us. At me.

It remembers me.

It charged toward me like a steam train careening off the tracks, one blade-clawed hand reaching back for a killing blow. I was quick on the draw, but Jessie was quicker. Her second blast sent the creature sprawling to the dirty carpet, the rags on its hip shredded and drooling with burgundy blood.

It bounced back up, somersaulting like an acrobat, and ran for the closet.

The air inside the closet wasn't right. A murky, swirling haze of gossamer fog. The Bogeyman plowed into the mist at full speed—and vanished.

"After it!" I shouted, racing for the closet. "Now!"

The fog started to recede, the portal between worlds closing in the creature's wake. No time to think, no time to weigh the consequences. I held my breath, shut my eyes, and barreled on through.

Into the House of Closets.

My feet suddenly clattered against rough wooden floorboards. I stumbled to a stop. Jessie came in right behind me, almost knocking us both over, and clutched my shoulder to get her footing back.

We stood in a barren room, maybe ten feet across on either side. A bare floor, a bare ceiling, and walls covered in peeling, yellowed wallpaper. Victorian roses. I recognized it immediately: it was the same wallpaper from Mitchum Kite's house. Edwin had re-created his family home.

It wasn't an exact match, though. Light shone from a gas lamp on one wall, shrouded under dusty frosted glass. Beside it, a window looked out—into another room, exactly like this one. I looked behind us, trying to get my bearings.

The door we'd arrived through was gone.

"Shit," Jessie muttered, echoing my thoughts.

The room wasn't entirely empty. A doll sat discarded, propped up in the corner. Just a little rag doll, with a gingham dress and no face.

There were two ways out, identical doors facing each other on opposite sides of the room. I picked one at random, and Jessie covered me with her shotgun as I slowly swung it wide.

On the other side was a small, empty closet. And on the other side of the closet was another door.

We passed through and found ourselves in another empty room. Another window, looking out into another empty room. Another identical doll, abandoned in the corner. Another two closets, and another two doors on the opposite side.

By the seventh empty room we passed through, I started to get nervous.

"It doesn't make sense," I said. "At this point, we've doubled back and covered our own trail, but look at the floor. No footprints in the dust. The geography just . . . doesn't work."

Jessie hadn't said a word. She stared ahead, steely eyed, clutching the shotgun at hip level like a gunslinger. As I glanced over at her, I saw her cheek twitch. A little involuntary flinch.

"The whispering needs to stop," she growled.

"What whispering?"

She blinked at me. "You don't hear it?"

Another three rooms, and I heard it, too.

Soft at first, so soft I thought it was my mind playing tricks on me, starved for input in the silence. As we stalked through Edwin's lonely kingdom, though, they grew louder. A chorus of voices, whispering, pleading.

Children's voices. Begging to go home.

I felt them as much as heard them. Feelings of loss washed over me, dread, memories of fears that didn't belong to me. I was five years old, and I'd let go of my mother's hand at the shopping mall. I stood alone in a crowd of giant strangers, knowing I'd never see her again. I took a wrong turn, walking home from school in wintertime, and found myself on an unfamiliar street in an unfamiliar town where all the windows were dark. The cold clawed at me, wind howling over snowdrifts taller than my head, stealing the breath from my lungs.

I was very small, and very alone, and the world didn't care.

"What is he—oh God, Jessie. Oh God."

"What?" she snapped, irritated.

I staggered to the closest wall, feeling unsteady, sick to my stomach, like I'd just chugged a bottle of some nasty bottom-shelf liquor. I put my ear to the wallpaper.

"The sound. It's all around us . . . because it's coming from the walls. He's not burning his victims, like Adramelech did. He's *absorbing* them. Jessie, they're *in the walls*."

I jumped out of the way just as Jessie swung the barrel of her shotgun around, leveling it toward me, and pulled the trigger.

The blast tore into the wall, shredding the old, rotted wood. Blood poured from the hole, guttering down the wallpaper in thick, dark rivulets. Beyond the wreckage, at the edges of the ragged hole in the wall, wet muscle and veins glistened.

The house was alive.

"You want to mess with my head?" Jessie screamed at the ceiling. "Fuck you!"

She fired again. Blood rained down from a fresh hole in the roof. I circled, keeping low, trying to stay behind her.

"Jessie, stop! Stop!"

Her shotgun clattered to the floor. She fell to her knees and pressed her palms to her eyes. I crouched beside her, resting a steadying hand on her back as she took deep, ragged breaths.

"It's okay," I said. "We can beat him, okay? Just keep it together."

"It's not okay," she whispered. "He knows we're here. I told you . . . my hearing is better than yours."

"Edwin? You can hear him?"

She didn't answer right away. She took a long, slow breath, her shoulders trembling.

"He wants me to hurt you."

"Just keep it together. We can beat him—"

"*I* want to hurt you," she said.

Her shoulders shook now. With laughter. A short, bitter, humorless chuckle.

"That's what this place is," she whispered. "Hurt or be hurt. It feeds on pain. And I'm trying, I'm trying so hard, but you need to do something for me, right now."

"Name it. Anything."

She pulled her hands from her face and looked up at me. Her eyes blazed like iced-over spotlights.

"Run."

FORTY-ONE

Halima had warned us. *Edwin Kite's house represents his own evil, animal hungers made manifest. When your beast awakens, smelling blood, do you think it will fight against him . . . or* for *him?*

She'd warned us, but I'd thought she was wrong. I thought we could beat him. I thought Jessie had more control over her inner demons than that.

And here I was, charging through closet door after closet door, as she hunted me down.

I ran blind, my lungs burning as I threw doors shut in my wake and charged through the empty house. I heard her behind me, bellowing, *howling*. A slamming *crunch* echoed a few rooms back, the sound of Jessie putting her fist through a wall.

Edwin doesn't even have to show up to the fight, I thought. *It's only a matter of time before she runs me down. Can't keep up this pace.*

Jessie had dropped her shotgun, though, and I still had mine, clutched tight to my chest as I barreled through another identical door.

One way into each room, one way out. No way to lose her or slip away. I'll have to kill her. Just turn around, wait for her to show up in the doorway, and take my shot. Only way to survive.

Then I thought about Willie.

It's proof, he'd said, telling us Edwin's sick philosophy. *Because when it's you or them? No matter how good you think you are, no matter how brave you think you are . . . you'll always choose yourself.*

No.

No, I wasn't doing this. I wasn't going to play the object lesson for some madman's amusement. I wasn't going to kill Jessie, and I wasn't going to let her kill me, either. There had to be a third way. A better way.

Where could I go, though? One door ahead, one door behind—

—and one window.

I ran for it at full speed, hugged the shotgun tight, and threw myself into the window shoulder first. I tucked my chin against my chest as I crashed through to the room on the other side in a rain of broken glass. I thumped to the floor, rolling, gritting my teeth against the sting of a half-dozen fresh cuts. As I pushed myself up on my knees, I did a quick inventory. My jacket was torn, and I could feel sticky wet lines blossoming along my arm, back, and legs, but nothing life threatening. I'd live with the pain.

My satchel had gone flying, spilling its contents across the hardwood floor. Nothing I could use anyway, except for one: I scooped up Angie's teddy bear.

Now I had two doors to choose from, and if I was quick enough, shutting it behind me, Jessie would have a fifty-fifty chance of going the wrong way. Staking my life on a coin flip, but those were better odds than I'd had thirty seconds ago.

Which way, though? I'd still be a mouse in Edwin's maze, lost in the endless chain of barren rooms. I lowered my shotgun and held up the teddy bear in the palm of my other hand, raising it like a lantern in the gloom.

Angie, if he's made you a part of this place—if any part of you is still here, if you can remember who you are—reach out to me. Please. Show me how to find you.

The bear's faded fur rippled in a breeze I couldn't feel on my bleeding skin. Its head nodded, ever so slightly, toward the door on my right.

I ran, following its lead, shutting the door behind me. I could still hear Jessie rampaging in the distance, slamming walls and breaking glass, but I couldn't tell if she was getting closer or farther away.

Another three rooms, and the bear stopped tugging toward the next door. Instead, it leaned back in my hand, pulling me toward the one I'd just closed behind me.

I'd already seen how the rooms overlapped and crisscrossed one another. Just like Halima warned us, the usual rules of space and physics didn't apply here. Maybe the house was rearranging itself behind my back. On the other hand, if it wasn't? I might run straight into Jessie's path.

Trust, I thought, and turned around.

A hallway waited on the other side of the door. Long, narrow, lit by gaslights in frosted-glass sconces. I stepped on through and shut the door behind me. I heard a faint crackling sound, and when I looked back, a bare wooden wall stood in the door's place. Committed now, I walked ahead.

The whispering grew louder, sounds of loss and despair that weighed on me like iron chains. *You're going to die here,* I thought. *You can't beat him. You've already lost your partner, Edwin is controlling everything around you, and all you have is a probably useless gun and a goddamn teddy bear. What can you do?*

"Try," I said aloud, and trudged down the endless hall.

A light bloomed at the end of the corridor. Not gaslight. Fire. I stepped out into the heart of the house, Edwin's temple.

Flames burned in great brass bowls all along the vast chamber, held on the shoulders of kneeling statues. The statues' faces contorted in pain, sculpted as though their burdens pressed them low and seared their marble flesh.

The whispers turned to echoing wails. Faceless shades floated through the air all around me, faint echoes of life in the shape of humans. In the shape of children. Children like the two sleeping infants in the center of the temple, lying in cradles of hammered brass spears that curled inward all around them like cage bars. Three more empty cage cradles flanked them in a semicircle, waiting for their victims.

"Yes," Edwin Kite said, "Willie's offerings still live, for now. I don't feast until I have a full plate. But . . . you aren't Willie."

Edwin had been human, once, but the giant that reclined upon a basalt throne barely qualified for the name. Twelve feet tall at the shoulder and clad in moldering robes of silver and gold, his skin was the texture of bark from a diseased tree. Faceted black eyes, like an insect's, studied me from across the room while he idly rapped curling claws upon his armrest.

Jessie paced wildly to one side of his throne, lost in her madness, muttering under her breath as she threw punches at the air. On the other side, the Bogeyman glared at me from behind its featureless mask. The wounds from Jessie's shotgun had already healed over, leaving its rags clotted with blood.

"No," I said, approaching the throne. "Willie is dead. My name is Special Agent Harmony Black of the Federal Bureau of Investigation. And you're under arrest."

Edwin's howl of laughter shook the temple walls.

"You have no power here, woman. Behold my glory."

"You mean," I said, "behold Adramelech's glory."

"Speak not that name!" Edwin thundered, pointing a claw at me. "He is not my master! No. *No.* I have taken his power and made it my own. I have fashioned this perfect form, this perfect kingdom, with my own will and magic."

"You mean, with the lives you've stolen. How many children have you murdered, Kite? How many lives have you destroyed, just to prop up this little prison of yours?"

"Murdered?" His gnarled lip curled in amusement. "Ah, you think this place is haunted by ghosts. By memories of distant agony. But I don't take their lives, woman. I take their *souls.*"

He leaned forward in his throne. As my stomach clenched and my heart dropped, he seemed to savor every second of my pain.

"Every soul I've ever claimed suffers to feed my power. To sustain my life and my strength. And they suffer still. You call this place a prison? No. I learned well, from my old teacher. *I built a new hell.* I am its keeper, and its master, and its *god.*"

"Why?" The word tore out of my throat, half question and half anguished plea. "Why *children*?"

Edwin leaned back and waved his claws idly, almost casually.

"Because of what I learned as a boy in my father's house. The same lesson I passed down to my own sons before I left the world of mortals. Children are unruly, savage beasts. They need to be taught. Disciplined. But if you raise them right—if you teach them to respect you, to *fear* you, as they should—they become something so much better. *Obedient.*"

The shotgun felt like a lead weight in my cold, clammy grip. More than anything in the world, I wanted to put Edwin's head in my sights and pull the trigger. *It won't work,* I thought. No, he wouldn't have let me get near him with a weapon in the first place, if he was afraid of what I might do with it.

"Why the long wait?" I asked him. "You take a handful of victims every few decades. Why?"

"The potency of a soul fades over the years. I feed best when they're new. When their anguish is most keen, and they haven't forgotten what it feels like to hope. Even an infant knows hope. Or a little girl. Oh, yes, I know you, Harmony. You were the first to give my ambassador a name."

He gestured toward the creature on his left. Still standing motionless, glaring at me, unblinking.

"You called it the Bogeyman. I like that. But I'm afraid I have to disappoint you. If you came here seeking revenge against the creature that murdered your father, you're far too late."

"What do you mean?" I said. "It's standing right there."

"No. This is *a* Bogeyman. You see, the process of creation requires me to invest them with a spark of my own power. They burn out rather quickly, forcing me to replace them now and again. The Bogeyman who killed your father? Long faded into oblivion. It exists only in your nightmares now."

Edwin rolled his head to one side, favoring the creature with a leering, toothy smile.

"I pick one child from each batch of new offerings. The one with the brightest spark. Then . . . I crush that spark. It requires a great deal of, shall we say, *special* attention. But they learn to obey me. And they serve my will in the mortal world, without question."

I suddenly thought back to what Fontaine told us at the diner.

"Bogeymen aren't born. They're made."

"Made, how?"

"Same way they always have been, miss. Same way as ever."

Both times I'd seen the Bogeyman—in my sister's nursery, and on Helen Gunderson's camera—they were crying as they took their victims.

Now I understood why.

"I changed my mind," I told him.

"Oh? About what?"

I squared my footing, standing before his throne. The whispers of despair washed over me, but they broke like an ocean wave against a wall of stone.

"I'm not arresting you anymore," I said. "I'm going to kill you instead."

Edwin chortled, jerking his claws toward Jessie and the Bogeyman.

"My little friends here might have something to say about that. And I must say, I'm disappointed. I thought you'd be happier right now."

"*Happy?* About what?"

Edwin's cracked lips curled back in a grin of pure malice.

"The reunion, of course!" He gestured to the Bogeyman. "Come, now. Don't tell me you don't recognize your own sister."

FORTY-TWO

Edwin howled with glee as the world collapsed around me.

If she recognized me, the masked creature didn't show it. She stared at me with a look of pure, seething malice in her bloodshot eyes. Still, I knew. I knew he was telling the truth.

"That little toy of yours," he said, gesturing to my shotgun, "holds no terror for me. Against your sister and your partner, though, it might save your life. I consider this an opportunity for enlightenment. Here you are, a crusader in your own mind. A self-styled upholder of justice and the right."

He clicked his claws. The Bogeyman—no, *Angie*, my *sister*—crouched low and let out a feral growl.

"You know this girl—your own flesh and blood, no less—is innocent. She doesn't deserve to die now, does she? But I promise you: you *will* slay her. You'll do it to save your own life."

Willie, all over again. Edwin had built his prison, his hell, as a mirror of his own twisted mind. An endless cycle of abuse, of punishment and fear, that he could feed upon and feel justified by. Like Halima said, this place was an extension of Kite's very soul. He *needed* to be proven right. Shaking his confidence would be like shaking the house's very foundation.

"My order against your chaos," I whispered.

He leaned forward on his throne. "Hmm? What was that?"

I threw the shotgun to the ground. It clattered on the stone at my feet.

"No."

Edwin's eyes narrowed to black slits. "Pick that up."

I ignored him and turned to face Angie. I held up the teddy bear.

"I don't know if you remember," I said to her, "but this used to be yours. And I came a long way to give it back to you."

I took a step closer to her. She growled and did the same.

"Pick up your weapon," Edwin snapped. "Don't be a fool."

"It used to be mine," I told her, "but the day Mom and Dad brought you home from the hospital, I put it in your crib. See, I thought it could chase away nightmares. And you were littler than me, so you needed it more than I did. That's how the world is supposed to work. We're—we're all—supposed to protect the little ones."

Edwin slammed his fist on his armrest, the sound booming like a peal of thunder.

"Who do you even think you're talking to? There's nothing of your sister *left* in there! Are you looking for mercy? Compassion? Love? I ripped it out of her!"

"That's not true," I said. To her, not to him. "That's not true. I bet he told you a lot of things that weren't true. Did he say you were alone, Angie? Did he tell you nobody cared about you? We never stopped looking for you. Never once."

We stood five feet apart now. Angie pushed her shoulders back, hissing like a cornered cat. A feral animal, trapped and confused.

"She'll kill you," Edwin said. "You're throwing your life away."

I shook my head. I held the bear out to her, cupped in my palms, and stepped closer.

"I'm so sorry that it took me so long to find you. But it's over now. You don't have to listen to him anymore."

I barely saw the claws coming. Just a blur of motion, then white-hot pain as my arm ripped open from my elbow to my wrist. The bear fell to the ground at my feet. I gripped my wound, blood trickling between my fingers while Angie let out a rattling hiss.

I bent down and picked the bear back up.

"Even after everything he did to you," I said, "even after all the lies he fed you, I *know* you're still in there. And I know you're scared. But I'm here now. And no one is ever going to hurt you again."

I took one more step toward her. Angie's arm shot up, claws tensed, a killing blow ready to fall. She could tear my throat out in a heartbeat, as easily as shredding a piece of paper. I could die just like my father. I took a deep breath, trying to ignore the blood dripping from my shredded sleeve.

"You think you destroyed everything human in her," I told Edwin. "But you don't have that power. Nobody does. All you did was hurt her. She'll heal."

Edwin squeezed the armrest of his throne, veins bulging under the gnarled skin of his face. He looked to Angie and waved a furious hand. "Enough of this. Kill her!"

Angie's claws trembled, held high and frozen. Behind her mask, her eyes flicked wildly between us.

"Your name is Angie Black," I told her. "You're my sister. And I love you. And I'm here to take you home."

She let out a slow, strangled yowl, a confused and anguished whine as her raised hand shook.

I looked over at Edwin. With my life on the line, a heartbeat from the end, I couldn't help but smile.

"My order against your chaos."

"You keep *saying* that, but what does it—"

Two quick steps, and I pulled Angie into my arms.

She spit and hissed, and her claws dug into me. Cutting through my jacket and blouse, gouging bloody furrows in my back, but I only held on tighter.

"I'm not letting go," I hissed into her ear, "I'm *not letting go.*"

She stopped clawing at me.

Her shoulders heaved, and her animal fury broke down into broken-throated sobs. Leaning against me, weeping.

"It's all right," I whispered. "It's all over now. I'm taking you home."

I held her as long as she needed me to. It felt like forever. When she finally pulled away, slowly, drained of tears, I reached up and gently took off her mask.

"No more hiding. Masks are for monsters."

I didn't flinch at the scarred, ravaged face beneath. She was still beautiful to me. I dropped the mask to the stone at our feet, the porcelain shattering.

I looked to the side. At some point, Jessie had stopped her mad pacing and raving. Her eyes still blazed, but she just stood there, watching us.

"And I'm not afraid of the Big Bad Wolf, either," I told her. "So get your shit together, Agent. We've got work to do."

Jessie grinned, showing me her teeth.

"Insolence!" Edwin roared, rising from his throne. The giant glared down at us, curling his mammoth hands into fists. "I'll kill you both myself. And then, oh, what I'll do with your souls. I will feast on you for—"

Jessie charged. She hit him from behind like a linebacker, driving her shoulder into the back of his leg. He went down, kneecap cracking on cold stone, and howled as he lashed out at her. She caught his wrist, twisted it behind his back, and snapped two of his fingers like brittle twigs. Then she went to work on the others.

As Edwin kicked and howled, the walls of his temple shook. The brazier flames spit and guttered, responding to his pain. Then I realized something else was happening.

He was shrinking.

He wasn't twelve feet tall anymore. No, now, as Jessie hurled him against his own mighty throne, he was the same size as us. His claws faded to yellowed fingernails, his armored skin to pallid, liver-spotted flesh.

The Edwin whom Jessie dragged before us was just a man. Just an old, feeble man with bottomless hate in his eyes. She forced him to his knees.

"Idiots," he spat. "You *can't* defeat me. This is still my fortress, my kingdom, and its magic still protects me. I can't be slain here, no matter what you do to this body, and I can't be removed unless I will it. So what can you do? What can you possibly do?"

"This," I said, and pressed my hand to his forehead.

As a tingling rush shot down my arm, I had a fleeting thought—*thank you kindly, darlin'*—and the sensation of a kiss on my cheek.

Edwin blinked. "What . . . what did you just do?"

"There weren't two of us, invading your kingdom. There were three. Edwin, meet Fontaine. Fontaine, Edwin. Fontaine was curled up quietly in the back of my brain, but I think *your* body will suit him better."

Jessie let go of him. Edwin rose on shaky feet, his eyes going wide.

"What is—what's *happening* to me?"

"You said it yourself," I told him. "You can only leave under your own free will. Only problem is, now your will kinda belongs to *him*."

"Just long enough to walk you right out of here," said the syrupy drawl from Edwin's lips, a voice no longer his. He glanced back at Jessie. "And did you have to beat him up that bad, sweetheart? This *hurts*."

Jessie folded her arms and smiled.

"Yeah," she said, "I really did."

I touched my sister's arm. "Angie? Can you open a portal and get us all back to the house?"

She frowned, lips moving slowly, trying to find her voice.

"Yes," she said.

Jessie and I ran to the crib cages and scooped out the stolen infants. Somehow, they were still asleep. Drugged or enchanted, I imagined, but they were still breathing, and that's what mattered. I cradled one in my good arm, wincing at my cuts.

Angie stood before a hovering miasma of violet light, concentrating as she held her claws wide, forcing the portal open. On the far side, I could almost make out the hazy impression of the upstairs closet we'd arrived through.

"You can't do this," Edwin begged in his own voice as his legs carried him one shaky step at a time toward the light. "Please!"

"We're not doing anything," Jessie said. "You're the one walking out of here. Sheesh, just stop if you don't want to."

He was screaming when Fontaine forced him through, back to the real world. Jessie jumped in after him.

"Come on," I said to Angie, holding out my hand. But she shook her head.

"Need . . . to stay," she said, fumbling for words.

I touched her face, tracing the curve of her scarred cheek. "No. No, Angie, you don't. You don't belong here; you never did. Come on. We have . . . we have people, out there. People who can help you."

"Help," she said, nodding. She gestured to the temple. Shades floated in the gathering dark, the temple fires dying one by one, and the whispers of despair swirled all around us. "Children still here. I have some of his . . ." She shook her head, missing the word she wanted. "I help. Fix this place. Set them free."

"When it's done, will you—"

The violet light flickered. Angie shook her head, cutting me off.

"Door hard to keep open. *Go.* I fix this place."

"Angie," I said, "I love you. Mom loves you. Never forget that."

She smiled. Maybe for the first time. Then she took hold of my shoulder . . . and shoved me into the light.

FORTY-THREE

"We're back," I called down from the second-floor hallway. "Coming down with a prisoner!"

Our team watched from the foot of the stairs as Edwin trudged down, followed by Jessie and me. Barry's jaw dropped.

"Who the hell is that, and where did he come from? Where did the *kids* come from?"

"They were hiding in a closet," Jessie said. The infant in her arms rubbed its eyes, squirming as it stirred. "Here, Kevin. I'll trade you. Baby for a shotgun."

He gave her a dubious look. "Uh, I'm not good with kids."

"Neither am I, but I'm *really* good with shotguns. Take the kid."

April opened her arms, taking the other baby on her lap, and passed me her weapon. Our job wasn't done.

Cody rushed over to me, looking me up and down. "Harmony, you need an ambulance. You're bleeding . . . what the hell *happened* up there?"

"Family reunion. C'mon. This is the tricky part."

The first rays of morning filtered through the dying trees, casting a faint golden shine upon the weed-choked lawn. A new car sat parked across the street—the Garners' Subaru. Ellen and Jacob huddled in the backseat, looking terrified. Not hard to see why, considering Nyx—wearing her blonde Russian bombshell disguise—sat behind the wheel.

"So that plan of yours," Jessie murmured.

I looked down at the street. My chalked circle stood between us and the Subaru, waiting to be finished.

"That incarnate I faced in Vegas," I said, "took a .454 round to the face. Didn't kill it, but it *hurt.* Slowed it down for a minute. Wait until she gets to the middle of the circle. If we all unload on her, that should buy me enough time to close the circle and trap her. Then, once she can't hurt anybody, I send her ass back to hell where she belongs."

Nyx got out of the car. The Garners stayed put.

"You brought this one a present," she said, smiling as she strode across the street.

Edwin stopped in the middle of the lawn. He shook his head.

"Sorry, Nyxy," he said in Fontaine's voice. "This one's already spoken for."

He threw his head back and bellowed an incantation that set my teeth on edge. The words—words from no human tongue—felt like acid burning my eardrums. I recognized only a single name, the last word he spoke: *Adramelech.* I glimpsed a shimmer of shadow as Fontaine fled Edwin's body. Edwin stood there, panting, finally free.

Then the earthquake hit.

The ground shifted, tossing me like a rag doll, and Jessie caught me in her arms. The earth split with a thundering roar and tore a jagged hole in the lawn. Light boiled up from the deep, orange and hungry. Edwin had just enough time to scream before a dozen greedy, grasping hands, their skin charred by flame, grabbed his legs and hauled him into the chasm.

Then, silence.

There was no chasm of flame, no earthquake. The lawn stood pristine, if overgrown. It was all over in less than ten seconds, and suddenly it seemed as if nothing had happened at all. A momentary hallucination.

Edwin Kite was really gone, though. Gone to pay the price for his betrayal. I had a feeling he'd be paying for a long, long time.

Cody stared, speechless, mouth agape. I reached over and touched his arm.

"That's the part I couldn't tell you about," I said softly.

"Did—did that just happen?" Barry asked. "Did any of you *see* that?"

I didn't get the chance to answer him. Not with Nyx standing in the middle of the street, pointing an enraged finger at us.

"You!" she hissed, and shed her human disguise.

Armored chitin blossomed across her skin as she grew, her clothes tearing and flames rippling down her back like a mane. She took one step forward, and a cloven hoof slammed onto the asphalt.

Barry stared at her, mouth hanging open. "What the hell?"

Unveiled in her full glory, the demon's serpentine tail cracked through the air like a bullwhip. Jessie leveled her shotgun. I stood beside her and did the same.

"Funny choice of words. That's a demon," I told Barry. "And we just ruined her day."

"Can we kill it?" Cody asked me.

"We're about to find out."

Barry shook his head. Some people break under that kind of revelation. Another man might have cowered or run for his life.

As Jessie, Cody, and I spread out, forming a firing line, Barry stepped up.

"Ma'am," he called out, "I'm the sheriff in this town, and I'm going to have to ask you to peaceably depart."

Nyx curled her claws and hissed, "This one looks forward to making you scream."

He sighed and brought up his shotgun. The four of us held her in our sights.

"Ma'am, it truly pains me to say this, because I've always prided myself on overseeing a fair-minded and racially diverse community . . . but your kind isn't welcome around here."

We got one shot off as she charged. Just one. Our shotguns boomed like a cannon battery as Nyx barreled across the street, slugs catching her in the chest and thigh and exploding with black ichor. I dropped my gun and pulled a stick of chalk from my breast pocket, lunging for the sidewalk where the tiny, open link in the arcane circle waited to be filled. I landed hard on my knees, ignoring the stabbing lance of pain, reaching out to draw the final line.

Nyx barely slowed down. She tore the weapon from Barry's grip and slammed the stock across his head, sending him sprawling to the lawn. Then she grabbed Cody by the neck, spinning him around and clutching him in her claws, using him as a human shield.

"You think this one is *stupid*?" Nyx hissed. "Empty your hand."

The chalk clattered to the sidewalk, the circle unfinished. I stood back up.

"I don't have a shot," Jessie snapped, trying to drop a bead on Nyx's head.

"Let him go, Nyx," I said. "He's got nothing to do with this."

"This one has been *insulted*," she seethed. "This offense will be paid for."

"Then come at *me*," I told her.

"This one is doing so. You *like* this man, yes?" Nyx's claws dug into Cody's neck. He bit back a grunt of pain as trickles of blood stained his uniform shirt. "This one saw, from the vents, when Willie died. Saw him try to protect you. Can you protect him now? No. Want to see the look on your face as you watch this one—"

"Oh, Nyxy-poo," Fontaine called. He sauntered up the sidewalk, back in his corpse body. "Job's done, sugar. That bounty's mine."

"This one *knows* that," she snapped. "But—"

"Ain't no buts about it. Job's done. Now, it seems to me that you're hanging about in a place where you've got no business, about to do a nasty number on some humans you've got no business doing a number on."

She showed him her teeth. "No rules against it."

Fontaine shook his head, giving us a "What can you do?" look. His gaze went to Cody, clutched in Nyx's iron grip. Cody fought to stay stoic, eyes hard and teeth gritted, fighting his fear.

"It's just unprofessional, is what it is," Fontaine said. "We're only supposed to interact with humans as part of a hunt. Hunt's over. You're makin' us look bad. And frankly, if you insist on besmirching the Chainmen's good name with your general unruliness and suchlike, I'm gonna have no choice but to break out the biggest, meanest weapon I've got."

Nyx stared at him in expectant silence.

"I will *tell your momma*," Fontaine said. "She's already gonna be ten kinds of pissed that you got skunked out of a bounty today. You really wanna make it harder on yourself?"

With a frustrated grunt, Nyx shoved Cody to the grass. She turned her baleful glare upon me and Jessie.

"Black. Temple. This one knows your names. This one will *not* forget."

With a whip crack of her tail, she turned and stomped away. Her image seemed to boil as she walked, a heat mirage striding toward the sunrise, until it finally dissolved in the open air. She left nothing behind but the stench of sulfur.

"She does know how to make an exit," Fontaine said. "Just a tiny bit lacking in the social graces. And on that note, it's time for this rambler to get rambling. It's been a pleasure doing business."

He strolled up the sidewalk, whistling a happy tune. Across the street, the Garners slowly clambered out of their car.

"Is it over?" Ellen asked.

"It's over," I said. "Go home."

# # #

Barry radioed for a couple of ambulances, one for me and one for the recovered infants, and called around to break the good news to their parents. I ended up lying on my stomach on a stretcher, getting fifteen stitches and enough bandage pads and antiseptic cream to stock a small clinic. *It could have been worse,* I told myself. Getting patched up stung more than getting the cuts in the first place.

The sunrise brought a new day to Talbot Cove, washing the streets in gold. A day with no Edwin Kite, no Bogeyman, no missing children. We'd ended the cycle for good.

And my baby sister was alive. She'd been through a hell I couldn't imagine, but she was *alive.*

I dug my nails into my leg, hard enough to leave cherry-red welts, to drive back the sudden torrent of emotion. *Lock it down,* I told myself. My eternal mantra. *Lock it down until you get home.*

Once I got the thumbs-up from the paramedics—and changed into a fresh blouse, tossing the tattered ruin of my jacket into my suitcase—it was time to have a couple of talks. Jessie and I pulled Barry aside.

"You've been involved in this from the start," I said, "so you deserve some answers. I can't tell you everything. I *won't* tell you everything. But here's what I can share."

So we walked him through it, leaving out half the story and a few key details he didn't need to know. Like what happened to Angie.

"So the thing that killed your dad—"

"Dead," I told him. "The Bogeyman is dead."

He chewed that over.

"You all right?" I asked.

"Just saw a man get swallowed into hell, then a demon clocked me with my own shotgun." He rubbed his temple, an ugly bruise rising up. "You might say I'm adjusting at my own pace. Figure I'll freak out later, in the privacy of my own home, once the adrenaline wears off."

"Please remember that everything we've just told you is highly classified," Jessie told him.

He chuckled. "And if I blabbed about it, I'd get locked up in the nuthouse anyway."

"Exactly," she said.

"Well, you got those kids back," he mused, "and put a stop to the whole damn mess. Guess that's some kinda win."

As we walked to the car, leaving him to deal with the grateful parents, I saw Jessie smiling at me from the corner of my eye.

"What?"

"It absolutely was," she said, "some kinda win. Nice job, Agent."

I looked up the sidewalk. Cody stood alone, gazing into the distance with a thousand-yard stare.

"Let me handle this one myself," I told Jessie. She gave me a nod and kept her distance as I walked over to stand at Cody's side.

"I get it," he said, his voice distant. "Why you couldn't tell me. I mean, I wouldn't have believed you. I wouldn't have believed in . . . any of this."

I thought of Douglas Bredford, drunk and hopeless in his booth at the bar. And the talk I had with Jessie on the drive to Detroit, about why we keep our secrets secret. *Imagine a nation of Douglas Bredfords,* she'd told me. Some people could handle the truth, and some people couldn't.

I could see the despair on Cody's face, and it terrified me. He was slipping under the waves, the weight of what he'd seen like a lead anchor chained to his ankle.

"Who *are* you?" he asked me.

I shrugged. "I'm just the girl next door."

"When we were kids, yeah," he said, "but that was a long time ago. Who are you now?"

I had to think about that.

"I'm the woman who makes the monsters go away. Sometimes I win, sometimes I lose." I looked back toward the empty house. "This time . . . we did all right. Talbot Cove is safe now, Cody. It's over."

He let out a bitter chuckle and touched the fresh bandages on his neck, covering the cuts Nyx had left him. "It's over for them, you mean. All the people who don't know the truth. The people who don't have scars on their neck from a goddamn demon."

"I've got a few of those, too."

"So you know," he said, "it's not over for me."

"No. I won't lie to you. You'll remember this day for the rest of your life. What matters is what you take away from it. The point *isn't* that demons are real, Cody, and the point *isn't* that you saw a man get dragged down into hell."

He shook his head. "What's the point, then?"

"The point is," I told him, "today? The good guys won. And you were one of them."

I let him think about that for a while. He strolled up the street, hands in his pockets, mulling it over, and I walked silently at his side.

He stopped, and turned to me.

"You remember what I said, about living in Talbot Cove? That night we talked outside the motel?"

"That you're moving on," I said. "Saving up a nest egg, and figuring out what you want to do with your life when spring comes."

There was something new in Cody's eyes. The despair faded, replaced by calm confidence. The cowboy was back. Maybe a little older, a little wiser—the kind of wisdom that comes only from getting kicked in the teeth a few times—but he was back.

"I put on this badge because I wanted to help people. I think, knowing what I know, seeing what I've seen . . ." He looked all around, taking in the sleepy suburban street. "I think my calling's definitely elsewhere."

"What are you thinking about?"

"Don't know yet. I need to process this. Think it over. But now I know that monsters are real. And I know I wouldn't be any kind of a man if I didn't *do* something about it."

I gave him my business card.

"When you decide," I told him, "give me a call. Day or night."

He took the card, read it over, and slipped it into his pocket. I looked back toward the cars. Jessie waited for me, making an effort to pretend she wasn't watching us.

"One last thing," Cody said, "before you go?"

"Sure, what—"

He put his hand on my shoulder and pulled me into a kiss. I lifted my chin, rising up on my toes to meet him, my body responding before my brain could catch up.

"Sorry," he murmured as he pulled away slowly, not sounding sorry at all. "But if I hadn't done that, I'd have kicked myself from one side of town to the other the second you left."

"You don't hear me complaining," I told him, swallowing down the butterflies in my stomach. "Talk to you, Cody. Stay safe."

I tried to ignore Jessie's smirk as I walked back to join her. To her credit, she didn't say a word.

"So how much of this is going in the final report?" I asked her.

She pretended to think about it as we got into the SUV.

"Oh, at *least* twenty percent," she said. "Maybe even twenty-five. We can leave out everything about your sister, for starters. Better drop Barry and Cody out of the picture, too. Don't want Linder sending anyone around to hassle them once we leave."

"Thanks for that."

"Hey," she said, "we take care of our own."

I looked over at her.

"Yeah? That mean I passed the audition?"

"Well, there's still a few formalities, like your membership dues and the mandatory hazing, but I'd say you made the cut. Welcome to the Circus."

I'd spent three years flying solo, working a case with nobody to talk to but the mirror. I'd thought I was fine with that. It wasn't until now, with people I could trust at my side, that I understood how much I'd been missing.

A team? Sure. That suited me just fine.

We watched Main Street wake up as we cruised on by. People flipping **Closed** signs to **Open**, setting out window displays. Just another ordinary, average day.

A day without monsters.

"So," Jessie said, "ready to say good-bye to Talbot Cove?"

"Yeah." I leaned back and stared out the window. Taking one last look. "Yeah. I really am."

FORTY-FOUR

We met up with April and Kevin back at the motel. April packed up, slipping her books into a battered suitcase, while Kevin huddled over his laptop.

"We just took down a two-hundred-year-old sorcerer," Jessie said, shaking her head at the swooping dragon on his screen, "and *this* is how you celebrate. You really are hopeless, you know that, right?"

"*Working*, thank you very much," he said. "One of my contacts is online, the one I had check out that Cold Spectrum thing for you."

"That phrase Douglas Bredford mentioned?" April asked.

"He's got nothing," Jessie said, "because it means nothing. The ramblings of a very sad and self-loathing drunk."

Still, she leaned over his shoulder just like I did, reading the tiny chat box.

DuLac: Encrypted voice. NOW.

Kevin shrugged. He ran a USB cable from the laptop to his cell phone, rattling out a string of commands in a second window.

"What's up, man? Why voice?"

"Because," burst a panicked, breathless man's voice from the phone's tinny speaker, "I'm not typing those fucking words again! What did you *do* to me, man?"

"Wait, what words?"

"*Cold Spectrum!* I barely even ran a surface scan. That's all it took. I—I triggered something. No, it's more like I *woke something up*. All of a sudden coded comm traffic starts lighting up the grid like an electrical storm. And none of it makes sense: there's, like, a four-star general at the DoD swapping encrypted e-mails with an IRS auditor out in Wichita. Elements in all of the alphabet agencies are getting involved, *all of them*. And near as I can tell, the big question on their minds is: *Who wants to know about Cold Spectrum?*"

"Did you get clear?" Kevin asked.

"Yeah, I'm clear. As in I'm five states away and burned two fake IDs getting here, clear. Still not far enough. I'm mobile, man, gotta stay in the wind until this blows over. Whatever you're involved in, just leave me the hell out of it, okay? There's only one thing that involves this much back-channel cooperation in DC: heavy, *heavy* black-ops shit. Leave it alone, man. Just leave it alone."

The line went dead.

Jessie stood there, tapping her chin with her index finger, staring at Kevin's screen.

"Okay," she said, "let's go. We need to have another chat with Douglas Bredford."

Kevin looked over his shoulder at her. "Uh, is that a good idea?"

"Nope. But we're doing it anyway. Besides, as a patriotic citizen, I have serious issues with shadowy government conspiracies."

"Jess, we *are* a shadowy govern—"

"Ones that aren't *mine*," she said. "God, do I really need to qualify that? Some things should be obvious."

# # #

We rolled into Bredford's sleepy little neck of the woods right around lunchtime. The narrow strip of gravel outside the Brew House sat empty, but the lights were on and I could hear the strains of a Conway Twitty song drifting out through the rickety screen door.

Douglas's booth sat empty, too. I walked over to the bartender. He gave me a grunt of acknowledgment, not looking up from his crossword puzzle.

"Looking for Douglas Bredford," I told him.

"So am I. He owes me for a twelve-dollar tab."

"Any idea where I can find him?"

The bartender nodded toward the empty booth.

"Seven days out of seven, he's sitting right there," he said. "More predictable than my granddad's pocket watch. Maybe he decided to go be miserable someplace else for once."

"Know where he lives?"

The bartender looked up, wearing his irritation like a medal of honor.

"What am I, the yellow pages? Last I knew, he had a place at the Greenglade Trailer Park." He pointed. "About four miles up the road, that way, on the left. Only thing but trees for ten miles. You're blind if you miss it."

He was right. There was no way we'd have missed the trailer park. Not with the conga line of fire trucks, police cars, and ambulances choking the central drive. Not with the plume of black smoke slowly wafting up into a cloudless blue sky.

I found a spot to squeeze the SUV in and killed the ignition. "Wait here," Jessie said to April and Kevin. She jumped out with me.

Firefighters rolled their hoses up and took photos of debris, while cops worked the gathering crowd. Locals stood on tiptoes, craning their necks to see the wreckage. The trailer might have been comfortable once, even expensive. Now it was a blackened, crumpled husk of twisted metal, sitting in a pool of mud. The trailers to its left and right sported blackened sides and blown-out windows.

We made a beeline for a bearded man with a notebook, a camera, and a fire marshal's badge clipped to his belt. I flashed my badge.

"FBI. Is this your scene?"

"For now. Damn, you guys work fast. Who called you out?"

"Nobody," Jessie said. "We're here to talk to a confidential informant. I hate to ask, but do you know who owned this trailer?"

He checked his notebook. My heart sank, even though I already knew what he'd say.

"Yep. Douglas Bredford. He's not your CI, is he?"

"Afraid so. You recover his body?"

He gestured over to a stretcher. A body bag lay out on top, but judging from the bulges in the black vinyl, there wasn't enough meat to make a Thanksgiving turkey inside.

"There are small parts of *a* body, but if you want positive ID, you're going to have to wait. I think they're trying to find enough teeth to run the dental records."

"What happened?" I asked.

"Explosion, but we're still working on the source. As it stands, from the blast pattern and the smell, I'm thinking meth lab."

We thanked him and walked back to the car in silence.

A woman stopped us on the far edge of the crowd. Fortysomething, with stringy brown hair and a worn-out Hello Kitty sweater. She clutched a long, tan envelope to her chest like it was made of gold. She didn't say anything, not right away, but she didn't move out of our way, either.

"Help you, ma'am?" Jessie asked her.

"I think . . . I think I'm supposed to give this to you."

She handed Jessie the envelope.

"I didn't open it," she said quickly. "He made sure to tell me, over and over again, not to open it."

"Who did?" I said.

"Dougie." She shot a glance over her shoulder and leaned in close. "Yesterday he came to me and said . . . he said soon, something *big* might happen. He said I'd know it when I saw it. And he said . . . if it did, I needed to look for two lady FBI agents and give them that envelope. He gave me twenty bucks just to hold on to it for a few days. I thought he was crazy, or just drunk again, but . . ."

She gestured toward the burned-out trailer. Jessie and I shared a look.

"I'm not in any trouble, am I?" she asked.

"No, ma'am," I told her. "You did the right thing. Let's just keep this between us, okay?"

She nodded, backing away slowly, disappearing into the crowd of onlookers. I followed Jessie a few trailers down, slipping around a quiet corner and out of sight. She tore the envelope open and slid the contents into her outstretched hand.

Photographs. Some black-and-white, some in color, even an old Polaroid. The Polaroid was a shot of Douglas Bredford in younger, more sober days, smiling with his arm around a pretty brunette in a sun hat. A scribble in black Sharpie on the back of the shot read, "Paris in New York."

The next photo showed the same woman. Dead, on a mortician's table, with a bullet hole between her sculpted eyebrows.

Everyone in the other photos was alive, though there wasn't any rhyme or reason to them. A tall, dark-skinned man in a beanie walking out of a convenience store, shot from a car half a block away. An intense-looking young woman in a picture clipped from a newspaper, but without the story or its caption. We recognized only a single person, from the very last picture.

Linder, at the back of a group of suited men, striding down the steps of the Capitol Building together. A circle of red ink put a bull's-eye around his face.

We got back in the SUV. Jessie handed the envelope back to April and Kevin. I brought them up to speed while they leafed through the pictures.

"Okay," Jessie said, "as of now, we've got a little side project."

"Maybe . . ." Kevin said, "maybe we should just take these to Linder? I mean, his photograph is in here. He could be in danger."

Jessie turned around in the passenger seat and stared at him over the headrest.

"I will slap the taste right out of your mouth," she told him.

"What Jessie means is," I said, "somebody just put a bomb in Douglas Bredford's trailer, not long after he dropped a name that triggered government back-channel chatter all over the country. There's no way that's a coincidence."

"It's a hot potato," April said, "and his dying act was to drop it square in our laps. Lovely."

"Until we know exactly how Linder is involved, and what Cold Spectrum *is*, nobody says a word to him," Jessie said.

April flipped through the pictures, one after the other, like a handful of puzzle pieces that just wouldn't fit.

"It appears," she said, "we've just become a conspiracy *inside* a conspiracy. Welcome aboard, Agent Black. Look on the bright side: at least you'll never be bored."

FORTY-FIVE

"Never bored" was an understatement. The ink on our report to Linder hadn't even dried before we got the next call to action. Vigilant had only so many field teams—three, Jessie believed, besides us—and there was plenty of work to go around, largely thanks to our jaunt to Detroit. Dr. Victoria Carnes was still on the run, and while Buck Wheeler had died in the plane crash, we still had his brothel in Los Angeles to follow up on. Then there was the case Jessie's team had been pulled away from, the one where they lost a member. That, Jessie told me in private, was the top priority no matter *where* Linder officially sent us next.

It's like Bredford said, I thought. *Take one monster down, more flood in. And there are always more monsters.*

But we did take one down, at least. Edwin Kite was in hell, where he belonged, and Talbot Cove could finally slumber in peace. Hard not to feel good about that.

I requested a couple of days off, made a brief stop in Chicago, and then I flew home. To Long Island Sound. The taxi dropped me off at the curb outside my mother's house. She opened the door as I walked up the steps, my battered overnight suitcase rolling behind me.

She didn't say a word. She just searched in my eyes for an answer. She looked as exhausted as I felt, the kind of exhaustion that comes from too little sleep and too many unanswered questions.

"She's alive," I said, and my mother pulled me into her arms.

She put on a kettle of hot cocoa, and I told her my story, told her Angie's story. And she reached across the dining room table and squeezed my hand, and we cried for what we'd lost and we cried for what we'd found, and it was all right.

It was all right.

The closet in my old bedroom was for storage now, piled high with boxes and bags, things we'd taken when we'd moved from Talbot Cove. Baby clothes, a broken-down crib, my father's old uniforms. Things we never needed but couldn't throw away. Not until now. We cleaned it all out together, filling garbage bags with the detritus of the past and carrying it outside.

The job done, I gently shut the empty closet's door.

Then I cleaned off the dresser by the door and set out a single decoration: the little cylinder of clay that Halima had made for me when I'd visited her on my way home. My fingers lightly played across its surface, stroking the beacon to life.

In an empty wall socket down near the floor, I plugged in a nightlight. It glowed, cool and blue, when I clicked it on. I stood back up, and my mother stood beside me.

"For you, Angie," I said to the closet door. "For when you're ready to come home. We'll always leave a light on. We promise."

Douglas Bredford was right, and he was wrong.

There were always more monsters.

There was always more hope, too.

AFTERWORD

My readers know that I have a thing for playing the long game. It's not uncommon for me to plan a story arc several books in advance, or leave tiny seeds that don't pay off until much, much later. When I introduced the character of Harmony Black in *Redemption Song*, the second Daniel Faust novel, I knew she'd be more than the straight-arrow adversary for Faust and his gang; a spin-off series would come about eventually, opening up my fictional world and showing it from a new perspective.

When 47North gave me the opportunity to do just that, I had a whole slew of challenges to face. Could I write a new series that both stood on its own for new readers and had lots of fun nods to the original books for the Faust fans? Could I take a character so straitlaced she "makes Joe Friday look bent" and turn her into a relatable and interesting heroine? Could I maintain the general feel of my other stories while treading new ground?

Could I? No, that's not a hypothetical: I'm asking you. I mean, you just read the book, so you tell me.

It's been a blast working on the new series so far, and I hope you enjoyed reading this first installment. There are some exciting adventures coming down the pike, and new mysteries to unravel. (And while

Harmony may think she's left her experiences in Las Vegas behind, there's a shadowy man with a Cheshire smile who might have a different opinion on that subject . . .)

If you want to be the first to know what happens next, head over to craigschaeferbooks.com/mailing-list/ and hop onto my mailing list. Once-a-month newsletters, zero spam. Want to reach out? You can find me on Facebook at facebook.com/CraigSchaeferBooks, on Twitter as @craig_schaefer, or just drop me an e-mail at craig@craigschaeferbooks.com. I always love hearing from my readers.

ABOUT THE AUTHOR

Photo © 2014 Karen Forsythe

Craig Schaefer's books have taken readers to the seamy edge of a criminal underworld drenched in shadow through the Daniel Faust series; to a world torn by war, poison, and witchcraft by way of the Revanche Cycle series; and across a modern America mired in occult mysteries and a conspiracy of lies in the new Harmony Black series. Despite this, people say he's strangely normal. He lives in Illinois with a small retinue of cats, all of whom try to interrupt his writing schedule and/or kill him on a regular basis. He practices sleight of hand in his spare time, although he's not very good at it.